Praise for Sop

"Telling the story of a child of slave owner and an enslaved woman, *Wild, Beautiful, and Free* focuses on the individual heartbreaks of slavery and especially on the heroine, a courageous young woman who has to find her own route to becoming a free woman. It's intensely readable—a page-turner set in a vividly described landscape."

—Philippa Gregory, #1 *New York Times* bestselling author

"Stunning in a thousand ways, this spellbinding declaration of wild and beautiful freedom burns so fearless and hot it fairly takes one's breath away. As the mixed-race heiress of a white, slave-owning father fights to survive enslavement, the danger of escape, and the Civil War to reclaim her life's rightful place, her fierce battle rewrites the essence of what it means to be home and free. Sophfronia Scott gets pitch perfect every word, moment, heartbreak, and victory of this young woman's determined struggle. From start to finish, it's a searing and stunning triumph."

—Patricia Raybon, author of *All That Is Secret: An Annalee Spain Mystery*

"Marvelously dramatic . . . brings its era to life with lush detail."

—*People*

"Dazzlingly dark and engaging tale full of heartbreak, treachery, and surprise."

—*Kirkus Reviews*

"Scott will most assuredly be recognized for her superb storytelling."

—*Booklist*

"Scott should take a bow for penning this delicious and infinitely enjoyable read."

—Essence

"Highly recommended."

—Historical Novel Society

WILD

BEAUTIFUL

AND

FREE

ALSO BY SOPHFRONIA SCOTT

Fiction

All I Need to Get By

Unforgivable Love

Nonfiction

This Child of Faith

Love's Long Line

The Seeker and the Monk

WILD

BEAUTIFUL

AND

FREE

A NOVEL

SOPHFRONIA SCOTT

Published by Lake Union Publishing, Seattle

www.apub.com

Amazon, the Amazon logo, and Lake Union Publishing are trademarks of Amazon.com, Inc., or its affiliates.

ISBN-13: 9781662507458 (hardcover)
ISBN-13: 9781542036061 (paperback)
ISBN-13: 9781542036078 (digital)

Cover design by Lesley Worrell
Cover image: ©Lukasz Szwaj / Shutterstock; ©Anatolir / Shutterstock; ©Ron and Joe / Shutterstock; ©Texture background wall / Shutterstock; ©KanokpolTokumhnerd / Shutterstock; ©ami mataraj / Shutterstock; ©Vectorgoods studio / Shutterstock

Printed in the United States of America
First edition

For my sisters,
Theodora (1967–2011), Denise, Jeanette,
and Michelle,
brave daughters of a strong southern man

Prologue

My papa, Jean Bébinn, the owner of fifty thousand acres of the finest land in Louisiana, used to say a man falling down stairs was one of the saddest sights you could ever behold. Not only could you be certain the one falling would feel his body battered like the devil having his day on your behind, but there was also the fact that the person was surely humbled because he'd been unable to master this simple creation man made to overcome the ups and downs of the earth.

Mr. Christian Robichaud Colchester looked like that when I first saw him in the winter of 1860. He tumbled and spun like a hay rake falling down the front stairs inside Fortitude Mansion. His eyes caught me in one hot moment as he whirled. Black marbles they were, and they flashed with shock like everything he believed about the world had betrayed him with a snap of a twig—eyes that looked like they had been somewhere and had returned to find me and were asking, Would I help? Now I know I couldn't have seen his plea in that quick of time, but that was how it seemed. Papa's words came to me, and I felt sorry for the man rolling down those stairs. I rushed to the staircase and stood there. Never mind I was probably two heads shorter than the huge beast falling. I was and still am nothing but a bit of a soul in slight packaging. My body didn't have any sense of what my mind was making it do. I stood there and let him land on me.

Air fled my chest, and a tingling sensation sprang up and down my spine. I thought I'd never breathe again, but I heard him coughing like he was too full of air, like he had taken all my breath from me.

I think about that moment when I try to figure out when it all changed. When did he reach out like he was falling all over again and grab my heart with both hands and hold on like his life depended on it? When did I start holding on with him? He knows that I did, because that's what's making him so bold to ask what he's asking of me now. He wouldn't have done it otherwise. And by the same vein I wouldn't be sitting here thinking about saying yes. Because that's how much of me he has, and I'm thinking it wouldn't be a great thing to let the rest of me go too. It's just like standing in front of those stairs again. Can I break this fall? Inside that man is every notion of what I know about myself. He stands tall, like there's a force inside him drawing him up to his full height, and that same force makes me feel large as well. Our eyes on the world are great and unyielding, like we've seen too much to close them now. We say the words we want to say and don't care about the consequences. I know a bigger hell comes of keeping your mouth shut. We're that much alike. And yet he doesn't know what he's asking of me. For what he wants, I'd have to deny myself in a way that would dismantle every aspect of my humanity. And his, too, but that doesn't seem to concern him, perhaps because he's already done it for so long. Maybe that's why I've loved him—he's burned himself down to this purity, and it's all I can see of him. I can't see anything else.

"Jeannette, the only people who would give a damn are the ones who give a damn for you," he said. "You don't have people like that in this world."

No.

Not in this world.

Because I do think of Papa. That's what gives me pause. That and the love of my Creator, my Alpha and my Omega. Anyone might look at me and wonder how, in all my strangeness, I could demand love of any human being. I know I'm unusual to look at, with pale skin telling one story about myself and tight coils of light-brown hair telling another. And I'm hard in ways most admired women are soft. I used to think my half sister, Calista, imprinted the world like a cloud. But my papa's my excuse for everything I'm about to tell you. I was born of great love, and Papa bore me well in that love for as long as he could. I was a beloved child. I think I knew that before I knew anything else. So now I can't settle for anything less than such love. That's just the truth of who I am.

Chapter 1

Within minutes of my birth Madame Bébinn tried to burn the bed on which I'd come into the world. If her husband, Jean Bébinn, with me in his arms, had not stood between her and my poor mama, her body still warm and soaked in blood from where the life had drained out of her, Madame would have set fire to everything: woman, sheets, mattress, curtains. It didn't matter to her the bed stood within the walls of her own home. What mattered was her husband loved a slave, loved her enough to bring her into his house, into a white person's bed, to bear his child. Is it any wonder that whenever I crossed paths with this woman, I wanted to see her hands to make sure she wasn't holding any matches? Forever I could sense her need to set my hair afire.

Madame Bébinn was the reason why, in the late afternoon of a late-spring day in 1851, I stood at the door inside my room, considering the wisdom of leaving it to go to the kitchen for some food. Dorinda knew I ate alone when Papa was away, but sometimes Madame kept her so busy with added chores—bleaching Calista's sheets—she would forget to bring a meal to my room. I knew I could take the back stairs and easily avoid an encounter with Madame. The house slaves used this route when they moved from room to room to do their work. But I was twelve years old, and by then my feet instinctively obeyed Papa's constant reminder that I tread the same floorboards as him, his wife, and their daughter. "This is your home, Jeannette," he said. "You don't need to hide your head here."

But he didn't account for his wife, his frequent absences for business, and how much she had to drink on any given day and by what time. I'd learned to stay more than an arm's length from Madame. If I got any closer, she was always pulling my hair or pinching my arms. I knew her hatred smoldered and all it took was a breath from me to make it blaze.

I'd spent the morning studying Papa's map of the area of Louisiana known as LeBlanc. He wanted me to understand the breadth of the lands of Catalpa Valley, his plantation, and to know the fifty thousand acres as well as he did. By sight much of the fields were familiar to me, as I had viewed them from on high, on horseback, for most of my young life. Now he wanted me to know where the sugar mill, made of red brick, lay within our boundaries and how far out the largest field reached. Through Papa I learned what I know of the earth because our land had names. Sitting with the maps, I'd recite the names of the parcels as if they were the roots of my family tree:

Belle Neuve

Baton Bleu

Siana Grove

Chance Voir

Belle Verde

Mont Devreau

I haven't said these names out loud for years. Now they are marked on my heart.

"This earth belongs to you, Jeannette," he would say.

Not all of it. That would be impossible. But one particular section I knew was in fact mine: five thousand acres, called Petite Bébinn. It was land Papa had set aside for me, on which he planned to build me a house so I could be free and safe. It was land that would give me a living.

I suspected he thought I would never marry. As bright as my skin was, my hair would always have the rough texture of a negress. That's just a fact.

"Jeannette," Papa would say in our lessons, "tell me about the southwest parcel."

"It is Siana Grove, where the new-growth sugarcane gets planted and where the swamp meets the edge of the fields."

I liked looking at the map, but at times it was hard to listen without growing sleepy to all of Papa's words about how and when he'd acquired each parcel and how he'd used the word *valley* to name the estate because he liked the word. He didn't care that it didn't make sense because Louisiana's as flat as the bottom of a cast-iron pot. I loved sitting with him. His clothing smelled of tobacco and his breath of the sugarcane he chewed. The map's paper felt thick and satisfying between my thin fingers. I did wonder why Calista didn't have the same learning, nor did it seem required of her.

This thought of my half sister made me wonder where she was. Madame, when I was a baby, used to keep us apart, or she'd tried her best to. With no other children in the house, Calista, four years old when I was born, was naturally drawn to me. Dorinda said she would find Calista rocking my crib if it took too long for someone to come see about me when I cried. I suspect our connection grew when I learned to talk and she realized we called the same man Papa. Once I was walking, she would help me climb out of the crib and go to her room, where we'd share her bed. Dorinda, knowing how Madame would rage if she discovered me in Calista's bed, retrieved me early in the morning and tucked me back into my own bed.

As girls we escaped Madame's scornful eye by playing outside. Our favorite game was to climb onto the thick branches of the oak that shaded our back lawn. Long, luxurious strands of Spanish moss curtained the whole tree, and we loved to drape the soft fronds over our heads like hair and pull it over our shoulders like shawls. We pretended to be old wisewomen, like Deborah in the book of Judges, who sat under a palm tree and provided counsel to the people who came asking for it. Only we sat in a tree, not under it, and no one came to me and Calista, so we made up the people and the stories of their requests.

There was the man who complained about a farmer having sold him a horse that was lame, and there were the brothers who couldn't agree who would care for their old mother. There was the old mother who accused these same brothers of neglect. As we judged the fates of our people, it became clear that Calista was more merciful than I. She was always looking for a reason to explain why the person acted the way they did.

My argument was always the same: "But they should know better!" Because that was what Dorinda always said when she scolded me—I was a big girl and should know better. If I, at age six, seven, or eight, should know better, why shouldn't big people older than that know the same?

One day Dorinda found us holding court in the tree and asked what we were doing.

"We are the old wisewomen of Catalpa Valley," Calista said. "Do you need counsel?"

Dorinda laughed. "Older than me?"

I nodded. "And wiser too!"

"Oh, I don't know about that." Dorinda leaned against the tree's fat trunk and looked up at us. "I can tell the future. Can you all do that?"

Calista looked at me, and we looked down at Dorinda. "All right," Calista called down. "What's our future?"

"Now that depends. Whatcha want most?"

"Want most?"

"Uh-huh. Most out of the entire world."

The day was so hot that it seemed the moss could drink from the sweat on our skin. Calista smiled and took my hand.

"For me and Jeannette to stay here always."

"How you gon' do that, Miss Calista? You don't think you ain't gonna marry? You don't think the men won't come after you when you grown?"

She didn't say this could happen to me.

"They won't find us," Calista said. "We will stay here, and this moss will grow over us, and no one will see us again."

I draped more of the Spanish moss over her head. Her words made sense because I believed the moss could support and sustain us, though I didn't know how. Everything about Catalpa Valley felt that way, full of life and growing—the water over our bare feet when Calista and I waded in the creeks; the air when it seemed to soak up all the water until it felt so thick we could grasp a breeze in our hands and squeeze it to our hearts; the ivory-breasted kites who built nests from this moss and lived in the branches over our heads; the low bellow of bullfrogs searching for mates in the swamps. Why wouldn't we stay here, on Papa's land, and grow season after hot season along with everything else?

"Girl," said Dorinda, "you'll leave this place when it's time. Even the sugarcane does that."

But now Calista was doing a different kind of leaving. Ever since Dorinda had started bleaching Calista's sheets, she had grown distant, and I missed her. When Papa wasn't home, we often became islands floating solo about the great house. Calista stayed in her room, sorting through her dresses and staring into her mirror, until her mother, who didn't like to sit alone, called for her. She made Calista play piano while she sipped her sweet wine.

Madame never drank enough to get drunk, but she drank enough to make her bolder, enough to say or do things I don't think she would have said or done otherwise.

That afternoon I felt bold too. I can only think the wrongness of being forgotten came over me, and I was hungry, annoyed, and tired of being afraid. So I left my room and went to the main staircase.

My luck was bad, for Madame was already on her way up the steps, most likely in search of her daughter. When she saw me, she started like she'd seen a rat scurrying across the floor. She grasped her skirts higher and flew up the last of the stairs to where I stood on the landing.

"What are you doing? Where are you going?"

She always sounded like I was about to steal something or set fire to the house. But burning things was her notion, not mine. Her eyes flew up and down, looking me over, and her blonde curls bounced against her cheeks. I wore a simple fern-colored dress with soft ivory petticoats underneath. Papa always made sure I had nice clothes, but they were not the bright silk dresses Calista wore. Still, I knew every aspect of me looked wrong in Madame's eyes.

I meant to tell her I was going to the kitchen, but the craziness in her eyes provoked me and made me lie.

"To Papa's study."

The shock on her face satisfied me.

"I want a book we have been reading together." I felt my tongue slow as it touched the roof of my mouth to form the word *together*.

She reached out for my shoulder, but I stepped away. She shook her empty fist at me.

"There's nothing in there for you."

"What is Papa's is mine. He said so. Because he is my papa."

"What about Calista? He's her papa too."

"But she has you, and she can have your things."

Her lip curled upward, and half a toothy grin cut into her face. "Then by that reasoning, you should have what belongs to your mama—nothing but dirt."

The mention of my mama made my chest swell. "Then Calista and I would be the same, because from what I see, you don't own anything either. Everything is Papa's."

Madame's face glowed pink. "Why, you ugly little . . ."

She slapped me. The familiar stinging warmth flooded my left cheek. I exhaled.

"I'm going to the kitchen," I said.

"That's where you'd stay if I had anything to say about it."

I thought the words *And you don't*, but I didn't speak them aloud. She must have seen them, though, in the way I met her eyes and didn't turn away, my lips a mute straight line. That was when she grabbed my arm and dragged me across the wood floor.

"And take the back stairs! I won't put up with this when Jean is away! I've had enough!"

I kicked her and tried to scratch at her arms. She lifted me—I was small for my twelve years, so this was easily done—and threw me away from her. My back hit the wall near the staircase. My left foot slid down to the next step, and my arm flailed out to grasp the handrail, but it was too late. I fell sideways onto my right hip, then rolled down the rest of the stairs. My ankle and hip bone were sore, my wrist bleeding where it had scraped against the metal handrail.

A door upstairs opened.

"Mama! Stop it!" Calista rushed down the stairs and took me by the hand. "What if Papa saw you?"

Madame's eyes widened. Of course, he wouldn't stand for what she'd done. I didn't know how he might punish her, but Madame was well aware of the consequences, because she flew toward me and shook a finger in my face. "If you say one word to him . . ."

"She won't! Will you, Jeannette?" Calista, tall for her sixteen years, placed herself between me and her mother. I put a hand on the small of her back and shook my head.

"No," I whispered.

Calista stood her ground until Madame turned and climbed the stairs again. Then she moved down the hall to the kitchen and pulled me with her.

Calista was right. I wouldn't tell because I didn't like seeing Papa angry. The noise he and Madame Bébinn made when they argued sounded so loud it seemed to make the floorboards tremble beneath my feet.

"Why does she hate me?"

"I could ask the same thing about Papa."

"Papa doesn't hate you!"

"No. He doesn't." She gently tugged one of the coppery curls hanging near my shoulder. She used to pull my hair this way when we were younger, thinking it would straighten eventually. "But he doesn't love me like he loves you."

Calista pushed open the wide wood door. "Now go. Show Dorinda your wrist. I will soothe Mama."

When I had crossed the threshold, she closed the door behind me.

Dorinda had midwifed my birth. She's the one who told me of Madame's fire and my mama dying. I believed her because I could see the heavy sadness that pulled down her face when she talked of how she couldn't stop the blood. I would sit in the kitchen listening to her and chewing on the pork crackling she had given me. She went back to kneading bread dough, her work punctuated by heavy sighs.

"I seen many babies come into the world, and I know one or the other, mama or baby, don't always make it. But I prayed for Lindy. Knew your papa might go crazy for losing her. Didn't matter what she was. I know love when I see it.

"He loved you right off too. Didn't matter you was the ugliest baby I ever did see—all that orangey-brown hair, just like his, and a face pinched up like a pomegranate. But he saw himself in you right away, like he done spit you out. Light skinned, too, almost white. I said, 'Can't call her nothing but Jeannette because that's just what she is, a little you.'"

She had warned Papa not to let me out of his sight until I was old enough not to get smothered or bagged up and dropped in a river. Dorinda knew Madame felt me under her skin like a nasty itch and would do anything to get rid of me. Dorinda fashioned a sling and bound me to Papa so he could ride with me daily into the fields. That was my first sense of infinity: an endless ocean of sugarcane flowing beneath me and growing high enough for the fronds to sweep against Papa's thighs.

He was the talk of the parish—Jean Bébinn and his nigger baby. So many landowners sired children with their slaves. Only Bébinn made anything of it, of one of them. Me. They made allowances for both his wealth and being mad with grief. He also had a wife crazier than him, and they pitied him for it.

I had my questions. Riding the fields with Papa, I saw how the women were made to work as hard as the men. I didn't see how it could be possible for someone forced to work under the blazing sun to love the ones riding above them and wielding whips. Made no sense to me.

But whenever I asked Dorinda about this, she'd only say, "You can't know your mama's mind. You can only know what you know. Does your daddy treat you with love? Ain't you treated like you matter?"

Of course, I could only say yes, despite sensing that Dorinda probably did know my mama's mind.

"Then you got something most slaves will never have. Whatcha gonna do with it, Jeannette?"

"Everyone at Catalpa Valley matters, Dorinda."

"No, they don't. Not in the way you think. But you keep saying that to yourself. And keep the land on your heart and on your mind. Maybe one day you'll make that true. Make it true for us all."

I didn't understand, but I trusted her, so I said, "I will."

That afternoon Dorinda gave me biscuits and jam, and I went out to the gazebo on the far edge of the lawn near our wisewomen tree to eat them. I could smell water in the swampy air. It made the air feel like a soft blanket on my shoulders. I was happy then, and the only thing that could make me happier came next: the sound of Papa's voice rolling to me from across the yard.

"Jeannette!"

"Papa!" I ran to him and pressed my sticky jam fingers to his cheeks. "Where have you been?"

He kissed my forehead. "Oh, I had business. But look—a gift! I ordered it for you long ago, and at last, here it is!"

He returned me to my seat in the gazebo and wiped my hands before taking a small box of blue velvet from his pocket. Inside shone a small locket made of a burnished brown metal.

"Here, Jeannette. Open it like this."

He took the small oval between his fingers and pried it apart until it became two ovals. I gasped. Each one contained a tiny painting. The face on the left I recognized at once—Papa, his red hair combed back from his blockish forehead and growing down the sides of his face in bushy muttonchops. He wore the sour expression that made him repugnant to others but Papa to me.

On the right, a face I didn't know but found familiar. Her brown hair was not ringleted like Madame's. She wore it pulled back from her face, a small dark bun visible at the base of her neck. Her skin was the color of sand except for a whitish blotch like a cloud on her lower right cheek and chin.

"This is Mama?"

"Yes. Your mama. I had it done long ago."

He ran a finger along the curve of the metal frame. "I couldn't bear to look at it for some time. Not since she died. You see the scar?" He pointed to the cloud, and I nodded.

"I told the painter not to include it, but your mama insisted. My wife . . ."

Papa's eyes filled with tears. I moved closer and put my head on his shoulder.

"My wife had burned her there. Threw boiling water on her. I shouldn't have tried to forget it. I'm ashamed I asked. But she was still so beautiful. *Ma belle!*"

And she was. There was a calmness in her face and a glow that felt like staring into the full moon on a summer night.

"I wish I looked like her," I said.

"Ah, but you have her strength, Jeannette. You have her gentle soul." He took me by the shoulders and held me in front of him. "You are beautiful in your own way, and it's good that you don't look like her. When you become a grown woman, it will be important."

"But why, Papa?"

"There may come a time when you'll have to pretend Mama was not your mama. That's why I wanted you to have this. Even if you must pretend, you don't have to forget."

"I don't understand."

Before he could speak again, Calista called out, "Papa!" and ran to join us in the gazebo. Papa caught her up in his arms.

"Calista! Oh, look how tall you are! One day I'll return to find my little girl all gone, and you will be a woman."

"Almost, Papa," she said. "Almost!"

"Look, a present for you too!" He reached into his pocket and pulled out another locket similar to mine. Calista knew how to open it, and she smiled even wider when she saw the portraits. The one of Papa was the same. Madame's portrait looked recent, and I guessed it had been done when she'd gone to New Orleans last summer. She wore a midnight-blue gown that made her yellow hair bright. Her shoulders seemed stiff with pride.

I held out my palm and showed her my locket. We sat close, examining the portraits.

Papa said, "So you and Jeannette will remember us when we're gone."

"Oh, Papa, we will never forget you!" Calista threw her arms around his neck.

"Yes, but you both need to remember that you are my blood. Catalpa Valley is my blood and sweat, and it's all I've got to give you. Calista, you will have what the law won't allow for Jeannette. You must make sure she gets the land of Petite Bébinn."

Calista laughed. "Papa! Jeannette and I will always be together."

Papa pulled us toward him, a daughter in each arm. "Oh, I hope so. I hope so, my little ones."

"Yes," I said. "The moss from the oak will grow over us and keep us here."

He laughed. "Let's pray that we won't need it. I can't have you all living in the trees!"

He held us, and I thought about how I had been right about Madame. She owned nothing.

"Calista, where is your mama? Does she know I am home?"

I saw her hesitation. By this time of day Madame could be in one room and her mind in another. My half sister answered simply. "No."

"Then go tell her. She'll want to get herself ready for dinner." He said the word *ready* like it had two rough edges he would sand down with his tongue.

"Yes, Papa!" Calista kissed him on the cheek and ran back across the lawn to the house.

When she was gone, Papa turned to me, took my wrist in his hand, and examined it. Dorinda had applied a soothing paste with a cloth, but the scrape still shone red on my skin. I lowered my eyes, but he lifted my chin with his other hand.

"You won't tell me how you got this, will you? Not the truth anyway."

I whispered, "No, Papa."

"Because Madame had something to do with it. You don't have to lie, Jeannette."

"Please don't be angry with her, Papa. I know she doesn't like me. But I'm all right. She won't really hurt me because of you."

"True, but you must learn to protect yourself, Jeannette. Life will not be easy for you because I loved your mama. More people will be unkind to you, even worse than she. I will do what I can, but Madame is only a taste of the rest of the world. You must be strong, Jeannette. And you must never forget your mama."

I would have said *How can I forget what I didn't know*, but then I held her face in my hands. I opened the locket and looked at her again. Mama's head was turned almost hesitantly as though she wanted to question someone about why she had to be in the frame. She had a fullness to her face—not fat like Dorinda but healthy, well cared for. I recognized this roundness in my own face and sought to find more similarities. We seemed to share small ears cupped like tiny seashells to the sides of our heads. But she would make you look twice. A spark in her dark eyes caught you, made you wonder. I looked more like Papa, and I thought nothing about my looks would ever inspire a second viewing.

As much as I loved examining her side of the locket, it was his face I would never forget. I wondered at how he could ever doubt it. To me the word *mother* is the same as *father* because he was so completely both to me. I mimicked his voice when I learned to speak. And he taught me how to read, sitting on his lap in the evenings in his study. His warmth was my sun, his calmness my moon. But I answered because I wanted to please him.

"Yes, Papa."

"Did you study the maps today?"

"Yes, Papa."

"Tell me where your land is, Jeannette. What marks Petite Bébinn?"

"Petite Bébinn is bordered on the south by the line of laurel oak that runs up until you get to the cotton fields in the west. It is the farthest parcel of Catalpa Valley."

"And what will you grow there, *ma chérie?*"

"Can I grow lavender?" I loved the fragrant plants that Dorinda grew in the kitchen garden. If I could grow fields of it, I would lie down among the thin branches and sleep there under my mosquito net when the summer nights were too hot to be in bed.

He laughed.

I kissed him on the forehead, then ran my fingers over his brow. It was damp ever so slightly, like dew on the morning grass. He'd never sweated so gently before. Papa's sweat had always poured forth like tiny waterfalls down his temples. It made me smile.

"Oh, my papa," I said. "Use your handkerchief."

He kissed me back and wiped his forehead. I didn't know it then, but that was when his sickness started. It sneaked up on him slowly, like the sickness had a mind and knew that sneaking was the only way it could take hold of Jean Bébinn. The film of wetness returned and persisted. In the ensuing days, Papa seemed to tire easily.

Then came the morning, in late August, when Papa did not get out of bed. In the kitchen I watched Dorinda prepare a tray for him and saw the same sad veil she'd always had when talking about my mama.

"Don't look like he's going anywhere for now," she said. "He's mighty ill, Jeannette. Poor man's shivering like he's got demons under his skin."

She lifted the tray and balanced it on her forearm so she could open the kitchen door. When she turned back, I stood next to her, waiting to step through.

"Where are you going, little miss?"

"To see Papa."

"His sickness might be catching. That room ain't no place for chilrun."

"If you can go in, so can I."

Dorinda gave me the look I'd seen her give Papa when she knew it was no use arguing with him.

When we entered Papa's room, I saw Robie, Papa's manservant, gently laying Papa back against the pillows. He held up one of Papa's nightshirts and showed it to Dorinda.

"Gave him a fresh one. This one's soaked clear through."

"Papa," I whispered. I drew near and touched his arm. His lips fluttered together like they were making words, but nothing was coming out.

The dew I'd seen before now had swelled into a stream. Dorinda set a bowl of water down on the bedside cabinet, wet a cloth, and swabbed Papa's brow.

"He can't hear you right now. Best you sit over there." She indicated the window seat across from his bed. "You can stay hid if Madame comes."

I scrambled onto the seat and carefully arranged the curtain so I could see Papa without being seen. That was where I stayed.

Not long after the clock on Papa's dresser chimed two o'clock, Madame Bébinn entered without knocking, followed by Robie and Dorinda. She held a handkerchief over her nose and mouth and spoke to Papa loudly, like he'd gone deaf in his sickness.

"Jean! Jean!"

Papa stirred and nodded slightly.

"Jean, I've called for Dr. Clarke. I don't understand why you have to be sick now! And harvest time already on us. Good Lord!"

Papa's eyelids slowly opened, and his eyes rolled about in a strange way. All the while Madame fussed at him. I wanted to jump on the witch and make her leave him alone.

"Wh—wh—" was all Papa could manage. It sounded like he wanted to say *where*, but then his eyes fell on me, sitting still as I could in that window seat. I put my fingers to my lips and held them up to him—a kiss. Papa coughed and seemed to gather himself, determined to speak.

"Where is Robie?" He spoke slowly, each word a struggle, and his voice sounded thick and wet like the swamp. He coughed again, and Robie brought him a tin dish to spit in.

"Tell Mr. Cleaton to come here," he told Robie. "I will direct him about the work."

"Stop foolin', Jean! Nothing will be right about Catalpa Valley until you're out of that bed."

"Rest assured, Madame, one way or another I will be leaving this bed."

She stifled a noise underneath her handkerchief.

"Now if you'll leave me, I'll work out which way that might be."

Madame made another noise of disgust, and I heard the rustle of her skirt as she hurried out of the room.

Papa spoke again. "Dorinda. Water."

She moved swiftly to hold a porcelain teacup to Papa's parched and swollen lips.

"Jeannette."

I pushed the curtain aside, but only a little.

"Come, child."

I climbed onto the bed and embraced him where he lay.

"Are you scared?"

I nodded and whispered, "A little."

He kissed me on the top of my head. "Ha! Yes, just a little. Only a little because you are Bébinn. Too strong to be scared a lot!"

"I will stay with you, Papa."

"Ah! I would like that. We will fight together."

"Yes, Papa."

He slept again, and we stayed that way, my arms around him, until Dorinda returned to warn me of Dr. Clarke's arrival.

Dr. Clarke brought medicines for Papa and advised Dorinda to keep putting the cool cloths on his forehead. He suggested bleeding, too, but Papa roused himself enough to refuse.

"If it's all the same to you, I'd like to keep my bodily humors intact."

I thought Papa said this to spare me the sight of his blood, but he coughed, and I heard him utter "Barbaric" under his breath.

Papa stayed in his bed for ten days.

I sat by his bed and chanted the litany.

Belle Neuve

Baton Bleu

Siana Grove

Chance Voir

Belle Verde

Mont Devreau

Petite Bébinn

The sound of Papa's breath moved through the room. As long as I could hear it, I felt safe. From my perch I'd open the windows a crack so Papa could take in the fresh air, the air of the land that had always sustained him. It made no sense to me how Madame wanted the room shut up. What made Papa sick wasn't out there. If it were, we'd all be in our beds suffering. Papa burned from the inside out. I didn't know if the air could heal him, but it helped him feel a little better. I hoped it did.

Papa's bedroom faced the front of the house and had large windows overlooking the front grounds. The sill was long enough, wide enough, for me to sit there. The drape, thick and scratchy brocade, with a bronze-and-yellow pattern, hid me from Dr. Clarke and Madame. Only Dorinda knew I was there. She brought me warm milk and bread with pieces of roast pork wrapped in paper so I'd have something to eat if she couldn't get to me for too long.

The first day I felt certain Papa would get well. The second day the fever worsened. By the end of the week a yellow pallor bled over his skin, and my insides began to feel cold.

At night when the house slept, I left my seat and crawled under the covers of Papa's sickbed. I wasn't afraid. I'd known Papa's warmth longer than I'd known the heat of the sun. But I could feel it draining away, and hard as I tried, I couldn't replace it with my own. I didn't waste time being afraid. If Papa was going to leave me, I figured there'd be plenty of time for fear when it happened. And I didn't want Papa feeling any fear from me. I was Jean Bébinn's daughter. Still.

Papa woke from a nightmare.

"Chérie, I've been wrong."

"Wrong about what, Papa?"

"All of my plans for you . . . Petite Bébinn." He struggled for another breath.

"Please, Papa. Rest."

"I thought I would be here." He coughed. "I thought I would be here to give you the land. That you would be grown and could have it."

"I am still your daughter, Papa."

"But I can't look after you anymore. There's no one to take care of you." A tear ran down his cheek.

"I will take care of myself."

"The world is set against you, Jeannette."

"I don't need the world. I will have my own corner of it. I will have the land—if not Petite Bébinn, then somewhere else. I will find it, Papa. I will."

"If you are to do that, you must be white. When you are old enough, go away from here. Go far, where no one knows about your mama. You are light. Your features are mine."

I grasped the bronze locket I wore around my neck.

"And you must never wear that, when you are grown. Even now, perhaps. Keep it hidden."

"Papa, I can't."

"You must, Jeannette. The law won't let you own land."

I wiped his tears with my pocket kerchief. "I will be all right, Papa. Please rest now."

He nodded, smiled, and put his arms around me. His breathing quieted, and in the calm we both fell asleep.

Madame's wail woke me.

The sound collapsed on us like a shattering glass. But Papa didn't move.

His arm lay heavy over me, and I felt a chill from his body like he'd been encased in a cloud. My papa was dead.

Her cries offended me. I couldn't believe she would shed one honest tear for my papa. There was something shameful about her behavior, and though I felt Papa's loss growing like a sad black fog inside me, I wouldn't show myself breaking into little pieces of pity like she was doing. I slipped out of Papa's embrace, stood on the bed, and pushed my hands against my ears. I shouted at her.

"Stop it! Stop it! You shame my papa with your noise!"

Madame looked up at me. Her hands shook at her sides. "How dare you!"

"You only cry for yourself! You know Calista and I are the mistresses of Catalpa Valley now."

She screamed and slapped me. "Get away from him!"

"No! You get away!"

I put up my arms to block her blows, and when she didn't stop, I pushed back. My forearm struck her on the side of the head, and one of the combs holding her hair clattered to the floor. I pushed her again, and she tripped over her skirts. Robie, stunned, managed to catch Madame before she fell. If he hadn't caught her, I'm sure I would have stomped on her where she lay. I didn't care how much I hurt her. It didn't matter. My papa was dead, and this wicked woman wasn't, and that wasn't right to me. It wasn't fair that I now had no one to care for me. I jumped from Papa's bed, grabbed the comb from the floor, and threw it at Madame.

"I am glad you are not my mama. I will build my own home now. I will live on Petite Bébinn, and you will never step foot on my land or in my house! Calista will have to care for you. I never will."

The comb struck her breast, and Madame's face froze. The tears on her cheeks glistened. Her voice, in a tone I shall never forget, went quiet and hard.

"That child will make herself sick with all that fussing. Take her to her room, where she can rest for a good long time."

Robie picked me up by my waist, and I kicked at him.

"Take her out of here!"

I spat at her.

She said, "We'll see who is the mistress of Catalpa Valley."

Robie kept whispering, "I'm sorry, miss, I'm sorry," while he carried me down the hall. He said it one more time when he locked the door after putting me down in my room. Only it wasn't like my room. The maps of Catalpa Valley were gone. My papa's books were missing. I sat in my newly empty world and waited.

Chapter 2

After a while that barren room—my room and not my room—got to me. Papa gone. The maps of Catalpa Valley gone. Papa's books, the ones I'd been reading—all gone. I lay on the bed and cried. They were a child's tears, full of grief and bitterness and frustration. I wanted to keep crying those tears. It seemed to me I should weep for the rest of my life. And I tried to keep crying. Brought up wails from the bottom of my throat and squeezed my eyes until they burned. But finally I felt empty, like I had poured myself all out.

I sat up and wiped my nose with a handkerchief from my pocket. A voice came to me then. Whether it was Papa's or an angel's, I don't know. It said, *Sleep now, Jeannette. You must rest, else the journey will be too much for you.*

I didn't question it. I climbed under the covers and fell into a deep and comforting sleep. When I woke hours later, the warmth of the morning sun shining in my face, I felt a settling had come over me. That was what it seemed like. I felt strong. I got out of bed, changed out of the dress I'd worn for over two days, and washed myself. I buttoned up a clean dress and opened my window, which looked out over the back lawn and the path to the gazebo where I'd sat with Papa. The Spanish moss on the grand oak tree shifted back and forth in a late-summer breeze. Where was Calista, and where was our future now?

Papa had prepared me for this time. He had known that one day the maps and the books might be taken away. It was why he had sat with me for hours, why he'd asked me the questions again and again. I stood at the window, and from my tear-soaked throat I spoke the words I knew as prayer, as litany. I spoke the words imprinted on my soul.

"Fifty thousand acres make up our plantation, Catalpa Valley. The parcels are named Belle Neuve, Baton Bleu, Siana Grove, Chance Voir, Belle Verde, Mont Devreau. There is a section Papa set aside for me, five thousand acres, called Petite Bébinn."

The words comforted me. I pretended that I could see the maps laid out as big as real life outside my window, and I pointed in the direction of each parcel as I said its name. The land was alive to me in a different way now—no longer mere lines on paper on Papa's desk. I would have to trust it and trust the feel of the dirt beneath my feet. I didn't know what would happen to me next, but I knew the daughter of Jean Bébinn would be ready.

No one came to me until the late afternoon, when Dorinda brought me a small bowl of grits, collards, and red beans and a cup of milk. I hadn't thought about being hungry, but when I smelled the food, suddenly I was starving. While I ate, she looked me over.

"You been taking care of yourself?"

I nodded.

"Good." She dabbed at my cheeks with the hem of her apron. "Crying in here all by yourself. Ain't right. Your poor sister don't know what to do with herself. Been crying nonstop since Master died, but Madame ain't paying her no mind. Miss Calista been sitting next to Master in the parlor."

"Papa's in the parlor?"

"Yeah, in his coffin, dressed nice and ready to be buried."

"When will they bury him?"

She looked at me, her eyes floating with pity. "I wouldn't be concerned about that, Jeannette. Not sure Madame's gonna let you go anywhere anytime soon. She talking about how you were with your papa all that time. How you might have what he died of. Said we gotta keep you away from everyone."

"Where is Madame?"

"Shut up all day in Master's library. Been in a fit, got all sorts of strange men coming and going."

I wanted to be angry and indignant, but again the reason—that's the best I can call it—settled over me. What did it matter if I was standing next to a hole in the ground when they put what was left of Papa in it? And I felt sure he wasn't there, that what they would put in the hole had nothing to do with Papa. I had been with him when it had mattered most, to hear the words he'd most wanted to tell me, to know how much he'd loved me. Madame could have the shell of what remained. It was all she deserved and all she knew she had had of him in his lifetime. She had to keep me shut away to keep from being reminded of it.

"Dorinda, you have to take me to Calista."

She gathered my dish and cup into her apron and looked around as though Madame might come in at any moment.

"Not now," I told her. "Tonight. After Madame is asleep."

"I don't think she's slept since Master died."

"I have to see her, Dorinda. Please."

"All right. I'll come after the house has settled."

Calista's room was in the east wing of the house and one floor below. For once I would be grateful to take the back steps, as it would be the quietest way for Dorinda and me to make our way there. I waited a long time, sitting by the window and watching the daylight fade. When Dorinda finally appeared, she said, "We gotta be quick. Madame ain't sleeping, just like I said. But she's in your papa's library downstairs. Come on. Miss Calista's waiting for you."

We padded softly on our bare feet down the hall and descended the back steps. When we reached the broad white door of Calista's room, Dorinda didn't knock but turned the knob slowly so it wouldn't squeak.

Calista sat up in bed, one candle lit on the table next to her. Her hair, yellow like Madame's, hung long and loose over her shoulders. Her blue eyes were swollen and pink from crying. I ran to her and climbed onto the bed. She clung to me. Dorinda stayed by the door.

"I'll wait out here. Say what you gotta say, then come on. Don't know when Madame might decide to go to bed."

But for a few moments Calista and I had no words. We held each other and cried for the longest time. Finally, she took my face in her hands and looked at me hard as though she would examine me. "Your skin is cool, Jeannette. You have no fever. You are not sick?"

"No, not at all."

"Mama lied. She said you were burning up like Papa. Oh, Papa!" Tears streamed down her cheeks. "What will we do without him?"

"I don't know. He will look after us. We must believe that. But what happened to my room? Papa's books, the maps of Catalpa Valley, my things are all gone."

"She put Papa's things back in the library. Your things . . ." Calista swallowed. "She said your things had to be burned. That you wouldn't be needing them anyway."

"Why is she saying I am sick?"

"I don't know. Something's changed about her. A man came to the house after Papa died, and she threw him out. She's been like ice since then, stopped crying about Papa. I sit with him in the parlor all by myself. And she won't tell me what's wrong. But now that I know you are well, I will find a way to take care of you."

I reached beneath the front of my dress and removed my locket. The metal warmed to my touch. I almost didn't open it at first, but I longed to see my father's face again. I snapped it open, and there he was. His whiskers, the glint in his eyes. He was on the left side of the locket, positioned so he was looking at my mama. She looked silent and resolute, as though she'd known all along this moment would come. I closed it and gave it to Calista.

"Papa said it won't be safe for me to wear this anymore. Keep it for me. I know it will be all right with you until I can wear it again. But I don't know, Calista. I don't know when that will be."

"Mama has to treat you properly. This land is ours, Jeannette. Papa saved Petite Bébinn for you. That must give us some rights. Papa always said the land is everything."

"Yes." I thought about the litany and agreed. I knew the land would save us.

Calista reached for the mahogany box she kept by her bed, a treasure box Papa had brought back for her from New Orleans on one of his trips. She opened it and removed a section that revealed a false bottom. She placed my locket inside and closed the bottom over it.

I put my arms around her again. "Are you afraid?"

She ran her hands over my hair and kissed the top of my head. "I was. Now that you're here, I feel better. Mama wouldn't let me see Papa after he got sick, and then I couldn't find you."

"I was hiding in Papa's room."

"Yes, Dorinda told me. Oh, Jeannette, how I wish I had been with you and Papa."

A floorboard near the door creaked, and Dorinda entered the room. Her eyes burned with urgency.

"Madame! She's coming."

"Go, Jeannette, go!" Calista crushed me in an embrace, and I kissed her forehead. I climbed from the bed and followed Dorinda up the back stairs.

We made it to my room and heard voices. Dorinda and I realized Madame was coming to me, not Calista. I squeezed Dorinda's hand and motioned for her to go away. I didn't want Madame to find her there. Didn't want her punished by a crazy woman.

I looked around the empty room and wondered whether I should sit on a chair or get in the bed and pretend to be asleep. It didn't matter. Madame was going to do whatever she was going to do. I would be Jean Bébinn's daughter, which to me meant standing my ground, ready for whatever she would bring through my door.

When she opened the door, that's how I was, standing straight and strong on my own two feet. Madame jumped like she'd stepped on hot cinders.

"What are you doing?" She looked around the room, but there was nothing to be seen. "Why aren't you in bed?"

"I've slept enough."

She looked me up and down like she was trying to figure something out.

"Dorinda!"

Dorinda appeared at the door almost too fast. No way she could have made it back downstairs. I figured she'd been listening down the hall.

"Yes, Madame?"

"I want you to get some cloth and cover this girl's hair." She eyed my dress, grabbed it at the skirt, and rubbed the material between her fingers. The gray calico must have satisfied her, because she mumbled, "Plain enough," and turned around and went back into the hall. "Bring her downstairs to Master's office when you're done."

"Yes, ma'am."

We waited until Madame was gone from our view, and then Dorinda hurried me down the back stairs.

"I got a bad feeling," Dorinda said. "Madame working up something awful. Come on."

In the kitchen Dorinda rummaged through her basket of scrap cloths and found a rough and faded piece of blue muslin. She wrapped up the curls of my hair so they were hidden. Then she pulled me close to her.

"Somethin's gonna happen. It'll be in the dark of night or the early morning, before anyone's awake enough to see. You gotta be ready, Jeannette."

She went to the larder and wrapped biscuits and corn cakes in a cloth. She put two apples in another.

"Keep this food in your pockets. If something happens tonight, you'll have it on you. If you sleep here, go to bed in this dress and eat the food in the morning. If you're here in the morning, God willing, I'll bring you a proper sack to keep with you, take with you. You understand?"

I nodded, but one thing I didn't understand—where would I be going? I had no other family, had lived nowhere else but Catalpa Plantation.

Like she had read my mind, Dorinda said, "I don't know, chile, I don't know. But God will go with you." Her eyes widened with a spark of a thought. She opened the door outside and motioned for me to follow her out into the backyard. We went over to the kitchen garden, a few steps away. In one corner she kept a small pile of stones that she collected on her walks down to the creek. She used them to mark new plantings. Dorinda grasped one, and we took it inside to look at it by the light of the fire. It was small enough to go unnoticed; big enough to not be lost. It was dark gray in color with reddish-brown and white streaks. She shoved it into the pocket of my dress.

"Take this rock from your papa's land. You hold on to it, never lose it. That rock comes from clear water, so your mind will be clear. Keep the land on your heart and on your mind. Maybe one day it'll help you find your way back. Your papa's always with you. Don't forget that, Jeannette. I'll be praying for you. Now go. She's waiting for you."

I hurried out, but when I came to the front hall, I paused. To the right was Papa's office. To the left was the parlor. I heard Madame moving about in the office, and I figured she wouldn't miss me for a few more minutes.

Papa's body lay in a box polished so well that its sides gleamed in the candlelight. He didn't look like he was sleeping, as I'd heard people say of the dead. He looked shrunken, more like a shell, like something left behind. His face held no expression other than that of a man who had dropped everything within himself and moved on. To see him that way confirmed what I had already felt in my heart. Papa wasn't there. He had flown from his room that night, and I had been with him when he had done so. Our goodbye had happened then. But this body had held his spirit, and I was glad to see it well cared for and to know it would go in the ground of Catalpa. It was where he belonged.

I heard a low and bitter laugh behind me.

"Every promise he ever made to me was a lie."

Madame stood at the parlor entrance. She wore a black silk gown and clutched a fine lace handkerchief, though I doubted she had cried as Calista or I had. Her eyes were not red. She moved past me and spoke close to Papa's ear.

"Wasn't it, Jean? You made damn sure of that."

I thought she would spit in his face, and I wondered what I would do then, because I couldn't let her disrespect Papa's body. Instead she turned to me, and I saw what Calista had meant. I was used to Madame being a crouching thing, pinching me, hitting me, pouring words of bitterness all over me. It was like the weight of the world bore her down. Now she held herself up, her shoulders back, her head level.

"When Jean Bébinn courted me, he said I would be the jewel of his life. He took me from my father's New Orleans mansion and said he would bring me to a place where I could shine and make his world bright. That place was Catalpa Valley Plantation."

She touched the gilded frame of a painting on the wall and then ran her fingers over the fabric framing the windows. "We were happy early on, I think. I loved how the air smelled of flowers and green things growing. The city stank to high heaven even on the best of days. Soon I was with child. I gave birth to a boy. And Jean? A man couldn't have been more thrilled. But my baby died of the fever before he was a year old. I had Calista, but I don't think Jean got over losing that boy."

She snatched me by the arm and pulled me into Papa's office. Again, I noticed a difference. She was resolute in her actions, not frantic like she'd been when she'd pushed me down the stairs. "Next thing I knew, he was whistling again. Laughing again. And I thought things were gonna get better. But he wasn't laughing or smiling because of me. He'd gotten himself enchanted by your nigger mama. Like she'd cast a spell on him.

"I had to put up with her in my house and then you! Now he's up and died, and what do I have to show for it?" She grabbed some papers from Papa's desk and shook them in my face.

"Nothing! He leaves everything to Calista! And leaves land to you! He thinks he's had the last laugh. Well, I'm the one left standing. I don't have to live on his lies. I can make my world the way it's supposed to be, and that starts tonight."

I smiled. "The land belongs to us. Papa always said so."

"We'll see about that. You may be fair enough, but at the end of the day you're just a little nigger girl. You have to go where you can remember that."

I heard a horse outside and the sounds that said the horse was pulling a carriage or a wagon. Madame went to the door and opened it herself, not waiting for Dorinda or one of the men.

The man at the door had something wrong with his left leg. When he stepped into the house, it was like the leg forgot to follow, and he had to drag it into the room. Wisps of thin gray hair hung from under his hat and framed his thin, sharp features—a strange chin that came down straight until the very last moment, when it turned slightly upward like a pig's. I'd never seen him before. He removed his hat and bowed his head at Madame.

"Madame Bébinn," he said. "Got your message. Came soon as I could."

"Thank you, Mr. Amesbury. She's in here."

He followed Madame into Papa's library, but he looked at me and stopped at the threshold. "She's a light one." He rubbed a scruffy chin. "How old is she?"

"On her way to twelve."

"You sure you want to sell? A few more years you could get a lot more for her at one of the fine houses in New Orleans. They always lookin' for new fancy girls." He reached out to touch my face, but instinctively I stepped backward. I know he didn't like that, because then he put his whole hand on the back of my head, above my neck, and pulled me toward him. He smelled of whiskey and rotted food.

"She can't stay around here." Madame said it like that notion was all too obvious. When Amesbury looked at her, she followed that with, "My husband favored her. I'd rather she go somewhere far from Louisiana, where Jean Bébinn isn't known."

Amesbury nodded, looked at me again, and seemed to under-stand the situation was different from his expectations. "What's your name?"

"What does that matter?" Madame tried to cut me off, but I spoke over her.

"I am Jeannette Bébinn!" I thought he would hear the name and go away. I could see a question in his eyes, and that made me think he would not lay hands again on a daughter of Jean Bébinn. But it was not the question I expected.

"Can she read?"

"No, she cannot." Madame walked toward Papa's desk as she said this, like she thought the lie would work better if she kept in motion. But I cut in front of her and made it to the Bible that Papa always kept open on a table near the window. I placed my fingers on the lines of a psalm and read aloud.

"'My God, my God, why hast thou forsaken me? Why art thou so far from helping me, and from the words of my . . .'"

"Stop it!" Madame shoved me to the floor. She went to Papa's desk and spoke urgently while she wrote on paper.

"I understand your concerns, Mr. Amesbury. I am prepared to compensate you for your troubles." She opened a drawer in the desk and removed money. She offered it to him along with the paper. "Take this for your travel expenses. Here is my permission for the sale. You may keep forty percent of whatever you get for her."

His eyes widened.

"But you must take her tonight."

Reading the paper and hearing her words made him grin, and he looked like a pig who had eaten his fill—satisfied.

"Madame, don't you worry. You'll never have to hear about this gal ever again."

I got up from the floor. If she was never going to see me again, then she would have my words. I would tell her everything. "Madame, you are evil," I said. "And all your evil will roost in your bad heart and torment you, because my papa will know what you've done. He may be dead to this earth, but Papa is still here and all around me. He will go with me now, *and* he will stay here and haunt you. I swear to you, Madame, you won't have any peace on this land until I step foot on it again. Papa's soul is bound to this land, and so is mine, and so is Calista's. You will never be anything but a trespasser. I will go with this man because the sooner I go, the sooner your evil can turn in on you and poison you like the witch you are!"

Her face went dead white. Her fingers pulled at her skirt as though itching to reach for my throat. Amesbury grabbed me by the arm and shook me until it felt like he would pull the arm from my body. "I don't know what you've been learned, but you have to obey now." He pulled me toward the door, and I caught a glimpse of Papa's casket in the parlor. I pointed at it and yelled.

"Bury him, Madame! Bury him soon! Or he will rise up and strike you down for what you're doing!"

Madame looked all around her as though Papa were about to walk in the room. "I will bury him," she said. I saw her moving toward the parlor. Perhaps she was going to do it right then and there, with her bare hands. But that was the last I saw of her. Amesbury dragged me outside, and the door floated shut behind us.

Chapter 3

Amesbury struck me. He struck me so hard that when I hit the ground, I was shocked I hadn't blacked out. I remember thinking about the force it must take to make a person lose consciousness if that blow of Amesbury's couldn't knock me cold. But then maybe I was just hard-headed like my papa.

"I don't want to hear you say another damn word. Ever."

He pulled me up and into a cart. He tied a rope tightly around my ankle. I gasped. "That hurts!"

Whomp. Another blow. I fell backward in the cart.

"You don't listen too well, do you, smart gal?" He clutched the front of my dress and held me close enough to smell the stink of his breath. "I said you will never say another word." He got in the cart, picked up the reins, and went on like he was talking to himself.

"All anyone have to hear is a few words, and they'll know you got some education. Madame lying something desperate. Ain't no overseer worth his salt gonna let an owner pay good money for a troublemaker. Got to tell 'em you dumb, and if you say a damn thing, I'll cut out your tongue and make it true. You hear me? You smart enough to hear that?"

He turned around, and though it was dark, his eyes cut through, daring me to say yes. But I nodded and covered my mouth with my hands. He snapped the reins, and this man took me away from Catalpa Valley. Away from my home. He wouldn't kill me. He was willing to make me suffer, but he wouldn't kill me. I was worth something to him alive. I didn't have to fear for my life, but everything else I wasn't sure about, like my tongue. I figured I had to do two things: find a way to remember not to talk, not even to myself, and learn where I was going so I could get back to Catalpa Valley as soon as I could.

I reached for the stone that Dorinda had given to me. Her words and thoughts had a power I didn't understand, but if she believed it would bring me back home, then I believed it too. It just had to be true. If I didn't, I probably would have wailed myself sick, and Amesbury would have beaten me into a rag doll.

As it was, my head was clear enough to think of Papa's maps. I pictured them in my mind as best I could. I listened carefully to the bumps in the road and for familiar sounds to keep me oriented. The bridge at Belle Neuve made the cart bounce in the way Papa's carriage had always done. And I felt the careful curve the horses took, like the way Papa did when he was riding around the swampy, damp patch of ground that sat two miles west of the cotton fields at the edge of Catalpa Valley. There was a gate five miles after the cotton field. Amesbury got out to open and close it. Tears sprang to my eyes when we didn't turn around but drove through the gate. At that point we were beyond Papa's land. Since I hadn't gone much beyond the boundaries of Catalpa Valley, I was lost. I burrowed my head into a corner of the cart, covered my mouth with my hand, and wept. After a while I couldn't keep my eyes open, and I cried myself to sleep.

I couldn't have slept long. When I woke, it was still dark, but I could smell water. Not fragrant like rainwater on grass—this was water full of mud and decay. I figured it was the Mississippi. We must be going north. The river was on the left side of the cart, and I could see dim fires that must have been from boats on the water. Knowing we were near the river settled me. Papa had shown me how the wide old river cut up and down in the South, leading straight down to Louisiana.

If Amesbury kept us close to the river, I'd be able to find my way back to Catalpa Valley.

He stopped by a glade on the side of the road and built a fire. He pulled out a bedroll for himself and set about making himself supper. He only let me out of the cart long enough to relieve myself in the woods with him watching over me. Then he gave me a cup of water and tied me up again. I waited until he was asleep to eat the food Dorinda had given me. My head and neck were still sore from his blows.

While I ate, I thought of Madame and of all the ways I might have her punished. My anger felt like a wild animal in my heart, and I wanted her to suffer. But at the end of these ruminations, I'd still find myself lying on the hard boards of Amesbury's cart with no sense of where I was going or what my life was about to be. It seemed I needed to be thinking about what I had to do and not waste my energy on Madame. I was old enough to know that being angry wasn't easy. Dorinda used to say that cursing someone wasn't a matter of spittin' out words. You had to stay focused on the curse, nursing the words and the hurt, and after a while you wouldn't even know that some part of you was still working the curse, because it got so deep inside you. I didn't like that. If a thing was inside you like that, it had to be eating you up. Just stood to reason. I didn't care enough about Madame, even in hate, to let her have that much of me. I didn't know what to do with the hate, though. I couldn't resolve it, so I put it aside. I figured I'd get back to it when I got back to Catalpa Valley. I'd find a way to avenge myself against her, and that would be that—at least that was my thinking.

The problem in front of me right then was how I was going to live wherever Amesbury was taking me without talking. Maybe it wouldn't matter so much once he went away? But since I didn't know our destination, that was a calculation I couldn't make, not with any certainty. All I could do was pay attention and take whatever chances came my way.

It rained once as we made our way. It was that kind of rain that feels heavy, like a cloud has been wrung out like a sponge. I felt the saddest I'd ever felt since Papa had died, because the rain made it feel like the world was weeping all around me. My dress stuck to my skin and made me cold and sunk, pulled down into darkness. I crouched into a ball in a corner of the cart closest to being underneath Amesbury's seat and fell asleep.

Wherever we had arrived, we got there in the dark. Someone pulled me from the cart and put a fire to my face. I couldn't see who held the torches, but I felt myself being handled. My head was jerked around, my limbs pulled. The hands tried to force open my mouth, but I was awake enough to know to keep my jaws clenched shut and not make a sound. I heard men's voices murmuring, and they kept murmuring when I was taken away to a place that was a circular yard of dirt. Buildings that seemed like stables lined the edges. I heard a man's muffled scream. I knew it was muffled because the sound was so deep and wretched that it should have been much louder—higher and louder. I guessed he must have had something forcibly covering his mouth.

I was thrown to the ground and told, "Stay!" Then a colored man, naked to the waist, was thrown near me. He landed heavy like a sack of potatoes and didn't move or make a sound.

"Nigger passed out," I heard a gruff voice say.

The man's face was half-concealed behind a length of leather strapped over his mouth. There was enough firelight for me to see he was unconscious. When he hit the ground, an awful smell reached me. I saw a huge welt in the shape of an *H* and a *W* together rising from his skin, and I realized I was smelling burning flesh. I threw up.

Someone grabbed me by the wrist.

"What about this one? Jeez, she's messed all over herself."

Again, a light was shone in my face, and I stared into the face of what I was sure was the devil. One of his eyes was dead blue, the other brown. He had thick, greasy lips that protruded from underneath a heavy, dark mustache.

The one who'd grabbed me said, "She's little, ain't she? Just a bag of bones."

The devil man spat out tobacco juice. "Amesbury said she's twelve."

"I'd sell my prize hog to slaughter if she is! I'd say ten at the most."

"Either way, we shouldn't brand her. She so light that Missus Holloway will want her in the big house. Gal almost white. Blue eyes and all."

"Go put her in Fanny's place. She'll look after her in the morning. Aunt Nancy Lynne can sort her out after that."

The hands carried me somewhere and shoved me into a dark space. I fell into something that felt like a table. My side hurt.

"Who's there?" The voice sounded high but calm. I said nothing.

"Ain't you got a name?"

I stayed quiet but breathed hard from the pain in my side.

"Come on over here."

I followed the voice in the darkness and felt smaller hands this time. They went over my shoulders up to my head and held my face between them.

"Lawd, you ain't nothing but a chile. Lie down here. Go to sleep."

The voice reminded me of Calista's—the voice of someone not yet a woman but no longer a girl. I obeyed her and, with my own hands out in front of me, felt my way down to a pallet on the floor. It had a roughness that made me think it was made of hay and with a rough covering like burlap. It wasn't bare wood floor like the cart, so I was grateful for the pallet and the voice that had led me to it. The voice's soft hands cradled me to her like a doll, and I felt warm and even safe. I fell asleep.

"Lawdy, help me!"

I opened my eyes and saw that my bedmate had drawn away from me. She'd pulled the cloth of her shift to her mouth like she wanted to muffle the sound.

"You a white girl?"

"No." Then I gasped and covered my mouth with my hand. I looked around the room and saw nothing but a rough table and the smoke of a small fire burning out black and dirty in the hearth. I whispered, "He said never to speak."

"Who?"

I moved away from her, the both of us at the ends of the pallet. I had more right to be scared. She had sounded like a girl, but to see her in daylight, she was much bigger than me, with heavy breasts and thick hips that made her seem full grown. But I sensed she looked older than she was in the same way that I looked younger than I was. I couldn't have scared an adult the way I had scared her. She must have seen I was more afraid than she was, because she lowered her voice too.

"It's all right. Nobody here but us."

"The man who brought me here."

"How come you can't talk?"

"They might find out. Find out I can read."

She sucked air through her teeth. "Writin' too?"

I nodded.

"Show me."

I went to the hearth and knelt near the ashes on the floor. She stood tall over me. I guessed she couldn't be much older than Calista. Her large breasts were barely contained by the loose cloth of her shift.

"What's your name?" I whispered.

"Fanny."

With my finger I drew the letters into the dust and ashes. When I was done, she stared hard at the word and traced the indentations with her own long fingers.

"That's me. That say me."

Her hands went to her face, and the ash dusted the cheeks of her tawny-brown skin. She closed her eyes, and I thought she might even lick the ash from her fingers. She looked again at the floor.

"Fanny."

She stood and shuffled her wide bare feet through the letters until they were smeared and gone, and I wondered how she could stand to have her feet so dirty. But we stood on a dirt floor, and I guessed dirt was the way of life in this place. Like Madame had said, dirt was all my mama had. Now dirt was how I had to live.

"That man right. Boss Everett, he the overseer, whip us both to death. But he don't know?"

I nodded, then asked, "Is that the man with the different-colored eyes?"

"Yeah. Don't say nothin' to nobody but me." She lowered her voice even more. "And whisper. Can't let anybody hear."

I nodded again.

"What they call you?"

"Jeannette. I'm Jeannette Bébinn."

"No Bébinn now. We all called Holloway. That's your name."

"I am Bébinn! My papa was Jean Bébinn and—"

"Hush! We got to eat and get up to the house. From now on we only talk at night. We be safe that way."

Fanny stirred up the fire and put a grate over it along with a small cast-iron skillet. She made bland hoecakes out of nothing but some cornmeal, water, and lard. She ate quickly and twice the amount that I managed to swallow. I chewed the makeshift breakfast best I could.

"I won't say any more until night," I said. "But Fanny, tell me now. Where am I?"

"This here's Mississippi."

Off the maps, that was what that meant to me. No longer on Catalpa Plantation, far from the dirt of my papa's land. But how far? I couldn't figure. Were we still near the big river? And how far north?

Fanny grabbed my hand. "Come on now. Gotta hurry."

We walked along a lane of shacks, rougher than the slave quarters at Catalpa. No steps or small porches. Just row after row of sadness— that was what it seemed like anyway. When the shacks ended, the lane curved to the right and moved under tall trees. Trees so tall I couldn't see the whole of the big house when we got to it. The house took all the shade while the wood of the shacks baked and dried out in the heat of the sun. We went to the back of the house, where she pushed down on a latch of a back door and we went in. Fanny took an apron from a hook on the wall of a small anteroom and tied it over my dress. Then she grabbed a large black dress from another hook and pulled it on over her shift. She tied on an apron and led me into the house kitchen. We put on soft-soled shoes that made no sound when we walked across the floor.

The room smelled familiar—corn bread, real corn bread and not what I had just eaten, cooled on a side table, and there was a big fire, coffee boiling. Just like Dorinda would have had it at Catalpa. The way it still was, going on without me. My fingers grasped the stone Dorinda had given me in the pocket of my dress, and I took in the whole of the kitchen. It was bigger than Dorinda's, where she sometimes toiled alone. Four women moved about in the Holloway kitchen. But I could see, or rather hear, they weren't in charge. A strong-looking tall woman wearing a black dress and white apron decorated with two lengths of white ruffle that crisscrossed her chest worked at tearing collards from their thick stems with her sandy-colored fingers and delivered a stream of commands and criticism while she did it.

"Mabel, that dough is too dry," she said. "Add a bit of milk to it. Corrine, you making them pieces too big. They ain't never gonna cook like that. Bess, go get them yams from the cellar—I ain't gonna tell you again." She stopped talking when she saw me.

"That the new gal?" she asked Fanny.

Fanny nodded. "Yes'm, Aunt Nancy Lynne. But she don't talk."

"What's her name?"

I held my breath. If Fanny told them my name, they would ask how she knew, me showing up in the dead of night and all and not talking. But Fanny was already ahead of me and being smart about what we had to do.

She shrugged. "I don't know."

"Why don't you know?"

"I told you, she can't talk!"

"Dumb?"

"Don't know, Aunt Nancy Lynne. Can't tell if I can't ask her."

"Fool child, you can ask her anything. The trouble gonna be figuring out what she ain't gonna say." Aunt Nancy Lynne put her face so close to mine I could smell the oil of her skin. "You got sense, girl?"

I took a moment to answer. It seemed good to have sense, bad to be too quick. Finally I nodded.

"Go cut up one of them apples."

She moved away from me so I could see the long wooden table where the other women were working. They pushed and shoved at dough, stirred batter in bowls, and sawed at slabs of meat. On the end closest to me was a bowl of red apples.

I wasn't used to knives. The long ones looked big enough for me to chop off a finger, and they scared me. I picked up a smaller one with a thin blade and chose a big apple. I cut through it, core and all, to make it two pieces, then kept going like that until the apple was a mound of messy chunks. I wiped my hands on the bottom of the apron Fanny had tied on me. Aunt Nancy Lynne muttered, "Humph," and went to a pot over the fire and returned to stirring and calling out.

"Lee, take what she done cut there and use it in the applesauce, but pick out them seeds. Child cut up core and all in there. Fanny, you best keep her with you for now. She'll be in the way in here. Don't know nothing about being in a kitchen. But I'll teach her when I got a minute."

Fanny hesitated.

"Go on now. She'll do what you tell her to; she ain't stupid."

"But I don't even know what to call her."

"She looks like a Ruth to me. Call her Ruth, maybe Ruthie. That'll be just fine."

Fanny turned her head away from Aunt Nancy Lynne and scratched her face, and when she motioned to me to follow her, I saw she was trying not to smile. I was a slave and an orphan, and I didn't care if I never spoke again, because no words could catch all the damn hopelessness running at me. That touch of a smile from Fanny didn't make me feel any better, but suddenly it seemed possible that I could step in the direction of better. And now I had a name that wasn't mine, and I was supposed to answer to it.

Fanny showed me up the back stair and put a finger to her lips to remind me not to say anything. For a moment, she couldn't say anything herself. The climb upstairs had winded her. When she had caught her breath, she explained the family and the house. The Holloways were Missus, Massa Holloway, and a daughter and two sons, all full grown. Missus would be getting dressed in the room we approached. We had to go in when she was done and empty the night pots and clean up the washbasins. We refilled the water pitchers. Then we made up all the beds on the floor and gathered anything that needed washing. When we finished, we went downstairs to help Aunt Nancy Lynne in the kitchen. "You know how to sew?" she asked me.

I indicated that I could, a little. Dorinda had taught me.

What I remember most about that day is how we never stopped and barely ate. Aunt Nancy Lynne gave us biscuits around midday, but we had to eat them while we carried out sheets for washing. My legs walked and climbed and my arms lifted and carried more than I'd ever done my whole life. I was so exhausted by the end of the day that I fell onto the pallet and would have fallen fast asleep if Fanny had not roused me and insisted I eat a bit of the collard greens and salt pork that Aunt Nancy Lynne had given us to take back to our tiny shack.

"You'll be all right," Fanny said. "You just ain't used to working. I fell asleep the same way when I first had to go work in the big house."

"How old were you?"

"I don't rightly know. Seven or eight, I guess."

"How old are you now?"

"Don't know when I was born. How old are you?"

"Twelve."

"It seem like I'm older than you, don't it?"

"Yes. I'd say you're fifteen or sixteen. Calista, my half sister—you remind me of her. She's sixteen."

I went quiet for a moment. "Fanny?"

"Yeah?"

"I don't want to get used to this life."

"What else you gon' do?"

"I don't know. Not this."

Those early days of no freedom could have been days of misery. But I was with Fanny. I followed her throughout the house every day emptying chamber pots, washing linens. At night we helped Aunt Nancy Lynne and the other women scrub down the kitchen worktables, wash the dishes, and prepare for the work Aunt Nancy Lynne did at night. Aunt Nancy Lynne liked that my hands were small and careful. She trusted me with the Holloway china, which I cleaned with a soft rag in a pot of soapy hot water.

I felt so grateful to Fanny that I wanted to teach her how to read. It was the only gift I had to offer. Maybe I could unlock something for her, help her feel some of the freedom I had known, give her a piece of the world from one of Papa's maps. But she refused to learn.

"Don't make sense for me to read. What would I do with learning? Where would I get a book to look at? If Overseer Everett caught a slave peeking at a Bible, even if it was nothing but the pictures, he'd whip the skin off the bones—man, woman, or child. Don't matter who."

But Fanny, as I suspected, was smart. She didn't want to read, but she had a curiosity about language. I'd been on the plantation about two or three months when we were doing our whispering before going to sleep and she asked me about a word.

"Other day Missus Holloway told me to tell Massa Holloway in the dining room that she gonna be there—" She stopped and slowly formed the *pr* sound on her lips. "Pre-sent-ly. What that mean? Like a Christmas present? Why she say that?"

"Just meant she was gonna go to him soon. Spelled like *present*, though. The word got two meanings."

"Two? How you supposed to know both? How can you read it if they look the same?"

"You just know—all the other words around it tell you which meaning to use."

"Oh Lord." She laughed. "That's too hard."

"You would remember it, Fanny. You're smart enough to remember."

"I remember the way my name looked in the ashes when you put it there. I'll never forget that, for sure."

Suddenly she gripped my hand.

"Shh!" she hissed.

We heard it far down the lane—a distinct sound of a foot leaving the drive from the big house and biting into the gravel with the first crunch of movement toward the slave quarters. Fanny pressed her hand over my mouth and moved her lips close to my ear. She spoke so softly I only caught the words "no matter what happens."

We lay still in the dark. The fire had burned out long ago. I prayed the dark would protect us, make us invisible so whoever was out there wouldn't find us and would keep on walking. My plea went unanswered.

When he opened the door, the smell of him flooded the shack. He stank of whiskey and sweat and the mustiness of a cellar. I crouched closer to Fanny.

Next thing I knew, he was on top of me. He didn't say anything. His large puffy hands fumbled over me and pulled at my shift. The shock of his silence kept me from crying out with words. I pushed at his chest and shoulders, but my thin, straw-like arms were useless. I felt another hand on me, on my shoulder, and I realized another set of hands was pushing and we were all tied into a wordless, grunting, whimpering ball of struggle. Fanny was pushing me off the pallet. I slid onto the dirt floor and rolled away. He must have thought she was fighting him. I heard the blow of his hand against some part of her, her head or her face. Then Fanny, I knew, was the one underneath him. I wanted to help her, but her left arm stuck out straight, keeping me away from her. I wanted to leap onto Everett, for this was certainly him, and rip at his hair and pull his eyes out to get him off Fanny.

He grunted and panted and sounded, at times, breathless. But Fanny's silence deafened me. I stifled the tears rising in my throat. It was over fast, and Everett stumbled out after, still without a word.

I wanted a knife in my hands. I thought only the cool of a blade pressed into Everett's white flesh could lessen my burning anger.

"I'm all right," Fanny finally whispered.

"Fanny." I wet a rag in the small bowl of water from our table and crawled back onto the pallet. I took a guess as to where her bruises might be and touched the rag carefully to her face.

"Shh."

"He does this?"

"Shhh. Yeah."

"You pushed me away."

"You too young. Wouldn't know how to take it."

"I'll never let him do that to me."

"Like you could've stopped him just now?"

I was silent. My anger soured into shame. I lay the wet rag on her forehead, and I turned away from her on the pallet.

"Jeannette," she said. "You don't know nothing about being a nigger."

"Me being a nigger is like you with reading. Something I don't want to learn."

"You don't learn, you get yourself killed. Or worse. Just pray. Pray for all of us."

I folded my arms beneath my head. "Pray to who?" I asked. "And what for?"

"God."

"God don't seem to be much good around here."

"You don't know that. All of us dumb when it come to that."

I sat up again. A warm bubble of anger formed deep in my chest. "What do you mean?" I said. "Like there's a reason for negro men to be branded like cattle? And you and, for that matter, my mama being taken against your will?"

Fanny touched my arm and shushed me. "God don't cause any of this craziness," she said. "He probably just as mad about it as you are."

"Then why don't he do something about it?"

"How do you know he ain't?"

I bowed my head. I thought about how I didn't have Papa or a mama; how Madame had sent me away.

"It's awful you here," Fanny said, like she'd been reading my mind. "But you ended up with me, and we can look after each other. That's something."

"Yes."

"So pray to God and say, *Thank you!* You can do that."

She pulled me to lie down again, and she put an arm around me.

"I guess so," I said. But I didn't see my way to it just yet.

Church at Catalpa Valley happened every week. It involved a lot of talk about hell, and that didn't interest me. Sounded like God caused plenty of trouble.

"What do you know about God, Fanny? Is there a church here?"

"I don't need no church. I feel God around me all the time, even when I was little. Don't need no white man waving a big old book at me to tell me about God. And I suspect that white man making up a lot of what he talks about anyway."

I didn't know what "worse" meant for Fanny, but I suppose there are other ways of dying. Like how, with each encounter with Boss Everett, my heart reconsidered the story of Jean Bébinn and my mama and my living in the world. I thought about what it had been like for my mama, whether Papa had gone stealing into her bed and, night by night, taking her soul away in pieces. When I closed my eyes, I tried to recall her face in the locket, her expression blank—neither serene nor frightened, neither happy nor sad.

"He come out here after his wife got big with a baby," Fanny said. I had asked her about Everett and whether he had a wife. "He stops messing around when you get big like that."

"What? You had a baby?"

"Naw." She paused. "Well, I did. But she was dead when she was born. Boss stayed away after it happened. Now he back."

"I'm sorry about your baby."

"I'm not good at carrying a baby."

I put my arms around her.

"It's not your fault," I said. "You're good at everything."

"Well, right now we have to take care of you. If he gon' start up again regular, you can't be here."

"Where am I gonna go? I don't wanna stay with anyone else. I don't know nobody else."

"Aunt Nancy Lynne will know. Maybe you can help her with her night work."

"Aunt Nancy Lynne, can Ruthie help you bake crackers?"

Aunt Nancy Lynne's crackers and pastries were famous all across the countryside. Neighbors requested her wares for their special occasions, and the Holloways allowed her to earn her own money baking. She did it at night, after her kitchen duties were over.

"Why would she want to stay up all night in the kitchen with me?" Aunt Nancy Lynne paused over the chicken she was carving up into parts. She peered over her glasses and studied Fanny. "Boss Everett bothering you again?"

Fanny's chin dipped to her chest, and she nodded. She squeezed my hand, and I didn't know what else to do but look down too. Because now I would be really alone and without words. When would I speak now? No one else cared for me. I received only cold looks from the quarters when Fanny and I walked to and from the house. Those looks came of my looking too strange, too white. To the other slaves, my looking like that meant I could only be a spy or some kind of abomination.

But Aunt Nancy Lynne spoke to that, too, like she knew what I was thinking.

"She gon' have to talk if she work with me. Don't look at me like that, Fanny. I know the girl can talk." She narrowed her eyes and peered at me. "Can't you? I hear you sometimes."

"It's not her fault," Fanny said. "Man who sold her threatened to hurt her." She lowered her voice. "And she can read."

"Can she work figures too?"

Fanny looked at me, and I nodded.

"All right then. Leave her to me."

That night Aunt Nancy Lynne laid out a pallet for me behind a curtain in the pantry. She gave me a biscuit and a bit of ham to eat for dinner and told me to lie down and rest. She would call me when she was ready for me to work.

And work I did. I prepared the ingredients—cut up butter, sifted flour—while Aunt Nancy Lynne performed the magic of putting it together the right way. I built up fires and moved the pans of buns, crackers, and rolls in and out of the oven. This became my existence at the Holloway Plantation. When I was done baking with Aunt Nancy Lynne, I would walk back to the barren four walls I shared with Fanny. If Everett had been there, he would be gone by then. I would fall onto the pallet and into a deep sleep.

We did eat a little better because of my work with Aunt Nancy Lynne. Instead of leftover flour and scraps of fat we were allowed to scavenge after the Holloways' dinner was done, Aunt Nancy Lynne would send me away with a fresh bit of bread or a small basket of crackers. It became poor comfort, though, as the months passed and the winter came on. The winters were mild but cold, and our thin clothes, made from scraps like the food we ate, provided no warmth. Aunt Nancy Lynne and Fanny worked through the autumn to stitch together new dresses of linsey-woolsey so we'd look presentable working in the house for the holidays.

Another thing I liked about night work: When the men who worked late or at other plantations came back, they would stop in the kitchen, and Aunt Nancy Lynne would feed them. This was how we got news. One slave, Silas, knew the most because he traveled with Massa and had gone on many journeys with him. He'd been on trains and had seen cities like New Orleans and Atlanta. His appearance was different, too—he was always clean shaven and wearing nice clothing that Aunt Nancy Lynne had made for him.

Silas was how we found out about what the abolitionists were up to and how the people of the Southern states didn't want to stop keeping slaves.

"If abolitionists had their way, we'd all be free tomorrow," he said.

Aunt Nancy Lynne shook her head. "Guess they don't have their way, do they? And I don't see them getting it anytime soon." She often sounded bitter, and I soon learned she had good reason to be.

Working so close to her as I did, I got to know her better. She was intelligent and highly valued by the Holloways for her wisdom. That was why they let her earn money. She'd wanted to buy the freedom of her children, a boy and a girl, who she had kept as close to her as she could. Her little shack on the lane was the nicest because the boy had learned carpentry skills and kept the shed in good repair. They were allowed to live as a family, and she thought that she could save up enough to buy their freedom.

"But my boy, Jacob, he got hired out on New Year's Day, 1850."

Every year on the plantation, after the holidays, came the day when the Holloways would hire out slaves to work elsewhere until planting season came around. It was always a fretful time. A scant few might better their situation if they went to a kindly owner who clothed and fed his slaves well. But mostly that wasn't the case, and any slave who knew better would rather shiver in their windblown shacks than work for a massa who could only afford to hire slaves and not have his own. They were the meanest souls because they knew nothing they had was any good. The only thing that kept them from working a slave to death was the knowledge that they had to bring them back in a few months.

Aunt Nancy Lynne's son had been hired to a good massa, but that had turned out to be a blessing and a curse. A blessing because he'd been valued and well fed. A curse because the man could afford to buy Jacob away from the Holloways.

"I still figured I could buy him back. Worked my fingers to the bones, didn't sleep for what seemed like a year. I had three hundred and twelve dollars. Three hundred and twelve dollars of good paper money."

"Was it enough?" I asked. I felt a twinge of hope despite knowing the answer couldn't have been in Aunt Nancy Lynne's favor. She was still shoving dough in hot ovens in the middle of the night, and there was no sense of joy about her.

"Won't never be enough. White folks will never let it be enough." She rubbed her hands against each other, and the flour on her skin drifted into the air between us. "One day the Boyce brothers came by the house with a brand-new chandelier Missus ordered for the front hall. Made of brass, it was. I was thinking about who the poor nigger gonna be to have to polish the thing. Then Missus asked me to loan her money to pay for it."

"What? Why?"

"She went all pouty. Say, 'Aunt Nancy Lynne, go in and get me the money to pay Mr. Boyce. You know my husband isn't home.' I said the Boyces could bring the chandelier back when Massa come home. She smacked me on the back of my head and told me don't be ornery. 'It's just a loan,' she say. That she didn't want the Boyces to take the chandelier all the way back to their place; it was too big and too heavy."

The corners of Aunt Nancy Lynne's mouth hung down. "So I went in there and got my money and gave it to her. That was six months ago. Ain't seen a dime from her since."

"But that's not right."

"Who gon' say so? Me? A court of law? Girl, I know you smarter than that. If the children I birthed from my own body aren't mine, what claim I got to three hundred dollars?"

I stared at the table full of finished breads. Why were we doing all this?

"The Holloways own me, and as long as they own me, I don't own nothing."

"Why do you keep baking?"

"Because I don't let on to Missus what I take in anymore. Not all of it anyway. I keep enough to give her when she asks for it. Got a hiding place for the rest. Gonna get some freedom for somebody one of these days."

The days stretched into months. My existence at the Holloway Plantation changed very little. I didn't call attention to myself, but I knew it would be harder to go unnoticed as I got older. Even at Catalpa Valley, when a female slave reached a certain age, it seemed everyone had an eye on her, negroes and whites alike. White women wanted to use her skills, like Missus did with Aunt Nancy Lynne, or keep her beaten down and away from their husbands. Men wanted to use her like Boss Everett used Fanny. But if the man was a slave, at least there was the possibility of marriage and a family. And this had me thinking about my mama again.

Chapter 4

Aunt Nancy Lynne said Silas could be trusted, and because I trusted her, I talked with him. I liked asking him questions about his travels. From him I learned that the Holloway Plantation was farther east than I'd known before. And there were places where a traveler could get on a train or board a coach and cross many miles. Silas had gone as far north as Virginia with Massa Holloway and didn't shy away from talking about it. In fact, I liked that about him—he didn't seem afraid or burdened by his lot. Seemed like he didn't have a fearful bone in his body. He laughed when I told him so.

"I used to be scared. Scared enough to be scared for every soul under this roof. Scared about being cold, scared about not having enough to eat, scared about gettin' whipped." He sat in a corner, cleaning and polishing boots.

"What happened?"

"Just got tired of being scared, I guess. It didn't do nothing. Didn't stop Boss Everett from burning me with the fireplace poker when he thought I was lookin' at 'im sideways." Silas pulled up his sleeve and showed me the long, thick line of blackened skin running like a mountain ridge along his forearm.

"That coulda been my head. But I was too quick for him." Silas shrugged. "Anyway, I figured right there I was gon' stop being scared.

Just gonna be me. If I'm me, I can handle things just like I did that burn. They not gonna make me live like a rat. Not Silas."

What Silas said made sense to me. Made sense when nothing else around me did. Being afraid wouldn't get me anywhere. I suspected it was the same as with Amesbury—a slave had a certain value; all of us did, from someone small and obscure like me to someone as polished and shining as Silas to every single soul laboring under the sun in the fields each day. The Holloways lost money if one of us died. That was why they were so invested in the whip and branding—pain induced fear, and the fear kept it all going. I don't know if Amesbury would have cut out my tongue, but it got me to thinking about how to figure out what was a real threat and what was a fear threat. And what could I risk when I knew which was which?

The summer after I turned thirteen, in 1852, I did my risking by not doing what I was supposed to be doing, at least not right away. I would do my work with Aunt Nancy Lynne, but instead of going straight back to Fanny, I would use the warm nights to explore on foot what I could of the Holloway Plantation. That was how I found the clearing where I had been the first night I arrived. Another night I followed Silas because I knew he slept somewhere in the woods but close to the stables. He had a place even nicer than Aunt Nancy Lynne's, with even boards, whitewashed and pretty. He had a small garden, and I figured that was why he was so well fed. This exploration would be harder to do when I got older. I had to do as much as possible. Take a few chances as they might come to me.

But one chance I didn't take: In late August, when I'd been at Holloway's about a year, I saw two slaves running away. It was a man and a woman, one following closely behind the other, slipping through the dark of the woods. The next night Aunt Nancy Lynne told me it was Laney and her husband, Montgomery. They hadn't been found yet.

"Do you think they will be?"

She was sewing and not looking up. "From now on, it's day by day," she said.

"What do you mean?"

"Every day they're gone is a chance they'll stay gone." She shrugged. "Dogs would have a harder time tracking them."

Fanny, when I got back to our pallet, said she liked that Montgomery and Laney had gone together.

"If one had gone without the other, they'd be lost forever, like one of them be dead."

"Seems that's what you have to do," I said. "We don't have anything else but trying to protect the people we love. I think that's what keeps Aunt Nancy Lynne going."

Suddenly a scream, raw and desperate, pierced the night air.

"Lawd, Jesus Christ, NOOOOOOOO!"

Then sounds of horses trotting and dogs barking. I wanted to go to the door, but Fanny held my arm tight.

"Don't," she said. "Stay here with me. It'll be worse if you see it."

"See what?"

"They done caught 'em. Montgomery and Laney. They been caught."

I gasped. I wanted to know how she knew, but then I heard Boss Everett's voice, loud and taunting.

"Welcome home! Hey, niggers! Mr. Montgomery and Miss Laney have come back! Why don't y'all come on out and greet 'em real nice."

I could hear movement, so I knew people were obeying, but their silence pained my heart. I didn't know what they were seeing, but it was clear Boss Everett was making an example out of the runaways. I shut my eyes and tried not to imagine the condition of the husband and wife. Fanny and I held hands and cringed with the sound of each lash of the whip. They were being whipped at the same time, so both man and woman cried out in a way that was both frightening and unseemly, like a man should never have to hear his wife screaming like that, and she shouldn't have to hear him plead for mercy. I didn't know how they could look at each other after that.

In the morning Montgomery and Laney were taken to a slave market and sold off separately.

There were things I had wanted to know from them—which is probably why they were sold: to keep other slaves from asking questions to figure out if they could do the same and be successful where Montgomery and Laney hadn't been. Which way had they gone? How far had they gotten? Had they seen any other runaways? Boss Everett meant to set an example, but with me anyway, he failed. Montgomery and Laney's running off inspired me to continue my explorations and see how I might make an attempt of my own.

By that December, though, Fanny was with child and so sick I couldn't think of leaving her. She threw up every morning, so bad on one day that I made her stay in bed. I worked for both of us. As her baby grew, I felt a resentment growing within me. It was like I was watching my papa and mama's story play out in front of me—my mama having no choice but to take Papa into her bed. Giving birth to a child who could never have any place or standing in the world. I began to see Papa's land for me, Petite Bébinn, to be poor recompense, for it wouldn't have been any better than another form of enslavement—me living there alone, almost no better than being a kept woman. Too light for the notice of some, my light-brown hair too rough and nappy, signaling I was in fact too dark to be accepted by the rest. The thought sapped my resolve. Where would I go if I left the Holloway Plantation? Would Catalpa Valley, with Madame in charge, really be a better place? I began to see that maybe a better place wasn't anywhere. I might as well stay with Fanny and Aunt Nancy Lynne and Silas.

"You don't ask me nothing about my baby," Fanny whispered. It was spring. Aunt Nancy Lynne had said the baby would come in the summer.

"I know where it is. Belly against my back every night. What else do I need to know?"

But I did ask her something.

"Fanny, where are your mama and papa?"

"Never knew my daddy. My mama looked after me and most of the babies here. Taught us how to pick seeds out of the cotton. Taught the girls how to sew. Made sure we didn't make no trouble."

"Where is she now?"

"Don't rightly know. Ran away when I was about your age."

"Ran away?" My heart thumped hard. "They never caught her?"

"They didn't miss her right away. I was working in the big house. Then they figured she would come back 'cause of me. She knew they'd whip me."

"Fanny, no . . ."

She took my hand and put it down the back of her shift. My fingers found the raised cords of flesh on her skin.

"Two lashes," she said. "Only two on account of my being so young. Corinne in the kitchen got five for spilling a glass of water on one of Massa Holloway's dinner guests. So I was glad it was two."

"Don't it make you mad?"

"Mad about what? Mad my mama left? About getting whipped? That's the way things are. What good would it do to be mad? I'd have to be mad every day."

I touched her back again. "I'm mad every day," I said.

"You been used to a different life, that's all. Now I can tell you what I'd be mad at."

"What?"

"If you let all that being mad turn you into something else, like a different girl from when you come here. That girl? She special."

"How do you know?"

Fanny made me turn around to face her. "Tell me about your mama and your daddy."

"Nothing to say. My mama was . . ." Suddenly I couldn't say the word. I hadn't known the meaning of it before—the true meaning of it—until I'd come to the Holloway Plantation. Slave. Nigger. Not human. Less than nothing. "Like us," I said finally.

"Your papa didn't treat her that way."

"How you know?"

"I know you."

I shifted on the pallet.

"My baby gonna be birthed right here on this pallet. Where were you born? Where'd your mama die?"

"In the big house."

"Yeah, that's what I figured. Your feet never touched the dirt in the coloreds' quarters. How'd he raise you?"

"In the house. With his wife and daughter."

"Uh-huh. Bet his missus pitched a fit about that. And the first words out of your mouth when I asked who you were—you just going on about being his daughter and talking about his land. Why you know all that?"

"He told me. He wanted me to know . . ." I stopped. Tears slid from the corners of my eyes.

"What did he want you to know, Jeannette?"

"That he loved me. That he loved my mama."

"That's right."

"But my mama didn't have a choice. She didn't get to love who she wanted to. What does that make me?"

Fanny placed a cool hand on my forehead. "You can't know your mama's mind," she said. "Only what you know—your daddy's love. Now you can go round here feeling bad like I seen you doing, or you can walk like you loved. Nobody can touch that—not even Everett. I know my mama, God rest her soul, loved me. I think about her, how she wouldn't want me to suffer no matter how bad things are. That's what gets me through when Everett is on top of me. It's what's keeping me going now—thinking about how I can protect my baby and let him or her know they loved. That's all I can do."

"It makes me mad, Fanny. Feel the anger like a wild animal on me, like Everett always on top of me, even though he's on you."

"If you were my child, I'd say you mad because you can't talk. Got everything bottled up in you like an old jar of canned collards rotting because it never got opened."

I put a hand to my eyes and felt the tears running down my face. "I miss Papa."

She put her arms around me. "He still here. You his girl."

I thought about what Dorinda had once said, how I looked just like him, like he had spat me out.

"What would you do, Jeannette? I mean, if you were him right now, what you be doin'?"

"I'd be working hard and planning—making lots of plans."

"For what?"

"Making sure his family was safe, protected."

"Huh," Fanny said. "Sounds like he doing something else too."

"What's that?"

"Lovin'. Sounds like a man spending more time doing that than being mad."

"I don't know what he had to be mad at."

"But you do know what he had to love. Just act like that for a while. See where it take you."

So that was what I did—I went about being a little Jean Bébinn. I walked upright and looked after what I loved—Fanny. I'd never been close to anyone having a baby, so I didn't know how to look after her other than to take care of whatever she needed. If she was hungry, I'd find her something to eat. If she got tired and thirsty while we were working, I'd make her sit down where she couldn't be seen, and I'd find her some water, even if I had to sneak it from the pitcher near Missus's bed. I rubbed Fanny's back at night when the baby grew heavy in her belly. I was able to do this because Boss Everett stopped bothering her, just like Fanny said he would.

Did I feel any better? A little. Maybe it was like not looking so much at what was bad and not feeling worse because of it. But I liked looking after Fanny.

Then one morning in August I woke up thinking it had been about two years since Papa had died and two years since I'd come to Holloway's. I was telling Fanny about it and helping her up from the pallet on the floor when I heard a strange pop. Fanny looked at me, her eyes huge and bright. She lifted her shift, and there was water leaking from between her legs, gushing like a waterfall. She sank back down on the pallet.

"It's the baby," she said. "It's time."

I didn't respond. I just ran and kept running. I got to the big house, threw open the back door, and found Aunt Nancy Lynne and Corinne starting breakfast.

I was breathless but managed to say, "Fanny's having her baby."

Aunt Nancy Lynne ducked into her sewing space and brought out some cloths. She went over to one of the big iron pots on the hearth.

"Here," she called to me. "Help me tote this." She swung up the metal handle and handed me a square of cloth so I wouldn't burn my hand. "Corinne, you know what to do."

"Yes, Aunt Nancy Lynne."

Aunt Nancy Lynne held the other side of the handle, and we made our way back down to the lane. I wanted to run, but the pot was heavy, and I could see by her steady concentration that Aunt Nancy Lynne didn't want to lose a drop of the water in it.

When we got there, Fanny was lying on her side, facing the wall and moaning. We put the pot on the grate.

"Build up the fire," Aunt Nancy Lynne said. "And bring some water for her to drink."

She put the cloths on the table and pulled a chair over to sit near Fanny. "Don't you worry, honey. We're here." She rubbed her back. "Just let yourself do what you need to do."

Aunt Nancy Lynne looked over her shoulder at me. "You ever seen a woman give birth?"

I shook my head.

"It's gonna be loud. She gon' be in a whole lot of pain. Don't be scared, now. You can't help me if you scared."

"I won't be scared."

But it wasn't the noise that affected me. Fanny's screams seemed to be a piece of all the screaming I'd heard since coming to Holloway's. It was seeing Fanny in pain, her eyes wide and wild with it, that broke me. Sometimes she would even lock her gaze on me like I could make it go away. And of course, I couldn't. Then there was the duration of the labor. Six hours later the baby still wasn't there. Aunt Nancy Lynne wasn't worried, so I wasn't either. I was just tired. But Fanny was doing all the work. No way I was more tired than her.

It must have been just after noon when the crazy white woman arrived. I first heard her in the lane yelling, "Where is she? Where is she?"

The door burst open and banged against the wall.

Fanny was writhing in the middle of a pain, and the white woman laughed like she had lost her mind.

"Does it hurt, bitch?" she said.

She pushed me aside and stood over Fanny and Aunt Nancy Lynne.

"I hope God splits you open like the whore you are!"

"Missus Everett, this ain't no place for you," Aunt Nancy Lynne said. She had to raise her voice to be heard over the woman's screams and Fanny's cries.

But the woman didn't stop. She ranted on, calling Fanny a bitch and her baby a bastard. Then she spit on Fanny.

That was it for me. I couldn't stand it, couldn't let her treat Fanny that way. So I did what Papa had done for my mama. I got between them and started moving toward the door, forcing Missus Everett out. She tried to get around me. I put my hands on her waist and pushed. Her focus, once we reached the door, shifted from Fanny to me.

"How dare you put your filthy nigger hands on me!"

I pushed her again, and we fell out the door and into the lane. She slapped at me, but I didn't fight back. I let her. Then she pinched my left ear between her fingers and dragged me out into the yard. She grabbed a whip, but I don't think she'd ever used one in her life, because her first lash at me jumped back, and she cut her own face. She kept trying, screaming, "How dare you?" all the while, and I wanted to laugh because it sounded like she was screaming at the whip for cutting her. She must be drunk, I figured. I didn't care. At least she wasn't bothering Fanny anymore. She managed to strike me on the arm I had raised to protect myself. The sleeve of my dress tore. She landed another lash on my shoulder.

My skin felt like I'd touched hot coals. I looked at Missus Everett and saw the purple welt bleeding on her chin and realized I could hate this woman, but what would I be hating? I saw a soul so sad and furious she didn't know herself. And I was no more to her than a spider she wanted to crush underfoot. I'd have to work hard, make numerous changes in my brain, to create hate for such a pitiful person. What would I have to mold myself into to conjure such hate? Fanny had been right. I wouldn't be myself if I did it.

Boss Everett must have recognized his wife's wails. He came out and stopped her. He scolded her for whipping a house slave, which redirected her anger onto him. While they fought, I ran back to Fanny.

"Sweet Jesus."

Aunt Nancy Lynne's hands were moving fast, and I went to help. Fanny was moaning and crying. Blood—I saw an ocean of blood. Aunt Nancy Lynne knelt in it, her lap covered with it. The entire pallet was soaked. I knelt next to her.

"Get me some more of those rags. Dip them in that hot water."

I got up and did what she asked, and when I brought the pile of cloths, I saw what Aunt Nancy Lynne held in her hands. It had the shape of a baby, curled up like a flower bud that wasn't open yet. She put the dark and quiet bud on Fanny's chest and put a cloth over it. Fanny was crying. The blood was still coming, flowing hard like from a broken levee.

"Talk to her," Aunt Nancy Lynne said. She tried to stanch the flow of blood with the cloths. "Keep talkin' to her."

I put one hand on the baby and my other hand on Fanny's head. Her lips were dry and cracked as she murmured a stream of words.

"He a boy, ain't he?"

"Yeah, yeah," I said, but I couldn't tell. The baby was too crouched up for me to see its privates. "What's his name?"

"Jeremiah."

"Jeremiah. That's a beautiful name, Fanny," I said. "Real nice."

Her teeth started chattering and making a loud clicking sound as they clashed together. Then Fanny's whole body shook violently.

"Fanny! Fanny!"

She looked down at the baby.

"I gotta . . ." She gasped for air. "I gotta . . . go take care of him."

"Don't leave me, Fanny," I whispered. I was crying, too, and I held her tighter and tried to stop her shaking.

"I'm . . . all . . . right," she said. "God's with us. Listen . . . Jeannette, listen."

"What is it? Listen to what?"

"You hear my baby laughing? Listen to him laughing."

She smiled then, and her body relaxed. The shaking stopped. Her eyes closed, and she didn't move again.

"No!" I sobbed and sobbed and kept kneeling there in her blood and holding on to Fanny and her dead baby. I wanted the ground to open and swallow us all, right there. Nothing mattered.

Aunt Nancy Lynne put her arms around me. "Come on, now. Help me clean them up."

"Why?" I wailed. "They're dead."

"'Cause it's the last thing you can do for her." She pulled on me. "Come on now. You don't want her going into the ground looking like this, like some animal Boss Everett slaughtered."

Mucus streamed from my nose, and I couldn't see for the tears. I stood, and she handed me one of the clean cloths. I wiped my face. I was still crying, but I was able to move and to help. We took the baby and unfolded its crouching form enough to see Fanny had been right—it was a boy.

Some of what Aunt Nancy Lynne had brought from the big house wasn't rags but clothing. She'd brought my housekeeping dress and hers too. When we were done, we washed our hands and put on the clean clothes. After I had settled some, I realized the lash wounds I'd gotten from Missus Everett still burned.

"Come on now," she said, but I sat at the table awhile longer. I didn't want to leave Fanny.

"You done good. Come on."

We walked down the lane back to the big house. I said, "I won't go back there again. I'm not sleeping where she died."

"All right, honey. Don't think about it now."

It wasn't just the shack. I couldn't stand where I was. Fanny's death had crushed me. I felt reckless. If Aunt Nancy Lynne hadn't been walking me back to the big house, I would have kept on walking down the road and then God knows where. I didn't care how or where I'd end up. I was leaving there. But Aunt Nancy Lynne had me by the arm. She brought me into the kitchen and sat me down with a bowl of green beans in front of me. I was supposed to snap off the ends, but I just sat there. When night fell, she put me on the pallet where I used to sleep for the night work. I kept on staying there and never went back to where I lived with Fanny.

I was heartsick after that. Nothing felt good. The sound of laughter was like cold water poured all over my soul. I know that's selfish, but that's how I felt.

"I know you thinking of running off," Aunt Nancy Lynne said. "You should wait."

"Wait for what?"

"To make a plan. You run out of here without a plan, you liable to end up back here like Monty and Laney. Back here in a day. You don't know a real whippin'. You'll know it if they catch you, though."

I shrugged and said nothing, but I waited. I didn't see how anything might change or what kind of plan would get me away from Holloway's without getting caught.

A few weeks later, when we were sewing, Aunt Nancy Lynne said, "Can you wait a year, maybe two?"

Two years seemed so far away. "Why?"

"Because you need to grow up a little."

"I can handle myself!"

"No, that's not what I mean. I mean you need to get a little bigger, look like a woman and not a little girl."

She glanced at my work. "And you need to be more careful with how you do things. Like you need to pull out them crooked stitches on that hem and do 'em over."

I put a hand over my eyes and sighed. I started picking out the thread. "Yes, ma'am."

"She right!"

Silas startled us. We heard his voice at the open window before we saw him. He came striding in and sat at the table.

"How long you been out there listening to business that ain't yours?" Aunt Nancy Lynne asked.

"Long enough to make it mine."

He looked at me and said, "I been thinking about Montgomery and Laney—about what the rest of their running woulda been like. No matter where they ended up, it woulda been trouble. They didn't look like nothin' but a couple of ragged runaway slaves. The kinda work you doin' there?" He indicated our sewing. "That's the key."

Aunt Nancy Lynne stopped and stared at Silas. Her eyes got really small, like she wasn't looking at him. She was thinking.

"When Massa take me with him somewhere, what the first thing he do? Make sure I'm cleaned up, wearing good clothes. Nobody say a thing because people see we're together."

"Yeah, but he white—" I didn't finish the sentence. I gasped and looked down at my sewing and then my hands. Aunt Nancy Lynne and I were now staring at each other.

"You can do it," Silas said. "If you wearing the right clothes, people would see nothing but a white gal."

"I could." I stood and paced around the kitchen. Aunt Nancy Lynne closed the window and checked that no one else was outside. Then she opened the drawer of the desk Missus used when planning menus for her parties.

"Girl, stop that. Come write some things down for me."

I went to the desk, and she called out types of cloth and measurements and colors. I wrote down types of buttons and lace.

"Silas." She gave him the list. "Don't make no special trip. It'll call attention to yourself. And don't take it into town. Wait until the next time Massa send you to Monroe. The mercantile man there won't ask no questions."

She checked the window and the door again, then went into another room. I looked at Silas and shrugged. When she came back, she was holding some paper bills.

"I'm gonna have to trust you with this. You gotta have it with you all the time. No telling when you'll get to go."

"But isn't that the money for . . . ," I began.

"You hush now," she said. "I told you this was gon' take time. Now time might be our friend. You'll see. It'll be fine. We're gonna have a plan."

Chapter 5

September 1855

The plan came together slowly, as did the clothing. Aunt Nancy Lynne and I had to make it on the sly on top of all our other work. Silas would join us in the middle of the night for fittings and to refine the plan because, out of the blue it seemed, he was going with me.

"You need to be thinkin' about how a massa can travel up and down every mile and every state, North and South, and take his slave with him. You're better off if I go with you."

Aunt Nancy Lynne and I looked at each other, and she smiled slightly.

"You'd be traveling with me," Silas said. "I know which way to go. Been waiting for a chance like this. Waitin' for years."

"I'm making a respectable-looking dress for her. She'd look just like Missus."

Silas shook his head. "Don't see too many white women from the South traveling alone. Can't stay out of sight like that. But we can make her look like a man. Nobody pay us no mind if she a man."

That was how we decided I would be a man—a sickly man who was dependent on my faithful man Henry, which was what I would call Silas on the road. It took some getting used to the idea. It seemed too big. I had doubts whether I could maintain the charade for miles, days, weeks. But I had to try and soon. I was sixteen, and as I was so light skinned, Aunt Nancy Lynne said it was just a matter of time before I was sold off as a fancy girl, forced to service men until I ended up like Fanny or grew too old for anyone to be interested in me. I had to go. She figured it best to keep me out of Boss Everett's sight as much as possible. If she saw him coming from down the lane, she would send me upstairs with a chore or two that had to be done right away for Missus Holloway. But Aunt Nancy Lynne didn't know that, really, she was keeping Boss Everett safe from me, not the other way around. Maybe she did. I was no longer awkward with a knife the way I'd been when I'd first come to the plantation. More than once I thought about slipping one of the smaller kitchen knives into the pocket of my apron and hiding it under my pallet. But she kept a close eye on me and even closer attention on where all her knives were.

We kept working on the clothing, which now included a suit for me as well as a nice outfit for Silas. But Aunt Nancy Lynne said I should still have a couple of nice dresses. I would need them once we got to where we were going. "You just gon' have to be patient," she told me. "The better we work this, the better chance you have of getting away and staying away."

She worked on a travel dress, navy blue, which I liked very much. There was also an everyday dress, made of plain gray cloth, and a nicer dress meant for evenings, but it wasn't formal. Just brown silk with black trim, keeping with my station. She taught me how I would keep them clean, with carefully placed rags between my legs, when I bled each month. It was vitally important that I not ruin the clothes, the suit especially. It would give away the disguise.

The changes in my body embarrassed me. Maybe this was why Calista had kept to herself so much before Papa had died. It felt like all I wanted to do was cover myself up. I think those were the loneliest days of my life. If this was what it meant to become a woman, then the condition didn't have much to offer, as far as I could see.

We were finally ready that October. Silas had the idea to ask for consent to be away for a few days, as he sometimes did, to do outside jobs in other homes. This would give us a head start. No one would miss me right away, and it would be at least three days before anyone realized Silas hadn't returned. It was decided Silas would take the clothing with him the night before, and the next night, I would go to Silas's place. We would make my transformation there and begin our journey.

On the last night, Aunt Nancy Lynne and I were carefully packing the clothing into a large sack so that Silas could look like he was carrying bedding or some other laundry back to his cabin. When we were done and waiting for him, she pressed money into my palm. It was $250.

"I told you I would buy somebody's freedom. It's gon' be yours. I don't want to hear another word about it."

I didn't protest—we would need the money for the journey. I put my arms around her and held her tightly.

"Thank you. I'll never forget you."

She smiled, then pulled away from me and looked out the window.

"Silas is sweet on you."

"I know."

"He's a good man."

"Yes."

"So how it gon' be when you get up north and he figures out you ain't gon' be his wife?"

I sighed and shrugged. "I'll figure it out when we come to it. Got too much to worry about until then."

The truth of the matter was I didn't know if I could be interested in any man after what had happened to Fanny. But I did find myself thinking about what kind of man I could love. It didn't seem like looks mattered much to me. If they did, I'd be smitten with Silas. He was easy to be with and smart and had a sly way of smiling that could make other women giggle. But he was Silas and not a person who could make me sit up and think differently about myself. Why I thought I needed that, I don't know. It was a thing—and I guessed I would recognize the man, whoever he was, whenever he presented me with a new part of myself.

I made my way to Silas's place. We sat up that night making final plans. He was glad I could read and write. With Aunt Nancy Lynne's money, I could stay in a hotel room and would be able to register my name in the establishment's logs. He laid out on his table a small bunch of herbs— eucalyptus, thyme, and mint. He used a pestle to crush them together into a fragrant medicinal poultice. I prepared the strip of muslin that would hold it, sprinkling the cloth with water and placing it near the hearth to warm it.

When he was done with the herbs, Silas removed my head wrap and cut my wild, unkempt hair. I didn't care because it was always too hard for me to gather it into a bun or make it look tidy in any way. Then we folded the poultice into its cloth and carefully wrapped it under my chin and around my head. Silas arranged it to obscure my face as much as possible. Then he put on me a pair of spectacles he'd bought at a shop in Monroe. He held up a piece of mirror so I could see myself. The spectacles, which I couldn't look through straight on, seemed to magnify my eyes and spread them to the sides of my face. The lenses were slightly tinted, making my eye color more ambiguous. The smell of the poultice made my eyes water slightly.

"That's good," Silas said. "The smell will keep people away."

With a hat on and the spectacles and wearing the poultice, I did look like a common, if slightly odd, Southern gentleman.

"I know you can talk good," said Silas. "But don't say nothing unless you have to. No telling what might cause people to look at you funny. Gotta keep our heads down and just go about our business. Remember to walk slow and lean on the cane."

We prayed first. Silas insisted on it. Since Fanny and her baby had died, I didn't consider myself on good speaking terms with God. I knelt with Silas, though, because I wanted God to know how mad I was still.

The October night was silent, the air and the leaves on the trees unmoving. We stepped through the door, and suddenly we were quiet too. Silas and I looked at each other. It was like we could see the hundreds of miles laid out in front of us, and it all seemed so strange and impossible that it scared us into stone. God only knew what they would do to us if we were caught. It seemed to me Silas had more to lose than I did—his favored position of trust, his relative comfort. If Massa Holloway learned Silas had used his experience of traveling with him to get away, he'd doom Silas to work in the fields and never come near even a horse again. That would be after he was whipped within an inch of his life. My eyelids flinched. I would be whipped, too—more likely branded. Aunt Nancy Lynne said they didn't like marking up the fair-skinned women on account of it lowered their value as fancy girls, but I was certain they'd make an exception for me.

I took his hand—something I'd never done before as a woman, and here I was doing it disguised as a man. It would be the last time on the journey I could do such a thing. Made sense to do it then. "Come on, Silas. We gotta be on our way."

When we arrived at the railway station, Silas and I parted. He went to the negro car and stood with the trunk, an old one that Massa Holloway had discarded long ago but Silas had had the foresight to keep. He would stow the luggage and wait for me, his new massa. I entered the small crowd of early-morning travelers. The cane I leaned on gave me an excuse to keep my eyes cast downward, but I made myself look forward as much as possible. I didn't want to look like I had anything to hide. It was like Papa used to tell me—I had to walk like I belonged. I had to put off my fear. At the window I purchased a ticket for the port of Savannah. That would be our first piece of the journey, about three hundred miles away. The clerk barely glanced at me.

I moved slowly with my cane over to Silas and gave him his ticket. He nodded, and I made my way to the front and climbed into the comfortable carriage. The surroundings fascinated me. The smooth wood of the trim of the compartment and the plushness of the cushions were such a stark difference from the straw pallets on which I'd slept for the past four years. But I couldn't allow myself to be distracted. I sat and focused on the scene outside the window and waited anxiously for the train to move. I paid no attention to the passengers walking up the aisles and arranging themselves on the seats across from me and in front and behind.

If I had been looking, I would have seen the devil, Boss Everett himself, sitting directly across from me. When I turned and saw him, I stifled a scream in my throat. How had he found me? When would he snatch me by the collar and drag me back onto the platform? But he looked at me—looked at me!—and nodded cordially. I coughed to cover the sound of my fear and managed to return his nod. The disguise was working, but I'm sure it helped that the man had never seen me straight on when I'd been in Aunt Nancy Lynne's kitchen. I turned back to the window so I wouldn't call attention to myself or encourage conversation.

The train moved away, but I didn't breathe easy. Not with that man, whose vile smell seemed to be cloaked with the scent of strong soap, sitting so close. After a few miles he spoke to me.

"Sir, it looks like we have a good day ahead of us."

He really could have been talking to any of the passengers around me, so I said nothing and kept my eyes focused out the window. Everett then repeated himself, but I kept ignoring him as before. Perhaps this wasn't the best course of action, because he didn't take well to being ignored. And the other passengers noticed, so he didn't want to be embarrassed. "It's all right," he said to no one and everyone. "I'll make the old man hear me."

He leaned more in my direction and raised his voice. "Sir! I said it looks like we have a very good day ahead of us."

I turned and, without looking at him directly, bowed my head. "Yes," I said. Slowly I moved back toward the window again and said no more.

"A sad thing to be deaf in age, ain't it?" Everett said. The passengers around him agreed, and I could hear him sniff and the pages of a newspaper unfold. "I won't bother the poor old soul again."

By God's grace my enemy didn't stay on the train. Everett's destination was Topperville, not Savannah, and we arrived there before lunch. The man disembarked without, as far as I could tell, looking again in my direction. When the train began to move again, I felt such relief that I either passed out or fell asleep. I was too exhausted to tell either way.

When I awoke, I discerned the conversation around me and found myself in the perfect position to eavesdrop. I only had to pretend to continue sleeping and take in the information. The men were complaining of abolitionists.

From what I gathered, abolitionists made a lot of trouble for Southern landowners who kept slaves. I was stunned when I realized they were talking about God-fearing white people who didn't believe in slavery—who thought it should be outlawed. In Aunt Nancy Lynne's kitchen Silas had spoken of people who opposed the institution of slavery. Now I was thinking about them differently. I knew Silas and I were headed north because we could be free. But I hadn't thought clearly about what freedom would mean for me or what it would look like. How could I make my way in the world? I had not shared these thoughts with Silas because my plan was to disconnect myself from him once we reached safety. It would be better for us to separate because anyone in search of runaways would look for a pair. Now, hearing that

I could find people, perhaps these white abolitionists, willing to help me sustain myself in my freedom, I felt heartened.

We arrived at Savannah early in the evening and got into an omnibus, which stopped at the hotel for the passengers to take tea. Silas stepped into the house and brought me a small sandwich and coffee. I sat outside and ate a little. Silas knelt next to me and tended to me like he would Massa Holloway. He dusted off my boots and checked and retied the poultice.

"You all right?" he whispered.

"Boss Everett was on the train," I said. "Silas—Henry, I thought I was going to die."

Silas took small, nervous looks around the area, moving from me to the street and back again. "Damn it," he said. "Where is he?"

"No, no." I patted him on the shoulder. "He's gone. Got off a ways back."

Silas sat back on his heels, took out a handkerchief, and wiped at the sweat trickling down the sides of his face. "Well, the Lord must be looking after us then," he said.

"Are you all right? Have you eaten? Here, take this." I carefully wrapped the rest of my sandwich. I had only managed a few bites.

"No, you keep it. Gotta keep your strength up. We'll be traveling over water soon. Might make you sick."

He was right. The omnibus took us to a steamer bound for Charleston, South Carolina, and then another steamer to Wilmington, North Carolina. On board, the up-and-down motion of the waves gave me a painful ache at the back of my head. My stomach felt so unsettled it was all I could do to sit up straight on the bench outside. We stayed outside on both steamers. Silas said it would help me feel better. Still, the journey wore on me badly. We boarded a train for Richmond, Virginia, and by the time we arrived, my slow sick-man walk was no longer pretended.

Silas thought some fresh air might help. He led me from the platform to the street, and we were walking like that, speaking quietly about where we should go next, when Silas suddenly took my elbow.

"Stop," he whispered. "You hear that?"

I wasn't sure what "that" was supposed to be. We were surrounded by people and horses and carriages, all making their own noises. But the sound came to me: a low and rich melodic hum, the way a mother might sing to a child. The hum rose in tone and volume, and then a woman's voice, deep and clear.

"Swing low, sweet chariot, coming for to carry me home. Swing low, sweet chariot, coming for to carry me home."

"That's a signal song," he whispered. "Someone from the Underground Railroad. They'll help get us someplace safe." He looked around carefully.

"Over there." Silas guided me to a shop stand of squash, collards, and potatoes. A colored woman wearing a dark-brown cloth wrapped around her head was stocking the table from a crate at her feet. She sang as she worked.

I pretended to examine the vegetables while Silas spoke to her.

"You lookin' to hire a carriage for your man?" she asked him.

Silas nodded.

She glanced briefly in a direction opposite us and a little way down the street. "Take that one with the man in the green hat. Tell him Miss Maude said he has the finest carriage in town."

I gave Silas a few coins to pass to her. She wrapped a butternut squash in brown paper and handed it to Silas. I gave her a slight bow, and we walked on.

When we got to the carriage, Silas repeated Miss Maude's message, and the man opened the door and helped me in. Silas got up on the outside seat with the driver. The man never asked where we wanted to go. He just started. We traveled out of Richmond but still, I could tell, in a northerly direction. We ended up not going far, but the man let the horses walk, so our progress was slow. I figured that was best. We wouldn't call attention to ourselves. There didn't seem to be anything to fear, so I sat back and relaxed and felt better. I even managed to fall asleep for a bit.

It was dark at the small farmhouse that turned out to be our destination.

Silas hopped down, and the man in the green hat opened the door for me. I climbed out and took off my hat, my spectacles, and the poultice. I could breathe deeply for the first time in days. But then suddenly Miss Maude was there. She slipped out of the shadows and approached the carriage. I looked at Silas. How had she managed to get there? Maybe that was why we had gone so slowly—she had been walking along with us.

"Thanks, Charley," she said to the driver. He turned his horse and went back toward Richmond. To us she said, "This here the Burke house. Come on." She moved fast. Her steps bounced up from the ground, one right after another. It was all we could do to keep up with her.

Miss Maude knocked on the door softly in a rhythmic pattern and then did something very strange. She ran her hand over my head as though she would press down any errant curls. Who would care what I looked like? The nighttime dew had already done its work, and I helped it along with my sweating despite the chill of the night.

The glow of a candle illuminated the face of the woman who opened the door. She was white.

"Missus Burke, I have a man and a girl with me."

The woman pulled the door wide open. "Yes, of course. Come in, Maude. It has been quiet for a while. I thought you would be here yesterday." She pulled out chairs at a wooden table, and I could make out the hearth and the walls of a kitchen. "Sit here. You both must be hungry."

"Yes, ma'am." I'd eaten very little on the journey, but I didn't tell her that the edge of the hunger had kept me going, even when I'd felt sick on the steamer. It made me feel alive, and I was happy to feel my body talking to me. It meant I was healthy, and I had that going for me, if nothing else.

She placed the candle on the table and moved about the room. She put bread on the table and put a kettle over the fire in the hearth. Miss Maude didn't sit but followed her around the room and whispered to her. I could just make out "need" and "help" and "don't know." Silas and I looked at each other. He shrugged.

Missus Burke put cups on the table and filled them with hot coffee. She sat, and Miss Maude sat with us.

"I'm thinking of that family stuck north of here. We could get them all to Philadelphia if we make it look like they belong to somebody, like they're traveling with a master like these two just did." She nodded at me, and I stopped chewing the bread. "Or a mistress."

Missus Burke looked at me and did the same thing Miss Maude had done. She ran her hand over the mess of my cropped hair. "What is your name?"

I hesitated and looked at Silas. Miss Maude nodded and said, "Go on. You can tell her about yourself. She's a helper."

By that I figured she meant an abolitionist, so I told her.

"My name is Jeannette Bébinn. I am the daughter of Jean Bébinn of Catalpa Plantation of the LeBlanc Parish in Louisiana. My father was master of fifty thousand acres, and the parcels are named Belle Neuve, Baton Bleu, Siana Grove, Chance Voir, Belle Verde, Mont Devreau. There is a section Papa set aside for me, five thousand acres, called Petite Bébinn. But Papa died, and his wife, Madame, sent me away with a slave broker. That was four years ago. I have been a slave at the Holloway Plantation in Mississippi until Silas here and I escaped."

Missus Burke listened, but it seemed like she wasn't listening to my story. She seemed to be studying me. She leaned on her elbows with a hand under her chin. I liked the voluminous sleeves on her purple-and-black dress.

"Jeannette, you speak very well. Do you know how to read? Did you ever have a teacher, I mean, before you were sent away?"

"My papa was my teacher. He taught me all about the land and how to read books and work with numbers. I would listen to him talk about politics and the weather and about how to think about the world."

"You hear it, right?" Miss Maude said.

Missus Burke nodded. "You have quite a presence, Jeannette," she said.

Miss Maude pressed on. "She wouldn't have to lie. She already talks like she would own land—and slaves."

"Like a diamond in the rough," Missus Burke said. "We'd have to get her some clothes. And a carriage."

"I have dresses—nice dresses," I said. "They are in my trunk. Aunt Nancy Lynne helped us. She made the dresses for me and these clothes we're wearing now."

"Oh Lord, what a blessing!" Miss Maude said. "But what about her hair?"

"She will wear a bonnet. No one will see it's been cut."

"I'm sorry, Missus, but what is it you want me to do?" My eyes moved from Miss Maude to Missus Burke and back again.

"Yeah," Silas said. "What's all this about?"

Miss Maude sat with us. "We got five runaways in hiding, just a little north of here. We were expectin' one or two, but they all came. From the same family. They won't separate, and we can't move 'em all without calling attention to them."

"Bounty hunters following the Fugitive Slave Act would notice," Missus Burke added. "They'd be looking for a group that big."

"What that got to do with us?" asked Silas.

"You'd drive Jeannette to the Quaker house where they hiding," Missus Burke said. "Tell the people there I sent you, and they'll know what to do."

I reached for Missus Burke's hand. "Other slaves? And we'd help them?"

"Yes. They could travel with you as if they were yours. You'd look like a lady traveling with her property. Maude, how dangerous do you think it would be?"

"There's no telling." Miss Maude sat back in her chair.

Missus Burke seemed to study me even closer than she had before. "Jeannette, what do you think of Maude's idea? You don't have to go along with it; it's your choice. If you're not willing, it'll be fine. We'll still help you get to wherever you'd like to go."

I was thinking it was kind of her to ask me, but I didn't have anywhere to go. I didn't belong anywhere. I didn't know what to want other than a safe place to lay my head. But if I helped Miss Maude, I would have a purpose, maybe even a purpose God meant for me to have. I thought of Fanny and how I would have helped her escape.

"I wouldn't be here at all if it weren't for you people helping. I have no one waiting for me and nowhere to be. If it's all the same with you, I will do it."

Miss Maude smiled and pulled a hunk of bread from the plate. "Then we better eat up and get some sleep. Got work to do to get you ready."

"But I said I have dresses. I can get ready myself."

"You know how to use a gun?"

I paused, my mouth open. Then I finally said, "No."

She nodded. "Like I said, we got work to do."

The next morning Miss Maude and I stood in the backyard wearing long coats to protect us from the cold autumn air. At one end of the yard I saw an old shirt and pants stuffed with straw and tied to a stake. She had planted the stake far from the house.

The gun was small but, Miss Maude said, powerful. It had to fit my hand and the pocket of my dress or coat. "I don't expect anyone to bother you, but you have to be ready."

She pointed the gun at the scarecrow and showed me how to raise my arm and aim.

"If you have to fire a gun, most likely it will be hard to think straight, but I want you to be able to fire with your head on right. You have to aim in the right places. Don't want you killing anyone. Hit a man in the leg if you can."

She fired the pistol and hit the upper thigh of the stuffed man.

"That'll stop him from coming after you. If they figure out what we're doing and you kill a man, you'll end up swinging from a tree at the end of a rope." She checked the gun, wiped it with a cloth, and handed it to me. "Even if they don't catch you, killing anything hurts your soul. Ain't none of these white men worth you harming your soul. Remember that. They've taken enough of us, and they don't get any more. Your soul is precious. You wound them, and that'll be just fine. Understand?"

I said I did and took the gun from her. The pearl of the handle felt warm against my skin. When I pulled the trigger, the gun pushed back into my palm as though it needed to brace itself so it could spit the ball out. My arm shuddered. I stepped back and thought I would fall.

"Yeah, it's got some kick to it," she said. "You gotta hold your body strong when you fire a gun. Don't matter if you're sitting or standing."

I thought about Madame and how she would behave if she were standing on the other side of this gun. How it would feel to have her at my mercy. I would have entertained this thought further, but what Miss Maude had said stayed with me. I understood. If I killed Madame, I would never be rid of her. She'd be in my blood, itching and impatient—a ghost underneath my skin. I didn't want that. And more in line with what Miss Maude was saying, Madame didn't deserve it. She didn't deserve to have so much of me. But, I decided, that wouldn't stop me from hoping bad things might happen to her all on their own.

We spent several days at Missus Burke's property. It was located in a place where no one thought anything about gunfire, because no one came to see about it or wonder why it was happening. Silas wanted to watch my shooting lessons, but Miss Maude set him to work with memorizing the route to the Quaker house, just outside Washington, DC. Once we picked up the family, we would head straight to Philadelphia.

Miss Maude had me try on the dresses Aunt Nancy Lynne had made. I hadn't had a proper dress since I was a child, so it was a strange thing to wear petticoats again and feel the softness of cotton muslin against my skin. Missus Burke liked the plainness of the travel dress. It was well made but not fancy. I only needed to look proper, like a Southern woman of means. They brought me shoes that fastened with tiny buttons. These made me think of Calista. It occurred to me that if I had to make up a name, I should call myself Calista. I could pretend to be my half sister. If anyone questioned, they would know such a person did exist and from such a plantation. But would it be too close to the truth? I would have to ask Miss Maude's advice on this. She would know best. I stared into the mirror and wondered what Calista was doing now. Was she married? Did she have children? She'd be about twenty. I could be Calista in the same way that Fanny had told me to be Papa. Papa had brought me this far. I could see how far Calista would take me, maybe even the rest of the way.

The night before we were to leave, Missus Burke came into the room I shared with Miss Maude. She explained that I would travel with the family during the day so our movements wouldn't look suspicious.

"The Friends at your destination will have papers for you to carry that will make it look like the members of the family are your property."

"But don't stop, and don't show nothing unless somebody ask," said Miss Maude. "Same thing with the gun. Don't show it unless you have to."

Missus Burke touched my arm. "You have to be in charge, Jeannette. Not Silas."

I nodded.

"Honey, what do you want to do when you get to Philadelphia?"

I sighed. It seemed this was the same question Aunt Nancy Lynne had asked, but since I wasn't there yet, I had no real answer, and I said so.

"Don't know, ma'am. Right now I'm just getting through each day. Can't think beyond it."

"You don't have family?"

"No. My parents are dead." I paused and looked at Miss Maude and Missus Burke. "Do you think I could go to school?"

"Now that's a fine idea. Some form of education would be good for you." Missus Burke stood. "I'll write a few letters and make inquiries. Friends can look into what you can do."

"I would appreciate that, ma'am."

I went to bed. I wasn't as scared as I'd been when Silas and I had first left, but lying in bed, I decided to pray. We had been brought far and safely. If God had been with us, I wanted to ask that he remain, even though we had more going for us—a means of transport, friends. I even had a gun. With God, it would be enough. It would all be enough.

The next morning Miss Maude arranged things with the carriage. Silas would be driving. She showed me where and how to sit in the carriage and told me to leave the window open even though the morning was cold. At a glimpse, one could see what looked like a white woman inside. I thanked her and Missus Burke, and Silas got us going.

Since the window was open and no one else was on the early-morning road, Silas kept talking to me. I'd noticed how he had been growing more and more annoyed during our time with Missus Burke and Miss Maude.

"I don't know about all this. We was fine with just us."

"It's still just us. But this could be better. If they're looking for you and me, they'd be looking for two. Not a woman with her slaves."

"But a sick man and his slave was better. Nobody paid us any mind. Now we're supposed to just ride into Philadelphia with a whole carriage of slaves. That's crazy."

"They know what they're doing. I trust them."

"Then you better be trusting for both of us."

"I will."

I think the cover of the morning fog made Silas bold to keep talking like he was, because once the sun burned it all away, he was quiet. The area became more populated, but we weren't noticed, and the short journey was uneventful. We arrived at the Quaker house after dark, around suppertime.

The Dillinghams were the people who greeted us—a man and his wife, who both seemed to be in their late forties or early fifties. Missus Dillingham had gray streaks throughout her dark-yellow hair. Mr. Dillingham, holding a lamp for us, took charge of the horses. He wore eyeglasses and a black vest and was bald except for a fringe of curly white hair along the back of his head.

"Go on in," he said when he helped me from the carriage. "I'll join you soon."

Missus Dillingham led us into the house, a low structure that seemed to branch off into sections. I couldn't see in the dark how far it went on.

From the outside you couldn't tell the house had a lower level, but it did. She moved a panel that, at first glance, looked like a piece of wall. Behind it were steps going down. Missus Dillingham handed a candle to Silas and told him to go first so she could close the panel behind me. "Be careful now."

I lifted my skirts and stepped down slowly into a room. Missus Dillingham came into it behind me and lit more candles.

"Please sit, both of you." She motioned to a long table set for a meal. Silas and I sat next to each other while she went around the room scratching at the walls in a funny way. But then those walls moved, too, and people emerged: two men, a woman, and a boy and a girl.

"This is Miss Bébinn and Henry," Missus Dillingham told them. "By God's grace this young lady will take you on to Philadelphia. But let's eat and talk."

Mr. Dillingham brought a tray of breads and cold meats to the table. Missus Dillingham went back upstairs and returned with a pot of soup.

"Where y'all from?" Silas asked.

One of the men bit into a piece of chicken and responded. "Anselm. That's in North Carolina."

"Yes," said Missus Dillingham. "But the less said about it, the better. We find it's easier if anyone asks questions to know as little as possible about your travel companions."

"Not even names?" I asked. I ladled soup into the bowl of the boy who had taken the chair on the other side of me. He looked to be about five or six years old. The girl must have been eight or so.

Mr. Dillingham said, "No, not even names. But Miss Bébinn . . ."

"Oh, but they allowed to know her name?" Silas said quickly.

"Why, yes, *Henry*." Mr. Dillingham said Silas's false name pointedly and looked at him over his glasses. "That is the name she's using, and yes, they have to know the name of their purported owner should anyone ask."

He turned back to me. "Now, likewise, you need to know their names—false names of course. We haven't written out the paperwork yet because we wanted to wait for you. If you name them, you'll remember better what their names are. Do you understand?"

I looked around the table. The woman put down her knife and fork and returned my gaze intently.

"That all right with you all?" I asked.

Everyone nodded.

"You go on, miss," said the shorter of the men. His voice was a high tenor. "We know it ain't for forever. We gon' choose new names for ourselves anyway when we get free."

I thought of the names I would remember best. "Then your name is Cal," I said. *Cal for Calista,* I thought to myself. The other man, across from me, had thick side whiskers that reminded me of Papa. "You are Jean."

Mr. Dillingham took a little notebook from his vest pocket. He wrote the names in it.

The woman looking at me so strong and straightforward—I called her Lynne. And I didn't hesitate on the children. They would be Jeremiah and Fanny.

I think there, in the room that night, was when I first sensed a true taste of God. Because right then I was surrounded by all the people I'd lost or left behind. I had a way to take them with me into the freedom that Aunt Nancy Lynne craved and Fanny couldn't even imagine. The strange miracle of it was that I hadn't even asked for such a thing. I just knew my heart had been aching for years, especially since Fanny had died, and I'd been sitting in that ache and stuck in it like a muddy swamp. It felt like God was saying to me, *Time to get out of this muck, Jeannette. Here's help to keep you going.*

The little girl said, "I like my name. Can I keep it?"

"Yes, baby, that would be fine," the new Lynne, who I figured was the mother of the two, told her. "Hush now."

Silas nodded as he ate. "I know all those names. Easy to remember."

Missus Dillingham glanced at her husband and then Silas.

"There's no need," Mr. Dillingham said. "You won't be going with them."

"What? I come all this way with her." Silas swung his head toward me. "Why can't I go with her now?"

"Henry, it would be difficult for three negro men on a carriage to go unnoticed. We think it's better for you to continue with me."

"How you figure that?"

"We will be just a day behind. That way we can help if there are problems. And we can continue the ruse that you began—you'll still be traveling with a white man."

I put a hand on Silas's arm. "I see what he means."

"You do?"

"Yes. If someone comes looking for us, it would be as a man and woman. If someone recognizes you or they guess I was dressed as a man, Mr. Dillingham can vouch for you, and they would see only a mistake on their part.

"And the folks at the Holloway Plantation never knew my real name. On paper it will all make sense. We're all going to the same place, Philadelphia. It'll be fine. Like Mr. Dillingham said, you'll be just a day behind."

When we were done, Mr. Dillingham took the men upstairs to discuss the route. Lynne put the children to bed behind one of the panels and came out to help me and Missus Dillingham clear the table.

"That man your husband?" Lynne asked.

I shook my head. "He a friend. Been looking out for me."

"Jean"—she paused and slowly recalled the other names—"is my husband. Cal is my brother." She motioned toward the panel. "My children."

I nodded.

"You afraid?"

"A little." I looked at Missus Dillingham. "But we have help. And we're going all together. It's not so scary that way."

The next morning we started even earlier than before. Mr. Dillingham thought since the carriage had arrived in the dark, it should leave in the dark. We decided Jean and Cal together should sit out at the top and drive. Lynne and the children would be in the carriage with me, but I would sit by the window again. Though they weren't hidden exactly, they had to stay out of sight as much as possible. Before I got in, Silas took me off to the side. "You got that pistol?"

"Yes, it's right here." I touched a pocket of my travel dress.

"Good. Don't be scared to use it if you have to."

"I won't be scared."

He shoved his hands into his pockets. "I'll be seeing you in Philadelphia then."

"Yes."

"I heard Mr. Dillingham say you might go to school."

"I might. Don't know what's gonna happen. We've got to get there first."

"All right."

"All right."

"You be careful."

He seemed to be waiting for something. I didn't know what else to do, so I just hugged him. "Goodbye, Silas."

"Bye."

When I climbed into the carriage, I was thinking it did feel like goodbye, like I might not see him again. The next part of my journey was beginning, and I was with the people I was supposed to be with even though I wasn't sure about where I was going—not just on a map but within myself.

The thing about this leg of our journey—it wasn't that long. Seemed the amount of time it took to get from the Burkes to the Dillinghams was longer. When we stopped in Havre de Grace in Maryland to water the horses and Jean said we were more than halfway there, I wondered what all the fuss was about. I looked out the window, and it seemed like a nice little town, not far from the water. I figured from its name that it was a kind of port town, and it was busy that way.

While I was looking out, I noticed a baking shop with lots of pretty little cakes in the window.

"Come with me, Lynne," I said. "I want to buy us some treats for the rest of our way."

"Are you sure?"

"It'll be all right. It's just here on the street."

I opened the door and helped her out.

"Jean, we'll be just a minute," I said. "Look after Jeremiah and Fanny."

He glanced around and nodded. Cal was on the other side of the horses, and he nodded also.

When I walked in the store, the delicious scent of sugar and dough nearly brought me to tears. Aunt Nancy Lynne's kitchen had smelled like this on the nights we'd done her baking. I thought of how much she might enjoy having a little shop like this of her own. But then I gathered myself and selected some small cakes with icing. The woman put them in a box, and I paid for them with Aunt Nancy Lynne's money. I gave the box to Lynne, and she followed me out of the store. I was stunned to see, just that fast, there was a white man standing very close to Jean and speaking to him. Cal was already up on the driving seat and looked ready to bolt if necessary.

"Jean!" I called out, keeping my voice nice and light. "We're all ready. Please help Lynne get my cakes in the carriage. I don't want them to be a mess of crumbs when we get to Papa's."

He moved quickly and did what I said.

I looked at the white man. A sense of something that felt like Madame—yes, Madame—came up within me. I knew at once how to look and what to say.

"I'm sorry, I don't usually speak to men to whom I haven't been properly introduced. Was my man causing a problem?"

He looked flustered. He took off his hat and opened his mouth to say something, but then a deep, huge voice boomed out.

"Tolins!"

The voice belonged to a tall, round-bellied man wearing pants with suspenders and a white shirt with his sleeves rolled up on his thick arms. He was wiping his hands on a cloth, and I realized he worked in one of the shops across the street. He walked slowly up to the man Tolins.

"I hope you're not interfering with this nice lady and her property." He put his hands on his hips. "Are you now?"

Tolins stepped back. "Not at all."

"Ma'am," the stranger said, "this here one of those abolitionists. They like to stir things up."

"I see."

"You go on your way. Don't mind him."

I curtsied to the stranger. "Thank you kindly, sir. I am much obliged."

Jean came round and opened the door and helped me into the carriage. I thought about giving Tolins a sign of some sort to let him know we were on the same side. I couldn't think of anything to do, but then I thought better of it. I didn't know what would happen between Tolins and the man after we left. The encounter helped me see more clearly the dangers of the route. I had been foolish.

Lynne's hands were shaking. I took the box of cakes from her. I had planned on giving the children the cakes in the carriage, but it would be better to wait until we were safe in Philadelphia. I took Lynne's hands in both my own.

"We're all right," I said once we were on the road again.

We were quiet for a while. Jeremiah and Fanny fell asleep against Lynne.

"How you come to talk like that?" she asked.

"I was raised in a white family."

"They didn't keep you?"

"No. They didn't keep me." I smiled. That was a nice way to put it. "But I'm glad I'm here with you and your boy and your girl."

That was the truth.

Mr. Dillingham had given me the written directions for the house that would be our destination in Philadelphia. I called out to Jean which way to go, and after a while he let out a loud whoop.

"We here!" he cried out. "We here!"

Lynne and I didn't wait for anyone to open our door. We jumped out and pulled the children after us, and we all embraced and just jumped up and down and laughed.

Laughed.

I looked at the children—it was the first time in two years I'd felt anything like joy.

A negro man—in a suit!—opened the door of the town house and extended his arms. I detected a smile under his thick black mustache.

"Welcome, my friends," he said.

He shook Jean's and Cal's hands.

"I'm Fenn, Fenn Mosher," he said. He rubbed Jeremiah's head. "Come in, come in. You must be tired."

"Naw, sir," Cal said. "Right about now, I feel like flying!"

Mr. Mosher turned to me. "You are the group's fearless leader."

"Don't think I'm a leader or fearless, but I was happy to help."

Inside we were joined by the home's owners, a Quaker couple whose name was Phillips, Robert and Deborah. Mr. Mosher, as it turned out, was a free man who also lived in Philadelphia and helped the newly freed get established. They had laid out for us what amounted to a holiday feast—roasted turkey and potatoes and yams and corn bread. I gave the children the cakes for dessert, but we had pie on the table too.

We told Mr. Mosher and the Phillipses what had happened in Havre de Grace. They all knew Tolins.

"He needs to work on being more discreet." Mr. Phillips laughed. He had a gentle voice and quiet blue eyes. I liked him very much. "Don't worry. We'll let him know you're with us and all right."

We had a good laugh over the Southern shop owner and his unintended aid. But I was thinking about how I had initially read the situation so poorly from the start. Tolins would never have thought he could speak to Jean if I had stayed in the carriage. It made me think to be, in the future, more watchful and cautious of any change in a situation.

It turned out Mr. Phillips was a photographer. He took portraits of the slaves who came through this way to celebrate their freedom. He said he would take these portraits before we moved on and would give us our own copies. I'd never had my portrait taken before and looked forward to doing so.

That evening I was in the parlor, and Missus Phillips sat next to me. She put her hand on mine in my lap and said that I was a brave and intelligent girl.

"You want to go to school; did I understand that correctly? Missus Burke has written to me."

I nodded eagerly. "Yes, ma'am. I haven't had any proper learning since I was about twelve."

"How old are you now?"

"Sixteen."

"Well, you're too old of a girl to be in a school with young ones. But what if I could get you a place in an institution where you would learn from a private tutor, a kind of governess, and live with other girls like yourself?"

"That sounds fine. Is it here in Philadelphia?"

"No, it's in New York City. The teacher is Miss Temple, and the school is called the Barbary Institution. Mr. Phillips and I are going to New York in a day or two and can take you there."

"Ma'am, I'll go whenever you are ready."

"You should rest first, Jeannette. You've been traveling a long time. I'm going to guess that you are more tired than you realize. Once the stress of the situation has lessened, you'll see."

She was right. I slept deeply and for a long time that night. I dreamed I was on a hill with sweeping views of a beautiful green valley with a wide curving river cutting through the land. I didn't know where it was. It didn't look like Catalpa Valley. But I felt fresh and alive standing on that hill. Maybe it was a place I was going. I felt good about it.

The next morning, we received a message that Silas and Mr. Dillingham had been obliged to delay their travel by a day.

"It's all right," I told Missus Phillips. "We can leave for New York when you want."

"Mr. Phillips will take your portraits today and we can go tomorrow, but are you sure, dear? You don't want to wait for your friend?"

"I said goodbye before. We always thought we might have to go our separate ways once we got this far. I'll leave a message for him with Mr. Mosher."

And this was true. But the message I left for him would have to be spoken because Silas couldn't read. I asked Mr. Mosher to tell Silas I had said "Thank you."

Chapter 6

The Barbary Institution was located in a brownstone building on Fifth Avenue near Twenty-Third Street near the St. Germain Hotel. Missus Phillips brought me there in December of 1855, when the small trees along the sidewalks were bare and the sky looked stark and white against the hard structure lines of the buildings that made up New York City. I couldn't imagine anything more different from Catalpa Valley, and yet this place would be my home. The parlor rooms downstairs had shelves of books covering the walls and two to three medium-size desks. Two girls who looked to be about my age, one white and one colored, sat together studying. Missus Phillips introduced me to Reverend Bell, the superintendent of the facility, and Miss Temple, who would be my teacher. The students—six, including me—lived in rooms upstairs, as did Miss Temple, who looked to be about twenty-five, and a Missus Fletcher, whom I met later. She was a widow who acted as a house matron and teaching assistant to Miss Temple.

My room was a garret-like space on the third floor that looked out on the small courtyard in the back. I was to share it with another girl who had been there for a year. Miss Temple sat with me while I removed my coat and bonnet and began to unpack my few belongings.

"We're going to do quite a bit of reading," she said. "And we'll see how much you know by way of math. But most importantly, Jeannette,

I'm going to teach you how to teach. That way you'll have a vocation when we're done. You'll be able to make a living."

"Oh yes," I replied. She had spoken what I most wanted to hear— that it was possible for me to be independent and look after myself in the world.

Miss Temple checked the silver watch she wore as a brooch with a small chain. Her dress was simple but well made from a navy wool with a black trim around the bottom of her skirt. She had a pale, thin face and soft brown eyes. I looked forward to getting to know more of her.

"You rest now and get yourself settled. We can begin your lessons tomorrow."

She was true to her word. I was under the tutelage of Miss Temple for a little more than three years. She became my friend and close companion—a mother, teacher, and guide all at once. The Barbary Institution, I learned, was funded by a group of wealthy, liberal-minded individuals who kept the building in good repair and made sure that its students were clothed and fed properly. There was another girl like me who had been a slave but could read and write. The others were white and orphans sent to the school and supported by benefactors. The donors and benefactors paid a salary to Miss Temple and Missus Fletcher. Reverend Bell, who served on the board of trustees along with the donors, was the administrator. I'll be forever grateful for the life and learning I had there.

I did love to study and fell back into it as though I were in my papa's library again. Miss Temple was so encouraging that I was eager to please her and thus was spurred to work even harder. She recognized that I could, because of the work I'd done with Papa, study geography very well. I read literature, enjoyed poetry, and learned math. I also studied French, which I'd heard so much of at Catalpa Valley but had never learned or spoken much on my own. I especially enjoyed discussing teaching, and after a year Miss Temple had me tutoring the newer girls who came to us. She influenced me with her calm and economy of emotion. I lived quietly at Barbary because she was my model.

Miss Temple modeled another important lesson: a quiet life didn't mean an unchanging one. On a spring day in 1859 she rose from the dining table and informed her students that she was going to marry and leave Barbary Institution. The gaiety that erupted from this announcement became the source of an ongoing hum of excitement that went on for several days as we celebrated Miss Temple and planned for her departure. When the newly wed Missus Herman Cain boarded a chaise with her banker husband and rode off for new adventures, that hum went with her.

I stared out of the window of my room at the pink dogwood in blossom in the courtyard and considered this new void in my life. At first I thought I was mourning the loss of Miss Temple, or Missus Cain, and thinking how I might distract myself until I'd recovered. But my thoughts quickly turned, and I found myself contemplating how to replace the scene and not the person. The scene, I realized, didn't have to be quiet. All the quiet I'd thought I had taken on from Miss Temple was, it turned out, only borrowed clothing. Now that she was gone, I found myself removing it and feeling a restless spirit within me. I had been content to stay in one place, hidden in the busyness of a city, and be obscure because my position as a runaway slave required it. I'd had no run-ins with the hunters who tracked runaways so they could, under the Fugitive Slave Act, return them to their owners. Of course, my appearance allowed me to blend in. My whitish skin and blue eyes always made me seem white on sight, especially with my hair hidden under a bonnet. I could take advantage of that now and move about a little beyond New York. It would have been easy for me to think Barbary was my entire world, but my geography studies with Miss Temple reminded me that the world was wide, and I could go into it and learn more of myself, of who Jeannette Bébinn really was.

Night fell. I opened the window and took in the heady scent of the hyacinths planted in the borders. The first evening stars were still quite dim. My eyes eventually rested on the horizon. If I went east, I would come to an ocean, a vast ocean. I could take a ship to Europe and cross that ocean. Or I could travel west and explore Ohio or even Canada. I thought about the hundreds of miles I had traveled to finally come to this place. I looked at the soft green leaves near my window and thought about how cold and bare everything had been three years before. In another year I would have been in Barbary as long as I had been at the Holloway Plantation. Aunt Nancy Lynne had told me that I had to have a plan if I were to have a chance of running from there and not coming back. She had encouraged me to wait. Should I wait now, and for how long? Maybe only long enough to figure out my plan. Not a day longer. Because suddenly I was that impatient—three years of calm had evaporated within an afternoon. I wanted my life to begin, a real life, with the independence Papa had once envisioned for me. But where could that life be, and what would it look like? Then I remembered: I had learned a vocation. I was a teacher. Where could I find for myself a position?

Isabella, my roommate, interrupted my thoughts when she summoned me to supper.

I couldn't return to my thinking until bedtime, but even then Isabella was eager to talk and rehash the details of Miss Temple's wedding and departure. I wished she would just go to sleep. If I could have quiet again, I could go back to the idea I'd had as I'd stood at the window and discover some answer for how I could find a position.

When Isabella finally drifted off, I wrapped a blanket around my shoulders and returned to the window. By then it was so dark I could see nothing but my own reflection in the glass.

Teaching—I am a teacher, I thought to myself. *I am qualified. I have taught at Barbary for two years. Now all I want is to teach somewhere else.*

It was an entirely sensible and feasible path for a single young woman. *But how do I find a new position?*

I sat on my bed again: it was a chilly night, so I crawled under the covers and continued to puzzle over the question.

What did I want? A new place, in a new house, with new faces and new circumstances. There was nothing else I could ask for, nothing better anyway. My avenues would be limited because of my mulatto blood. What should I do? I could ask my friends—people like Reverend Bell or even Missus Phillips, who often sent notes of encouragement during the holiday season. I could ask if they knew of any places that might accept me. These answers soothed me. I resolved to start in the morning by writing a note to Reverend Bell, asking him for an appointment. If the conversation didn't prove fruitful, I would write to Missus Phillips. I went to sleep at last, satisfied that I had, at least, an initial plan.

My meeting with Reverend Bell was delayed because he was traveling, but in a few days I did sit before him in his office. He looked severe in his long black suit and collar, but he looked over his glasses at me with kind eyes, so I wasn't nervous presenting him with my request.

"I will admit, Miss Bébinn," he said, "that I had hoped you would take Miss Temple's place and become a teacher here."

It felt good to know he had such faith in me. If he had asked me before Miss Temple had left, I might have accepted and happily. But I was different now.

"Yes, sir. I would like, I think, a change of scenery."

"Of course, I understand. You haven't ventured much beyond our little neighborhood since you arrived. Grace Church on Sundays and really nothing more."

"Yes, sir."

"Well, I may have something for you. I've been reading the letters that arrived during my absence. Let me find the one I'm referring to."

He leafed through the various pages of stationery on his desk until he came to one that he perused closely.

"Yes, this is it. A friend of mine referred a Missus Livingston to us. She lives in southern Ohio at a place called Fortitude Mansion. It's in the vicinity of an unusual community—a small village founded by a population of former slaves freed from a single plantation. She is seeking a teacher to establish a school for the children and, if I guess correctly, most likely the adults too."

I couldn't believe it. Hadn't I just considered Ohio as a place to explore? And now here was an opportunity to not only teach but create a school where there was none, and my pupils would be new Fannys and Jeremiahs, and I could open up the world for them.

"Does this interest you, Miss Bébinn?"

"It is exactly the type of situation I had hoped for, sir. Can you help me secure it?"

"I'll write to Missus Livingston today to recommend you."

"Thank you, sir. I'd like that very much."

And so it was that the arrangements were made. Missus Livingston accepted me and sent directions, and in about three months' time, I was on a train with my trunk and headed west.

When I arrived in Dayton, I left the train with a handful of people. It must have been easy for the man with the bushy yellow hair to find and approach me. He had a hat pushed down over his hair, and it seemed to escape and fluff out when he removed the hat and addressed me. I thought he was badly in need of a haircut.

"Are you Miss Bébinn?"

"Yes, I am."

"Missus Livingston sent me to fetch you. I'm Stephen. Let me get your luggage, and we'll be on our way."

"Thank you, Stephen."

At the carriage he loaded my trunk and I got in.

"How far are we going?"

"About ten miles, miss."

The horses ambled along. I was excited to be so near the end of my travels and very curious about Fortitude Mansion. I wondered if it would be as grand as the name sounded. I touched the cushions of my seat. The carriage was comfortable, but it wasn't as big or as fine as one of Papa's or the one the Holloways rode in to church on Sundays. Judging from the plainness of both Stephen and the carriage, I guessed that Missus Livingston would be just as plain. This would give me a better chance of liking her. But she must be kind. She must be some sort of benefactress of the village for her to inquire about a teacher for the children of former slaves. I wondered if she had any family living with her in the mansion, how far it was from the school, and where I would live. It was only at the end of these ruminations that the question of *Will I like it there?* entered my mind. When it did, I realized I didn't have to be concerned, because if I didn't like it, I didn't have to stay. I was free to do as I wanted.

I let down the window and looked out. Dayton was behind us. It was nowhere near the size of New York City, but it was a city of considerable size. I was grateful there was plenty of daylight left so I could see the countryside that was to be my new home. There was a large river twisting through the land. Eventually the road rose away from this river. When we made the final approach to the mansion, I saw that it was situated on a generous but not-too-steep hill.

We slowly ascended the drive, which wove around into a semicircle in front of a large house. But it seemed more like a cross between a house and a small castle. It had a porch that went all along the front like a house. But the posts supporting it were made of stone and were wide and rectangular, not the elegant white posts of a Southern home. The part above the supports had the up-and-down block pattern that I'd only seen in illustrations of castles. But above that Fortitude looked again like a house, with two stories of windows and topped by a red-tiled roof flanked by four chimneys, two on each side. The coloring of the stone was a light sandy brown, which I guessed must have come from an area quarry. It was a curious house, and I liked it right away.

A young woman in a black dress and blue-and-white apron opened the wide mahogany door. "Welcome to Fortitude, miss," she said. "Missus Livingston is waiting for you." I followed her across a square hall with high doors that, I assumed by their height, enclosed large rooms. The one I stepped into, though, located more toward the back of the house, was a small room that seemed to be a combination of parlor and office. There was a small writing desk by the window, which looked out over an immense garden. Near the fireplace, empty for the summer, were a round table covered with a burgundy cloth and two wing chairs. Some knitting work lay on one of the chairs. A vase of yellow roses decorated the table.

A lady sat writing at the table, and when I came in, she rose, and I saw that she was tall and elderly but moved with ease and elegance as she walked toward me and extended her hand. She wore black as well, but her dress was made of silk, and her apron was a pristine white. Her light-brown hair was streaked with white. She smiled kindly, and I knew at once I had nothing to fear.

"How do you do, my dear? I'm Missus Livingston. Come sit. You've had such a long journey."

"I have," I said. "But I'm glad to be here." I sat in the chair without the knitting. She picked up the blue yarn and needles and sat in the other.

I removed my bonnet and looked around the room. In a moment, the young lady returned with a tray of tea and small sandwiches. Missus Livingston poured tea for us and spoke to the woman as she did so. "Leah, please tell Stephen to take Miss Bébinn's trunk up to the blue room."

"Yes, ma'am."

I enjoyed the attention, but I was surprised. Missus Livingston treated me like a visitor. I had expected a more formal reception, with a serious recital of a list of what was expected of me in my position. But perhaps she wasn't my supervisor, I thought. Perhaps the severe person had yet to appear.

She handed me my cup and then a plate with two small sandwiches. I hadn't thought about food since I was on the train, but suddenly I was quite hungry and found the sandwiches, made of ground-up ham and dressing, delicious. Since Missus Livingston was so natural and comfortable, I decided it would be all right to ask questions instead of waiting to be told what I should be doing.

"Will I meet my students today?"

"Oh, dear, that can wait until tomorrow. The village is within walking distance, but I need to take the carriage, and I won't ask you to get in it again so soon. Just rest this evening, get your things unpacked, and I'll show you the school tomorrow."

I had wanted to ask about her connection to the village but realized that might be too intimate. Instead I asked about Fortitude Mansion.

"As you can see, it's a lovely place. You might enjoy taking a walk in the garden later on, when you get settled. I am so glad you are here. The house really should be filled with guests, but recently there's been just me, Leah, Stephen, and the kitchen staff. Oh, and there's Founder. She lives in a suite on the third floor. But she keeps to herself so much. I've often invited her to sit with me as you're doing now, but she prefers her solitude, I suppose."

"Founder? Who is she?"

"She is a fine woman who came north with the other slaves, but she stays here, not in the village."

The mention of the village and its people made me forget about Fortitude. I wanted to know more about their story, which was sure to be impressive.

"Where in the South did they come from?"

"Well, I don't know the state well enough to give you an exact location, but they came from a plantation called Belle Meade, in Louisiana."

"Louisiana!"

"Yes. Do you know it?"

"A little." I could have said more but thought better of it. I should learn more about the people first, see if there was a chance that they might know Papa or Catalpa Valley. But the state was large; I knew that from Papa's maps. It was possible that they knew nothing about my home.

"I know it's unusual," Missus Livingston continued. "But the owner denounced the practice of keeping slaves. He sold his property, gave the people their freedom, then assisted those who wanted to do so in moving here and getting established."

"That is . . ." I searched for the word. "Stunning."

"Yes, isn't it? Quite extraordinary. But I'll not keep chattering on. There's plenty of time to learn all this. You have been traveling for so long. You must be tired. I'll show you your bedroom. I've had the room down the hall from mine prepared for you. I hope you'll be comfortable there."

"I'm sure it will be fine." I said this, but I knew it in fact. I hadn't had my own room since I'd lived at Catalpa Valley. This room would be, for me, an unexpected luxury.

She led the way upstairs. The steps were wide and flanked by beautiful banisters made of oak and polished to a shine. A window near the top of the stair was decorated with stained glass in the pattern of a bluebird sitting on a branch of green leaves. We walked a little ways down the hall. Missus Livingston was opening the door to my chamber when we heard another door close. I turned to see a fine-looking colored woman, dressed in brown silk, about to make her way downstairs. A black net gathered her hair behind her head, and she wore gold hoop earrings. She was an older woman with a stout frame. She moved slowly, but it seemed like she moved that way not because of age but because she had all the time in the world to get where she was going. Missus Livingston called out to her.

"Oh, Founder! Come meet Miss Bébinn. She will be the teacher for the new school in the village."

She strolled our way and looked me up and down with striking black eyes that felt like she could bore right through me.

"How do you do?"

I curtsied. "I'm fine, Miss Founder. Glad to meet you."

"I ain't a miss or missus. Just Founder."

I was unsure how to respond to this, so I only said, "Thank you, Founder."

She nodded and turned back to her progress toward the stair. She raised her chin, spread her arms open wide, and seemed to speak to the air in front of her.

"Welcome to Fortitude!"

I looked at Missus Livingston, and she shrugged. "Well, yes, that's Founder." She quickly opened the door to my room and showed me in.

Though there was still some daylight remaining when Missus Livingston left me alone, I decided to leave a walk around the grounds to another time. I was exhausted, and being alone in the well-appointed room made me loath to leave it. I sat on the bed, decorated with magnificent blue curtains, and the relief of such comfort brought tears to my eyes. I slid down to my knees by the bed and prayed out my immense gratitude. I felt heartened that whatever force had brought me safely to this place would continue to guide my heart and soul. It didn't take long to unpack my few dresses. I removed a small box in which I placed my Catalpa Valley stone at the end of each day. I still carried it with me, though I had no thoughts about if I would ever see Papa's land again. But the stone reminded me of Dorinda and Calista and the love of my papa. I undressed and fell asleep before the sun had fully set.

When I awoke, I realized my room faced east. The sun shone brightly between the blue chintz window curtains and warmed the beautiful oriental carpet on the floor. I was simply happy. My surroundings inspired me, and I was thrilled by not knowing what the day would bring. All would be new.

I rose and washed in the basin by my bedside. I put on my gray dress—it was simple and neat, and I thought it seemed like schoolteacher attire. It had always been my sense that I could look neat and mindful of my appearance. On a good day, I might even consider myself pretty. And I wanted to please, which was a fancy of my young heart. I brushed my hair and pinned it up in my usual way. I straightened up my bed and looked around the room to make sure all was in order. When it seemed satisfactory, I went out to make my way downstairs.

My curious surroundings kept my head turning with my every step. A large bronze chandelier hung from the ceiling over the hall; an enormous black clock that I hadn't noticed the day before solemnly ticked; paintings of landscape scenes decorated the walls. I pulled the front door open and stepped outside. It was a fine morning with a slight crispness that hinted at autumn's slow approach. I crossed the drive and onto the lawn so I could study the house more closely. The castle-like details I'd noticed yesterday and the stone made the mansion seem larger than it really was. While it was three stories high and very grand, one could see that it was a house and not a school or some other institution. And for that reason it had a kind of warmth. I turned around and took in the view from the hill. I wondered if it was the view from my dream months before. Indeed there was a river and a bucolic aspect. It was so much pleasanter than the dirty bustle of New York City. I appreciated the seclusion of this place and opened my arms wide as if to embrace it. Once the leaves from the surrounding trees fell, I guessed, the view would be even broader. In the distance I saw what must be the little village. Its roofs mingled with the trees and straggled down toward the river. A wonderful breeze came up from the water, and I enjoyed the feel of it on my face.

"What! Up already?" I turned to see Missus Livingston at the door. "I see you are an early riser, like I am. But you went to bed very early and had no supper. Come to breakfast; you must be hungry."

In the hall she put an arm around me, as though we'd been friends for years, and asked, "How do you like Fortitude?"

"It's so beautiful," I said. "I never imagined I would be in such a lovely place."

"Yes," she said, "it is quite lovely. But it would be a good deal livelier if Mr. Colchester would make up his mind to be here more often and socialize in the neighborhood as a young man of his station should. If we were to have a big affair now, I don't know how we would handle it. There's not enough staff, and I fear the kitchen is out of practice feeding such a crowd."

"Who is Mr. Colchester?"

"Why, he owns Fortitude," she responded quietly. "He is the one who sold Belle Meade, founded the village, and moved its population here from Louisiana."

"Oh," I said.

"Reverend Bell didn't tell you about him?"

"No. I've only known your name. I thought you were the proprietress."

"No, dear. Mr. Colchester brought me on after he moved here. I was housekeeper for the longest time for a family in Dayton proper. But since my husband died, I'd been wanting a quieter servitude."

"I see." Perhaps this Mr. Colchester would be the severe person. He paid my salary and would soon make it known what was expected of me.

After we had breakfast, Missus Livingston and I boarded the carriage, and Stephen drove us down the road two miles or so to the village.

"It's called Lower Knoll," she told me. "It's about five years old. Most of the attention, as you can imagine, has been spent on building housing and then town necessities. They only got to the school this past year. But even now some supplies must come from elsewhere. It's not self-sufficient just yet."

Lower Knoll, from what I could see, consisted of a single long street with small houses dotting the surrounding land. One tiny side street led to a small clapboard edifice. The carriage stopped there.

"Here, Miss Bébinn, is your school."

I left the carriage, took in the sight, and found myself whispering under my breath, "My school."

Inside, the large room featured a wood-burning stove in the center. There was a chalkboard on the wall at one end and student desks of various sizes arranged in rows. My desk was to one side, underneath one of the long windows. Primer books were stacked on the desk, but a few shelves were nailed to the walls, and more books, I saw, could live there.

"I think you can do some good work, here, don't you, Miss Bébinn?"

I placed my hand on the desk. "Yes. It's the best place I've ever been."

The door opened and closed, and a little girl ran into the room and straight up to my desk. She looked up at me with bright dark eyes. Her skin was a clear, deep shade of hickory brown. "It's you! It's you!"

"Me?"

"You!" She grabbed my hand and looked at Missus Livingston. "This our teacher?"

Missus Livingston seemed to enjoy the scene. "Yes, Jelly. This is Miss Bébinn."

"Hi!"

"Hello"—I paused—"Jelly, is it?"

"My name is Najelle! But everybody calls me Jelly. You can, too, if you want."

"I would like that very much. Thank you, Jelly."

"I want to read!"

"Well, we can start working on that."

"When?"

I laughed. I already loved her eagerness and couldn't wait to get started myself. "Let me get the school set up, and our first day will be tomorrow. Is that all right?"

"Yeah! Can I help?"

Missus Livingston laughed too. "Jelly, let me finish showing her the town and her cottage. Come back in a bit. You can help then."

The little girl agreed, but she didn't go away. She followed us outside again and over to a small edifice under construction.

"What is this?" I asked.

"This will be your home, when it's finished," Missus Livingston said. "Of course you'll want your own place, your own privacy. It will be a small cottage, just one or two rooms."

"Oh my goodness, Missus Livingston. This is more than I ever dreamed of. I didn't know I would have my own house."

"Well, I wouldn't mind having you always up at Fortitude, but yes, I hope you'll like it. But it may not be done for some time. There is a larger work going on, and that build has all the attention of the men in the village. That's why there's no one working here now."

"That's okay; whenever it's done will be fine with me. I'm happy with just the idea of it."

That was true. It seemed the blessings were pouring over me. I marveled again and again at this Lower Knoll, this miraculous place. Missus Livingston introduced me to some of the woman residents, who must have heard the carriage and come out to see what it had brought. I was delighted with everyone I met and with all that I saw.

Once the school opened, my days took on a certain shape. I rose in the morning, drank a bit of coffee, and walked down the hill into Lower

Knoll. In the schoolhouse I laid books on the desks and wrote out lessons on the chalkboard. I'd go to the window and pray silently so that all that came out of my mouth might be right and good things. When I was done, I rang the school bell and waited for my students to fill the room.

At noontime the children would take wrapped bread and meat from their pockets (a scene that made me miss Dorinda something fierce) and settle themselves outside to eat. I would walk down the road a piece and look in on the progress of my cottage. Most days there wasn't much to look at. The men had other work to do, and Missus Livingston said that with the weather growing colder, the work most likely would not pick up until the following spring. But I liked going to the cottage anyway and thinking about its little square of land that was the closest anything was to being mine.

My students weren't used to regular study, so there were times when they were, as children are, chatty and distracted. I was patient and determined to enjoy their playfulness. Jelly dived into learning with a hunger that reminded me of my own. I could give her a bit of extra reading or more math figures and know she would apply herself to them.

At the end of the school day, I returned to the mansion and strolled its confines so I could learn its structure. I did this until it was time for supper. One afternoon I was exploring the third floor to see what the view of the river valley would be like from that height. I knew there were small windows at that level, and I thought those rooms might be open. There was a larger center window with a small balcony. I figured that room must belong to Founder. The stair to that level was behind a door on the second level. The third-floor hall didn't have windows like the ones on the floor below it, so it was rather dim, with indirect light that came through the open doors of its rooms.

I jumped when I heard someone clearing a throat. I turned and there was Founder, leaning against her open door like she had been waiting for me.

"Got some tea set out," she said. "Come sit for a bit."

Her room was large, more than twice the size of mine. It was more like an apartment, for it had space for a sitting area in one end and her bedroom area in another. The wall of the sitting area was covered by a large tapestry depicting a Bible scene—the baptism of Christ. In the middle was the large window and its balcony. She saw me looking at it. She motioned her head in that direction. "Go have a look."

"Thank you."

She went to her table and poured tea while I unlatched and opened the double window. The view looked like one of the great paintings downstairs. In this living painting the artist was illustrating early autumn and had touched the tops of the trees with red, gold, and orange.

"It's so peaceful here," I said.

"It wasn't peaceful where you come from?"

"No. I came from New York City."

"But you know peaceful." She sat down and motioned for me to do the same. When I did, she peered at me closely. "You wouldn't feel it if you didn't know it. Must have had peace sometime."

"I did. The place where I was a girl was peaceful. But I was taken from there."

I drank my tea, but she said nothing more. Finally, I asked a question.

"Missus Livingston said you were from Louisiana. Maybe you know where I'm from?"

"Where you from? Who your people?"

I told her. I don't know why, but I felt I could tell her. I spoke of Papa and recited the litany of our land. I told her about Catalpa Valley and Madame and how she'd sold me to Amesbury after Papa had died.

She sat back and considered me again closely.

"You're free with that information," she said when I was done. "You don't seem concerned about being half-negro."

"It's just who I am. I don't have anything to be ashamed of."

She drained her cup and wiped her mouth. "It's not about shame, girl. It's about safe."

"I'm sorry, I don't understand."

"How old are you?"

"I am twenty."

"Then you old enough to know."

She got up and opened her door.

"Time for me to nap now. You can come on back another time. I ain't going nowhere."

I was confused, but I accepted her dismissal. I thanked her and returned to my own room.

That evening, at dinner, I thought about how my interview with Founder had only brought on more questions. I figured the absent Mr. Colchester must hold the answers to what I didn't know about Lower Knoll.

"Have you had any word," I began, "of when Mr. Colchester might return?" I uncovered a fragrant dish of stew with roasted vegetables.

"No, and I must admit, he is often negligent on that count. When Mr. Colchester does take up residence, it's often on a whim. Founder likes to say, 'You look for Christian when you see him!'" She chuckled.

"Christian?"

"Yes. His name is Christian Robichaud Colchester. Founder and I call him Christian, but of course he's Mr. Colchester to most everyone else."

"Is he very informal?"

"Not particularly so, but he was born and raised a gentleman. He's twenty-eight years old. He was very young when he inherited his father's estate. I find, sometimes, he needs to be reminded of his manners. He can be, well, rough sometimes."

"But you like him?"

"Oh yes; it's obvious he has a kind heart. You can see that from Lower Knoll. But he's restless and sometimes, I think, unhappy. No more than other young men, though."

"What is his personality?"

"He is clever and well read but comes off as rather peculiar. He has traveled a great deal—I believe he is in Europe now. I never know for certain."

"Peculiar?"

"I don't know—how can I describe it? When he speaks to you, it can be hard to tell whether he is serious or making a joke, whether he is pleased or not pleased. I admit, I often just don't understand him. I'll leave it at that."

October, November, and December passed away. If it seemed I was settled and satisfied in my life at Fortitude, it was an untrue image. Missus Livingston spoke of the restlessness of young men. She didn't know that young women could have the same energized spirit. I was such a woman. I'm sorry to say I was perturbed, maybe even more than when I'd lived in the slave quarters at the Holloway Plantation. Because then I'd had a sense of something I had to do, of vital work coming up next. My whole body had been bent on leaving that place and then on making sure I didn't get sent back. What reason was there to have such a focus at Fortitude? And yet I had this feeling of something to come. I didn't know if I had to do anything to help it along. It felt strange. Ungrateful. Here I had good work I could do, I had good food to eat, and I lived unharmed.

Perhaps my restlessness was stoked by my connections. Missus Livingston was kind, and I enjoyed our evening hours together, but our conversation was neither challenging nor inspiring. I didn't develop any particular friendships in the village, though I hoped that would change once I was living in the cottage. On the odd occasion that Founder allowed me to sit with her, she seemed more interested in speaking generally about human nature and "the way people are." She saw me as hugely naive and needing guidance in this area. She intrigued me, but she was not a close friend, nor did it seem she would become one. So I was dissatisfied with my society but unsure of what connection I did want. Were all women supposed to be as placid as Miss Temple and Missus Livingston? Aunt Nancy Lynne had something of a fire about her, and that determination had lit me up on days when I'd thought I would never leave Holloway's. Would I ever have such a friend again?

There were times when I would walk down the hill from Fortitude and I had a sensation like the valley, the world, was laid out before me on a table like a feast. It was like that faraway dream I'd once had. But in the real-life picture, I thought I could hear a voice that was either my papa or something bigger talking to me.

Anything you want, ma chérie. Anything you want, Jeannette.

The thought scared me. Thrilled me. What could I want beyond a full belly and a place to rest in relative safety?

With Mama's blood running through me, the things I might want would have, as I was a mulatto, a natural limit. I wasn't one to dream outside my head, yearning for fantasies. Where I was, at Fortitude, was a small miracle in itself. Who was I, Jeannette Bébinn, with my papa dead, to think I could have anything more?

But something messed with my peace of mind. It felt like seeds in a cotton boll. In my quiet time I picked at the seeds and tried to clear my thinking. I didn't think too kindly of the world, that's for sure. I was prone to believe I had value because I'd seen it in Papa's eyes. And I was God's child, too, which meant everything. That was what I believed, and because I believed it, it was hard for me to accept what little was offered to me, a girl the world only saw, as Madame had pointed out, as a little nigger girl. It didn't seem right, not when Papa had meant for me to be more. Surely the lives of the children I taught meant more.

And yet the land ran with crazy white men willing to fight a war because they didn't see it that way.

One day I went to visit the cottage. It was built out of wood and had two rooms, one meant to be a kitchen. At the back was a plain set of stairs that went up to a sleeping area—not a full room, really, and not an attic since it didn't go the length of the building. A man couldn't stand up straight in the space, but I could, and that was all that mattered, all I needed. That was all the cottage was: a roof, walls, window holes with no glass, and those stairs. I felt drawn to the little house, though. I would climb the stairs and look out the opening where a round window would eventually be. I could see the road leading to the riverbank and the oak trees bare of leaves and acorns.

I had just finished looking out the window hole and was going down the steps, which I always did carefully because there was no rail, when I heard a rustling noise that seemed to be coming from under my feet. I stopped and listened and thought maybe I was hearing the sound of my own petticoats against the stairs. But then, standing there, I heard a bump and another rustle. I knew the space under the stairs was meant to be a closet or cupboard, but right then it didn't have a proper door, only a thin slab of wood leaned against it. I thought a squirrel or raccoon had gotten in there and needed to be let out.

When I got downstairs, I went around to shift the piece of wood, and when I did, I saw a pair of dark eyes look up at me, and I just about jumped out of my skin. I recognized the child right off. She sat with her legs crossed underneath her and held in front of her the book she'd been reading.

"Jelly! How did you get in here? You scared me."

"I'm sorry, Miss Bébinn, I didn't mean to."

She crawled out of the closet. Her dress was dusty from sitting on the unswept wood, and the tips of her fingers were pale with cold. "It's quiet here. I can't rightly hear the words in my head when I'm around everyone else. Reading is easier when I'm in there."

I nodded. "Yes. I find I can think in this cottage better than anywhere else. Maybe because it's not finished."

I walked her home and thought about how I'd probably needed to see her just then. She reminded me of my work and how much I enjoyed it. Jelly's eyes always seemed eager for filling. When I saw the ten-year-old sitting in the classroom with her big eyes, I felt like I'd need buckets to pour into her the knowledge she was looking for, but I only had a cup, maybe a small pitcher at most. It wasn't going to be enough no matter how hard I tried, because I had to see to other students who didn't take to learning as easily as Jelly did. It was something of a relief to know she was taking it on herself to read and add onto whatever I managed to relate to her in school. Maybe one day, if things changed, she could go to college. She could certainly become a teacher.

After I took Jelly home, I walked on to Fortitude in the growing darkness. The new year had been celebrated the week before, so it was 1860, and I considered the new decade as I climbed the hill. Missus Livingston had said that a new president of the United States would be elected this year. Who the new president was would tell me whether I had a chance of returning to Louisiana. But it seemed too far off to contemplate in that moment. I pulled my cloak tighter around me and sat on the front steps. I didn't want to go in just yet. The moon was rising. Missus Livingston would probably have with me a conversation about the election very similar to the one we'd had the night before. She tended to repeat herself unknowingly. It didn't seem polite to keep alerting her to this. I thought it better to just listen. If I stayed on the steps, I could delay our little scene for a few minutes longer. I got up and walked down the drive. There must be some remedy to my discontent. I refused to believe such a remedy involved moving on to another position. What change would there be other than location? I could travel the world and still feel this way. The restlessness was within me.

It would follow me wherever I went. My heart trembled at the thought because it seemed to foretell a restless life. I looked up at the evening stars and felt a wordless prayer rise from my chest. I didn't know if it would go anywhere or whether it would find someone who could interpret it. It was just out there floating in the cold winter air. Behind me, I heard the hall clock in the mansion strike the hour, and I knew I was late. Missus Livingston would be wondering where I was. I answered the clock's summons and turned away from the moon and the stars. I slowly climbed the steps of the mansion and went in.

A few moments later I would be standing at Fortitude's main staircase, and Mr. Colchester would roll down those stairs and crash into me.

Chapter 7

Winter 1860

I was twenty when Mr. Christian Robichaud Colchester went tumbling down the stairs of Fortitude Mansion and knocked the air out of my body. He didn't say he was sorry for landing on me, and he didn't thank me for breaking his fall. Instead he started asking questions and making demands, as most white men seem born to do.

"Who the devil are you, and what the hell are you doing in my house?"

I couldn't yet speak, but if I'd had breath, it would have been my right to ask him the same thing. I had been a resident of Fortitude Mansion for five months at that point. I'd wandered its floors and halls and walked the rolling hills of the property down to the Great Miami River and back again countless times. But I'd never laid eyes on this man with skin like onion-colored parchment. I gasped and rolled over onto my hands and knees, the better to find my footing again. The servants came running.

"Mr. Colchester! Are you all right?" Porter knelt and tried to take him by the arm. The man peevishly pushed him away. George appeared by my side, and I sighed and groaned when he pulled me upright.

"Stop it! Stop fussing!" Mr. Colchester took hold of the banister and rose to his feet, which were bare and pale. "Who is this person?"

I composed myself and took a deep breath. I was determined to speak for myself. "I am Jeannette Bébinn."

He wheeled his wild eyes over to Porter, who bowed his head slightly. "Mr. Colchester, Miss Bébinn is the one Missus Livingston brought here to teach at the school you built on the little knoll down a ways."

"That doesn't explain what she's doing here."

"Sir, the teacher's cottage isn't done yet. Doesn't even have windows. Weather was too bad at the end of the season, so come winter they couldn't finish it."

Missus Livingston arrived from her parlor office. "Christian! What was that noise? And why didn't you tell us you were coming home?"

"Because it's my home and I can come and go as I please."

She crossed her arms and looked over her glasses and down her long nose at him. "Well, if you were more regular in that coming and going, I suppose so. But we haven't seen you since the spring."

The fact seemed to knock the air out of him a little, too, like he'd forgotten he hadn't been there. He turned away from Missus Livingston and looked at me. "Never mind that. This is the teacher you found?"

"Yes. I thought it proper for her to stay here, in the empty suite on the second floor, until the cottage is ready in the spring."

"But who is she? Where is she from?"

"I can speak for myself," I said. I stepped forward. "I am a learned woman and a good teacher."

Missus Livingston came over and put an arm around me. It felt comforting and helped me be steadier on my feet. She said, "Reverend Bell from the association wrote a letter of recommendation for her and sent her here. She's been doing an excellent job with the children."

"I will be the judge of that." He turned his dark-eyed gaze on me and seemed to assess me from the top of my reddish-brown hair, the topknot loosened by our collision, down to the instep of my shoes. "Are you hurt?"

"No, sir."

He waited like he expected me to say more, and when I didn't, he sniffed and raised himself up and puffed out his chest. "I'll get to the bottom of this myself. We'll talk more. I'll receive her in the parlor."

I didn't see how there was any mystery to get to the bottom of, but since I was used to doing what I was told, I moved toward the room. Missus Livingston gently grasped my elbow and made me pause. "Christian, you're not fit to receive anyone," she said.

Mr. Colchester looked down on himself and seemed to notice for the first time his bare feet and unbuttoned shirt. His forehead scrunched up, and he put a hand to his eyes like he'd forgotten something. "Damn it!"

"Language, Christian!" Missus Livingston moved toward the parlor and drew me with her. "Miss Bébinn and I will have some tea. When you've made yourself respectable, you may join us."

We turned away from him and toward the library, a room I'd never been in. As the door closed on us, I heard him speak sharply.

"Leave me alone! I can walk for myself!"

Missus Livingston led me to a seat at one of the round tables in the room, which was handsome and large. I was stunned by the collection of books lining the walls. In another moment Leah brought in a tray with tea and a plate of small corn cakes. After she left, Missus Livingston looked me up and down like a china doll that might have been scuffed.

"Are you all right, Miss Bébinn? What happened?"

"He fell down the stairs, then onto me. That's all. I'm not hurt."

"Well, I'm sorry you had to have such an unfortunate introduction to Mr. Colchester. You'll find he's not always so . . ." She seemed to search for a word and finally settled on, "Unreserved."

I chewed on a piece of corn cake and thought about who Mr. Colchester's connections in the South might be. Would he have known my papa or any of his people? Would he have heard of a fair-skinned slave who'd fled the Holloway Plantation in Mississippi? Founder's caution made my skin feel hot, and I saw how I needed to watch my mouth when it came to Mr. Colchester. Even if he was friendly to colored people, as it seemed on the surface, there was no telling who he associated with and what they all said to each other. As much as I felt at home at Fortitude, I couldn't be careless.

"Is he a God-fearing man?" All the abolitionists I'd met seemed tied to some religion. Maybe this man was one of those Quakers or an Episcopalian like Reverend Bell. It might make him more trustworthy if he was.

Missus Livingston laughed. "His name is Christian! And I'm sure his family brought him up in such a way as to give it meaning. But honestly I have never known him to step foot in a church. What he does when he's away from here, I can't rightly say."

A half hour later Mr. Colchester joined us. He sat in an armchair, close to the fire, and near a table where his coffee awaited him. He motioned for me to sit in a chair across from him. I looked at Missus Livingston, and she nodded, so I left her. He ignored his coffee, leaned back, and laced his fingers together. He seemed to be studying me, and I didn't like it.

"You're a learned woman?"

"Yes, sir."

"But you obey too easily."

"No different from anyone else of my gender."

"Are you like Missus Livingston? I don't think so! She is a woman used to giving orders, as you can tell from her treatment of me just now. She is not used to obeying."

"And yet I'm here."

"What?"

"If Missus Livingston hadn't obeyed your order to find a teacher for your school, I wouldn't be here."

"True!" said Missus Livingston. "But I considered his order a reasonable one."

"You're saying others are not?" He turned his head slightly in her direction, but his eyes stayed on me.

"I won't tire Miss Bébinn with tales of your nonsense."

"No, but you will interrupt my interview! Let us find out what we're to learn on our own!" He accentuated his words so each one seemed like a poke with a stick. "You don't have to leave the room, but with respect, I ask you to be silent."

She stared at him for a moment.

"As you wish, Christian." She refilled her cup and took it to the other side of the room and sat at a small table to read the newspaper set upon it. Her stiffness as she went proved Mr. Colchester's point. Missus Livingston didn't take kindly to obeying.

He tilted his head back toward me. "And so, Miss Bébinn, as you so rightly observe, you are here."

"Yes, sir, that I am."

"But where were you before here? You didn't sprout up on my property like an errant seedling in the yard."

"No, sir."

"Then where is your family?"

"Dead, sir."

"And you came here from?"

I paused, and I could tell he would be on my hesitation like a magnet on iron. I thought of what Founder had said only a few months ago.

You're free with that information. It's not about shame. It's about safe.

"New York," I said.

"I detect something of an accent. Perhaps one you've tried to conceal?"

I heard Missus Livingston's cup touch its saucer and felt her eyes on my back. "I'm not hiding anything. I was born in the South, in Louisiana. I know you would have asked in another minute, and I would have told you so then."

"Miss Bébinn, you have nothing to fear. For all the rabble-rousing going on down there, you don't strike me as the rebel type. And I know Louisiana."

He bent the word *know* into two syllables in a careless, lilting way that I thought almost sounded like how my papa would have said it. But I ignored the notion and believed he meant to make fun of me. I said nothing. Mr. Colchester cleared his throat and sat up straighter in his chair.

"How is the school coming along? Do you enjoy instructing your students?"

"It is my work. I don't rightly see how my enjoyment has anything to do with it. I mean to make myself useful, and I see a chance to do that here."

"You don't care for the children, then?"

"I didn't say that, and that's not what you asked before. You asked about my teaching, and I'm telling you I take it seriously. The school is warm and comfortable, and I'm grateful we have enough books for study and paper for writing. I care for these things because I care that the children should have what they need. They are eager. They try hard. I want them to have every possible comfort that will help them succeed."

Mr. Colchester stared at me for a moment. "You surprise me, Miss Bébinn. I had expected a simple *Yes, sir.*"

I shifted in my seat. I didn't have the sense of having said something wrong. But if I had, it seemed the best course of action was to let him tell me what he expected now. Whether it would be apology or explanation, I was ready to give it. But I wouldn't, couldn't, give him words for all I'd been trying to figure out for myself since arriving at Fortitude.

Mr. Colchester stood up and positioned himself in front of the fire. My eyes fell on his feet, no longer bare but encased in shiny black riding boots. These could not have been the boots he had arrived in unless a servant had been quick to clean them.

"What?" he said. "Nothing to say to that?"

"No, sir. Not to your expectations. They're yours. Ask me questions, and I'll do my best to answer."

"You are a strange creature!" He laughed and leaned against the mantel of the fireplace. The way he did it pulled at something inside me. It felt like he was relaxing in my presence and like I had gotten him to do so. I didn't know how, but I liked the thought of it. And the sound of his laugh—like deep, warm folds of velvet I could wrap around my shoulders. But his eyes were still on me, and I couldn't raise mine to meet them. A warmth rushed up from my chest to my cheeks, and I lowered my eyes farther.

I wasn't used to being looked at anyway, but Mr. Colchester's eyes made it harder. I'd noticed a range of colors in them—not straight black or brown or even blue. It was like so many hues, greens and browns, washed through his eyes, and they had a light that made it feel like they could take in everything around him and not just the object in front of him. So him looking at me like that? It seemed like a world raining down, and I didn't know what to make of it.

"How do you like Fortitude? Will you be sad to leave it when your cottage is ready?"

"I like it well enough, sir. But I've known many places. I can make do wherever I need to lay my head."

"Can you? I envy you. Home can be an elusive thing."

"Oh, I know my home, sir. I just don't go wishing for it in places where it can't be." I thought of the litany of the land, the prayer I still whispered before I slept each night.

He started as though he wanted to say something fast, but he remained silent. Instead he took his seat again and said my name so I would have to look at him. "Miss Bébinn."

"Yes, sir?"

"In New Orleans in November, right before a good fall rain, there's a grayness to the sky. Gray and white, really, like a cotton boll. But it's not cold yet, and the air is thick with water waiting to be squeezed out. Makes me think I can walk on that air. I like walking on days like that. Do you know New Orleans?"

"No, sir. But I know that gray you're talking about. And I know that air. Like walking on the floor of the barns after the cotton gins been running."

He nodded. "We have something in common, Miss Bébinn. Let's leave it at that for tonight."

"Yes, sir." I rose and said good night to Missus Livingston. I was eager to go back to my room and out of his sight. But he had something more to add.

"Miss Bébinn, sometimes, not often but sometimes, we have air like that here in Ohio. We'll keep a look out for it, you and I. When it comes, we'll take a walk and compare it to the air in Louisiana."

I didn't know what to say. I stared at him a moment, then gave him a bit of a curtsy. It was all I could think of, and it seemed the right thing to do. I left the room.

Chapter 8

Missus Livingston checked on me before I went to bed. She worried I might be bruised from my fall. I took the opportunity to inquire more about my employer.

"Mr. Colchester is a strange young man, isn't he, Missus Livingston?"

"Well, I suppose so, but not much different from any brash young man too full of himself."

"More than that, I think. He is very abrupt. On the verge of rudeness."

"True, but he has been drinking tonight. He is not like that all the time, so allowances can be made for him. He is not vicious; that's what matters. I wouldn't put up with him if he were. But then I am used to him. And he deserves some compassion."

"Why?"

"He is responsible for so many. This whole community, really. Many of the inhabitants of Lower Knoll were once slaves of the Colchester family. But a good number are runaways. We have to be on the lookout for bounty hunters. They could kidnap one of our people and send them back south."

I flinched at this. Missus Livingston seemed to forget that I would be under the same threat. Perhaps my fair appearance made her set me apart.

"Why doesn't he stay and ensure the community is protected? Why does he leave it to others?"

"Well, he's young." She shrugged and looked toward the door as though she wanted to leave our conversation. "He has no friends here, no proper company."

"What about his family?"

"None."

I nodded. What she said fascinated me. Where was Mr. Colchester's property in the South? Louisiana? I burned to know, but I didn't think it wise to question further. And I could tell, by the way Missus Livingston increasingly avoided my direct gaze, that she didn't want to say more. We parted with a fond but brief good night.

When I came down for breakfast the next morning, Mr. Colchester was sitting there at the table, just sitting there straight and proper like he was waiting. Leah brought out a plate of hot eggs and grits for me.

Mr. Colchester leaned forward. "Good morning."

"Good morning, sir."

He asked me questions in a careful way, like he didn't want to scare me. He asked about my plan of teaching, how my students were. He wanted to know when I would start teaching the adults. I found it strange—he didn't sound like a patron or even my boss when he asked. It sounded like he knew the names, knew the people. I ventured to ask a question of my own.

"How long have you been away, Mr. Colchester?"

"I suppose I left right before the spring went away, before the hot weather started sneaking in. But I'm not fond of this winter weather. Of being covered up."

That would explain his bare feet, I thought. It's not like one sees men's naked feet that often. You'd think some men sleep in their boots. But he had been drunk before.

Much as I loved Leah's soft-scrambled eggs, I couldn't eat while Mr. Colchester was sitting there. Not that I wasn't hungry. But when he was sitting there, it was like all my being, all my mind, needed to be focused on him and the blood all went to my head instead of my belly. I put down my fork. He didn't seem to notice or care.

"Miss Bébinn, will you accompany me down to our little village this morning? I know you have no classes on a Saturday, but I've brought some gifts for the children, and I'd like to assess the progress on your cottage."

"Yes, sir, we may go as soon as you like."

When I went out to meet Mr. Colchester, I found him seated in one of the horse-drawn carts. The cart was filled with parcels of goods, and he seemed congenial, perhaps even proud of the abundance he obviously intended to bestow on Lower Knoll and its inhabitants.

"Come, Miss Bébinn. I'm eager to play my role of the good provider!"

He held out his hand, which I accepted, and I stepped up to the seat next to him. I positioned myself on the side, as far as possible on the bench away from him.

"No, sit here," he said. He motioned me to move closer. "I wish to talk, and I won't be able to hear your small, thin voice over the clopping of my eager horses."

I obliged him, but there was little reason to do so. He proceeded at a leisurely pace; the horses didn't make as much noise as they could have. But I didn't object. I considered it an opportunity to study him, which was only fair since it seemed this was his intention for me.

The sun was not yet too high in the sky and cast a whitish winter light over the brown grasses and bare trees. I wasn't cold. My coat and gloves were plain but well made. They stood up well against the windless morning. All signs foretold a fine day, with a clear sky once the mist burned away. Everything was still, save for the sound of the horses as we made our way down the winding hill.

Mr. Colchester, as he sat on the bench with the reins in his hands, looked healthier than he had seemed the night before. His skin was no longer flushed from whiskey, and there was a slight smile on his lips. He seemed to appreciate the strange, plain beauty of the morning and the brisk nature of its air. The light fell in such a way that I could still perceive his features under his hat—the swirl of colors that painted his irises, and the fine dark hair now flowing down and pressed against his neck. From the way he held the reins and the encouraging clucks he would give the horses, I sensed a gentleness about him that I wasn't sure I could trust.

He turned suddenly, caught me looking at him, and laughed. "Am I captivating, Miss Bébinn?" he asked. "Am I that handsome?"

"I wouldn't say handsome, sir. Striking perhaps. Different."

His laughter stopped, and his face clouded.

"I'm sorry, sir. I don't mean to offend you."

"Different? Do I stick out sorely in the world? Am I unlike other . . . men?"

I felt as though he'd meant to say *white men*. I had no reason for such a suspicion, but something about him planted the thought in the back of my mind. I couldn't place his concern otherwise. Mr. Colchester didn't seem vain. I sought for the words that might console him.

"Sir, I beg your pardon. I meant that the only white man's face I've had the opportunity to examine so closely was my father's. You are different from him."

"Tell me about him."

"Mr. Colchester, I would rather not."

"No? I suppose you wish to keep your privacy. But surely you can tell me how differently we look?"

"Looked," I correct him. "He died several years ago."

"Yes, you said you had no family. But what did he look like?"

"He had red hair that was darkening to brown with age. You are taller than he. But he was strong, I suppose one would say muscular. He had freckles and—" The words caught in my throat. It had been so long since I thought so specifically about Papa's face, and he seemed suddenly there, so clearly in my mind.

"You miss him?"

"Yes, sir."

"I envy you your paternal felicity." He paused and clucked at the horses before he continued. "Not that I wasn't cared for. Nothing was deficient in that department. In fact, your experience of your father is more unusual than mine, I would think. Men dote on their sons in ways they cannot or perhaps will not with their daughters. But such attention can be a blessing and a curse. Or a ridiculous game of blindman's buff. It's as though my father tied my hands, turned me about in circles, pointed me in a direction, then pushed me out into the world. He removed the blindfold but, unfortunately, forgot to unbind my hands. And now what chance do I have?"

"To do what, sir?"

"To break free. To move in the direction that I can see and would most like to go."

I didn't know how to respond. How could I when I knew neither what bound him nor where he hoped to proceed? If he had asked such a question last night, I would have put it down to his drunken state. But in the clear, cold sobriety of the winter morning, I couldn't dismiss his query as utter nonsense. The best course of action seemed to be to remain silent.

"I have puzzled you, Miss Bébinn. Good. While you search for answers in the air, you are not looking at me. It's just as well. By the by, you are not pretty any more than I am handsome." He turned and seemed to study me again. "But you are . . . striking."

"I take after my father."

"Not even a wince! You say that with such acceptance."

"I don't concern myself with what I can't change, sir. I know who I am. I know what I look like."

"Yes, well, the world makes much of one's looks, doesn't it?"

"I suppose it does, sir."

"But you and I aren't willing to be bowed by it! That must lend us some measure of superiority."

"I'm not sure about being superior. There is something wise, though, about accepting one's lot in life."

"Ah, but now we return to my original query. When must one be accepting, and when must a man do everything in his power to break free?"

"I think, sir, it may depend on the consequences."

"Humph!" Mr. Colchester shook his head. "I have underestimated you, Miss Bébinn. You are wiser than I."

He was silent for a bit, and this allowed me time to formulate a question of my own.

"If I may ask, sir, what binds you?"

"We have come upon the village now." Indeed, the main street was coming into view and the inhabitants of the small houses were emerging, perhaps in response to the sound of our cart.

"I will answer you another time," Mr. Colchester continued. "But I will make one last observation. I believe your silence and restraint are not natural to your character. Our village is filled with a population once enslaved. I know the imprint such an existence has made on their lives. But I do not see such marks, explicit or otherwise, on you. Your reserve comes from something else. I will learn more about this. You'll find I am a determined investigator."

Mr. Colchester reined in the horses, and within a moment an older man who went by the name of Poney was at my side and offering his hand to help me down from the cart. Though he greeted me warmly, I could see I was soon forgotten because of the general delight from those who gathered over Mr. Colchester's presence. He'd brought provisions, yes—fabrics for clothes to be sewn, coats for the children, pantry staples for kitchens. But the people of Lower Knoll had for Mr. Colchester a relaxed, congenial familiarity that I'd rarely seen colored folk have with a white man, even those considered friendly. The men embraced him, the women shook hands with him, and warm conversation flowed. He asked after their families and shared what news he had of the political landscape. All wanted to know if there would be a war, a topic that inspired both fear and a nervous excitement.

I would have felt an outsider in this scene if it hadn't been for Jelly, who approached with some of her classmates, took my hand, and began a narrative of their activities punctuated often by a "Did not!" from her friends. I listened poorly. I wanted very much to hear what Mr. Colchester said but could only manage pieces of disjointed information. I was also, I must admit, distracted by my thoughts. Would I have my own role in this scene once my cottage was done and I lived in the village? Would I feel at home and welcomed? Then, I found, my inner reflection took a different turn. I saw myself in the cottage and hearing the sound of the cart and of Mr. Colchester being greeted by name. Would I come out and join this festive display? Or would I sit quietly and wait for a knock on my door? Would he visit me? Certainly, he would want to ask about the school and if I needed anything for it. Was that what I wanted?

Soon I sensed movement in the group. Mr. Colchester was making his way through the village accompanied by a talkative young man named Templeton, whom I knew to be Jelly's father, and Evan, Templeton's cousin, who was as silent as his relation was chatty. The two of them had been working on my cottage. Poney followed, guiding the horses pulling the cart.

"It's a thing of beauty!" Templeton was saying. "Should be going full force in another month. We'll ride on down there with you."

"Yes, yes, of course. But Miss Bébinn's work cannot be forgotten. I want to see how we've left it with the roof to be over her head."

"That's about all there is to it," Templeton said. "A roof and not much else. Well, some stairs. Hadn't had time to think too much about it."

The site of the cottage, viewed in winter, didn't have much to recommend it. Set down the road from the school, it seemed separated and lonely. Why hadn't I noticed that before? The fine buckeye tree, meant to shade the dwelling in the summer, offered only bare branches, empty and uninviting.

"Nobody's blaming you, Templeton. Miss Bébinn is not impatient." Mr. Colchester opened the door.

One could see the whole house, front to back, upon entering. At some point Templeton and his men would add walls and, of course, windows. A chimney rose from a fireplace centered at the core of the building. It only wanted surroundings—a wall and perhaps a simple mantel. I walked over to the stairs to the loft and placed a hand on the makeshift door of Jelly's hiding place underneath the stairs and smiled. The little girl must have discovered the space while her father was working.

Poney now spoke up and loudly. "No need to wait until spring. You order up some windows, and I can put 'em in by myself. That's all she needs. We can do the rest later."

There seemed to be some affirmation of this thought from the other men, but Mr. Colchester disagreed. "Wouldn't be good for you to be out here in the cold working by yourself, Poney. By the time any windows got here—and the order would be slow owing to the time of year and the general unrest—we'd be in the thick of winter. Snow up to your knees. Leave it be for now."

"We could spare some glass from the factory," Templeton began.

"I said leave it!" Mr. Colchester's skin grew flushed, but he quickly recovered himself. "The factory is what matters now. Come, I want to see it."

Outside Mr. Colchester helped me back onto the now-empty cart, and the men mounted horses. I didn't know the factory he spoke of, but it was obvious I would soon see it. We ventured down a road I'd never noticed before, one that went quite a ways away from the village. Eventually it turned eastward, traveling uphill for a bit before plateauing on a large parcel of land not far from the river. And there it was—a building made of red brick, three stories tall, and smoking in a long thin stream drifting up from a round smokestack made of the same brick. It was functioning, whatever the place was. If I had come upon it on my own, I never would have thought it was associated with the village.

"Do you work here, Templeton?" I asked when he had dismounted.

"I have a shift tomorrow," he said. "Right now we gotta split the labor. Some of us working in the factory, getting the shoes made. Some of us working on the factory, finishing up the building."

"I see."

"Do you, Miss Bébinn?" Mr. Colchester took me by the arm and guided me toward the structure. "Manufacturing is the future; at least it will be for the people of Lower Knoll." We entered a warehouse type of space, hundreds of yards long and filled with machinery. The men, all negroes, worked the machinery. A structure that seemed to be an office jutted out from an upper floor, and a flight of stairs connected it to the main floor.

"Once this factory is at full capacity, it will provide a comfortable living for the community. The workers will take what pay and profit they need for their families. The rest will go into maintaining the business—purchasing materials, keeping the building and machinery in good repair. My visits and provisions will no longer be necessary."

"Sir, do you want to sever your connection to Lower Knoll?" This seemed strange, especially in light of his warm reception.

"Miss Bébinn, if the community can't sustain itself, if it were reliant on me for its upkeep and the payment of necessities such as yourself, a teacher, then how would the place be any different than the way the people lived in the South, enslaved and dependent?"

While I considered this, he continued.

"The product created here is a necessity and made well. Such a business will not be influenced by the whims of nature. In fact it is positioned to benefit from certain tides."

A gentleman emerged from the office, waved to Mr. Colchester, and moved downstairs to join us. He wore a white shirt with the sleeves rolled up to his elbows, and a set of wire-frame spectacles was perched high on his forehead. His complexion was similar to mine, but while my fairness contained yellow tones, his was more beige, like sand. He greeted Mr. Colchester with a warm handshake.

"I take it you bring good news, Christian?"

"Yes. I signed the contract in Washington. Stanton himself agreed to it. He's pleased that the Union Army's shoes will come from Ohio."

"He is? Christian, what a success. You've secured our survival, should it come to war."

"Don't sound so mercenary, Richard. We're not profiteers."

"No, but do not doubt—a war would be the making of us."

The two men walked away from us to discuss their business in private. It was hardly necessary—they only needed to move two steps before the machinery muffled their voices considerably. I continued to watch them. After a few minutes, the warmth of Mr. Colchester's good news seemed to cool, and their expressions, though I could see them only in profile, no longer smiled. Richard tried to throw an arm around Mr. Colchester, but he stepped away from the embrace. Were they angry? No, not quite. Some disagreement persisted, though. After a brief glance in my direction, Mr. Colchester concluded the conversation and returned to me.

"Come, Miss Bébinn, let us return to Fortitude. Mr. Mason has our productivity well in hand."

The sun was high and headed toward midday. Mr. Colchester took a hat from underneath our seat on the cart and pulled it low over his brow. I turned my head up into the light and was grateful for the measure of warmth it provided. He was silent, and I stayed the same. He led the horses, I noticed, down a road bypassing Lower Knoll. It went through a scruff of thin trees divided by a low creek.

"Tell me, Miss Bébinn," he said at last. "How many times should a man pay for a sin?"

I looked at him. He stared at the dusty road. Nothing signified that he was anything but earnest in the question.

"I'm not sure, sir. Seems to me once is plenty."

"Plenty?"

"Yes, sir. And if the sin is forgiven, it is more than enough."

"Ah, forgiveness! Now that is something. Who should forgive the sinner?"

"Sir?"

"What if the sin was not against one person but many? Must the sinner receive forgiveness from all?"

"I suppose so."

"What if they were a score in number? What about five score? Hundreds? Shall our sinner go hat in hand to each one?"

I didn't know how to respond.

"Let me tell you a story, Miss Bébinn. Maybe that will help you construct your answer. My father's father was a British farmer who traveled to America and made a fortune by purchasing land in North Carolina and starting a tobacco farm. My father expanded the family's interests further south and moved into cane and cotton."

I nodded. "It was the same on our plantation," I said.

"Then you'll know that such wealth was only possible with slave labor."

"Yes."

"My father was particular about my education. I was sent away to the best schools, and I had tutors in Europe. You may wonder at that—I probably don't strike you as refined. I wasn't a great student because I wasn't particularly interested in reading. But I did like to debate and think about how society works, about the way we live our lives. One of my professors was a Quaker, and when I studied philosophy, he and I would talk a great deal about slavery. He knew I was from the South and was interested in how we ran things. He asked a lot of questions about the slaves. He wanted to know how my father acquired them, about whether they could marry and who owned their children.

"That last part hit me—when he asked about the children, I was going to say right away that they were our property. I realized how wrong that was. The words stuck like a lump in my throat. Then he took me through a kind of meditation. What would I do, he asked, if I were walking back to my room and were suddenly accosted by strangers who attacked me and put me in chains?

"I would fight them with all I had, I told him. 'But ah,' he went on, 'you can't get away. They put you on a great ship, let's say in Boston Harbor, and chain you to hundreds of other men like yourself and send you off to parts unknown. You arrive on the shores of a foreign country where you can't speak the language, nor are you allowed to learn it. You are forced to work, subjected to painful punishments, and live in the most inhumane of conditions.'

"I laughed at him, Miss Bébinn. I said it was ridiculous to think such a thing could happen to me, and there would be many to step in to recover me should such an event ever occur. He looked at me and said, 'How can you say that, Colchester, when you have been a witness to it your whole life?' He asked me where I thought the people on our plantation had come from, and I was ashamed that I couldn't answer him. I tried to say that we didn't treat our slaves badly, but of course that was such a shallow argument. We were holding human beings in bondage.

He said to me, 'When you die, Christian, will that be your argument to God? That you enslaved his creation but treated them well?'

"I wanted to be angry. I wanted to rail at him for upsetting my peace of mind. For four nights I didn't sleep because our conversation ate at me so badly. Something came to me. It was like seeing a bit of candlelight in the darkness. I realized my professor had brought me awareness to sin so large that I thought it might consume me. But in that awareness was a chance for me to save my soul.

"My father, you might imagine, wasn't pleased to have his educated son come home and tell him how to run his plantation, with the insane notion of freeing his entire labor force. He said I was unfaithful to the family, that the Yankees had turned me against him. That I was ungrateful for the life that the plantation had afforded us. He kept asking how the plantation would run without the slaves. I told him I didn't see why we couldn't pay people. Did we really need to make the level of profit that kept us in luxury?

"It tore a rift between us, so much so that my father changed his will to act against me if I did not handle my inheritance in the way he saw fit. I didn't know he'd done this. When he died, I thought I would be free to do as I liked. Unfortunately, his will bound me in ways that I find disheartening. I have done what I could. As you know, I founded Lower Knoll by selling my father's plantation and freeing the slaves with the offer to come here and have their own community. I knew how hard life was for freed slaves, how they could be kidnapped and sold again into bondage. That's why I thought of creating Lower Knoll.

"But I refuse to be solely tied to it. I don't want to create another form of plantation where it only appears that the people are free. And I also want to be able to find my own life, to figure out where I'm supposed to be in the world."

"I can understand that," I said.

"Can you?"

"Yes, sir."

"Of course. You've had to seek out your place, too, haven't you?"

"Yes, sir."

Mr. Colchester stopped the carriage at Fortitude's front door. He got out, and when he turned to help me down, I found myself with a vantage point of looking down on him. He offered me his hand, but I didn't take it right away.

"Sir, if I may say so . . ." I paused.

"Yes, what is it?" He looked up at me and took off his hat. My eyes went to his brow, tracing the length of his forehead. His expression was so open.

"You have more places where you can be. You have money. You have land. And forgive me for saying so, but you're a white man. This country is made for you because men like you made it. Someone like me? I'm not even supposed to be here, let alone have the freedom to live like I want. It's not the same; that's all I'm trying to say. We're not the same."

I was going to take his hand and step out of the carriage then, but he wasn't offering it. He stood there staring up at me, and I figured I might have offended him. I looked away. Stephen held the horses and waited for me. After a few more moments Mr. Colchester gave me his hand.

"I'm glad you have found a place here," he said. "Thank you for listening to my rambling."

He stared at me a little longer as we walked into the mansion. Before we parted, he said, "I hope my story will help you think compassionately if I ever seem—strange."

He entered the library and left me standing alone in the hall. Whether he realized it or not, this was a time when he seemed strange.

I did consider his story, many times. I thought about it in bed as I waited for sleep. I considered it as I walked to the school each day.

And soon I had more to consider, because he seemed to enjoy speaking with me in the evenings and presenting me with some philosophical question or his view of the world. I couldn't tell whether he wanted me to affirm his thoughts, and I didn't feel equipped to do it. But I liked that he found me worthy of his confidence. He seemed more relaxed with me than when I'd first met him. I even allowed myself to wonder, in the most secret part of my heart, whether I was capable of affecting his humor and his character. Did I tame him?

Sometimes he asked me to speak of Louisiana, and though I still carefully kept from him the precise location of my upbringing there, I enjoyed remembering the sugarcane fields, the fronds of Spanish moss that hung low into the swamps, and the air thick with water in the storm season. He seemed to appreciate it all, and this drew me to him. He felt like family to me, a sensation I had not felt for any soul in so many years.

And my life took on a new color, new vivacity. I no longer dwelled on what I had lost, and the stone from Catalpa Valley, which I still kept safe in a bureau drawer in my room, held less of my thoughts. I could begin to think of Lower Knoll, and even Fortitude Mansion, as my home. Work on my cottage proceeded slowly in the spring of '60, owing to the men being focused so much on the factory and a war that seemed more certain every day. I considered myself quite settled in my room on the second floor, but that summer Poney began what he had offered to do months earlier: finish the cottage himself. He worked slowly, yet he made steady progress.

Gradually, ever so gradually, Mr. Colchester grew in my heart. I felt gratitude for his accomplishments and for his care of the Lower Knoll village. I was proud of him, unaccountably so, when I perceived he had attained some new level of maturity. He drank less, and even Missus Livingston acknowledged his apparent stability. He was not perfect, of course. What human could be? He could still be sarcastic and impatient, especially when he perceived he might not get his way. But I put it down to general moodiness. Again, excusable. Missus Livingston had known him to be different. Now, in my presence, he had improved. Could I be the reason?

These were my thoughts on a late afternoon in January 1861. There had been no school that day owing to my preparations to move into the cottage. For Poney had finished it just before Christmas, and after abiding by Missus Livingston's request that I stay in the mansion for the holiday, I packed my belongings. Poney would come with a cart in the morning to take my few things to Lower Knoll. But that afternoon, seeking solitude, I wrapped a heavy cloak about me and walked to the schoolhouse. There I swept the floor, wiped chalk dust from the children's slates, and put in order the books that had been hastily discarded before the holiday. The room grew dark while I worked as dusk fell on the brief winter day. When I finally left, I encountered the last of the sunset glowing near the edge of the wood.

The sight made my fingers suddenly grow cold as they tried to tie my cloak. That wasn't west—the light was not in the western sky.

Fire!

My cottage was on fire.

My steps flew. Why would I hurry to an empty house in flames? Because I knew, in fact might be the only person to know, that there was a chance it wasn't empty.

The structure wasn't entirely engulfed, but there was a great deal of smoke.

"Jelly!"

I untied my cloak and pulled it over my head before I opened the door. A thick curtain of smoke poured out. I threw myself onto the ground and crossed the threshold, crawling on my stomach.

"Jelly!"

I heard something—a whimpering in one moment, a groan the next. I crawled in the direction of the sound, for all was dark and I feared the flames and smoke. I kept the cloak close over my head. I found the steps first. My hands followed the shape of the cupboard over to the right, and I ran my fingers over the wood until I found the leather string to pull the door open. Jelly was crouched in a tight ball. I reached in and covered her with my cloak and tugged. We rolled backward.

Flames licked the ceiling above me, and I tried to take in breath so I could cover us again and get out. My lungs stung and my eyes watered. A plume of smoke seemed to reach out, and I thought it would consume us. But the smoke had firm hands and a pair of arms. Suddenly Jelly and I were upheld and moved swiftly out of the cottage. What happened next is unclear. I remember lying on the ground and coughing. We were surrounded by people and tended to. I remember shouts and the thunder of running feet. Then I was floating, like I was covering miles and miles with no effort at all. I enjoyed the sensation. It was like I was a baby again, riding with Papa through his fields. I thought I might see him again, and I took hold of this thought and allowed it to guide me into unconsciousness.

When I woke, I felt a heaviness on me on my right side. I thought I had been injured or lost feeling in that part of my body, so I shifted to assess my condition. I heard a child's excited whisper below my ear.

"Miss Bébinn!"

It was Jelly, lying next to me, holding on to me.

"You're all right!"

"Yes, honey, I'm all right."

She jumped from the bed and ran into the hallway. "Daddy Daddy Daddy! She's awake!"

I heard a commotion on the stairs and a rumbling down the wide gallery. But instead of Jelly's father, Mr. Colchester appeared in my doorway. His face was colored in pain, and his eyes glinted with a wild energy. But he didn't come into the room, and he didn't say a word.

In another moment Jelly had returned with Templeton and Missus Livingston.

"Thank the Lord! How are you, child?" Missus Livingston brushed past Mr. Colchester and laid a cool hand on my forehead.

I tried to sit up, but she pressed down gently on my arm. "Don't try to get up."

"No, it's easier to breathe," I said. "Please, I just need to sit up."

I rose, and she adjusted the pillows behind me so I was comfortably supported.

"Miss Bébinn, thank you. Thank you. I would've lost her for sure." Templeton stood at the bottom of the bed. He held Jelly tight against him; her eyes were trained solidly on me. I saw no burns and guessed she had been scared more than anything else.

"I thank God I was there."

Mr. Colchester stepped forward. "Missus Livingston, she must be hungry."

"Yes, perhaps some tea, Miss Bébinn? And something light." She left the room quickly.

"Templeton, please leave us. I want to talk to Miss Bébinn."

"Yeah. Come on, Jelly."

She wouldn't budge.

"Come on, Jelly, she ain't going nowhere."

The girl came to me, threw her arms around my neck, and kissed my cheek. Then she ran from the room. Templeton bowed to me and followed her.

Mr. Colchester closed the door behind them. "In the name of God, what the hell did you think you were doing?"

"Sir?" I hadn't expected to be berated.

"You both could have died! In another moment the roof would have fallen in on you."

"I didn't think. I acted."

"How did you come to be there?"

I briefly related to him how I'd visited the school, witnessed the flames upon leaving the building, and rushed to the cottage when I realized it was on fire.

"Jelly likes to read in the little closet under the stairs," I said. "I knew she might be in there. I had to check."

He listened. His level of upset increased as I went on.

"You found the girl. Did you see anyone?"

"No, sir, but I didn't look around. I went toward the fire and went in. That's all I remember."

He made no reply but paced the room back and forth twice. Then he stood silent with his arms folded, looking at the ground. At the end of a few minutes, he finally said, "I knew life here would be different because of you, that you would bring goodness and light to this place. I cannot tell you how I came to think this. You have been a great help to me ever since you broke my fall down the stairs. It hurts me to know that goodness could put your life at risk. That we could have lost you. I have never known such bravery."

"I did what anyone would do."

"No, not anyone! And you could have suffered a horrible and excruciating death because of it! No, I will not allow you to be modest about this."

He stood silent again and seemed to be waiting. Then, awkwardly, he held out his hand; I hesitated but finally gave him mine. He took it first in one, then in both of his own. He gazed at me; his lips trembled as though he would say something more. His eyes blazed with their colorful glint.

He wouldn't release my hand.

We were suspended like this how long? I hardly know. I heard Missus Livingston on the landing. In another moment she was at the door with my tray.

Mr. Colchester moved swiftly to open the door for her. Once she entered, he swept through the door himself and was gone.

Missus Livingston set the tray before me and chattered on, but I could listen to only half of what she said. I didn't want to eat, but she watched me closely and encouraged every bite. A fierce energy whipped about within me. I wanted badly to be alone so I could nurse the burgeoning bubble of joy forming within me.

Chapter 9

The next morning I awoke to a soft knock on my bedroom door. I felt buoyed on some happy dreams I couldn't remember—the sense of delight dissipated from my brain like an early fog. I both hoped and feared that the knock belonged to Mr. Colchester. I wanted to hear his voice, to know if the strange tones of yesterday would be repeated again, yet I didn't know if I had the confidence to look him in the face. Of course it was silly of me to expect such a visit; before yesterday, he had never set foot in my room, nor did he have any reason to. It wasn't proper. But nothing about the fire or the events that had followed had been ordinary, so I thought I could expect different behaviors. It seemed right that he would come to see me.

I sat up and smoothed my hair back and away from my face as best I could. "Come in," I said.

It was not Mr. Colchester. It was Founder.

She stepped slowly into the room, surveyed its contents, then approached my bed. She wore a light-blue scarf wrapped around her head to form a kind of turban. Her simple brushed cotton dress was a darker shade of blue, with a brooch in the shape of a silver rose pinned to her left shoulder.

"You all right?"

I nodded.

"Got any smoke still in you?"

I took a sip of water from the glass at my bedside, then took a careful deep breath. I felt nothing resisting the flow of air.

"No. I think I am well enough to go to the school today."

"That's crazy talk. You ain't leaving this house just yet." Founder went to the door and delivered quiet instructions to whoever stood behind it, out of my sight. When she was done, I thought she would take the seat near my bed, but instead she went over to my small bureau and leaned on it on her elbows. She stared out the window. "Had yourself a day yesterday."

"Yes."

She shifted her feet under her and didn't say anything else.

"Will they be able to salvage any of the structure?" I doubted this, but it seemed like a safe line of conversation.

"Naw, nothing but a pile of ashes, still smokin'."

"I suppose they can rebuild in the spring."

"That's what Templeton said, but I told him don't bother. This spring ain't gonna be like other springs. Can feel it deep in the bones of my soul. Supplies for a house will be hard to come by."

I assumed she meant the impending war, and I was ashamed to think how far it had been from my mind. South Carolina had announced its secession last month just before Christmas. But Lower Knoll had the sense of another world, like what was going on out there had little to do with us. I should have known better. The contract Mr. Colchester had secured for the factory was proof of that.

"What's happened?"

"Mississippi, Florida, and Alabama done seceded from the Union. Louisiana like to follow soon."

"Louisiana!" I wanted to leap from the bed, get dressed, and search for Mr. Colchester. I wanted to know his thoughts, to condole with him on the disconnection from a place we both cared for. But Founder stayed put at the window. It didn't seem right to do anything until she left.

"Of course Christian is sick about it. Went railing on about this and that, but I reminded him he got work to do. Responsibilities."

"He wouldn't—" I wanted to hold my breath. "He wouldn't fight on the side of the rebels?" The thought cut through me like a saber, but I also knew if I were in his position, I would be torn. I'd want to protect Papa's land, and yet—oh, the sad irony of it!—the very things the South was fighting for would keep me from doing so.

"No. He knows what he needs to be doing, though." She stood up and pressed her palms against her lower back. Without looking at me, she asked, "What about you? What you need to be doing?"

I didn't understand why she would ask such a thing, but I decided my best path would be to go another way.

"For right now, getting out of this bed. Would you excuse me? I won't go to the school, but I would like to go downstairs."

She shrugged, murmured something about being glad I felt all right, and sauntered out of the room.

At breakfast Missus Livingston scolded me for not staying in bed and forced me to sit next to her at the table so she could better fill my plate without my going to the trouble of lifting it.

"I shudder to think what could have happened to you and that little girl."

I sipped from the cup of tea she handed me. I realized I knew nothing about the story of the fire, and I told her so. "I don't remember anything after I found Jelly. I pulled her out one moment, and then the next I was in my bed."

"Thank the merciful Lord!" she cried. "Others saw the flames, same as you did, and came running. They tried to put it out with buckets of water from the creek, but it was too far gone."

The thought of the people of Lower Knoll rushing to my aid brought tears to my throat. They had worked in unison to save the spare place meant to be my home. And one of them, at least, had risked his life to carry me and Jelly out of the fire.

"Who pulled us out, Missus Livingston?"

"You don't know?"

"It was very dark and smoky. I was holding on to Jelly. That's all I remember."

"Mr. Colchester," she said. "He carried you both out."

I put down my cup. Ignored my food. "What? How was it he was there? And so quickly?" I had been first on the scene. Whoever had saved us had to have been hard upon my heels.

"He was coming from the factory. Saw the flames, just as you did, and rushed there on his horse. Said he saw you rush in just as he arrived."

Missus Livingston didn't notice that her words had struck me dumb. I stared at her, unhearing and almost unseeing because I was so distracted by the thoughts racing through my mind. They formed two specific and fantastic specimens:

Mr. Colchester had saved my life.

I had been carried, most gently, in Mr. Colchester's arms.

What a debt I owed him! And it didn't feel burdensome to be connected to him in such a way. He'd obviously felt the same, and I indulged myself by remembering last night's scene: what he'd said, how he had looked. It was all so vivid, so clear, so (dare I say it?) wonderful.

Now I was desperate to see him. My ears were trained on every movement in the hall, every voice just out of range. Whenever the door opened, I expected him to walk in. But it didn't happen. By the end of the meal, I had grown impatient and was on the verge of asking directly where Mr. Colchester was when Missus Livingston rose to draw open the blind. The late-morning brightness flooded the room.

"Clear and calm," she said as she looked through the panes. "Mr. Colchester has a good day ahead of him for his travels."

"He's gone? Where?"

"Oh yes, he set off early this morning. Didn't even take breakfast." She seemed to think this was the most natural thing in the world, so much so that she left out the information I most wanted. I repeated my question.

"Where did he go?"

"Well, of course the news is more alarming every day. And poor Mr. Lincoln hasn't even taken office yet. Christian has gone to gather our friends. It's about time we get ready before a battle is on our doorstep."

"Who are our friends?" In all the time I'd been at Fortitude, I'd never experienced a visitor.

"They haven't assembled here for some time. Christian prefers to travel to them and stay at their homes. Now it has to be different."

"Why is that?"

"The factory is supplying the Union Army. It will be protected from attack, and Fortitude as well. Naturally this would be the safest place to organize support operations."

"Who will come?"

"There's Mr. Parma. He owns a large farm about ten miles north of here. His son Nicholas runs it with him. Mr. Ingram, the Eshtons, the Morgans. And of course, Mr. Chamberlain. His son is Joseph and his daughter is Belinda. Christian has been fond of her for quite a while now."

I felt the blood drain away from my face. "He has?"

"Oh yes." Missus Livingston now opened the newspaper and perused the articles. "When he's gone for any length of time, that's usually where you can find him."

"What is Miss Chamberlain like? You've seen her?"

"Oh yes. We've known the family for three or four years, and they've been here for Christmas parties. She is a beauty, very intelligent too."

Of course she was. My heart seemed to sink in my chest. "What does she look like?"

"She is tall with a long, graceful neck and a lovely, fair complexion. She is blonde and wears the most beautiful trinkets in her hair to accentuate the color. One Christmas she had a blue rose pinned to her plaits in the back. Her eyes are a very dark blue. You'd almost think they were black until you see her up close."

"And he admires her?"

"Who wouldn't? She's such a capable young woman. Captivating too. She's run her father's household since her mother died. Belinda wasn't yet sixteen."

"Why is she still unmarried?"

"Christian has been slow footed, to be sure. But he's matured so much recently. And the war will nudge him to be quick."

"Perhaps there's a great difference in age?"

"No, they are contemporaries. Christian is nearing thirty; she is but twenty-five."

"An equal match in every way, then?"

"Yes. And he will make it. But you've eaten nothing. Are you really all right? Should I call for the doctor?"

"No, Missus Livingston, I am fine. I just want tea for now. May I have another cup?"

Alone in my room, I reviewed what Missus Livingston had told me and turned the facts over and over in my mind. Then I recalled what I had felt only the previous evening—the hope, the sense of joy and possibility. I had to admit I had indulged in my fondness for Mr. Colchester even longer—almost a year! I was mortified. How had I duped myself so well?

To think that I could influence him, please him, amuse him—I blushed with shame. And even if he did have some interest in me, what could it be beyond mentoring me as though I were a pet? He could never marry me, a penniless girl of mixed blood. I could barely hold that sentence in my head. And he would be well aware of these differences, would never have intended to inspire my affection. I obviously wasn't and so had read him all wrong. Madness! That must be my excuse. Madness and loneliness. God, how pitiful!

The blonde features of Belinda Chamberlain haunted my thoughts. I walked up and down my room, berating myself. I stopped in front of the mirror and surveyed my image. I wore a simple dress of linsey-woolsey, not unlike the dress Aunt Nancy Lynne had once made for me. My hair, which tended to look more brown than red in the winter, was pulled back into a plain bun at the nape of my neck. Nothing obscured the freckles dotting the sides of my face unless I wore a bonnet. Missus Livingston had called Miss Chamberlain capable. I envisioned a strong young woman, not unlike the abolitionists I had met in Philadelphia and in New York. A beauty who could lead people, who could give orders in a household and have them followed to the letter. The perfect partner for Mr. Colchester. I could see her living under the roof of Fortitude Mansion, hosting parties when they were in residence, and accompanying him on his travels to New York or even to Europe.

I had been Jean Bébinn's daughter. Now I was a simple schoolteacher with few friends and no prospects. I would always be a stranger no matter where I went. This thought made me open the drawer of my bureau and hold the stone from Catalpa Valley in my hand. Here was another split, for the ground the stone had come from would soon be no longer a part of the country in which I stood. I allowed myself a few tears. If I'd ever held the tiniest hope of seeing Petite Bébinn, its small bright candle had been snuffed out. I slipped the stone into my pocket so I could reach for it and its consolation when I needed it.

Days passed, and Mr. Colchester did not return. Soon it was a week, then ten days. Missus Livingston didn't seem concerned, and I tried to imitate her attitude. But my disappointment increased with every hour that slipped by without word from him. I tried to tamp it down by reminding myself that Mr. Colchester's movements had nothing to do with me. I repeated these words to myself:

"You are a schoolteacher. He is your employer. You have, as long as you do your job well, a right to his respect and kind treatment, nothing more. Be grateful you have that and be content."

I did this, but I also found myself considering how I might leave Lower Knoll. It was a broken notion—where could I go during this unrest, when the Fugitive Slave Act was still enforced stiffly in most areas? I didn't know where I would be safe.

I continued to teach my students. One day Jelly was helping me put the classroom in order after lessons were over. Her wide dark eyes seemed to be examining me as she took a small stack of books from my hands.

"Miss Bébinn, are you sad?"

I smiled weakly. "Now, Jelly, why would you say such a thing?"

"I don't know. You just been different after the fire. If you're sad, it might be my fault."

"Oh, Jelly, no, no. I am not sad, and nothing is your fault." But since the child had brought up the fire, I asked, "Do you remember anything about it?"

"I was sitting reading like I always do. It grew dark, and I was gonna leave because I had no candle. Then I heard a noise."

"What was it?"

"I don't know—sounded like somebody outside. Footsteps." Jelly shrugged. "I didn't want to get in trouble. That's when I went under the stairs."

"Did you see who it was?"

"No. Didn't see anyone. It got smoky and I got scared." She paused, and her lower lip quivered.

I put my hands on her shoulders and kissed her on top of her head. "You're fine now," I told her. "Don't think about it anymore."

Mr. Colchester's absence stretched past two weeks. February approached. Rumors that the Southern states would form a confederacy floated north. Finally he wrote to Missus Livingston. She read the letter during our breakfast. I drank my tea and pretended to be occupied with my own thoughts. The letter wasn't for me.

"It is just as I thought," Missus Livingston said.

"Oh?" I refilled my cup and helped myself to some eggs.

"He will be here in three days with all the people I've told you about. We shall have a full house of it." She left the table swiftly to follow whatever directions Mr. Colchester had sent.

Without her there to encourage me to eat, I allowed the tea and eggs to grow cold. He would return. He would return and bring with him the woman he intended to marry. I had three days to prepare for the confrontation of this reality. I didn't know how to be, whether I could even look him in the eye. My fingers trembled. I twisted a napkin in my hands to steady them.

Then, a small miracle—it was like my mind came to me. Papa used to speak of moments like this when it was like the world calmed down and reason walked in the door. I felt it—another version of me, sitting down next to me. She talked plenty of reason. It sounded like this:

They will not notice you. Remember, you belong in the village, and you will live there, at some point, in a cottage near the wood.

Who are you now? A schoolteacher. You only need care about your students.

Did you have his affection before? No. Do you have it now? No. Will you have it in the future? No. Nothing in your circumstances has changed or will change. You are the same. What is there to mourn?

This last struck me as the most sensible. *I am as I was.* The notion settled me. I only had to remember how I'd been when I'd first come to Fortitude. It was a map already laid out in front of me. I could allow this idea to guide me.

I rose from the table and went to gather my things for the school day. I discovered the mansion was newly alive with movement. I could hear a flutter of activity in the kitchen. Two chambermaids, Kick and Jocasta, were dragging out carpets to beat them on the back lawn. Poney was wiping down every surface: banisters, mirrors, clocks, and sideboards. I saw Founder going upstairs with a pile of fabric that looked like curtains draped over her arms. I followed her.

"We're in for it now," she said when I had caught up to her on the landing. "It'll be a push to get all these rooms ready. Not had company for a long time."

"Do you know them? The Morgans? Mr. Ingram?" I swallowed hard. "The Chamberlains?"

"Who hasn't heard of the Chamberlains? They order Miss Belinda's dresses from Paris. Can't miss hearing about folks with that kind of money."

"Founder." I touched the sleeve of her dress. "Is it true about Mr. Colchester and Miss Belinda? Will they marry?"

She turned to face me. Her lips pursed into a sour expression, and she looked me up and down with sharp, scolding eyes.

"If I were you, I wouldn't pay much mind to what white folks do. They have their own sorrows."

Before I could ask what she meant by sorrows, she continued down the gallery and disappeared into one of the bedrooms.

The three days, which I thought would proceed at a snail's pace, came and went as the hours do. On Thursday I returned to Fortitude at the end of my teaching duties to the news that Mr. Colchester and his friends were in the house. They'd eaten lightly on their arrival and were gathered in conference in the library.

I paused at the door and listened to the busy stir. I heard men's and women's voices, blended together. Though I couldn't make out what they were saying, I was certain I could distinguish the deep tone of Mr. Colchester's voice. I didn't allow myself to linger. It was likely someone could come through the door at any instant. Besides, I reminded myself, nothing they discussed had anything to do with me. I continued on to find something to eat.

The kitchen was in full commotion with preparations for the evening's dinner. I saw strangers sitting around the fire and assumed they must be the servants of our guests. I reached the larder and procured for myself some cold chicken, bread, an apple, and some water. I picked up a plate, knife, and fork as well as a newspaper I had noticed on a table, then retreated quickly to my room. It was late afternoon, and though the days had grown longer, the sun was low in the sky. I watched it set while I sat at the window and ate.

Since I'd eaten so little during the day, I was hungry. I focused on my food and dined undisturbed. When I was done, I read the newspaper. The conversations in the library must include whatever had been reported in the pages. The new president, Abraham Lincoln, would be sworn in soon, and it was expected that an armed conflict would begin in earnest not long after. I thought of Calista, Dorinda, and all the inhabitants of Catalpa Valley Plantation. Even Madame. I prayed silently for their safety.

When I was certain the dinner for the large party was in progress, I went downstairs to return my utensils and the remnants of my dinner to the kitchen. Missus Livingston met me in the hall and said I should come to the library when Mr. Colchester and his friends had finished eating.

"Why?"

"I don't know, dear, but there is much being discussed. We'll all have roles to play in the coming days."

"Will these people remain long, do you think?"

"The men will probably leave within a few days. The ladies might stay as long as two or three weeks. Miss Belinda has begun plans to assemble medical supplies, and she will need help. After the president's inauguration, Colonel Eshton will likely go to Washington to see about plans to raise a militia; Mr. Colchester might accompany him."

"Will he go to battle? Mr. Colchester will fight?"

"All the men will fight this war, I'm afraid. God only knows where they will go and when."

The war had seemed very far from my mind. Indeed, until that moment, Belinda Chamberlain had presented more of a threat to my peace of mind than the coming conflict. Again, it was a mark of my selfish and foolish thinking. I could still cross paths with a married Mr. Colchester. I could cherish my former admiration, laugh with him in certain moments, and take these fond memories away with me when the opportunity to leave Fortitude presented itself. But to lose him on a battlefield? To think that he might no longer exist in the world? I could barely hold the thought. My heart would be broken. Irretrievably broken.

I didn't like being summoned to meet with the party, but I had already formed my plan. After depositing my items in the kitchen, I returned to my room to wash my hands and face. Then I quickly made for the library. I thought it better for me to be in the room when they arrived. It would keep me from calling attention to myself, which certainly would have happened if I had entered the room solo and interrupted their conversations. I was surprised to find the room in a kind of ordered disarray. Some sort of work was already underway. In one corner spools of what looked like bandages formed sloppy piles. In another area were small hills of knitted socks and shirts half-sewn. I decided to take up something simple while waiting to be directed. I positioned myself in the corner and began to cut the strips of cloth to be rolled into bandages.

A soft sound of voices rose from down the hall and grew in loudness as they came closer. I held my breath as the double doors at the end of the room were thrown open and the small crowd poured through. They numbered four women and nine men, Mr. Colchester included. I lowered my gaze but kept watch from the corners of my eyes. The men looked elegant in long evening coats and white ties. The women seemed to float in colorful gowns decorated simply but smartly with small touches of bows or flowers.

I was determined to remain unnoticed, so I kept my head down and paid attention to the cloth in my hands. Because of this I didn't notice right away the navy-blue dress that had paused before me. When I saw it, I looked up into a pair of eyes that matched its shade. The owner of both stood frowning at me.

"You're doing that all wrong," she said.

I bowed my head and waited for further direction. Instead Belinda Chamberlain motioned me away.

"Move. Sit there." She pointed to a seat adjacent to where I sat. "I'll cut them. You shall roll them as you see these have been done."

"Yes, miss." I rose, curtsied to her, and did what she had said.

Slyly I watched her take my seat, and as the others populated the room and took up their places, I began to understand her calculation. Where I had been sitting was perfectly positioned. One had a full view of the entire room and all its occupants. Likewise, the seat, heightened as it was on a kind of bench near a window, put her on display. She took full advantage of it, making quite the show of cutting the cloth. She raised her right arm high with each swipe through the fabric, demonstrating a kind of flow and grace. She looked like she only wanted a beau to take her hand, and they would be dancing about the room.

I watched to see if Mr. Colchester was observing her unusual performance. He stood near the fire, deep in conversation with a man I eventually learned was Colonel James Eshton. Colonel Eshton had dark hair he wore parted on the side and a silky mustache that turned up at the ends. One of the women who took up some of the knitting was his wife, Caroline. She was handsome and smiling and seemed to enjoy the comfort of the party. Her daughter, Amber, a small and childlike young woman, chose needle and muslin and sat herself near Belinda, where they proceeded to whisper in confidence. An older woman, Sally Morgan, joined Missus Eshton at the knitting. She was the wife of Mr. Thomas Morgan, who sat on the couch across from the hearth and smoked a cigar. He had attended West Point with Colonel Eshton but, owing to some failure of health, had not fought in the Mexican War with his classmate. He had two firebrand young sons, Robert and Colson, and from his conversation I gathered he was eager for them to experience what he had missed out on.

These sons played at billiards with Nicholas Parma, the heavy, round-faced son of Mr. Parma, the farmer. I'd seen Mr. Parma before in the village, and Mr. Nicholas was the spitting image of his father. Both were stout men with thin hair on their heads but thick scruffy beards on their chins. Between shots he sipped from a glass of whiskey he kept perched on the corner of the billiards table.

Sitting opposite from Mr. Morgan was Miss Belinda's father, Phillip Chamberlain. He was a tall man with white hair and a thin body that reminded me of a grasshopper's when he sat and bent his long legs to cross them. His son, Joseph, with eyes like his sister's, stood behind the couch with Mr. Parma drinking brandy.

Miss Belinda, employed with her elegant cutting and whispering to Miss Eshton, gave me the opportunity to quietly study her. Her gold ringlets shone in the light. Her face was open and unfurrowed. She was confident in her expressions. I detected a trace of haughtiness. Nay, more than a trace—how else would she have the nerve to enter the room and order me about without knowing my name or position in the company?

Very carefully, I turned my gaze to Mr. Colchester. It had been weeks since the night he had saved my life and Jelly's, and I had not seen him since. I wanted to take the vision in slowly lest I be overwhelmed and thrust into emotional confusion. But I had underestimated what I would see. Mr. Colchester in formal clothing was a new sight to behold. Though his person and features were the same—the striking eyes, the dark hair, now beautifully tamed, and the strong figure—they were all now polished in this costume. Add to this the energy that came of being in communication with a group, much as I had seen in the village, and I found myself drawn to him yet again. As much as I resisted, I felt attached to him and knew this attachment to be more than fondness, more than kinship. I loved him.

I compared him with his guests. What was the gallant grace of the Morgans, the languid elegance of Mr. Chamberlain, even the military distinction of Colonel Eshton, contrasted with Mr. Colchester's look of authentic expression? Yes, anyone else would call this assembled dozen attractive, beautiful, handsome, gracious, imposing. They would deem Mr. Colchester acceptable, but with an alien nature and a heart not easily touched. But I took pleasure in his smile and the way he looked by the light of the candles. When he spoke, the eyes that were often so wild and disconcerting seemed searching and sweet.

And I will say this about Belinda Chamberlain: For all her beauty and intelligence, she did not attract him. He allowed her a share in the conversation, which she attended to carefully, tossing in comments during pauses in her talk with Miss Eshton. He deferred to her whenever there was a disagreement. But she seemed more concerned with pleasing him than he was concerned about pleasing her. I felt certain it would be difficult for her to secure his affection. There was something lacking in their connection.

He is not to her what he is to me, I thought. *He is not of her kind. I believe he is of mine—I am sure he is. I feel akin to him; I understand the language of his looks, the odd bents of his humor. We can never be attached in the world, but I have to confess to myself an aspect of my body and my being will always be drawn to him by a natural, irrefutable force. This is how it must be, though it breaks my heart to think it. While I breathe and function upon this earth, I must love him.*

These thoughts were overtaken by the conversation of the room when Mr. Colchester and Colonel Eshton's discourse on the war drew in everyone.

"The South will strike first," Colonel Eshton was saying. "Lincoln, as president, would never invade another state without a clear declaration of war, no matter how many Southern states secede."

"A mistake in my opinion," said the young Mr. Parma. "We should march straight to Alexandria and give those rebels a good spanking."

Mr. Colson agreed. "Finish it all before it gets started."

"In that case," said Mr. Ingram with a broad smile, "our ladies are working too hard. The army won't need so many provisions for a war that will be over within a month."

There was some general laughter over this, but then Mr. Colchester said, "You underestimate the Southern spirit."

"Ah, that's right!" Mr. Nicholas rapped the end of his billiards cue upon the floor. "You know something about it. Them rebs may as well be your brothers, ain't that right? Do you know what side you're on, Colchester?"

"You wouldn't be guests in my house if I didn't."

The elder Mr. Parma gave his son a hard, cold look, and the young man bowed his head slightly in Mr. Colchester's direction.

"Beggin' your pardon, sir. I didn't mean to offend."

Mr. Colchester returned the bow. "I only meant to say some folks don't know when they're whipped. The South is full of them."

Captain Morgan shook his head. "But if the fighting grows hot, come winter they will freeze—and starve. Their farms are planted with cotton and tobacco, unlike the bounty we enjoy here. We have the wheat and the corn."

I had a thought in response, and it seemed like it walked through my mind and emerged from Mr. Colchester's mouth:

"But the South has sugarcane," he said. "Molasses, sweet flour, cane juice, soup, even rum. Not a good diet in the long term but enough to keep an army on its feet."

"Colchester's right," said Mr. Morgan. "Our advantage lies in our factories, the ability to manufacture artillery, ammunition, footwear, and uniforms."

Coffee was set out, and the ladies left their stations to fill their cups and join the men. Missus Livingston and two of the maids who came with the guests slipped in silently to replace them. No one took up Miss Chamberlain's task, however, and I saw I would soon be done rolling the strips she had cut.

"How will you get your wares to the soldiers in the field?" Mr. Colchester asked Miss Belinda, who had taken a seat near him.

"Yes, they are hers, aren't they?" Mr. Chamberlain beamed at his daughter. "For those of you who don't know, my Belinda raised the funds for these provisions herself."

"I suppose it is my duty, then, to see that they go to those who are intended to use them." She swept an elegant arm through the air. "I will drive them to the battle lines myself if I must."

"The devil you will!"

I raised my eyes slightly to observe Mr. Colchester's protest.

"What will you do, Christian? Accompany me?" She touched him playfully on the shoulder and ran her fingers up the nape of his neck. "Don't be a fool. I'd be safer to travel with another woman than with a man. You would be considered a threat."

"Your wisdom is infallible, as always."

"Then no more need be said: let's change the subject," she commanded. "We have been serious enough this evening. We have worked long enough."

"I couldn't agree more."

"I propose we clear up and have some music."

"I'll agree, but only if I may have the first dance."

I sneaked a glance at him. Mr. Colchester danced? Would he really? Would she?

She smiled and leaned toward him. "You know my hand is always yours for the asking."

She rose and, without taking her eyes off him, proceeded to the piano. "I will begin and give us something cheerful to change the mood. Joseph, you can spell me when I'm ready to dance."

"Sister, I am at your service."

She seated herself at the instrument and began a bright divertimento. Missus Livingston took this as a cue to begin clearing our work to make space for the dancers. I followed her example and began to stack the completed bandages into a large basket.

The men gathered around the piano. Miss Chamberlain spoke while she played and seemed intent on engaging their attention. Her words and posture were provocative. She was evidently bent on striking them as dashing and daring.

"I wish I could go to war!" she said. "You men will leave us, and we women can do nothing but wait and pine. But to be in battle—in the thick of the smoke and the roar of the cannons. Christian, I would accompany you! Charging forth together, weapons drawn, everything on the line. Kill or be killed!"

"You tramping through mud? Sitting on the ground around a campfire, eating goober peas from a can, and not a washbasin in sight?" Mr. Colchester laughed. "Now that would be something to behold, my sweet."

"You doubt me?" She seemed pleased at eliciting a reaction. "But you are right. Loveliness and cleanliness are the particular prerogatives of women. They would be difficult to give up. Still, it would be worth it." Her divertimento quieted to a gentler song. "If it meant man and wife didn't have to be parted by war, it would be worth it.

"Whenever I marry," she continued after a pause that none interrupted, "I am determined to be that kind of partner to my husband—equal to the hard tasks as he must be. Ready to take up whatever must be done. I know it's unusual, but the times call for it. We must be more than what we are."

We had nearly cleared the dance area. Miss Chamberlain, who had been eyeing our progress, called to her brother. "I'm finishing now, Joseph. Play a reel for us. Let's be merry while we can."

She concluded her recital with a flourish, and her listeners applauded.

I was grateful to leave the room. As petty as it may seem, I will confess I couldn't bear to watch her in Mr. Colchester's arms. But I wasn't jealous—no. Indignant. Indignant is what I felt, to the depth of my aching heart. Because as capable as she might be—and she might be able to fire a musket for all I knew—she was also frivolous and self-absorbed. What she did that looked like charity was not done out of compassion—she acted for her own glory. But the wealthy were allowed to behave as they liked. Who would check them? Only Mr. Chamberlain could have such influence over his daughter, and he was either unwilling or unable to wield it. This might have been from the loss of Missus Chamberlain. Miss Belinda would have been thrust into the center of attention at an age when it couldn't help but shape her character and make her yearn to stay at that center. Mr. Chamberlain would have been proud of her. As a cherished daughter—and here I understood something of her position from my own experience—she could do no wrong in the eyes of a loving father.

Mr. Colchester, though, had the advantage of free will. He chose to be close to this creature, to connect himself to her intimately. He must have perceived her faults as I did. I could have thought less of him—perhaps even should have thought less of him. If he were any other man, I would have. But for Mr. Colchester? I believe I grieved for him.

Another idea reached me as I opened the library door. What if he excused her faults because *he loved her*? I had been considering all the ways he could not possibly love her, standing in judgment as though I knew how love should operate.

But what do you know of love, Jeannette Bébinn?

I knew, and it pained me to think it, that love flourishes when it is least supposed to do so. Wasn't that the story of my own parents? Had reason had any influence in that case? And love had made a great leap there, spanning a gap of race, position, morality, propriety. No such chasm existed between Mr. Colchester and Belinda Chamberlain. In fact, their match was sanctioned, perhaps even encouraged, by all around them. The path to love her was an easy one indeed.

Heartsick now, I entered the hall to carry my basket of bandages to the storage room. The basket was full, and in my haste, a few rolls of cloth fell out. I stopped to gather them up. I heard the door open again behind me and thought Missus Livingston or one of the other women would follow. I turned and was determined to make some sort of fake, cheerful comment, but the person who came out wasn't a woman. It was Mr. Colchester.

"How are you?" he asked.

"I am well, sir."

"I have not seen you since the fire. You've suffered no lingering effects from the smoke?"

"No, sir."

"And the little girl?"

"Jelly is fine. She is in school and learns well, like all the other children."

"Is that what you have been doing during my absence? Teaching at the school?"

I was confused by the question. What else would I be doing if not the job for which he employed me? I didn't respond.

"Excuse me, Miss Bébinn, but you seem sad. If you are in good health, I cannot account for it. What is the matter?"

"The talk of the war, sir. It disheartens me." A partial truth.

"Yes." He nodded. "There are trying times ahead. But here, return to the library when you are done. The lively music may cheer you up."

"I am tired, sir."

"So much so that you would be on the verge of tears?"

I turned my head.

"All right. If I had time, we would both stay here and talk about Louisiana and what we hope to see there again. But I have guests to attend to. Put your things away and go to bed. We shall see what tomorrow brings. Good night, my dear friend."

Chapter 10

Missus Livingston had been wrong about how long our visitors would remain. They slept only two nights at Fortitude. Each family had its own home to look after, duties to prepare for. But this didn't mean they would be long absent from Mr. Colchester. There was much coming and going by the men, who would hole up in Mr. Colchester's study for hours. When the women visited, I took care to be elsewhere. But this was easy to do. By April Lower Knoll was likewise busy, with the factory in full swing and the adults working in shifts around the clock. Every hand was needed. Even the smallest child could sort buttons or sweep a floor. I insisted my students spend something of every day, if not a proper school day, reading and practicing their lessons. However the world was changing, they would need some education—would need it more than ever. I stayed at the school so the children could come in when they were free. I asked for permission to take a screen from the mansion to be placed in a corner of the schoolroom. I put a cot behind it and took naps.

So much movement—so much life. In ordinary circumstances I would have described these days as merry. Fortitude was no longer quiet, no longer yawned with emptiness. But one day this activity was broken and silenced. I had gone up to the mansion to pack a basket of food for myself to take back to the school for dinner. I moved through the dining room and found Missus Livingston there along with Colonel

Eshton, Mr. Colchester, and some of the servants. I was shocked by the sight because I'd heard no voices, nothing to signal the room was occupied. The colonel was in uniform and wore a saber at his side. Mr. Colchester paced the floor with his arms crossed, his brow clouded with thought.

"Come in, dear," Missus Livingston said when she saw me.

"What has happened?"

"Fort Sumter has been fired upon. The president is calling for a militia to stop the insurrection."

"Fort Sumter?"

"Yes. In South Carolina."

South Carolina—the place where I'd feared to draw breath when Silas and I had traveled through its boundaries. *This is the place,* I thought. *Here is where it begins.*

"We must protect Washington, DC, and secure as much of Virginia as might be possible," said Colonel Eshton. "I will rally troops at the river and hope to march east by the end of the month."

"I will see what men can be spared here and join you at camp by June at the earliest."

The colonel looked confused. He took Mr. Colchester by the elbow and moved him closer to the wall. He whispered, but I could hear his words.

"Christian, leave the men of Lower Knoll where they are. They are more valuable to the cause in the factory. The president didn't say anything about the coloreds fighting."

Mr. Colchester pulled away from him, glanced at us, then threw open the doors and headed for his study. "Damn it, Eshton, what's this fight about then?" The colonel followed him, and they were gone.

Missus Livingston closed the doors behind them and, evidently determined to calm the unsettled energy in the room, began discussing how the running of the house might change. Economies might be necessary. There might be times when our normal processes would be in disarray. I admired her words, but I didn't think them necessary. Missus Livingston ran a well-ordered house with no frivolity in how she managed expenses. If ever a place was prepared for the uncertain vagaries of a war, this was it. I assumed I would continue my teaching as always until directed to do otherwise.

But I will admit, with the conflict now underway and an uncertain future forced upon the entire population of the Union, I thought only of two people in it: Mr. Colchester and his future bride.

For the party did gather again at Fortitude. I suspected it was at the behest of Belinda Chamberlain, for she seemed to be justifying merriment at every given turn.

"Who knows when we may meet like this again? I say tonight let us enjoy ourselves while we can, and let it be a kind of prayer that the next time I welcome you here, it will be to toast the victory of our Union soldiers!"

She raised a glass to the exclamations of "Hear! Hear!" I wondered if I was the only one to notice that she had as good as named herself mistress of the house—that she would be the one to welcome them at the end of the fighting. Perhaps she felt bold enough to do it because Mr. Colchester wasn't in the room. I had called him out myself to alert him to Mr. Mason's arrival from the factory. He had seemed agitated and eager to speak to Mr. Colchester. I remained in the room only long enough to observe how his visitors would weather his departure. After Miss Chamberlain's splendid toast and without Mr. Colchester to provide the bridge between the men and ladies, the room split. The men circled with their cigars around the hearth to discuss the insurrection. The women sat on the sofas and focused solely on Miss Chamberlain, nodding vigorously to whatever certainties she laid out for them.

In my imagination she conspired with them to make whatever final maneuvers were needed to secure her engagement with Mr. Colchester. I took issue with her seeming to have her prize already won. When she laughed, I felt she belittled him. When she smiled sweetly, she took him for granted, assuming he was like other men who could be played upon this way.

I lingered in the hall. Mr. Colchester had to return that way, and I wanted the opportunity to speak with him about his plans for joining the fight. When he didn't appear, I moved in the direction of his study, near the front wing of the mansion. He might have left with his foreman and gone to the factory. But I heard raised voices—impatient, even angry voices. I recognized Mr. Colchester's tones, though I couldn't make out the words. There was Mr. Mason, too, and—a woman's voice. It was Founder. She spoke fast, with sharp, punctuated diction, as though she were delivering blows with her speech. I flinched as though I were on the receiving end.

I feared the door would open at any moment. I fled.

In the privacy of my room I drank a glass of water to settle my nerves so I could sit quietly and think about what I'd heard. Mr. Colchester had disagreed with Mr. Mason on some matter before—I'd witnessed it. And if it weren't for Founder's presence, I would have thought this argument between the men was a similar disagreement. But why was Founder upset? What did she have to do with their business?

Chapter 11

I began having dreams of a strange infant. I didn't realize at first that it was the same child. I couldn't see its features clearly, but I knew it was a small child by the way it pulled at me and by its weight when I held it. When it pulled at me, it was insistent, angry. When I held it, it cried continually, and I felt faint with exhaustion because I'd carried it a long way and had more to walk with it still. In one of the dreams I discerned it was a boy—he wore tiny breeches and stood wading in water. I was trying to coax him to come away because I feared he would drown, but he only grinned at me with a child's careless joy.

Aunt Nancy Lynne used to say it was bad luck to dream of a baby. She'd had such dreams before her son had been sold away from her and the night when Missus had taken her money. I don't know if I believed in bad or good luck, but I do think that anything that comes out of us—dreams, words, looks—has its foundation in something rooted inside of us. Nothing comes out of nowhere. I figured this child was some remnant of my past. Maybe it was Fanny's child coming to tell me about his mother. Or he wanted me to remember her. The child could be some aspect of me, come to tell me about myself. In none of these dreams did I take joy in the child. He scared me, and I was fearful for him.

I had dreamed of the child for one week running and was thinking about him as I left the schoolhouse one afternoon in early May. I was making my way down the street when the door of Templeton's house flew open and a heavyset colored woman came running down the steps. She seemed excited, and she rushed to me, crying out, "That's her! That's her! I'd know that child anywhere!"

She threw her arms around me, nearly knocking me to the street. I was stunned. I didn't know her, nor could I, held tight in her embrace, see the face of my happy captor. Finally she pulled away and held me at arm's length. She examined me up and down. When I looked at her, I saw a puzzle, a face that seemed familiar and yet had been manipulated in some way or transformed into something strange by time. She must have read my confusion, because she said, "Do you know me, chérie? Do you remember?"

"Dorinda!"

I wanted to scream. I wanted to fly. It was Dorinda—Dorinda after all these years. It felt so good to see her I could have devoured her with my eyes. I guessed she was in her fifties—she was older but not yet old. The way she had descended the steps had affirmed that.

"Oh, Dorinda! How did you find me? How did you get here?"

Templeton followed from the house, and Dorinda reached for him. "This is my youngest sister Lottie's boy. Some of the people here are from the Archinard family's plantation. That's where she used to be."

Templeton nodded. "Ever since Mr. Colchester sold Belle Meade and gave us our freedom, I've been looking for my mama to buy hers."

"And he found me first. Found me at Catalpa Valley."

"And your mother?" I asked him. "What about her?"

Dorinda shook her head. "Poor Lottie, God rest her soul, died of the yellow fever in New Orleans. Not long after Madame sent you away. But Templeton wrote to us."

Templeton interrupted her. "Naw, Jelly wrote the letter for me. I told her what to say, how I was grateful to know what happened to my mama. I told her about the fire and how you saved Jelly's life."

Dorinda squeezed my hand. "You know I can't read. But Miss Calista, she was kind enough to read it to me—Lawd, how we jumped up and down in my kitchen! We screamed, 'It's her! She's alive! Thank you, Jesus!'"

"Calista?" My heart thumped hard like it had bumped into the wall of my chest. "She knows where I am?"

Dorinda pulled me close and looked around. "Come on in and I'll tell you. Can't be puttin' our business out in the street."

I smiled—she had been the one to run out into the street! But I was too happy to argue or scold.

We sat at the family table. Jelly sidled up to me at once, and I put an arm around her. Templeton frowned. "Jelly, go play."

I kissed her on her forehead. She pouted, but she went.

Dorinda was rummaging through a cloth-covered bag. Her hands shook. She pulled out a small and square box with a metal hinge at the back. "Miss Calista said to give this to you."

I knew at once what it was. My hands began to shake, too, and I cried even before I pried the box apart. My locket. I grasped it in my hands, held it to my forehead, then hugged it to my heart. I sobbed. Dorinda held on to my arm with one hand and wiped tears from her eyes with the other.

"Go on, chérie. Open it."

I wasn't sure I could bear to do so, but I did. There he was. Papa. And my mama. I'd thought I hadn't forgotten his face, thought it had always been before me, in my mind. Now I saw how much it had been enshrouded in a fog, the fog of time and memory. This image was so clear, like he was sitting there with us. I wanted to tell him everything, all that I had done, all that I had endured. I looked at Dorinda and took her hand. Our tears flowed.

"Oh, Papa! I miss him, Dorinda. I miss him so bad."

"I know, honey. I do too. Miss Calista, she about lost her mind when she found out Madame sent you away like she did."

"What happened, Dorinda? What happened after I left?"

"They fought something terrible! Madame locked Miss Calista in her room for days. Said she couldn't come out until she could act like a lady."

"Oh my God. What did you do?"

"I looked after her best I could, but Madame was crazy. Every time she think one of the coloreds look at her cross-eyed, she'd have 'em whipped. Man, woman, child. Didn't matter. Screams, crying, day and night."

Dorinda paused and mopped her forehead, damp with sweat.

"Miss Calista said she was ready to come out. She knew she had to calm Madame, make her stop. And she did. But as time went on, Calista turned the tables on her."

I wasn't surprised. I knew my sister was probably much stronger—and smarter—than Madame knew. "How did she do that?"

"Madame wanted to marry her off to make a wealthy connection. Had a fancy party with the Prudhomme family—it was young Noah Prudhomme that Calista was supposed to marry. Everyone was gathered, and they were about to make the announcement. Miss Calista stood up, bold as anything, and said she wouldn't marry. Said she'd never marry until her sister, Jeannette, came home. Said she couldn't think of marrying without you. The Prudhommes didn't know what in the world was going on. Madame nearly fell over from the shame."

I sat in wonder and pride. Calista was so strong. "What did Madame do?"

"She was licked. It got out what she had done, and of course most folks knew how your papa doted on you. She didn't want to leave the house after that. After a while she got sickly. Miss Calista runs everything now."

"How did you get here?"

"She wrote me a pass, but the man she sent with me, Mr. Louden, who sells the plantation's cotton, didn't dare come across the river with me. Said it wasn't safe for him to cross into a Northern state because he might be taken as a spy."

"He's not one of the rebel soldiers?"

"Naw, very few of the young men around Catalpa are. They just waiting to see what will happen. They might join the Union soldiers."

"Where is Mr. Louden now?"

"He brought me as far as Barbourville. Paid an old farmer to get me as far as Cincinnati. I walked the rest of the way."

"Oh, Dorinda."

"It's all right. Lawd help me, I could have flapped my arms and flown here. That's how happy I am that you're alive."

I stood up and walked around the table three times. I couldn't sit anymore. The prospect of seeing home again was so big, so glorious. "Is Mr. Louden waiting for you?"

"Yes. He's staying at that farmer's house. If I'm not back by the first of June, we agreed he'd go on back without me."

Templeton chafed at this. "Why you got to go back at all? We live a good life here. You'd be free."

Dorinda sucked her teeth and said nothing. She looked at me. She looked at me because she knew I knew her answer.

"I can be ready in the morning, Dorinda. I'll go back with you."

"Believe me, I'd like nothing better. But Miss Calista told me to tell you it ain't safe for you to come home yet. Madame could cause trouble, and on account of you running away from where they sent you, they might come get you. That man she sent you off with even come sniffing round to see if we'd had sight of you."

"Amesbury," I whispered.

"Yeah, that's the name. Anyway, she figures things might change 'cause of the fighting. She wants you home, but when it's safe."

I dropped my head and palmed the locket in my hand. "Not yet?" I asked. I sat next to her again and pulled from my pocket the stone she'd given me. Her hand flew to her mouth.

"No, chérie. Not yet." She touched the stone and nodded and smiled. "But soon. Soon!"

I sighed. "All right. But I will take you back to Mr. Louden."

"You?"

"Yes. You can't go alone, and none of the men can be spared."

"What if someone stops us?"

"If necessary, I'll be white. In fact I will dress carefully and speak as though you are my servant. Can you do that?"

"Miss Bébinn," said Templeton, "I can't let you do this. She's my aunt, my blood."

"You have a family and work here that must be done," I said. "Don't worry." I looked at Dorinda and kissed her forehead. "She is my family too.

"Dorinda," I told her, "get some rest. We'll leave in the morning. I don't know how long the trip will take. We can't risk you missing Mr. Louden."

"Thank you. I know it'll be all right. Got this far. Going back will be nothing. I'll have you with me."

"Templeton, find us a small cart, anything a horse can pull. I'll bring food for us when I come back in the morning."

"You'll tell Mr. Colchester? He won't like it."

"Yes, I will do it now."

But I didn't want to leave. I fell to my knees at Dorinda's lap and took her hands. I held them to my face, wet them with my tears.

"It's gonna be all right, honey," she said. "You go on. I'll be here when you get back."

Mr. Colchester was in his study with Mr. Parma and Mr. Morgan. I knocked at the door and entered. They seemed to be studying a large map spread out on his desk. Mr. Colchester looked up, and I noted his surprise.

"May I have a word with you, sir?"

He nodded and escorted me to the library, where he closed the door, took a seat, and waited. "Yes, Miss Bébinn?"

"Mr. Colchester, I want a leave of absence for two or three weeks."

"Now? When we're on the brink of a war? What to do—where to go?"

"To escort a lady friend back to her chaperone, who will see her the rest of the way home. She came all this way to see me."

He stood, alarmed. I wished he had stayed in the chair. It was easier to speak to him when he was at my eye level. He paced the room. "What lady? Where does she live?"

"She is Templeton's aunt, but she's a slave in the home where I was a child. At Catalpa Valley Plantation."

"Louisiana? You can't make it that far, two women alone. You can't be serious!"

"She was sent with a man who brought her as far as the river. I intend to help her cross again and meet him in Kentucky."

He frowned. "Why would her owner allow this? And why, if she's Templeton's aunt, doesn't she stay here and remain free?"

I swallowed. "Her owner is my half sister. She is Calista Bébinn."

"You've always said you had no relations."

I lowered my eyes to the floor. "Sir, I didn't mean to lie to you. Calista's mother sold me into slavery, and she is still the mistress of Catalpa Valley. She was jealous and angry that Papa left land to me. Calista didn't know where I was. I was as good as dead to them and they to me."

"This is madness. I won't let you anywhere near such a place or such a person."

"Yes, sir, but I am not going back. My sister has sent word that it is not safe. But I do intend to help Dorinda, who came all this way to bring word of my family."

He went to the window and stood looking out, silent.

"How far will you go?" he finally asked.

"If he is not at the river, then I will take her into Kentucky. There is a Union camp nearby. But if I must, I'll travel as a white woman and pretend Dorinda belongs to me. I've done this before."

"The devil you have."

"I can do it, sir."

He came back to me. "But you would return alone."

"I will use the carriage circuit, a road well traveled. I will ride where there are people."

"Promise me to return in a week—"

"I cannot. We will be too slow, and I don't know what the road holds for us."

Mr. Colchester moved closer. "When do you go?"

"Early tomorrow morning, sir."

He went to a desk, took out paper, and began to write. "Carry this letter with you. It says I am your employer. You may need it if you have to go into Kentucky and anyone questions your freedom. And you must have some money."

He pulled a wallet from his pocket and offered me bills totaling about twenty dollars. I wanted to protest—he paid me a salary, after all. But I thought better of it. Some circumstance might require a large sum. A bribe perhaps. I could give most of it to Dorinda for her journey with Mr. Louden.

While he wrote, I took the opportunity to voice what was most on my mind. "Mr. Colchester, you may have joined the militia before I return."

"It is possible. My plans are not yet made."

"It is my understanding, sir, that your plans include—" I paused. "You are going to be married?"

He stopped writing, put down his pen, and looked up at me. "Yes. What then?"

"In that case, sir, I should move into the village, even if the cottage is not rebuilt."

"To get you out of my bride's way, I suppose?"

"Sir, I am not a servant, and she may protest that I have no role in the running of the household."

"True!" he exclaimed. "It would not fit in with her orderly ways." He looked at me some minutes.

When he didn't continue writing, I finally asked, "Before you go, sir, could you make arrangements for me? I have a cot in the schoolroom. Perhaps a room can be added. Or I could stay above one of the stores?"

He nodded and finished his writing. "I will take care of it. But I do hope to take leave of you properly before I go off to war."

"I shall pray for that, sir." I took the money and the letter and folded them carefully. "But for now, farewell. Thank you."

"You say farewell now? But you go tomorrow?"

"Yes, sir, as early as we can."

"You will not join us after dinner?"

"No, sir, I must prepare for the journey."

"It is to be farewell."

"Yes, for the present."

He said nothing else, and I grew impatient. I wanted to pack and rest. I had no time for his confusing behavior. I bowed slightly and hurried away.

That night I opened the trunk I kept stored in my closet; the trunk I had arrived with and not touched since; the trunk that held, in a small compartment, the pistol Miss Maude had given me. I remembered how to clean and load it, which I did, but I wished I had the time and a place to practice firing it. I would have to trust my memory. Next, I wrote a letter for Dorinda to give to Calista. It was a joy and a relief to know she would read the words. I thanked her for the locket and told how I agreed with her that I should stay away from Catalpa Valley for now. But I begged her to write to me if she could get anything across the battle lines. Most of all I was grateful at the prospect that I might see her again and come home at last.

Dorinda and I started our journey at first light. We took a leisurely pace so as not to call attention to ourselves. But if anyone had noticed us, they would have seen what we appeared to be: two women in a small single-horse carriage talking pleasantly with each other. There was much about Catalpa Valley that I still wanted to know.

"How is Madame?"

"She's getting on. I think the news has got her down. If you ask me, I'd be surprised if she lasts another four or five years."

"Does she mention me?"

"Lawd, no. 'Bout had a stroke when Miss Calista said what she said in front of all them people."

"I really have been dead to her, I suppose."

"Humph. She done brought all her suffering down on herself. She knows it too. That's why she can't look no one in the eye."

"Dorinda," I asked quietly, "did she have you whipped too?"

She sat up straighter in the seat and didn't answer.

Instead she wanted to know if I was happy at Fortitude Mansion and what sort of a person Mr. Colchester was. I ran a hand down her back. I knew where the marks would be. But she kept talking.

"Templeton say he a good man."

I nodded and held the reins tighter in my fingers. "He is kind. He treats everyone well. I knew everyone in the village were once slaves. I didn't know right away that he brought them all up from Louisiana."

In such conversation we passed our time. Despite our slow pace we were able to gain the northeastern portion of the river by the end of our second day. I procured lodgings for us with Dorinda posing as my servant. The next day we continued following the river.

Once Cincinnati was within reach, we began to be on the lookout for Mr. Louden. I had been right about the roads being full. We were often passed by militia on horses and on foot. Dorinda and I pulled to the side of the road and watched them go by. The dust from their feet, most likely shod in shoes made in Lower Knoll, floated in the rising late-spring heat. I marveled at the baby-faced youth and the grim determination etched on their faces. I thought of Mr. Colchester's question to Colonel Eshton: What were they fighting for? Did they know?

Only once did I pull out the pistol. It was when we were near the Kentucky border. A man with a rifle slung over his shoulder approached us on foot. I saw him coming and whispered to Dorinda, "It's all right. Don't say anything to him." I tried to assess what he could be. He wasn't ragged, and yet he was on foot. He could be on his way to join a regiment. But for which side? I slipped the pistol out of my pocket and held it in my hand on my lap, like I always held it there. I kept the reins in my left.

"Good afternoon, miss." I could see his eyes going from the gun, to Dorinda, to me, and then back to the gun again.

I nodded. I decided it was best not to volunteer information, so I said nothing, not even *Good afternoon*.

"On your way to Cincinnati?"

I smiled. "I'm on an errand for my daddy."

He looked again at Dorinda. "She your property?"

My answer to this question meant everything. I couldn't tell if he was on the slave-owning side of the conflict or not. I listened for a tilt of his voice, for a different accent, but I couldn't discern one. Finally, I decided I would tell the truth, or a kind of truth. He would hear it the way he needed to.

I smiled again. "She has looked after me since I was a child. I almost feel like I belong to her! We are indeed together, sir. And as I said"—I moved the gun ever so slightly on my lap—"I'm running an errand for my daddy."

He nodded. "Good for you, miss. Don't let that Yankee trash bother you. If I were you, I'd go around Temsun way and avoid the Alma road. There's a Union camp set up near there."

"Thank you kindly, sir. We'll do that." I clucked to the horses to get them moving. "Good afternoon," I said as we passed by him.

We drove for a bit without saying anything. After I was sure the man was out of sight and not following us, I put the gun back in my pocket. Dorinda smiled and put an arm around me.

"You reminded me of your daddy just then. Just as brave and bold as can be."

I smiled and kissed her on the forehead.

She went on: "Brave and bold like he was when you were a baby, carrying you with him everywhere he went."

It was an image I hadn't thought of in a long time. It made me feel happy and settled.

"Thank you, Dorinda."

We found the old farmer first. He overtook us just past Cincinnati and, on glancing at us, recognized Dorinda.

"Is that you, ma'am? Are you looking for your man?"

She put up her hands and waved. "Mr. Smith! Thank the Lord!"

We pulled our carriages to the side of the road, and I helped Dorinda step down.

"Mr. Louden been sending me up and down this road every other day. Said you might come this way."

I was so glad we hadn't taken the directions the stranger had given us.

"He still waitin' for me, then?"

"It ain't June yet, so yeah, he's there. But I think he's itchin' to go. He'll be right grateful to be off."

"Well, I'm ready for him."

I helped Dorinda with her things. Templeton and I had made sure she was returning with more than she'd had when she'd left Catalpa Valley. I parsed out what food I might need for my return trip and gave her the rest. I did the same with the money Mr. Colchester had given me.

"Traveling mercies, Dorinda."

She kissed me. "We shall meet again, ma chérie. I know this now. I am glad of it."

Chapter 12

My journey back to Lower Knoll felt tedious and longer without Dorinda's company. I took fewer breaks and traveled more miles a day. During the drawn-out hours I thought of what Madame must look like now. I remembered our last encounter, her face disfigured with jealousy and anger, outside her wits from Papa's death. I wondered what his funeral day had been like—the coffin, the walk to the family graveyard, the black train of slaves and family following the horse-drawn hearse. Would there be such a gathering when Madame died? It didn't seem likely. I thought about what it must have been like for her to lose Papa's son and Papa's love almost all at once. I felt sorry for her. I decided if I ever saw her again, I would try to make peace.

I was going back to Fortitude Mansion and Lower Knoll, but how long could I stay? I had asked Mr. Colchester to find another residence for me, but I didn't think it could ever be far enough away to keep me from witnessing him and his bride every day. But now that I had a hope of returning to Catalpa Valley, perhaps I needed only to wait until the end of the war, which, if men like Colonel Eshton were right, would not last long. Mr. Colchester would be away fighting, so I would not have to see him, but would he be safe? Would he return whole? He might already be gone to join Eshton's regiment. For all I knew, he had married Miss Chamberlain in my absence.

I wrapped the reins around my hands until my fingers throbbed and ached. *Oh God.* If he was married, if he was under fire in a distant field far from me, I could make this prayer, perhaps even a sacrifice? I would stay near, endure the witness of his attachment to this woman, if it meant that he might survive. It seemed a meager, useless bargain, but it was all I had to offer.

But if I were being truthful with myself and my God, I'd have to confess that if I were to come upon a resident of Lower Knoll and call out to him for the news of the village, and he said, *Mr. Colchester is married!* and proceeded to tell me about the celebration, I would hail the news, thank the person who gave it to me, and then bypass the road to Lower Knoll. I would keep driving and never return.

It was a dull hot evening when I did make my way into the vicinity of the village. There were haymakers from the local farms at work all along the road. The air was hazy, thick with water but with no promise of rain. The clouds hung above in soft blue-gray folds. It felt like everything around was heavy with waiting—waiting for the heat to break; waiting for rain; waiting, perhaps, for the sound of cannon fire in the distance. It reminded me of my first conversation with Mr. Colchester about the air in southern Louisiana. What we had not discussed was how such air often preceded awful storms that flooded the land and blew wind so powerful that it flattened the sugarcane in the fields. Maybe we both had the sort of minds that chose to recall what was pleasant and forget what was not. It might be better for me now to pay close attention—to read the signs that the earth offered. Would there be a destruction waiting at the end of my journey?

And yet as I drew closer, I was aware of an energy, a small star of excitement igniting deep within me. It stirred with anticipation, conscious of impending joy. I tried to tell myself it was because of the hours I had been in solitude. How I would be happy to be home safely, among familiar faces. I was eager to tell Templeton that I'd delivered Dorinda and that she was now on her road to Catalpa Valley. But I knew that while all this was true, none of it was what sparked my hope. I thought of his eyes. I whispered his given name, chewing on the sound of the letters and enjoying the sweetness as if it were sugarcane.

I also told myself the prospect of seeing him, who didn't think of me at all, should not spur me on. This journey should have been my practice, my adjustment to being without him. It had been easy enough to not think of Mr. Colchester when I'd had Dorinda to keep me company and no expectation of encountering him. Now it was as though my heart knew its proper place and delighted in returning. But I checked myself. I resisted the urge to coax Bella, my mare, who had been so patient with my less than expert mastery of the reins, to trot faster. Instead I cherished the pace, savored the anticipation. My destination would be in sight soon enough.

Eventually I did recognize the landscape, the curve of the river and the hill that would dip into Lower Knoll. As the road stretched upward, I saw a lone figure walking ahead in the same direction. I couldn't see any distinguishing features other than that he wore no coat and his shirtsleeves were rolled up to the elbows. His hat sat back on his head, like its owner had pushed it there off his hot forehead. The man walked with purpose, not speed. But his stride, I saw at once, was familiar—long and powerful, the foot striking the ground with his heel on each step. His arms swung and propelled him up the growing slope. To see him was such a surprise that I doubted my senses. Perhaps I had fallen asleep and out of my carriage, and I was now unconscious and dreaming this odd scene. In speaking, I hoped to prove to myself that I was awake and alive.

"Mr. Colchester!"

He turned, waved, and stood with his hands on his hips, waiting for me to pull up to where he was. He patted the horse's neck. "Well done,

Bella!" he said in her ear. Then he came around to me. "Back from the river Styx, I see."

"Yes, sir."

"And you have delivered your friend to the other side?"

I nodded.

"I feared for you, my little friend. You didn't cross any battlefields? You're all right?"

"Yes, sir, a little tired."

"And hungry. Here, let me take you the rest of the way."

He climbed onto the carriage and took the reins from my hands. I leaned against the side of the seat. I was more exhausted than I'd realized. The shock of the happy meeting had shaken me as well. I'd known there would be pleasure in meeting him again, but I was ashamed that I took such pleasure. I was feasting on the crumbs he deigned to scatter my way, to a poor servant who could hope for no better. And yet in this moment I had no better home. He was the home I had returned to, the one I most loved returning to.

"I didn't know you would be here, sir. I thought you would be in Washington by now."

"Yes, well. I still have one more matter to settle before I go. You know what it is?"

"Yes, sir."

"Because you know me. You know where my life is headed."

I turned away from him and said nothing.

"My bride will be the queen of Fortitude. I doubt she would have it any other way. She will rule well in my absence."

"She is—" I sought out Missus Livingston's word. "She is capable, sir. Quite capable."

We rode on in silence. I noticed he turned away from the road through Lower Knoll and took a side route to the drive and stables of Fortitude.

"I have a request," he said after a while. "A promise, if you will."

I looked at his profile. He stared straight ahead and seemed to be gathering his thoughts. His eyes had the look of someone seeking within and calculating.

"You must promise me never again to take such a risk."

"Then you ask me not to live." I sat up to face him more directly. "What is this life for if not to willingly give it up for those we love? Mr. Colchester, I have attended the deaths of two people I loved most in this world, and it was hard knowing I couldn't do a thing to save them. To help Dorinda was a cherished privilege. There was something I could do, and I did it. I would never give up such a chance."

The words emboldened me. I felt them deeply, and it struck me that in a moment when he could have asked anything of me, he wanted a thing I couldn't supply.

"Dorinda risked greatly for me. She did not have to come here. I am happy, sir, to have inspired such love. I am blessed that I can show it in return."

"Do you not find such love in Lower Knoll? Or Fortitude?"

"I am appreciated and respected. Of course, Jelly loves me. And Missus Livingston treats me as though I am a daughter."

We were pulling into the drive now, and George approached quickly. I stood, but before he reached us, I turned to Mr. Colchester.

"You have always been a kind friend. Thank you, Mr. Colchester. I am glad you are still here. You are what makes Fortitude a home for me."

I took George's hand, stepped quickly from the carriage, and hurried into the house. Missus Livingston exclaimed at my arrival and proceeded to sit me down to get me fed and rested as soon as possible.

I was so grateful to have made it back to Fortitude that I went to bed refusing to think about the future. It was enough to be safe in my bed. Enough to know he was under the same roof. I would deal with the separation when it was before me and not torture myself by suffering it repeatedly in my mind until then.

But strangely, the time of separation did not come. A quiet fell over the mansion. I supposed it was because of Mr. Colchester's impending departure, but I'd thought there would be some activity around preparing for his marriage. When nothing happened, I assumed all the preparations and the wedding itself were taking place at the Chamberlains' home. However, that didn't explain why no one prepared Fortitude for its new mistress. I wasn't the only one curious about the circumstances. I overheard Missus Livingston asking Mr. Colchester when they should expect Miss Chamberlain, but he laughed and answered her only with, "My bride is indeed nearby."

She took it as a joke. She scolded but could get nothing else out of him.

I began to speculate. Perhaps the fighting and Mr. Colchester's impending departure had made them think better of marrying early. They had decided to wait. Or—and this was a fond hope—they had broken off the engagement. It was possible. I couldn't read his face—the insurrection was forever before us. Colonel Eshton had gone, and Mr. Colchester was organizing a small band to follow. He seemed grim at times. But then he would still meet me with some measure of contentment. He still sat in the evenings with me and Missus Livingston. We spoke as before, only now he shared his thoughts and plans about the growing army. I admired his bravery. I feared for his life. One evening I returned from the schoolroom to find him in the library trying on his uniform with Missus Livingston suggesting alterations. The dark-navy wool set off his brilliant eyes. Chevron stripes marked his left sleeve. I was proud of him and had never loved him better.

June was nearly done. The summer settled over Lower Knoll and the neighborhood. Roses exploded with riotous blossoms and seductive scents. Wild strawberries grew in the wood near the ruins of my cottage, and the children gathered them in the late-afternoon sun. I ended classes earlier so they could enjoy these free moments before going home to chores. I felt they should be outside as much as possible, and I thought the same for myself.

One evening I ventured out to the back terrace of Fortitude. It had been a favorite gathering place when Mr. Colchester's friends had been there, and I had not had the opportunity to visit it in recent weeks. The left side of it afforded a distant view of the river. At some point the moon would be visible, too, but it wasn't late enough yet.

I paced awhile across the length of stone. A measure of contentment steadied me, and I was grateful for the solitude. But I heard voices, including Mr. Colchester's. To avoid them, I moved down into the yard and sat on a bench at the edge of the wood. The seat was hidden by a small portico and shaded by large oak trees. None of the trees was as old or as grand as the oak Calista and I had once played in, and their branches, even with full leaves, seemed naked without Spanish moss draped over them. Still, it reminded me of home. I settled myself and enjoyed the gathering darkness and the growing scents of the garden's roses, jasmine, and lavender.

Within a few minutes, though, I realized Mr. Colchester was coming across the lawn to my place. I became self-conscious. I felt I was out of bounds, enjoying the grounds in a way that only Fortitude's owner and his guests had a right to do. I moved quickly to go back into the house, but he was soon at the bench.

"Where are you going?"

I performed a brief curtsy. "I don't want to disturb you, sir. You must want your seat."

"What?"

"You want to be alone."

"Nothing could be further from the truth." He moved to the bench and sat down. "On such a night I want to be in the company of a friend."

He motioned for me to join him, but I remained standing. "The night, sir?"

He sat back and crossed his legs. "Do you ever feel homesick on nights like this, Miss Bébinn?" He tilted his head backward and inhaled deeply.

I looked up and surveyed the line where the sky's pink hue had deepened into a pale blue now darkening. "Yes, sir. Summers in Catalpa Valley are very hot, but I never minded. It felt like everything was overgrown and would keep growing just luscious and crazy." A small smile formed on my lips. "I guess I thought Eden must be like that. The earth smelled rich. The flowers were like perfume."

He nodded. "Louisiana is like that," he said. "Not always so beautiful but magnetic still."

"How do you mean?"

"New Orleans is crowded, smoky. On a night like this the streets can stink so bad you don't want to go outside. But you do because New Orleans is like a huge front porch, and the city stands there greeting the world. All sorts of people come through the port. All over the place, people are making deals; people are making love. The energy radiating through the air. I adored it."

My face burned.

"But come away from the city, and it's all wild and beautiful—the moss hanging long like lace from the trees; the still waters croaking with life in the bayou."

"Catalpa Valley is closer to the Mississippi," I said. "A little further north. But just the same. Just like that."

A sensation like a warm, loving river flooded my chest and overtook me. I wanted to say more and knew what I wanted to say—in fact, I hungered for the words in my mouth:

"Fifty thousand acres make up our plantation, Catalpa Valley. The parcels are named Belle Neuve, Baton Bleu, Siana Grove, Chance Voir, Belle Verde, Mont Devreau. There is a section Papa set aside for me, five thousand acres, called Petite Bébinn. That is my home."

"You must have wanted to go with your friend, to go all the way back home."

"I did, very much."

"Why didn't you?"

I shifted back and forth on my feet. If he knew what he was asking me, he'd know I could have started walking south right then, at that very moment, and not stopped until I saw Calista's face again and wrapped myself in Dorinda's arms. I put my hand in my pocket and touched the stone from Papa's land.

"It's not safe," I said. "Fugitive Slave Act will keep it that way for now."

"You'll go back someday?"

"I hope to. Maybe after the fighting if slavery is finally abolished." I grasped the rock but kept it hidden in my pocket as I stepped toward him. "Even if it isn't, I will find a way to return and free the people on our plantation. I miss it. But I haven't grieved it all this time, because I had a home here, Mr. Colchester. I grieve it now because this home is going to change, which is just as good as losing it."

Tears crept into my throat, but I kept speaking to keep them at bay. "I've known freedom here, true freedom. And I have been given the space and the attention in which I could become fully myself—with attention from you. In our every interaction, with every gesture, I've come to know what it is to be appreciated for myself, my thoughts, my words." I looked up at the sky again. It was a deepening shade of indigo. "And now I must find another place, and until then I'll be lost."

He leaned forward and clasped his hands.

"Will you be sad to leave me, Jeannette?" he said. "I would be sad for you to go."

He paused, and I, startled, tried to see his face. In the gloaming it was hard to discern his features. He'd never called me by my name before. I was sure he was making fun of me. It seemed with each word he breathed life into an ember within me.

"It has been a mystery to me," he said, "how I could be surrounded by people who have all come from the same place—for almost every soul in Lower Knoll fled Louisiana—and yet you are the one, the strange one, who still holds it within you. You hold it as I do. We have shared this bond, and I think I will lose something of myself if we can't go on like we have."

God, what sentimentality was this?

"And yet we can't go on," I said. "Times are changing, sir. The fighting—nothing will be the same. Some bonds will have to be broken."

He stood and stepped toward me. "That's strange talk! Explain yourself."

"As a people, we come together to preserve the Union, but in other ways we must fend for ourselves, each individually."

"How so?"

"Those of us who have no family to influence our decisions, we can make choices for ourselves. We can decide whether or not to fight, whether to seek the field or stay at home, whether to find a way to profit and seek fortune."

"What do you care for fortune?"

"I don't. I only use it as an example." I sighed. "But if I had it, I wouldn't have to wait to go back home."

"Fortune has its own anchors." He took another step toward me and this time touched my arm. "But you and I are not alone."

"You are not. I am, sir. You'll have a wife soon."

"You are sure of that?"

"Yes, it's as good as done, from what I understand. So really, sir, you are the one leaving me."

I walked away from him, but he stopped me before I had gone three steps. What wicked game was this? I refused to play any longer. The ember burst brilliantly into flame.

"Stop it!" I said. "You are cruel to stand there and make me call to mind all that is dear and lost to me! Do you want me to break down in front of you? Do you want to see me cry? Here! Here you are!" I let the tears flow. He had pressed them from the depths of my being, and now I would have him feel the force of this river flooding. It no longer mattered to me what got carried away or who was drowned.

"You don't care!" I said. "But maybe you don't have a heart! That's why you can make an amusement of me. That's why you can marry such a woman."

He laughed. *Laughed!*

"She is vicious," he said. "And mercenary. Don't forget that."

"Then you are the same, a perfect pair!"

"The same? Jeannette Bébinn!" Now it seemed, in this strange play, it was his turn to be indignant. "That vixen doesn't know a damn thing about me."

I crossed my arms and stared. I spoke slowly. If I were a man, I would have grabbed his face and held it close to mine so he wouldn't miss a single syllable.

"Then I'm sorry for you. You've just confirmed what I have suspected. That you care nothing for her. She is your inferior, and you know it. I am ashamed for you."

I tried again to move away, but he pried open my arms and seized my wrists. He dropped to his knees.

"Look at me," he demanded. Like he'd read my mind, he lifted my hands to his face and held them there. His cheeks were damp, but I refused to believe it was from tears. "*You* know my mind. *You* know my heart. We were born of the same earth."

"What does that matter?"

"It does matter!"

"No, it doesn't. Not when I can't win you." I hardly knew what I was saying. My skin tingled from the feel of his whiskers under my palms. If I leaned forward just a little, my lips could touch his forehead or blow away the dark locks sweeping down over his brow. "Not when the world holds me worthless.

"But I know my own value," I said as I pulled away from him. "I'm not afraid to be alone, because it is what I have always been. I know how to be apart and solitary and still know that I am loved."

He grasped the cloth of my skirt. "By me, Jeannette! You are loved by me."

I stared at him. It was impossible to see his features clearly. I smacked at his hands. "How dare you say my name! How dare you say it and make it a joke? You think because I am mulatto and small and unconnected that I can be toyed with. But you're wrong." He let go of me, and that small victory made me bold. "Yes, we are the same. But not because we hail from Louisiana, and not because we can speak with like minds or love the same earth. We are the same because that is how we've been made. How we have all been made. I am a human being, as are you. And I will stand here and demand respect on that account."

He stood and grabbed for me again, this time by the shoulders. He had the advantage of me now. His height gave him purchase, and he towered over me so I had no choice but to hear him.

"Yes, yes, that's what I'm trying to tell you, Jeannette. You have always been my equal from the moment I fell down the stairs and you stood there like a wall. I knew my grace when I saw it. That night when I pulled you from the fire, I never thought you were in my debt for saving your life, because you had already saved mine. I knew from the way you spoke to me, from the way you challenged me to be better, you made me realize I was worthy of love."

"Is that why you brought Belinda Chamberlain here? Did you think she was all you were worthy of?"

"Forgive me, but I wanted to make you jealous."

"What?" I felt like a gear inside my head had broken. I couldn't comprehend his words. Me? Make me jealous? What was he talking about?

"Jeannette, I'm slow. So slow and so stupid. I didn't know how to earn your love. I wanted to be worthy of you. I didn't know if you felt anything for me. It was all I could think of to do. Please forgive me."

It was all too fantastic. I held myself straight, stiff, and proper. "I don't believe you," I said.

Again he fell to his knees, only now he pulled me down with him. "I swear on this ground I'm telling the truth. You don't need to believe me; believe what you've already witnessed, what you've already said to me." He took both my hands in his and held them to his chest. "You recognized that I couldn't love her. You saw that she was inferior to me. But did I ever show her any sign of affection? Did you sense any sort of attachment, true attachment, between us?"

These had been my exact thoughts. Every single day that Belinda Chamberlain had been at Fortitude, I had read his disdain for her, clearly written across every scene I had beheld. Her clumsy attempts to enchant him had been empty of any intimacy. She wasn't close enough to him to know how to attract him with anything but the most shallow of enticements. And yet I couldn't believe he was affirming these thoughts.

Mr. Colchester took my face in his hands. "Marry me, Jeannette! Say, *Christian, I will marry you. I will marry you because you love me as I do you.*"

I was speechless. I stared up at him in awe.

"Now you are the one being cruel," he said. "You won't answer me?"

Oh God.

"Sir, I'm afraid to speak. My heart might break into a thousand pieces."

"I swear I love you, Jeannette. You are my helpmeet; you are my equal. You alone are my bride."

I was overcome. My heart seemed to swell like a river blown out and overflowing after an abundance of long-awaited rain. All I could manage was one word.

"Yes."

"Yes?"

"Yes."

He kissed me. Suddenly my senses were full of him. He smelled of witch hazel and cigar smoke and of the jasmine and roses all around us, and I felt as though I had fallen into myself.

He held me tightly. "Are you happy, Jeannette? Because you have made my happiness, and I'm determined to seize it. This is my chance to own my own heart. And I gladly offer it to you."

"Yes, Christian, yes."

It was the truth. I was happy. I'm not sure I had understood the meaning of the word before, but now I felt like a child. Simple joy, like I was riding horseback floating over a sea of sugarcane as I'd done with Papa all those years ago. It was a simple, clear, shining bubble of happiness. I felt the wind shift, and a breeze blew about us.

He pulled me to my feet and kissed me again, and as he embraced me, I happened to look up at the house. There was a light burning in one of the upper windows. I saw the shadow of a figure behind the glass and felt a strange twisting sensation in my stomach.

I realized how we must look, but I couldn't do anything about it. Everyone would know everything soon enough, I figured. I allowed him to take my hand, and we ran into the house. The clock struck ten.

We embraced again in the hall. His scent seemed deeply familiar and exotic all at once. It mesmerized me enough to place a small kiss at the base of his throat.

"My angel," he said. "Sleep well. I will see you in the morning, and we will plan our lives from there."

I didn't think I could sleep. I spent at least an hour listening to the wind pushing through the trees. It sounded like an ocean flowing past my window.

When I did sleep, I dreamed again of a child, only now the child was a girl, and she stood silently very close to my face and stared into my eyes expectantly. I didn't know what she wanted or what she was waiting for.

Chapter 13

When I awoke, the sense of delight was still all over me. It could have all been a dream, wrapped in darkness and softness. I pulled the covers close and shut my eyes tight. If it had been a dream, I would still have the sensation that I could return to it, that I could dip down into sleep again, draw aside a curtain of Spanish moss, and cross back into that same softness, that same darkness.

Only I couldn't, because I, with my waking eyes, had the memory of Mr. Colchester's voice filling my ears and anchoring me to the daylight world. It had been no dream. Mr. Colchester loved me. *He loved me.* As I rose and dressed, I played last night's scene over again and again, every touch, every word. If I did doubt the reality of any of it, I couldn't deny the proof of what I saw in the mirror. When I looked at my face, I found a smile, natural and warm, on my lips. I had smiled before, but this smile seemed unused, like it had always been there but had been saved or even hidden under the surface; like this smile showed how my face was always meant to look. My eyes had borrowed the spark and liveliness of Mr. Colchester's—Christian's—eyes. A sense of hope and abundance filled me, and my new eyes saw a world of intense, vibrating color. I hurried my dressing. I wanted to show him this face, to lift up to him these eyes and have him see all that he had poured into me.

A rain overnight had washed the air clear, and the sunlight sparkled in a crisp deep-blue sky. A refreshing breeze blew through the mansion. I left my room and ran down the gallery, taking the steps so fast that I nearly stumbled into Founder. She was standing on the landing looking out of the window. Her expression, sad and grave, made her face look heavy with care. It seemed necessary for the hand beneath her chin to bear the full weight of her head. Again I felt a discomfort in my stomach, but I was determined to ignore it.

"Founder! Good morning!"

She glanced at me and frowned. "Who says it is?"

"Well, I suppose I do, but the day can speak for itself!" I joined her at the window and opened it. "It's a glorious day. And feel that breeze!" I raised my face to the light and took in the sweet air.

"What's got you acting bright as a button?"

It seemed like a trick question. I was certain she was the one I'd seen in an upstairs window last night, standing like she was now. It occurred to me that Founder was always looking out the windows, like she was always looking out for someone. I wanted to tell her about me and Christian. I wanted to blast that sour look off her face, to shout about my love to the heavens. But it didn't seem right, not until I had spoken to him again. For all I knew, it had been a dream. I wanted to see him first. Needed to see him above all, to have our love, for now, still between the two of us and unspoiled.

"Sometimes, we just have to believe it's going to be a good day, Founder," I said. "Just a blessed, good day."

She seemed about to say more, but I flew away from her and down the stairs. I was determined to believe my own words—determined to believe that all would be well.

I found Christian in the library, ready to embrace me, to kiss me.

"*Mon chéri!*" I blushed to use the words. Since I'd never properly learned Creole, the French fell awkwardly from my mouth. But I'd always heard this phrase with such love from the likes of Papa and Dorinda that I wanted to give it to Christian now.

"My angel! Good morning! Look at you! Your eyes are as clear and as blue as the morning sky. Here is my new day. You are my sunrise."

"Sir . . ." I caught myself. "I mean . . . Christian . . ." He laughed at me, and I easily laughed too. "Christian. I've wanted to call you that for such a long time." I rested my forehead against his chest. "But some part of me will miss calling you *sir*."

He raised my eyes to him. He had transformed too. His bright eyes seemed relaxed, even content. All aspects of cynicism seemed to have melted from his smile. He sounded kind, not arrogant. "Well, erase the word from your vocabulary," he said. "At least when it comes to me."

"You really meant it, Christian? You want me to be your wife?"

"Yes, Jeannette, of course, yes." He pulled me to a couch to sit with him. "Last night seemed like a dream to me. I'll have to keep reminding myself that we are together so I won't wake in the night in my tent and wonder if I didn't make it all up. Colonel Eshton waits for me in Washington."

"Will we come to regret this? When you have gone to battle, will it be worse because we will miss each other so badly? If we had been as we were . . ."

"We would have still loved each other, even if we didn't know it. It would have been a different kind of pain but pain just the same." He touched a hand to my cheek. "You've given me a reason to fight, Jeannette. You've given me a reason to want to come back to Fortitude. I go with a lighter, braver heart than I would have done before."

"When will you leave?"

"If you'll agree to it, let's marry before the week is out. And I will join Colonel Eshton soon after."

"But can we have a few days, at least, as man and wife?"

He sighed. "I've already been here too long. I didn't want to leave Fortitude until you were safely home, and when you were, well, I didn't want to leave you. But we can steal a few days more. No one would blame us. Who knows how long we'll be separated?"

I felt my bright energy lessen. So much time had been wasted. I wished I had known how he felt. I wished the whole month could have been ours. My eyes fell, but he lifted my face again and kissed me.

"Jeannette, don't think of it now," he said. "We have today. Let's celebrate today. Let's go to Dayton and order a wedding dress for you. We'll tell Reverend Jordan to expect us at the altar."

"I don't need a fancy dress. One of my own will do well enough. It doesn't seem right to be so extravagant now."

"I suppose you're right. But let me spoil you another way. I can take you somewhere when the fighting is over. We can discover the world together—Paris, Florence. You've never traveled."

I laughed. Was this what it felt like to have prayers answered? "It's almost too big, too beautiful, to think about," I said. "But I will imagine it every day, us at sea, riding over the waves in a mighty ship. It will keep me going while you're gone. You will write?"

"Always. As much as I can. You will never be far from my thoughts, dear Jeannette. But here we are again talking about separation. Let's go out."

"In a bit, Christian. First, can we share our news with Missus Livingston? She may have seen us in the yard last night. I don't want her to think wrong things about us." I was silent a moment, then added, "And Founder."

He furrowed his brow, and I saw a note of concern flash across his face. "What about Founder?"

"I've known her since I came to Fortitude. She is a solitary being, but I like her. I think she is suspicious."

"Of us?"

"Christian, who is she? I know she belongs here just as well as Missus Livingston or I. But why?"

He nodded slowly. "Like everyone else, she came north with our population from Belle Meade. She has been"—he paused and seemed to be searching for words—"a kind of counselor to me. She looks out for me."

"Like Dorinda did for me?"

"Yes." He lit up like he'd found what he'd been looking for. "Yes, you could say that. Very much like your Dorinda. Founder has indeed looked after me since I was a boy."

Before I could say or ask anything more, he stood.

"Now," he said, "we must go. Get your things. I'm eager for our new life to begin."

He kissed me again with such warmth and eagerness that all I could say was, "All right."

I went to my room for a bonnet and shawl, though I was sure the day was too nice to need them. When I came downstairs, I found Missus Livingston near the storage, taking inventory of the supplies that had been collected for the soldiers.

"We must get a wagon packed up," she said when she perceived me next to her. "It's time for these goods to go where they are needed." She held a list in one hand, a short pencil in the other, but she held the pencil floating just above the paper as though she'd forgotten that one needed to touch the other. She stared vacantly at the neat stacks and bundles.

"Where will it all go?"

"Colonel Eshton has written, and likely it will go to troops on the western side of Virginia, not far from here. Someone from the village will deliver everything."

I placed a hand over her hand with the floating pencil. "Missus Livingston," I said, "you've spoken to Mr. Colchester?"

"Yes, he was just here. I must confess, I'm stunned by what he's told me. He's going to marry you?"

"Yes, isn't it wonderful?" I smiled and squeezed her hand.

She looked at me, and I could see her forehead, right above her eyes, was pinched with doubt and concern.

"Are you sure?" she asked. "Sure that this is what you want?"

"Yes, of course! I think it's the most beautiful miracle ever."

"But dear, that's what I mean. It's so unexpected. I know this may sound old fashioned, but really, a man like Mr. Colchester doesn't marry schoolteachers or . . ."

She turned away, and I let go of her. I knew the rest of her unspoken sentence, but we had gone beyond that.

"Say it, Missus Livingston. I need to hear it."

"He is a white man. Are you sure he means to marry you? I know you both have history where white men are accustomed to having mixed-race mistresses . . ."

Still she couldn't say it. I knew the word, though I had not heard it spoken aloud since I was a child: *placée*. It is what my mother would have been had she lived—as good as a wife but less than a wife. Many fair-skinned negro women lived this way in Louisiana, with their white husbands in their own homes while they maintained white families elsewhere. Placées even bore them children, but nothing was sanctified by church or law. One could say they were only a step or two above the fancy girls in whorehouses. I refused to believe I had escaped that fate in Mississippi only to end up as Christian's mistress now. I'd rather die alone.

"We are not going to be like that! He wants to marry me."

"My dear . . ."

"No!" I cried and stomped my foot. "I believe him. Why shouldn't I?"

"Jeannette Bébinn, from the moment you entered this house, you have felt like a daughter to me. I blame myself for not speaking to you sooner. He changed so much after you arrived. I thought he might be fond of you, but—"

I interrupted. "You admit I have been a good influence on him?"

She hesitated. "Yes, but what about his influence on you? He may mean well, but . . ." She paused. "There are laws. And you have no one else to protect you."

I chafed. I didn't think of myself as needing protection. I hadn't thought of legality. Laws, in my mind, never existed in my favor. What Madame Bébinn had done to me was proof of that. I did believe, though, that Missus Livingston had my best interests at heart. I couldn't be angry with her. Still, I was unsettled. By law, I might not have a choice about how I lived with Mr. Colchester.

"It will be all right," I told her. "Please. Just leave us alone."

My mind was so thick with worry that when I got to the hall, I walked with my hand on the wall to steady myself, like a blind woman in somebody else's house. Mr. Colchester met me there. He held a picnic basket and had a plain gray blanket folded and draped over one shoulder. He took my hand, and we made our way on foot away from the mansion and toward the river. We walked awhile in silence before he finally spoke.

"Jeannette? You are not the same as you were earlier. What's wrong?"

"Missus Livingston is worried. And now so am I."

"She has scared you. I see that." He stopped and turned to face me. "What did she say?"

"Nothing that wasn't true. I forgot about your position and didn't think about the consequences."

"Position? Consequences?"

I felt his agitation growing and gently pulled my hand from his tightening grip.

"Christian," I said quietly, "white men don't marry women like me."

"And do you think I've been just as thoughtless? Truthfully, Jeannette, I erased any doubts on that score long ago. I don't care what the world thinks."

"What about Founder? What did she say?"

"She is a puzzle, and I'm sure you already know that. But she will be what she will be." He reached for me again, but I evaded his grasp.

"You said she counsels you?"

"It doesn't matter! I know my own heart; I don't need counsel. Let's not think about it anymore, Jeannette. I could get blasted to kingdom come by the end of the summer, and none of this will matter. The time is precious. We're here now. Please. I don't want to waste it."

He took my hand and led me down to the riverbank, where he spread out the blanket and placed the basket on it.

"Let's sit here and talk as lovers—an experience neither of us knows well."

I sat on the blanket and sighed. Lord knows how much I wanted to put away my worry. I was happy enough to ignore Missus Livingston and Founder, but there were questions in me that demanded more. I wouldn't be easy until he delivered the answers. "Christian, I need to know."

"What? Ask me questions. I will do my best."

"Don't laugh. How did you come to love me? I must ask. If I don't understand it, it will be hard for me to trust it."

"You don't trust me?"

"No, I do. Right now I do. But if I don't understand why you love me, I'll question it. Thoughts will come to me as time goes on, and they might make me doubt you. And you'll be off fighting. You won't be able to reassure me then."

He ran his hand over my hair, and the rough curls came loose from their clasp and fell to my shoulders. I let them stay that way. "You seemed so open, so self-possessed. That night when we spoke in the library, drunk as I was, I could tell that you knew your own mind. You weren't easily influenced by others."

"I was different from what you'd known before?"

He kissed me on the forehead. "In the past I have been fond of women with the same intelligence. But I never had the confidence to pursue them. You, on the other hand . . ."

"I encouraged you?"

"No, not directly anyway. But you made me think better of myself. The way you listened to me, challenged me." He laughed. "Even scolded me! But strangely you made me feel I could be a different person. I could come to not care about certain things."

"You said last night that you didn't think you were worthy of love. Why? You've never loved before? You are a man of means, Christian. It seems so strange that you've never been attached to someone. Not even before Miss Chamberlain."

"I am not as confident as I might seem. And I have loved only to realize later that a beloved's beauty did not always match up with what was within. I've been disappointed by Miss Chamberlain, for example. I was once fond of her. In fact, it took me a while to learn what you seem to have gathered after only a few hours of observing her."

I was glad he mentioned this, because I had a deep curiosity about what had happened.

"I feel badly for her," I said. "It doesn't seem fair that I should gain what she's lost. I know what I felt when I thought I couldn't have you. I wouldn't wish those feelings on her."

He stretched himself out on the blanket, leaned back on his elbows, and laughed. "Believe me, she is not feeling what you would have felt. I overheard her talking about what would happen if I were killed in battle. She was worried for herself—what money she would have, whether all my possessions would be left to her. Hell, she even declared she'd have a lawyer look into it once we were married and I had gone away."

I shook my head.

"Now, I will confess, this is the one wicked thing I did: I created a rumor that I had arranged for my estate to be sold and the funds donated to a charitable institution upon my death. My widow would receive only a modest living. You can see for yourself how the scheme worked out. You haven't seen her lately, have you? She is absent of her own accord."

I tilted my head toward him. "So she will not join you in battle after all, sir?"

"Sarcasm? From you, Jeannette?" He laughed, and I couldn't help but laugh myself.

"Perhaps she'll go with her next conquest," I said. "The Union needs eager soldiers."

We laughed a good deal more and enjoyed the bread, cold meat, and fruit he'd brought for us. I pushed aside my doubts and was determined to hold on to this frail bubble of happiness. Our days after that continued in the same vein. We feasted on joy, and for the first time in my life, I felt full.

In the back of my mind, though, I still thought of what Missus Livingston had said. And I did consider whether it would be better for me to keep Christian at arm's length until the wedding. But I had a strong sense that our time was short. I wanted to store up kisses and caresses, as many as I could, enough to carry me through the long and unknowable time we would be separated.

I gloried in his attention. He became my sole focus, my whole world. For those short, sweet days I didn't pray because I thought all my prayers had been answered. He was at once my hope and my heaven. The grounds around Fortitude became our Eden.

Too quickly the days of courtship slipped by. I laid out the elegant brown silk dress that Aunt Nancy Lynne had made for me so long ago. It might not be fashionable, but it seemed right to wear it now when I was about to step into a world where I felt truly free. Mr. Colchester insisted on one gift, which I accepted: a small but exquisite lace veil sewn in the fashion of the calottes, the veils that New Orleans women wore to church. It represented our connection to Louisiana and made me hopeful that, even if we never returned there, I would have some memory of the land in him, and he would have the same in me. The next day I would pull on the silk, drape the lace over my head, and walk hand in hand with him into my new life as Missus Colchester.

When I went to bed that night, I had nothing to trouble me. A full moon illuminated slivers of cloud floating through a serene sky. I was determined to sleep and not dream of strange children or unfulfilled longing. I would dream of union and of my husband in his dark-blue uniform coming home from the battlefield whole and fit.

Only I didn't dream at all. I dropped into sleep as though I'd fallen off a cliff into a dark cavern. My sleep was deep but not refreshing. When I awoke, it was as though I had a rope looped around my chest and hands were pulling on it, drawing me out of the depths. The sensation was so powerful I felt the rope tugged me to sit straight up from my pillows. I awoke and opened my eyes to see Founder, sitting at the foot of the bed, staring at me like she would burn a hole into my soul.

Chapter 14

I stifled a scream.

"What are you doing in here?" I pushed back against the bed's headboard, trying to get as far away from her as I could.

"Came to get you ready." She moved closer and regained the space I'd put between us. "For today."

"Founder, I can dress myself, thank you."

She put her face close to mine. "Yeah, you can do a lot of things," she sneered. "You one smart gal, I'll give you that. But when it comes to what's life and what's death? You ain't nothing but a baby."

"Founder . . ."

"White men don't keep promises on their own," she whispered. "You have to hold them to the fire."

I stammered. "What?"

"I was a placée."

"I see." My hands shook, and I gripped the covers.

"Blind fool!" She slapped the bedding and, by default, my leg underneath it. "You don't see a damn thing. If you were blind, I'd have pity for you. But you just stupid. Stupid little girl." She pointed a finger at me, and for the first time I noticed a ring, thick and gold, on her index finger.

"You have to make a white man keep his promises. I was on him every day about my babies. I told him it was a sin keeping people in chains, profiting off their blood and labor. He'd go to hell if he didn't atone. Never let him forget that.

"Don't think he listened until he started getting sick. Probably even saw the gates of hell opening up to greet him because fast as you please, he had a lawyer in the house settling matters."

"Did he—did he . . ." I hardly knew what to ask. ". . . keep his promise?"

She sniffed. "Yeah, in that lopsided way that white folks do. They give you what you want from one hand while stealing from you with the other. But I made do." She leaned back, crossed her arms, and looked me up and down. "Now, what we gonna do about you?"

She was crazy. Must be crazy. I surveyed the distance between us and the door, but like she had read my mind, she grabbed me by the wrist. I cried out softly.

"You've done crossed a line, child. I don't fault you for it—you didn't know a line was there. I ain't got nothing against you. Just remember that."

I raised my free arm to defend myself, but just as quickly she let me go. She pushed herself up from the bed and lowered herself to the floor. She walked stiffly, like her joints were sore. I wondered how long she'd been sitting there while I slept. And had she stolen my dreams, drawing them out of me with a magnet or some other item full of voodoo and ill wishes? I got up and looked over my dress and veil. The veil seemed wrong, like it had been handled and replaced, but not in the way I had left it. I had a sense that Founder had done this, perhaps even cursed the veil. I wouldn't wear it.

I rushed to my door and opened it. I wanted to run to Mr. Colchester. I wanted to tell him how Founder had frightened me and how I needed him to tell me again that we would be married. I went five, maybe six steps down the hall before I stopped. The first rays of the morning sun were washing over the gallery. Standing there in the light must have brought me back to my right mind, because I looked down at my bare feet and at my plain calico nightgown. What would he say to see me running through Fortitude like that?

Founder's words had hurt like she had reached inside me, grabbed pieces of my soul, and scattered them across the bedroom floor. I needed to gather the pieces, to gather myself again so I could think properly. I withdrew into my room, turned the key in the door's lock, and sank to my knees.

"The wedding is today," I told myself. "The wedding is today. The wedding is today. The wedding is today."

I said the words as a reminder and a comfort. As long as Christian and I married today, nothing Founder had said would matter. He would show her to be wrong, so simply and utterly wrong. If we spoke of it at all, we would do it after the wedding, when Christian would make me laugh about it and probably make me promise never to doubt his love or his intentions ever again.

I was so eager to get to that moment. I poured water from my pitcher, and after I had washed, I felt better. I dressed carefully. Instead of the veil I fastened in my hair a white lily, taken from the vase of blooms on my bedside table.

I couldn't eat. I didn't want to sit with Missus Livingston. I only wanted to get to the church, so I stayed in the hall and waited for Mr. Colchester. I heard a carriage outside and opened the door to find Poney ready to take us to the church. He waved and smiled at me. For the first time that day I felt hopeful.

Then I heard her voice—Founder's voice, weighty and heated, raining down words on someone's recalcitrant head. It could only be Mr. Colchester's. They were in the library.

I ran to the door and berated myself for not going to him sooner. If I had, we would have been standing together against her onslaught. We would have been together. Instead I found him alone in front of her, his arms crossed and his head bowed. He looked, for all his height above Founder, like a small boy being scolded.

A small boy.

Suddenly it was like a bolt of lightning struck the room, filling it with clarity and danger all at once. Mr. Colchester saw me, and his head sank lower, again like a boy. Founder came at me full of bluster like a storm. She grabbed my arm and pulled me toward him. She sounded like . . . she sounded like . . .

A mother.

"I don't care how many thousands of acres her daddy owned—she ain't got none of that now. And in the eyes of the law you won't be legal. We've come too far for you to mess this up now."

I wanted to ask him what she was saying, but there were too many layers I didn't understand. I could only stare at Founder's mouth moving so fast, and her eyes creased tiny with her anger.

"She may talk nice, and she may be educated, but she's still colored. And the world knows it." She looked at me and shook a finger in my face. "You don't get to have him. My son was meant for something better."

"Your son?"

"Yeah." She clapped her hands hard, twice. "MY SON. Stupid gal, he ain't white! No more than you!"

She dropped my arm, and by the grace of God, I didn't fall. I grasped the folds of my skirt in front of me so I could hold on to myself. I had nothing else.

"What is this?" I couldn't get the words out. I stared at Christian until he finally had to look at me.

"Promises," he said. "It's about promises I didn't make."

"Promises I worked hard to get! For you! For everyone!" Founder shook a fist in my face. "Like I told you, I held that man to the fire— wouldn't let him get out of it." She turned to Christian again. "And where would we all be if I hadn't done it! Now you standing there whining like you done had to sacrifice something. You who've never done a lick of fieldwork in your life."

"But we are here!" he protested. "Safe! And I got us here! Why can't I have my own life now?"

"You know why!"

"Christian," I said. "Your father?"

"My father," he said. "He put restrictions on my inheritance. Remember, I told you that."

"Yes."

"From the moment he was born, I told him!" Founder was sparking, leaning on one foot and the other, dancing with the energy. "'My baby can pass for white! You've got to claim him! You've got to!'" She stomped her foot. "'I will curse you, Louis Colchester!' That's what I said. 'I will curse you to my dying day if you don't do right by our boy.'"

"Jeannette, he raised me as white," Christian said. "Founder looked after me, but . . ."

"He didn't know I was his mama. Not right off. His daddy wouldn't let me, but I didn't argue that. He was right. Wasn't safe, not when you was young. And you went to school, got educated, wore good clothes."

"What happened?" I asked.

"The old weasel got sick and died—that's what he did. Had the nerve to leave a will with conditions. His conditions."

Christian faced Founder, but he spoke to me. "I could only inherit the estate if I keep living as white."

"But how could he do that?"

"Oh, he did it all right," said Founder. "Lopsided, like I said. Gave me what I wanted with one hand but took away our freedom with the other." She laughed. "At least that's what he thought!"

I looked at Christian. "You sold Belle Meade," I said quietly.

"Yes. Founder thought of it. As long as the estate was mine, I could do what I wanted. I freed our people, sold the house and land, then moved everyone who wanted to come north to establish Lower Knoll."

"Had to do it," Founder said. "Who was gonna honor that freedom if they all stayed down there?"

"But," I said slowly, "what does this have to do with us?"

"The restriction still exists. It's possible that if it were discovered that I'm not white, I could lose everything. Any distant family member could challenge my right to dispose of the plantation, including the slaves."

"That ain't gonna happen," Founder said. "Not if you married to the right family."

I sighed. This I understood. She meant to a white woman. With money.

"That would seal it. No one would doubt a thing. You see how the people round here look up to him. Like that Chamberlain gal." She pressed a finger against my shoulder. "He marry you? How that gonna look? How long before he's the talk of the neighborhood and that talk gets around and somebody start asking questions."

Tears rose in my throat. "Christian, why didn't you tell me?"

"I'll tell you why! He thought he was white enough to do what he wanted, just like his daddy. I guess he's white enough after all." She planted her hands on her hips. "And I'll tell you another thing."

"Founder!" He spoke in a tone I hadn't heard since the night I'd met him.

"No! She got to know it all! What does it matter, if she loves you like you say!"

She twisted her hips and drew out the word *loves* in an ugly sneer. I stifled a sob.

"What?" I stammered.

She leered at me. "You wanna know? Ask him how that fire got started—the one that nearly killed you and that little girl."

Suddenly the room seemed crowded—crowded with questions, with unspoken words. And even more—it was as though Founder had flung the library doors wide open and every soul that owned a role in making this moment had stepped right through: the residents of Lower

Knoll, Louis Colchester, my papa, and my mother. The room felt so full I thought I couldn't breathe. I saw my mother's face before me—her steady eyes, her stillness.

He was not who I'd thought, and I wanted to believe it didn't matter, but it did. It mattered for all the people of Lower Knoll, and it mattered that he hadn't told me any of this himself. He said he loved me. But my mother's face on my mind made me think of how large a man's love could be—that he would burn down a house to keep me near him. Her face said that when there was love so big, there was no room for your own. That was why she had looked the way she did in the locket—acquiescence. Because she'd had to carry her love small, like in a pocketbook, out of sight. Or worse—she'd had to carry the small love in her bare hands, the fingers gently clenched as though she were walking around holding two butterflies. With her hands like that, my mama couldn't hold anything else. Not even me. For all I know, that's why she died when I was born.

Now, standing there, suffocating in that too-full room, I got a sense of how small my love was. And I felt the stupid girl in me that Founder saw. Christian didn't come to me through all those souls. He didn't reach for me or try to hold me. I had no words. I thought of Madame. This was what it was to love and have the heart betrayed. This must have been what she'd felt when she'd realized Papa didn't belong to her. A kind of crazy did open up inside you, and it would be easy to just fall into it. The crazy felt like it might be comforting, like I could scream and scream all day and no one would pay me no mind because they knew I had a right to do it. Madame had been screaming for years.

From the crazy I could find the right to be uncivil, then the right to be mean. Nothing would matter much after that—I could do any evil that came to mind and call it vengeance. Madame had gone that far.

Why didn't I go that way? Because I felt what only could have been my mama's hands, firm but kind, on my shoulders. The force of them turned me, turned me away from the awful I could have released into that room. She turned me away, and I ran.

In my room I sank into a chair and stared out the window. I dropped my head in my hands as his words of the past several months came back to me. How many times had he stressed our similarities? He'd already known: we were indeed exactly alike. But only I, not he, had been prepared to come to the altar on my own and free. He would have had an entire village on his back, and he had tried to hide this burden from me.

I don't know how long I sat there. I didn't eat; I didn't drink. I watched the light shift and fade. I changed into my plain gray dress, removed the lily from my hair, and marveled over the change that had broken my life in only a few hours. I felt too tired and weak to cry. The shock wound its way through my body.

Finally there was a soft knock at the door.

"Come in, Christian," I said.

His hand grazed my cheek, but I didn't rise to greet him. He sat on the end of the bed, almost in the exact spot where Founder had been.

"Tell me one thing about Founder," I said. "Why was she placée?"

"He didn't have a white wife to complain."

Like Madame, I thought.

"Neither do I."

I looked at him sharply. "Do you expect that of me? And then what? You would marry Miss Chamberlain or someone like her?"

"It doesn't have to be like that," he said. "I love you."

"My papa loved my mother." I took the locket from my neck and placed the opened piece in his hands. "And she died with a white woman screaming over her body. Your father loved Founder, and she lives up there by herself and haunts this house like a ghost. Is that what love does to a life? I don't want it."

He closed the locket and returned it to me but held on to my hands. "Then come away."

"Where?"

"Anywhere we're not known. No one would have to know that you're not white. You can pass as I do. You've done it before."

"I did it to save my life," I said. "*My* life. Not so that I could live as someone else."

"What does it matter?"

"It matters. I knew what it was to live under another name and have no voice. And I lived in fear, every single day. I won't live that way again. It would be like being enslaved, only from inside me." I pulled away from him. "That's the truth of why you haven't married before, isn't it?"

"What do you mean?"

"You were afraid of being found out by your wife! You knew you had to live with that possibility, even more so than you do now, and you'd have even more to lose."

I stood and paced the room, the realizations coming quickly.

"That's why you wanted to marry me. Because you knew if I did find out, I wouldn't leave. I would have to stay. Stay attached to you. And I'd have to live on those terms because—oh my God, Christian—you thought I valued a white husband more than I valued you."

I stopped in front of him.

"What about the fire?" I demanded.

His shoulders slumped. "I wanted to keep you close, to stay in the mansion. I didn't intend for anyone to get hurt. I didn't know the girl was in there."

He lunged for me and gathered me in his arms. "Don't you see? I couldn't stand for you to be far from me. For the first time I felt a true connection with another human being—you. Without fear, without remorse. You loved me as I am. I couldn't risk losing you."

I didn't return his embrace. I removed myself from his arms as I would shed a coat or a wrap, and I sat in my chair again.

"Christian," I said quietly. "You don't know or have any respect for who you are. I can't be expected to make up that deficit for you."

He fell to his knees and grasped my hands. "We talked about sin once, remember? You said a man shouldn't have to pay for one sin over and over. I have atoned. I have freed my father's slaves and provided them a way of making a living if they choose it. Why can't I have my life now?"

"But their living can't be maintained without you."

"They are not free if I must be their caretaker. And neither am I free."

"I pity you, but I can't enter this jail with you." I moved away from him and opened the door.

"You love me," he insisted.

"God help me, I do." I pushed my forehead against the door so I wouldn't have to look at him. "And I shall suffer a good while because of it. I'm tired now. Please go."

He crossed the threshold and turned. "What are you going to do, Jeannette?"

"I don't know."

"Then do one thing for me. Consider a life away from here. Please, Jeannette. We've been through too much to lose each other now."

I nodded.

"You will think about it?"

"Goodbye."

"I love you."

I pushed the door closed behind him.

I was too exhausted to undress. I lay on the bed, fully clothed, and closed my eyes. The darkness that overcame me seemed palpable—thick enough to float on. I was Ophelia on the Miami River, drifting away. There was an ease about it, an effortless drifting in which my clothing didn't weigh me down or make me feel cold and wet. I longed to open my eyes and see sky and green branches passing overhead, but there was only darkness. And that was all I was—loneliness and darkness. As my awareness returned, I remembered the wordless prayer I had uttered last year. I could summon aid again. It would be one grasp at light. I had to believe God would not forsake me in this. I uttered a simple bit of scripture, remembered from years ago:

"Be not far from me; for trouble is near; for there is none to help."

That was what I needed: Help. Divine help and loving aid. I had to believe it would come. And because I believed it, I felt calmer. I fell into a deep and nourishing sleep.

Chapter 15

This was what our love made me, I decided: someone capable of great love and compassion. I knew from Papa what it was to be loved. Christian taught me that I could return it and grow from it. It gave me a new kind of strength and certainty. And clarity. I awoke the next morning with a clear idea of what I was going to do—what I had to do if I was going to go on being this person who had grown from our love. I would have to go on and be this strong self and do it without him.

The only thing I could do was walk away from him. And it would be easier if I allowed myself to love him even as I was leaving him. Trying to stop loving him would be like trying to pretend I was fully white. I'd have to twist myself up too badly for it to work. If I'd sat there in my room and tried to make myself stop loving him before I left, then I would have had to sit there forever. My love wouldn't break like that. Instead I let it be. I figured I could breathe like that, move like that.

So I whispered "I love you" even as I packed my few belongings in a small black case. I whispered "I love you" as I slipped each finger into my gloves. I said "I love you," letting the words float up the staircase into the air of Fortitude Mansion, where he might find them later when he woke.

I slipped outside and started walking. I told myself to think like I was planting love into the soil with each step, because that was what would make the next step possible. I just kept walking, and with those steps he was soon behind me, and I began my journey into another new world.

I walked to the village as though it were any other school day. I was wondering what would be the best way to go without being seen or having the children make too much of a fuss. But then I saw Poney coming toward me, heading in the other direction with the wagon of supplies. I waved him to stop. "Poney, may I ride with you?"

He shook his head. "Oh, Miss Bébinn, I'm going far. Taking these supplies to the Union soldiers in western Virginia."

"Yes, I know. I need to go far, far away."

He looked down at me, his face clouded with doubt. He shifted his feet and pushed his hat back on his head. "Mr. Colchester ain't gonna like that."

I put my hand on the wheel closest to me. "That's why you can't tell him, or anyone else, where I've gone."

He didn't move to help me into the wagon, so I put my bag on the floor and pulled myself up onto the seat next to him.

"Just keep on going like you were, Poney. It'll be fine. Just go."

We thought it was thunder in the distance. An odd breeze blew about us, changing direction one way to another. Poney whistled to the horses to settle them, and we moved into what seemed like a summer storm. It was cloudy, but I couldn't see any dark masses of rain. Maybe it was around the bend or across a field. Maybe the storm was on the other side of a hill in the distance. We kept going.

Suddenly Poney and I looked at each other. The ground now shook fiercely, like a giant was pounding it with his fists. He slapped the reins, and we went faster. I thought I glimpsed movement off to my right— someone, maybe many someones, running. A tremendous boom split the air, and I grasped the sides of my head, pressing my bonnet to my ears. Then a series of shots volleyed through the trees. We were riding into danger, but there was no way to tell which way to go to get out of it. A sidetrack veered off to the right, and Poney took it, still urging the horses on. It took us alongside a field, off the main road, but still the ground rumbled beneath us.

Then a sound like a rattle being shaken over us. A small piece of wood from the side of the wagon splintered and struck me on the right side. On my left—Poney fell against me.

"Poney!"

He grasped his left side and sank down to the floor. The reins slipped from his hands, and I grabbed them. I stood to reposition myself and put my weight behind the horses. I pushed them on. Poney groaned.

I was turning us when I saw a man in gray running toward me, his musket in one hand. With the other he was trying to grab the bridle of one of the horses. I pulled up the horses and pulled the pistol from my pocket. I stood and fired. Miss Maude would have scolded me. I didn't aim for his leg. He had a weapon, and he was trying to control the cart. I had to aim high.

The shot got him in the shoulder. He fell backward and seemed shocked. That was his arrogance, I suppose. I got the horses moving, and in a moment Poney and I were past him.

Suddenly a horde of men advanced on my right, some firing, some running with bayonets on the end of their rifles. I was relieved to see a swath of navy blue. Union soldiers. One of them ran up alongside and yelled, "That way! Get behind us!"

I nodded, and as I turned, I saw now how the positions were. I pushed through the line and went a few hundred yards until I was past the fighting but still close enough to hear the commotion of gunfire. I stopped the wagon and climbed into the back to find a parcel of bandages.

Poney's face had turned gray. He pulled open his shirt and looked down.

"Good God," he said.

I pushed him to lean forward. He bled from two places, front and back. The musket ball must have gone through him. I bound up the wounds using what were probably the bandages I'd made that night with Belinda Chamberlain.

"It's all right, Poney." I kept repeating it because I didn't know what else to say. "You'll be all right."

I climbed up and took the reins again. There had to be doctors somewhere. And they couldn't be far. I figured that they would be behind the battlefield, so I kept going in the direction away from the rear of the advancing soldiers.

Soon I came upon a large pavilion made of canvas, and I could see people moving about underneath it. Then I saw the rows of cots—it was a field hospital.

"Help!" I cried out. "Help us!"

Two men reached us first—one white with a thick beard and wire spectacles and the other a colored man who jumped up to help Poney to the ground. The white man examined his wound.

"We brought supplies from Dayton for the Union soldiers," I said. "Got caught in the fight just over there." I climbed down from the wagon.

"Get him a bed," the white man said. He seemed to be a doctor.

"Thank you, sir," Poney said. He looked at me.

"Go on. I'm all right," I said.

He leaned into the colored man, and they walked carefully toward the tent.

"Are you all right, ma'am? Do you need food?"

My legs felt weak beneath me. "I want to sit down."

I took his arm, and he led me to the front of an enclosed tent. A small folding table and a few chairs made of wood were set out there. I sat, and he went into the tent and returned with a small metal cup filled with coffee.

"Drink this," he said.

The warm liquid revived me. "Thank you," I said.

He went back in the tent and brought out a bound cloth that he put in my lap.

"You'll be hungry soon if you aren't already. Eat those."

The cloth contained two biscuits. My stomach suddenly rumbled to see them.

"Take your time. Not like you'll be going anywhere anytime soon."

He walked away. The wounded were coming in quickly now. Some walked, and some were carried on makeshift gurneys. There was yelling everywhere, filling the air—men yelling commands, men yelling in pain.

And yet I fell asleep in that chair.

I awoke to the sound of my name, from a voice that was warm and familiar. But it wasn't Poney's.

"Jeannette! Jeannette Bébinn!"

I opened my eyes. The face, now weathered and bearded, was still handsome. He pulled off his hat. I would have known him anywhere.

"Silas! What are you doing here?"

"I assist Dr. Nelson. Probably be a doctor myself after all this. I help him, especially when we get colored patients like the man who came in with you."

"Poney—is he all right?" I blinked, and the events of the afternoon began to come back to me. I sat up in the chair.

"He's gonna be fine." Silas went into the tent and returned with more coffee. He knelt down and looked at me while I drank. "You did a good job getting him bandaged and all. Wound like that, a man can bleed to death."

"Where are we?"

"Not far from Philippi. Fighting been going on here for weeks. We follow the action. We'll have the wounded here sent to proper hospitals in a few days. Then we'll move on. Like I said, we follow the action."

"Silas, can I go with you? I can help."

He sat back on his heels and rubbed his beard. "That's up to Mother B. She looks after the nurses."

"Who is that?"

"Missus Baxter. We call her Mother B."

I stood, removed my bonnet, and brushed away what I could of the road dust on my dress. "Please, Silas. Take me to her."

He escorted me to another tent. Inside a woman was seated at a desk writing. She looked up as we entered. She had soft white hair parted in the middle and cut almost as short as a man's.

"Mother B., this here is Miss Jeannette Bébinn. Rode here with the wagon of supplies that just came in. Wants to be one of your nurses."

The woman checked the watch she wore fastened to her waist and wrote a few more lines. Then she addressed me and examined me with calm, watery blue eyes. "Do you faint at the sight of blood?"

Her voice had a firm gentleness that reminded me of Missus Livingston. My heart ached to realize she might be worried sick about me. I resolved to write to her when I could.

"She and the elder gentleman who got shot rode through the fight today. He was sitting next to her. She got him here—bound the wound herself."

Mother B. stood and looked me up and down. "This is true?"

I nodded.

"Take me to him."

We walked through to the cots under the pavilion. At times she paused to put a hand to a forehead or check a pulse. When we got to Poney, he was asleep. His wound had been cleaned and freshly bandaged. Mother B. went to a nearby table, where she took a cloth and dipped it in a bowl of water. She wrung it out and placed it on Poney's forehead.

"He's a good deal bigger than you," she said. "How did you manage?"

I described how he had fallen—my struggle to get pressure on the wound and to bind him round. Mother B. nodded her approval.

"All right. We can use you. I have an extra cot in my tent. You may stay there tonight. We will make arrangements for you tomorrow."

Fanny had spoken often of God, and I am certain God brought me to this place, where I would have both shelter and purpose. Poney had been wounded, but he would survive. When he was well enough for the return trip home, I reminded him not to tell the inhabitants of Lower Knoll where I'd gone.

"Are you sure? Mr. Colchester be something frantic by now."

"He won't be there. He's joined the fighting," I said. "As for anyone else . . ." I paused and thought for a moment. "Tell them I took the train to New York."

Chapter 16

When Mother B. made me a field nurse, I felt like I had my own part to play in the fighting. I even had a uniform: a white cotton cap that I wore over my hair and a dress with a high neck and long apron, both white. The white didn't make much sense to me, considering how we worked in such dirty circumstances—dressing bloody wounds, walking through mud. But then I realized our camps were sometimes not too far from the battlefield. Wearing white, we could stand out, especially if we were outside—an enemy shooter wouldn't aim for us.

I didn't do much by way of healing care in those early days. The wounded who could survive were taken to schoolhouses, homes, or churches—buildings that were transformed into makeshift hospitals. The ones left in the pavilion tent under the watchful eyes of Dr. Nelson and Mother B. were dying. We kept them as comfortable as we could with whiskey and sometimes laudanum. But it seemed the best thing I could do was sit with them and talk. Some wanted to hear a friendly voice. A few asked questions about my life, how I'd turned up "in this godforsaken place."

One man, a young lieutenant we called Teddy, asked me that one evening.

"Is it really godforsaken, Teddy?" I said. "You're here, aren't you? You're not lost in that field out there."

He grimaced and turned away, but I leaned in closer. He had the metallic smell of dried blood, dirt, tobacco, and gunpowder mingled about him. His shirt was yellow with his fevered sweat, his torso bloated with infection.

"I'm not supposed to be here either, Teddy. Look at me."

He squinted at me. I realized he probably needed glasses to see and had lost them in the fighting.

"I'm colored, Teddy. Had a white papa. My mama was a slave."

His eyes widened. "You were a slave?"

"I was. I ran away."

He grasped my hand. His skin felt cold and thin. "What the abolitionists say—it's true?"

I unbuttoned one of my sleeves and pushed it up. I showed him the dark line on my forearm where I had defended myself from Missus Everett's whipping. "Here is a scar from being whipped. I can't show you the rest. Wouldn't be proper."

I told him a bit about Fanny and how Aunt Nancy Lynne had lost her children but helped me run away.

"The worst part," I said, "is the white people making us think we're not human. That we're beneath them and this is the way the world is supposed to be."

Teddy lifted his head slightly, then rested it back again, like it was too heavy for the effort. "It's worth it, then."

I wet a cloth in the basin near his bed and put it on his forehead. He was burning up. "What is, Teddy?"

"The fighting. If we can right that wrong, get people free, it's worth it."

He didn't say anything else. I thought he'd passed out or fallen asleep. But when I got up to leave, he stirred.

"Miss?"

"Yes, Teddy?"

"Would you mind writing a letter for me? To my mother?"

When he asked this, Mother B. happened to be going by and stopped. She came over to us.

"You know how to read and write?" she asked me.

"Yes, ma'am."

She went away and quickly came back with a wooden box that she put on my lap. She showed me how to lift the lid. Inside were paper, a pen, and ink. When the lid was closed again, I could write on it.

"Teddy, tell Miss Bébinn what you want to say. I'll make sure it gets to your family."

He began to talk. I wrote down what he said. He wanted to tell his mother some things. Like how he'd met up in his regiment with a boyhood schoolmate and had a chance to laugh over the mischief they'd gotten into when they were young. They'd let the pigs out into the garden for the fun of rounding them up again, but they were sorry for the damage they'd caused to his mama's squash plants. He talked about the cold soon coming on but said not to send socks or anything. "I'll be just fine. Got everything I need."

Tears welled up in my throat. He was not going to tell his mother, not directly, that he was dying. He was doing it another way—by telling her that her mothering duties were done. That he knew right from wrong, that he loved her, that she had provided for him and he was grateful. He told her about me and why I was writing the letter for him. He said I'd been a slave and he was happy to know many more souls would be saved than lost from the fighting.

When we were finished, he told me how to address it, and he thanked me. I took the box and the letter to Mother B.'s tent.

"Thank you," she said. "The men often need this service. You don't mind?"

"No, ma'am. It's something I can do. Can't keep them from dying."

I went back and sat with Teddy. His face had turned even paler, and I could see he had gone beyond his pain. I heard a percussive rattling in his chest, and I grasped his hand.

"You've been so brave. Your mama is proud of you, so proud." I kept repeating that until the sound in his chest stopped.

I've observed that in those moments, sitting with a dying soldier, everything else falls away—the awful smell of limbs black with gangrene, the noise of horses and wagons coming and going, the thunder of cannons in the battlefield. The world just shrank, and it was me and him, and then, slowly, there was only me. The further his spirit sped away, the more the world recrystallized and I was in it again. But I was aware of what was missing, of a soul departed, and of the space left in the veil where his soul had gone through.

A few weeks later, with the autumn of 1861 bringing a chill into the air, we packed up the field hospital and left for Kentucky. I was relieved to be traveling in that direction. If we had stayed on in Virginia and moved east, I would have feared seeing Mr. Colchester or Colonel Eshton. There was also the chance, however slight, that I could retrace Dorinda's path and make my way eventually to Catalpa Valley.

Silas drove one of the supply wagons, and I rode with him. It seemed like we were made to travel together, like we'd been when we'd run away. Only I wasn't wearing a disguise.

"I heard you telling a man you half-colored. Why you do that? You're light enough to pass, just like when we were on the run."

"I don't want to live that way, always being afraid of who might find out. That's the way I felt when we were running. I can't live like that, living a life that's not mine, like I stole it or something." I thought of Mr. Colchester. "My papa didn't want me to hide."

"You brave, Jeannette. Them soldiers? They do the fighting in the field, but you just as brave as they are."

"I don't know what brave has to do with it. What would you do, Silas? If you were lighter, would you pass?"

He shrugged. "I don't know. Can't imagine looking any other way. But there's one thing that would trouble me, keep me awake at night."

"What's that?"

"I wouldn't want to think like white people do. If being lighter means I might see myself as better than someone else, I don't want no part of that."

He was quiet a few minutes.

"You still young. How come you ain't married?"

I looked away and swallowed. "Almost was."

"What happened?"

"He wanted to pass. I couldn't abide with him like that. And I just told you why."

Silas shook his head. "He a fool, whoever he is."

I smiled.

"Where is he now?"

"I suspect he's fighting now. Not sure where." My throat tightened. "He could be dead for all I know."

After some silence I decided to ask the question that had been on my mind since he'd discovered me in the camp weeks before.

"Silas," I began.

"No." He said it quickly and glanced at me. "No, I wasn't mad at you for leaving me in Philadelphia. You were right. Safer for us to be on our own."

"And you've made your way pretty well since then?"

"Yeah. Being free? Nothing better. I thought it felt fine traveling with Massa Holloway. Thought that was a measure of freedom. But it wasn't. Now that I know real freedom, I know that was nothing, nothing next to this. I'm my own man now."

"How come you aren't married?"

"Ain't ready to set up house. Wanna go where I can buy some land. Be out in the open air. Much as I was grateful to be in a city like

Philadelphia—and I seen New York, too—don't seem a good way to live. Too many people."

I thought of the hills winding down to the river in Dayton and the breeze blowing through the cane of Catalpa Valley. "Yes, I feel the same way."

"When this fighting done, maybe I'll find the right place. Maybe you can think about coming with me then."

I nodded but said nothing. I couldn't see my way into tomorrow, let alone after the war, whenever that might be. I thought of what Mr. Colchester had said—to just think about today. That was what I had, and my hands were full of it—today. In that moment I was sitting with my friend Silas, and a sliver of moon still hung in the morning sky. It was enough.

By April of 1862 we had gone as far south as Tennessee. We were supporting a division of the Army of the Ohio when we got word that we had to pack up quickly and march to aid Major General Grant's regiment, which had been attacked by Confederates the day before. There would be a large counterattack, and Dr. Nelson feared great numbers of dead and wounded, maybe more than we'd ever had. While we were getting ready, I asked him a question.

"How far are we going, sir?"

Like Mother B., he had learned that I could read and write and also fire a musket. I would help clean the guns we used for our defense, and he would talk to me about the fighting while we cleaned the guns and fired them to make sure the cartridges were dry.

"Grant is based near Corinth, Mississippi. We will meet him near the Tennessee River."

I gathered my things, but I was a little scared and confused. I hadn't been in Mississippi since Silas and I had fled it. I ran about looking for him, hoping to ride with him. I figured I'd feel better if I were with him.

But his wagon had already gone, and I had to pile into one carrying Mother B. and two other nurses, Carrie and Martha. The horses trotted fast down the road. Suddenly this thought came to me: I was going to Mississippi, but I would also be closer to home than I had been in years. Could the fighting take us as far as Louisiana? I didn't know what battles, if any, were being fought there. I prayed for Calista and Dorinda, and I touched the stone I still carried in my pocket. It was a small hope. I let that be my comfort as we rushed toward the next battle.

We arrived in the evening and stayed up all night preparing for the incoming wounded. Silas and the men lined up cots. Mother B., Carrie, Martha, and I readied the supplies with the other nurses. Then, at about two in the morning, Mother B. urged us to sleep a little if we could.

"You'll need your rest," she said.

The musket barrage, thundering in the distance like kingdom come, began at daybreak. I pressed my hands over my ears, said a prayer, and got up and dressed as quickly as I could. I ran out to the pavilion tent and waited. Mother B. joined me. Times like this, I wished I had a place where I could see what was going on, like on a hill. The waiting was so hard. It would get to a point, before the first wounded came in, when I could trick myself into thinking that none would come. The Union had been so successful in the fight that none had been hurt and the rebels had all been taken prisoner. But this was nothing but a childish dream.

Silas and the other men soon came running with the stretchers cradling mangled bodies. He stayed to assist Dr. Nelson while the others returned for more. The doctors all did what they could. They extracted musket balls, sewed up bayonet wounds, and, in the worst cases, wielded the amputation saw and removed limbs. Martha and I were the best at bandaging, so once a doctor had completed an operation, like taking a musket ball from a man's leg, she or I would step in and bind the wound while the doctor moved on to another soldier. And another. And another. The pace quickened as the sun rose high in the sky. Cannon fire exploded through the air. No one stopped. No one ate.

Around three o'clock a soldier came riding hard into the hospital area. I was at a table near the edge of the pavilion working on a soldier when I saw him come in. It was Colonel Eshton! His horse was swaying in a strange way. Silas saw what was happening and ran up and pulled Colonel Eshton off and got him on the ground. Turned out the horse had been shot. The ball had struck through the saddle. The colonel had been hit, too, in the leg. Silas had gotten to him just in time, because the horse fell over and died right after. Colonel Eshton would have been crushed under it.

My fingers went cold. Was Mr. Colchester out there in the field? I shut my eyes tight and said a quick prayer. Then I looked to see where they were taking the colonel, but he was past my sight line.

Slowly, as dusk fell, the sounds of the battle, which would be called Shiloh, died away. At dark the stretcher-bearers were sitting on the ground near the tents and eating hardtack. Mother B. went up to them and asked when they were going out again to search for more wounded.

"Ain't no use going out there till morning, ma'am. Ain't worth gettin' shot at in the dark for a man who'll be dead in a few hours anyway."

"Perhaps, sir," she said. "But they don't deserve to die out there alone."

She went over to her tent, and I saw her lighting lanterns. When she came out, she motioned for me and Carrie to come with her. Carrie refused, but I knew what Mother B. was going to do, and we had to do it. We were going to walk the battlefield and look for more wounded.

I don't blame Carrie. If it weren't dark, I'm not sure I could have done it. I could only see a little bit at a time, just what was within the circle of my lantern light. That was hideous enough. The thought of that sight multiplied a thousandfold was too much to bear. I saw torsos with limbs blown off. Young pale faces tilted up, their mouths gaping open, as though trying to catch rain for a drink. Men crumpled, like their souls had just slipped off the bodies and discarded them. At every moment I feared seeing Mr. Colchester on the ground.

My heart broke. It wasn't right—all this life, all this blood spilled out. The river had to be running red. All this precious life gone. From the outline of Mother B.'s form, her shoulders slumped, I could see she was bereft too. It made us desperate to find a man alive, to hear a voice, to detect some movement. Miss Maude had taught me not to kill. She'd said it would harm my soul. With that reasoning, all our souls were broken, the living and the dead. Who would pay for this killing?

When we returned, Silas met us at the fire and poured cups of coffee for us. "Find anyone?"

Mother B. shook her head. She took her coffee into her tent. I sat down with Silas. He seemed agitated.

"There's talk of an emancipation order coming," he said. His fingers drummed on his thigh like he was trying to figure out a thought. "President could just free the slaves outright."

I wasn't sure how to feel about it. "I guess we wouldn't have to worry about getting caught or resold to slavers," I said.

I tried to sound hopeful, but from what I'd seen, the world didn't make sense. Seemed like humans were killing humans so that humans could have the right to be humans. I drank my coffee.

Silas stared into the fire. "I tell you what. I'd get as far away from this hell as I could go."

"Where would you go?"

"West. Maybe California."

How would any of us live after this? After so much death, there would be too many hard feelings on both sides. Was there enough forgiveness in the whole world?

"Didn't think we'd still be fighting," I said. "Can't believe it's been a year since Sumter."

"Still a lot more to do. This ain't over." Silas got up, shoved his hands into his pockets, and walked off into the dark.

I got to my feet. Exhaustion was starting to overcome me, and I turned toward my tent. But then I remembered Colonel Eshton. I had to find him. As much as I feared the answer, I had to ask about Mr. Colchester.

I went into the pavilion and walked up and down the rows between the beds. He wasn't there. I prayed again. I'd seen his leg wound, and it didn't seem like much. But if a ball struck a man in the leg in the right place, in his thigh, he could bleed to death fast. I saw Dr. Nelson coming down a row, and I stopped him.

"Sir, I thought I saw a man I know, Colonel Eshton, come in. He was the one on the horse that died. Where is he?"

"He's in my tent reviewing some maps of the area. His wound wasn't bad."

"Would it be all right if I spoke to him?"

"Yes, go on in."

Dr. Nelson's tent was on the other side of the pavilion and closer to it than the nurses' tents. I pulled at the entrance flap.

"Excuse me, Colonel Eshton?"

"Yes, who is it?"

I stepped in. The colonel's coat lay across the bed, and he sat at a table with his sleeves rolled up, studying some maps by candlelight. His bandaged right leg was propped up on a chair.

"You may not remember me, sir. I'm Jeannette Bébinn. I used to be the schoolteacher at Mr. Colchester's school in the Lower Knoll village."

He looked surprised, but to my relief, he recognized me. "Why, yes, come in. Forgive me for not getting up. I am indisposed, as my mother would say. Here, sit here." He motioned to a wooden chair near him.

"Sir, the fighting seemed really bad today. I was in the field just now searching for more wounded."

He sighed. "Yes. Don't know when we'll have a proper count of our losses."

I gripped the arm of my chair. "Sir, when I saw you come in today, I got scared. I hope you don't mind my asking—do you know if Mr. Colchester is all right?"

"Colchester? I'm sorry to say he's no longer with us."

My heart froze. I thought it would stay that way, because I didn't see a way it could beat in the next moment, a moment without him in it. But Colonel Eshton was going on, and I had to fight to process his words.

"He joined another regiment," he said.

My right hand moved instinctively to my heart, and I exhaled deeply. "Another regiment?" I managed to say.

"Yes. Colchester marched with them into the Deep South. He'd heard an infantry was going to attack New Orleans, and he wanted to be a part of that action. He asked me for leave, and I gave it. He joined them straightaway. They managed to secure it from the rebels just a few days ago. They've been guarding the port for the Union ever since."

"Oh!" I couldn't think to say more. He was alive. Mr. Colchester was alive. I felt caught up in the dual nature of these strange moments. Mr. Colchester had been dead, it seemed, only a few moments before. And now he was resurrected and thriving. The speed at which the range of emotions occurred made me dizzy. I managed to thank the colonel and meant to go back to my tent, but Colonel Eshton stopped me.

"Wait, Miss Bébinn. Now I have a question for you."

"Yes, sir?"

"In fact, I'm mighty glad to see you. I know this might seem like a strange thing to ask in light of what we went through today and, most likely, tomorrow. But a number of my men, well, they can't read or write. A lot of them were raised on farms, you know, and never had the reason or opportunity to learn. I think it might help their morale, raise their spirits, if they learned. Would you mind teaching them?"

"I'd be honored, sir. But I have to ask Mother B. Don't know if she can spare me from the hospital."

"I know it's a lot to take with everything else. Tell her it would be for the men recovering and for the other men when they're waiting." He paused. "Waiting for the next battle. I think those times of waiting are mighty hard on them."

I nodded. "That would be fine. Might I ask, sir, if it's possible for you to have some simple books sent? I won't need them right away; I'll start with teaching them their letters and such. But we'll need books."

"Absolutely, Miss Bébinn, I'll get right on it. I'll have one of the men send for you when they can do a lesson."

He reached out his hand, and I shook it.

"I appreciate it. I know they will too."

I left the tent. I was pleased with the chance to teach, but my head was full of Mr. Colchester. He was alive, and he was in Louisiana! He had gone home. And he had defended New Orleans, and now he guarded it. It was a dangerous enterprise—so dangerous I could barely think of him in a hail of musket fire. But I was proud of him too. So very proud.

In my excitement I wrote a letter to Missus Livingston. It shamed me to think I hadn't done so before. I told her about my service and how she didn't need to be concerned for me because the nurses were kept safe, well removed from the fighting. I told her how I'd seen Colonel Eshton and the news he'd given me about Mr. Colchester. I hesitated to add the last. I wasn't sure why. Maybe I thought she would have further news about him to offer? I didn't know if she was in correspondence with him or whether she might tell him where I was. But it seemed to me that even if he knew, he couldn't come to me, not without deserting his regiment. I was glad to know news of him. And though it felt like putting a message in a bottle and throwing it out to sea, I liked the possibility that he might learn something of me.

Chapter 17

I began teaching in the makeshift camp school about a month later, and I pursued it with the same faithfulness I had demonstrated with the school in Lower Knoll. The work was, surprisingly, quite hard at first. It took a moment for me to understand my students and their occasional impolite behavior and jokes. But I came to see that, being inexperienced with schooling, they were simply embarrassed to learn like children and frightened of me because they thought I would scold them for being dumb. With time, though, we developed trust. Some of them had excellent, if unpolished, minds, and I could see a light in their eyes when they made a connection or could read pages they had always wanted to read, like the psalms. The speed of their progress surprised me. They were more motivated than the restless children who sat in my Lower Knoll schoolroom, who sometimes questioned why they had to be there. These soldiers knew the value of what I taught, and they devoured everything eagerly.

I came to admire and respect them but fear for them, too, because the war still lived over our heads. It was a new pain to lose one of my students in the fighting. Now I knew more than their names and ranks, which was all I knew of the soldiers in the field hospital unless I wrote a letter for them. With my students, if one died, I knew the potential lost, the great things he might have done had he lived. Whenever the school gathered again, we would mourn the lost student, but then the men

would throw themselves into their learning with even more vigor. And
the material, fortunately, matched their enthusiasm. When I'd asked
for simple books, I'd thought Colonel Eshton would provide the types
of primers that children learn from. Instead he'd provided the likes of
Walden, by Henry David Thoreau; short stories by Edgar Allan Poe; and
Moby-Dick, by Herman Melville, which fascinated the men to the point
that I was asked to read it to them at the end of each lesson. They read
too slowly on their own and were excited to know what would happen
next. I enjoyed the time with them. All reading had been lost to me
since I'd joined the nurses. There was no time for it, and I didn't have
books. So Colonel Eshton's choice of books benefited me as well as the
men. They knew I wasn't paid for teaching, which went on for more
hours and with more students than Colonel Eshton had estimated. (Nor
for nursing, really, since I considered having room and board blessing
enough and had not asked for my wages.) So many wanted to learn. I
knew they appreciated the opportunity and my time. I would find small
gifts left in my writing box: a tin of sardines, a fresh roll, or a small doll
carved out of wood.

I enjoyed the company of my sister nurses too. There were more
of us and much needed after the terrible fighting at Shiloh. We began
to share quarters, and I stayed with Carrie and Martha and learned
more about them than I'd had the chance to learn before. Carrie was
negro and a former slave like me and Silas. Only she had been given
her freedom after her master had died. She hadn't known what to do
with herself until a chance encounter with Mother B. had brought her
to the hospital.

"I'd told her I used to help birth the babies," she said. We were
getting ready for bed, and she was braiding her coarse brown hair. "I
didn't see how that had anything to do with men gettin' all shot up, but
here I am anyway!"

She was smart in practical ways that I wasn't. When the icy winter
winds blew, Carrie knew to take one of the mess pans from which we

usually ate dinners of stew and vegetables. She'd clean it out and put some dirt in the bottom. Then she'd take it to one of the fires outside and put a few burning coals in it. She'd cover it with another pan and bring it into our tent. It heated the whole space, and we were comfortable and grateful for it.

Martha was white and had attended college in Oberlin, Ohio. She'd gone to one of Mother B.'s lectures before the war and joined up with her to nurse when she'd found out Mother B. would be running some field hospitals. But even though she'd been educated, she seemed more shocked and scared than we were by what we saw and heard during the fighting. I can only guess it was because Carrie and I, having been slaves, already knew the extremes of the world. Though the battlefield horrified us, it didn't necessarily surprise us. She held one fascination for me: she knew French and offered to help me fill in the missing pieces of the language I'd studied only briefly.

Carrie and Martha were the first female friends I'd had since Fanny. I enjoyed a different conversation than I would have had sitting with Missus Livingston or Founder when I'd lived at Fortitude. Carrie and Martha talked about which soldiers were handsome, which were the most gentlemanlike, which were the strongest. They laughed while doing chores, and we talked idly about nothing before falling asleep.

Eventually I noticed Carrie always seemed to be looking at me and Silas when we were together talking. I suspected she had taken a liking to him. But she would have to work hard to get his attention. I don't mean I was jealous or wanted Silas to myself. It's just that in the days after Shiloh, Silas and I took to looking after each other in a different way.

One day after a summer battle in northern Mississippi, I found him praying over a Confederate soldier whose leg Dr. Nelson and he had sawed off earlier in the day. The man was unconscious, but Silas held his hand and, with head bowed, fervently spoke words I couldn't hear. Later I asked him about it.

"Praying for his life. Praying for my pardon." He paused, and I could see he was fighting back tears. "I almost didn't bring him in."

"Oh no. Silas . . ."

"He the other side, right? He want us in chains, would take you and me right back down to Holloway's. Probably wouldn't lift a finger to save my life."

I went to him and put my arms around him. "But you did bring him in."

"That's because I realized"—Silas swallowed and pulled away— "under the uniform his body was the same as all the other wounded. He a man, somebody's baby. Like we all one.

"My soul felt sick, Jeannette. Like I could feel all the wrongs—them to us, us to them—coming back at me. Like a hell opening up, about to swallow me. That's when I picked him up and got him on a stretcher and ran us both out of there. All I can think to do now is pray, like I need to be praying for the rest of my life."

And he was true to that. When he wasn't working, he was in his tent, on his knees. Or he sat deciphering a copy of the Bible. Dr. Nelson had taught Silas to read some, but he needed help from me sometimes with words or understanding. I wasn't sure how Carrie could fit in unless she picked up a Bible and started studying with him. That didn't seem to be her thing. Instead, she sat next to him when we ate. Hoped her jokes would make him laugh. I made it a point to stay out of the way. I thought her high energy would be good for him.

But she didn't follow him to the battlefield, still smoking, at night, where he had taken to joining me and Mother B. as we searched for the wounded who hadn't been found during the day. It was important work, but for Silas it became his mission and his penance. We went out no matter the weather, and he often stayed out long after Mother B. and I made our way back to the field hospital. If Carrie could have shared this with him, she would have learned more about the man.

He became very particular about his hours when we weren't tending the sick and wounded. In the morning he woke early and did his praying and Bible reading. When he was done, he'd take a walk around to soldiers' camps. He'd offer to pray with whomever he found, but really he wanted the men to know him, to recognize what he looked like. That way they would have, if they got hurt, a familiar face in the surgery area. The soldiers did have their own chaplain, but I'd never met him. His name was March. The men seemed to prefer talking to Silas even though he was colored. Silas wore his faith all over him. It wasn't words that promised or threatened. He talked about love. He talked about salvation.

Because of this schedule, Silas didn't spend a lot of free time in the field hospital. When he was around, he was quieter, doing more watching than talking. Maybe he was listening, but I don't know what for. Sometimes he'd be sitting in front of his tent, his hand on his chin, staring at nothing. I think he was contemplating preaching—what he would say, how he would do it. Next thing I knew, that was what he was doing. He didn't preach on Sundays, like the chaplain. He would let the men know that he'd be talking one evening during the week. He'd build a campfire, and they'd gather round.

I only went one time. It seemed his focus was more on the men, which I didn't mind. I wanted to hear how he talked about God. When he started, it didn't seem like he'd begun. He spoke like he was just talking. I can't say exactly what he said, but it was like this: When he was just talking, it was like walking next to a creek—a bit of water trickling by your feet, the sound comforting and keeping you company. Then Silas kept going, and his tone changed. The creek became a river, and it was exciting because it was bigger and full of life. The river was running large and fast, almost to overflowing. You stayed with it because Silas had ahold of you, and the river felt like it was sweeping you away. Then the river broadened, the movement slowed, and you saw that it was opening into an ocean. The scene was awe inspiring in its depth and breadth. And suddenly it was like Silas was standing next to you, taking in the sheer abundance.

Silas's talks had a deep effect, and I saw it and understood it. But I also felt sadness after hearing him. I don't know if others experienced this. Here's how it was for me: I could tell his fervor grew from the pain of the fighting. It came from a place without light. He was serious and thoughtful—not bad things by themselves. But Silas used to shine and laugh in a way that made me feel he was one of God's fine creations. Just the way he was spoke to me about faith. It made me think about the brief time when I'd first learned Mr. Colchester loved me. As much as I ached to remember it, I know the joy brought a feeling of God to me. Silas was a good speaker. I missed the way he had been, though. I didn't understand why being devoted to God meant he had to shed the God-given good parts of himself.

The fighting continued as the Union regiments gradually made their way south. One day in early December I heard from my students that the army divisions in the whole general area would split. One set of regiments would go east toward Atlanta. The other would continue south and west to try to capture the port at Vicksburg on the Mississippi. The field hospital would be divided up too. I had no doubt which way I'd go. If the Vicksburg-bound regiments continued their progress, we would reach Louisiana and perhaps the parishes near Catalpa Valley. My fear of approaching home lessened. Madame couldn't do anything to me if I arrived protected by the Union soldiers I had taught and tended for over a year. I had great hope that emancipation would make her entirely powerless. Silas, bent on his Bible and working out his own salvation, had his own thoughts about freedom and where it should take me.

One late afternoon we stood at a campfire, warming ourselves and talking about the movement of the regiments.

"Proclamation go through, gotta think about where you want to be," said Silas. He was kicking at the dirt, his head down.

I pulled my cloak closer around me. "I thought you wanted to go west?"

"Not now. Need to be around the living. Preach the Lord's word. You need to come with me. Being the way that you are, you need to be with someone who understands you."

"Because I have mixed blood?"

"No. Because of how you don't fit with the way people think. And you don't care. Always by yourself. That ain't no way to be in the world."

He wasn't right about that. I had companions in my sister nurses and spent time enough with Carrie, Martha, and, on occasion, Mother B. But I did enjoy solitude and, when I had the chance for it, would often choose it instead of being with them.

"Even if I'm fine with it?"

"Maybe I want better for you than you want for yourself."

"Maybe I'm not thinking about myself. If I can get back to Catalpa Valley, I can make sure our people can make a living after they get their freedom." I was thinking again of Mr. Colchester and had wondered often how many of the boots and shoes on the feet of the soldiers around me had come from the factory in Lower Knoll. He had been right about how it wasn't enough to free slaves. I found myself puzzling over how Catalpa Valley could become like Lower Knoll. Would Calista be in favor of such an endeavor? I could guide her—tell her what I'd seen and what might be possible.

"And I can help my sister," I told Silas.

"You mean be her maid."

"We're not like that." I believed this deeply. Calista would not have sent Dorinda on such a treacherous errand to bring me Papa's locket and with it her love if she did not look on me as her equal and her sister. I would have been less confident without these assurances. We'd still been girls when Madame had ripped me from our home. While I knew and loved Calista the girl very well, I didn't know the woman. Nor did she really know me. And yet we seemed to still feel the tug of our filial ties. We had to believe those ties would pull us together again.

"And what makes you think your Catalpa Valley will still be there? Our soldiers been burning fields and big houses for miles to make sure the rebels don't have no food."

A bitter taste crept up my throat and into my mouth. I hadn't thought of that. Catalpa Valley destroyed?

"It may not be," I said quietly. "But I'll find out for myself."

"Are you still in love with that white man?"

"He's not white."

"He may as well be from what you told me."

"He's got nothing to do with this."

"Then there's no reason for you to go back there. You meant to be talking about the Bible, just like me. People would listen because of the way you sound, like you know God for sure," he said.

I shook my head. "If I'm supposed to be doing it, wouldn't I know that by now? Wouldn't I be moved like you? Wouldn't I hear a call?"

"Maybe you're not listening good." He took me by the wrist. His voice took on the gravity of thunder. This was a different Silas, one I didn't recognize. The Silas I knew would never lay a hand on me. "Listen to me. I'll say it right now. Jeannette Bébinn! You need to come with me to Atlanta."

Silas drew on God's power to be his own, and he would bring that power down on my head. I struggled to resist it, to know it for being Silas and not God pulling on me. But he used words to help him, words he knew to be the scripture I held closest to my heart.

"Thus saith the Lord, I have redeemed thee. I have called thee by thy name; *thou art mine!*"

The fire was too hot, and I felt sick.

"No, Silas, no! Have mercy!"

"You already had plenty of mercy from what I can see. Mercy all up and down the years of your life. What you think allowed us to get on that train, with Boss Everett sittin' right next to you, and us still making it up north?"

"You think I don't know that? But who's to say how I answer to that? It should come from me, from God speaking to me in my heart. I don't feel the spirit you feel for this, Silas."

"Then ask your heart, Jeannette. Pray with me right now and see where God wants you."

He pulled me down to our knees, there in the dust in front of the fire. He concocted a plea to Jesus that he spoke out loud, calling on the Lord to plant a seed in my breast and bring me to righteousness. I couldn't think for the sound of his voice, let alone pray. But after a while he was quiet, and I began the work of soothing my now-agitated state.

The way he talked, it all seemed too big—the dream of remaking Catalpa Valley, creating a community of free people. Even still harboring a hope of seeing Mr. Colchester again seemed fruitless. But I thought of him every night. I wondered where he laid his head, whether he was in health. Sometimes I closed my eyes and tried to conjure his face. I craved to see it again, to be ignited by his wild eyes. Where would I go if I failed? If Catalpa Valley was gone? What would it mean to me if Mr. Colchester was dead?

I opened my eyes and looked at Silas. His eyes were closed; his lips moved with whispered words. I had fled such horrors with this man. He had helped bring me to this current home, where I'd found meaningful work and sustenance. His arguments pointed to continuing a path with him that we seemed to have been walking for years. I was already living a kind of life with him. Catalpa Valley was nothing but a dream. But if all this were true, and if what Silas offered felt right to me in any way, it seemed I would, if I left him and found Catalpa Valley in ashes, want to go find him again. I didn't have that kind of desire. The thought crystallized within me: *I can't go with him because I don't love him.*

I stood up and left Silas and walked a little ways into the piney woods. He didn't follow—maybe didn't even realize I'd gone—and I was glad of it. The tall straight trunks were like pillars all around me, forming a space that felt, to me, like somewhere God could walk in and just sit and listen. So I knelt at the base of one of the trees, took out the stone from Catalpa Valley, and put it on the ground in front of me. Then I pulled the locket from underneath my shirt, took it off, and opened it. I laid it there next to the stone. I prayed to God and to my parents to guide me. My heart beat fast, and soon a sensation spread through me like the earth rumbling within me, like the moment before a cannon fires. The feeling set my whole being astir, like it was about to be broken open. It felt familiar, like home, and the sensation was bringing me back to myself. I heard the rest of the scripture passage that Silas had begun, and I spoke aloud these words, which struck a chord that went ringing through my soul.

"Fear thou not; for I am with thee."

I was not alone. Yes, called by my name, but free to run toward my heart, toward whatever my life held in store for me. And it would be all right. God would not, would never, forsake me.

I knelt on the cold ground, breathing cold air, but gently, ever so gently, the air changed. It held a hint of warmth, and I detected but couldn't identify a slight scent. I didn't dare move; I didn't want to disturb it. I folded myself up on the ground and closed my eyes and waited. There was water in this air and a hint of jasmine and magnolia blossom. None of these features fit the time of year or the place. I knew this because I soon recognized what I was taking in: Louisiana; the air of soft evenings; the air before storms; the air that carried water and flowers and endowed even the grayest of days with possibility. My home.

I unfolded from my prayer as though emerging again from the womb. I would turn in the direction of my mother's blood, of my father's voice, of my heart's love.

"Thank you," I whispered. "I am coming."

Silas's steps were behind me, but I ignored him and headed for my tent. He couldn't force his will anymore. I had come into my own power, and in the gloom of those woods I could see as clearly as if it were a bright summer day. I rode that energy, and I knew for certain that it would take me, forever, away from him.

"Leave me alone," I said.

The heat from the coals in the mess pan engulfed me when I entered the tent. I'd lost all thought about the cold until I'd been hurrying from the woods and felt it sharp against my face. Carrie and Martha, making their preparations for our departure, dropped their tasks and rushed to me.

"Are you all right?" Martha asked. "Silas looked so strange. Then I saw you go into the woods."

"I'm fine," I said. I took the blanket from my cot and wrapped it around my shoulders. Despite the warmth of the tent, a chill had come over me. "He wants me to go to Atlanta with him instead of Vicksburg."

"But Vicksburg would get you closer to where you came from," said Carrie. "You told him that, right?"

"Yes. I'll only be a few hundred miles away. Gotta keep moving toward it."

Martha sat near me. "What happened?"

"He said I needed to pray to God about it. That's why I went in the woods over there. I got my answer. He's not gonna like it."

"You're not going with him, are you?"

"No. Haven't told him yet, though. Too tired to keep arguing with him tonight. I'll tell him in the morning."

Carrie clutched a handkerchief that she wrung between her hands. "What do you think he'll do?"

"Oh, he'll be angry with me. That's for certain. But he'll get over it." I looked at Carrie. "You'll have to help him."

"But you . . ."

"He doesn't love me," I said. "If you'd heard any of what he said to me out there, you wouldn't have heard the word *love* at all. Not once. He talked more about me serving God than he did about my becoming his wife."

"Then why does he want you to go with him?"

"He thinks I'm supposed to be his partner on his mission. It's not my mission, though. He can't see that. You care for him, though. You can cheer him up better than I can."

"You don't mind?"

I shook my head. "He's like a brother to me, nothing more. This fighting has been hard on him. Leaning on his faith is helping him get through it. Maybe after the war you can help him come back to himself, see that God still loved him the way he was before."

"What if he wants me to be like you?"

"Don't let him do it, Carrie. Just keep being yourself. His resolve is strong. You'll have to be stronger."

Martha sat on her cot and sighed. "Will we see each other again?"

"We live through this war, God willing, yes," I said. "You'll always be welcome at Catalpa Valley."

As the day of the split came closer, a curtain of melancholy dropped over us. We packed and prepared as usual, but we couldn't hide the sorrow of losing each other. I felt as though I were leaving my sisters. I'd miss their comfort at the end of the battle days. The feeling was especially keen when, in spite of our hopeful thoughts of previous days, we began to doubt whether we would all cross paths again. Carrie and Martha had become my kinswomen. Silas, as broken as the relation might be, was as good as my brother. We had toiled together and developed genuine affection and admiration for each other. It was another kind of love— again in abundance!—by which I had been made whole. I didn't feel as singular as Silas thought me to be. I felt connected, indeed bonded, to all around me, the soldiers included. The melancholy taught me this. I couldn't have felt the split so deeply if I hadn't been so invested in this unusual community.

On the morning of the movement east, I helped Carrie and Martha load their things into the wagon we knew Silas would drive. They went to say their goodbyes to Mother B., who would be traveling west with me. I was standing nearby when Silas brought the horses and hitched them to the wagon.

"You ready?"

I patted the neck of one of the horses, grateful for the warmth of its body on my hands. "I'm not going to Atlanta, Silas."

"You just gonna let me go, betray everything we been through together?"

"Betray? I never promised you anything. And what we been through, we went through because we happened to be in the same place at the same time and helped each other as friends."

"What about your betrayal of God? What he wants for you?"

"I act in the name of what God wants for me! My purpose is here and, if I can get back to it, with the land my papa left me." I looked away from him. "And there are other things I need to know."

"Like what?"

"Nothing you need to know."

"You gonna go looking for that white man."

"I can't go looking for him. But I do want to know what's happened to him. It would ease my mind."

He climbed into the wagon and gathered the reins. "I'm gonna pray for you, Jeannette. You could be on your way to hell for all I know, but I'll pray for you."

I flinched at his thought of my damnation, but I wouldn't let his stubbornness keep me from parting well with him.

"Goodbye, Silas. I'll pray for you too."

Carrie and Martha returned. We said our farewells, and I helped them into the wagon. They joined the noise and movement of the procession of soldiers and supplies making their way onto the road. I felt so small in the middle of the whirl of change. But the change brought on a bit of energy and excitement. I realized I was hopeful in a way that I hadn't been for a very long time. I went back into my tent, sat on my cot next to my bag, and waited. I had to settle myself and remember that I wasn't getting in a wagon and going straight to Catalpa Valley. And yet home felt like it was right there, on the horizon, and within reach.

Chapter 18

I remembered Vicksburg from Papa's maps. It was an important shipping port, especially for cotton. I knew a person could take a train from Vicksburg and travel west. Or take a steamboat up and down the Mississippi. Back then it had been a name on the flat paper, written in pretty script. But approaching Vicksburg from the north in the winter of 1862, I could see it was not flat at all. Vicksburg itself was like a fortress that rose up and lorded over the Mississippi from magnificent bluffs. Such high ground, I thought. From what I knew of history, it seemed the longest and toughest battles of any war involved high ground like a hill or a castle. My stomach ached when I saw the city in the distance. I didn't like thinking about what was to come.

We arrived near the city in December, and the Union men were already planning to attack the rebels by surprise. I wasn't sure how that would be possible, since the Confederates did have the higher ground and a clear view of all that land around them. But I wasn't a Union general—it wasn't any of my business. I went about my own work. We established the field hospital a little north and east of the city near a plantation called Peterson. I recognized the name and knew we weren't far off from Holloway's. I wondered right away whether I would see anyone from Holloway's or whether anyone might recognize me, but

I decided I shouldn't think about it. I didn't want to be distracted by the looking around and worrying. Besides, I figured, everyone else had a lot more to think about than me, a small and insignificant mixed-race nurse. And if I needed any reminding of that, I had only to see what was already around me. I was surrounded by a sea of soldiers, doctors, nurses, aides. The fight in this area was a massive undertaking, with troops numbering over seventy thousand. I'd never dreamed I'd ever see so many people in one place, bearing down with singular intention.

What I came to understand about the attack was that it was supposed to have an element of distraction. General Sherman and his men, over thirty thousand of them, were approaching Vicksburg from the river and would surprise the Confederates while they were engaged with General Grant's men from the other side at another river. But there had been problems and miscalculations by both Sherman and Grant. Grant, for his part, simply wasn't there. Grant had learned that his army's stockpile of supplies had been raided by the rebels, and they didn't have the food or the ammunition for a lengthy assault. He'd been forced to retreat to Memphis. Otherwise, his troops would starve. With Grant gone, the Confederates could fully engage with Sherman, something Sherman had not expected. To approach the bluffs, his men would have to cross swamp and bayou—unfamiliar landscape to a Northern army. And they would only emerge from there in open fields that would make them vulnerable to rebel gun batteries positioned on the hills. This was the circumstance I had speculated on when I'd first seen the bluffs. It played out all too well.

One night, right before I went to bed, Mother B. came to my tent and said General Sherman and the regiments had failed. They couldn't take the city. She told me about General Grant's men and how they were in full retreat.

"We will be here awhile," she said. "The generals will have to rethink things. The port is vital. They won't abandon the effort."

"How long do you think?"

"Months. I wouldn't be surprised if we were here well into the spring."

And that was exactly what happened. The battles continued, and the noise was breathtaking, like the whole sky was going to fall on us. It was a mad dance, with advances, retreats, and circles. Fires too. Though I didn't see an instance directly, I heard about the troops on both sides burning plantations. The Union soldiers were stripping the homes of all their supplies and valuables and burning the structures to the ground. The Confederates in Vicksburg destroyed them to improve sight lines along their front. I knew the soldiers, like Mr. Colchester, had been in Louisiana for months now, so similar destruction must have been happening there. I thought of what Silas had said and wondered what would be left of Catalpa Valley if I ever made it back.

That January, in 1863, President Lincoln's Emancipation Proclamation became official. Finally. Exhilaration came over me, and I was so happy I wanted to do something crazy, like jumping on a horse and riding to the Holloway Plantation so I could spit and stomp on the ground in front of the big house. I know I wasn't the only one wanting to celebrate, because the generals ordered a barbecue party. But first we had a kind of service where we all gathered together and a Reverend Grisholm prayed a thanksgiving prayer and then read the whole of President Lincoln's proclamation out loud.

By the President of the United States of America:

A Proclamation.

Whereas, on the twenty-second day of September, in the year of our Lord one thousand eight hundred and sixty-two, a proclamation was issued by the President of the United States, containing, among other things, the following, to wit:

"That on the first day of January, in the year of our Lord one thousand eight hundred and sixty-three, all persons held as slaves within any State or designated part of a State, the people whereof shall then be in rebellion against the United States, shall be then, thenceforward, and forever free; and the Executive Government of the United States, including the military and naval authority thereof, will recognize and maintain the freedom of such persons, and will do no act or acts to repress such persons, or any of them, in any efforts they may make for their actual freedom.

"That the Executive will, on the first day of January aforesaid, by proclamation, designate the States and parts of States, if any, in which the people thereof, respectively, shall then be in rebellion against the United States; and the fact that any State, or the people thereof, shall on that day be, in good faith, represented in the Congress of the United States by members chosen thereto at elections wherein a majority of the qualified voters of such State shall have participated, shall, in the absence of strong countervailing testimony, be deemed conclusive evidence that such State, and the people thereof, are not then in rebellion against the United States."

Now, therefore I, Abraham Lincoln, President of the United States, by virtue of the power in me vested as Commander-in-Chief, of the Army and Navy of the United States in time of actual armed rebellion against the authority and government of the United States, and as a fit and necessary war measure for suppressing said rebellion, do, on this first day of January, in the year of our Lord one thousand eight hundred and sixty-three, and in accordance with my purpose so to do publicly proclaimed for the full period of one hundred days, from the day first above mentioned, order and designate as the States and parts of States wherein the people thereof respectively, are this day in rebellion against the United States, the following, to wit:

Arkansas, Texas, Louisiana, (except the Parishes of St. Bernard, Plaquemines, Jefferson, St. John, St. Charles, St. James Ascension, Assumption, Terrebonne, Lafourche, St. Mary, St. Martin, and Orleans, including the City of New Orleans) Mississippi, Alabama, Florida, Georgia, South Carolina, North Carolina, and Virginia, (except the forty-eight counties designated as West Virginia, and also the counties of Berkley, Accomac, Northampton, Elizabeth City, York, Princess Ann, and Norfolk, including the cities of Norfolk and Portsmouth[)], and which excepted parts, are for the present, left precisely as if this proclamation were not issued.

And by virtue of the power, and for the purpose aforesaid, I do order and declare that all persons held as slaves within said designated States, and parts of States, are, and henceforward shall be free; and that the Executive government of the United States, including the military and naval authorities thereof, will recognize and maintain the freedom of said persons.

And I hereby enjoin upon the people so declared to be free to abstain from all violence, unless in necessary self-defence; and I recommend to them that, in all cases when allowed, they labor faithfully for reasonable wages.

And I further declare and make known, that such persons of suitable condition, will be received into the armed service of the United States to garrison forts, positions, stations, and other places, and to man vessels of all sorts in said service.

And upon this act, sincerely believed to be an act of justice, warranted by the Constitution, upon military necessity, I invoke the considerate judgment of mankind, and the gracious favor of Almighty God.

In witness whereof, I have hereunto set my hand and caused the seal of the United States to be affixed.

Done at the City of Washington, this first day of January, in the year of our Lord one thousand eight hundred and sixty three, and of the Independence of the United States of America the eighty-seventh.

By the President: Abraham Lincoln
William H. Seward, Secretary of State.

The phrase *forever free* sent a wonderful shiver across my shoulders. As Reverend Grisholm went on, though, the sensation faded. The language was confusing. It included a list that seemed to be the states in question. But why was the list necessary? Why couldn't slaves just be free throughout the Union? Since Mississippi was on the list, I was certainly free. Louisiana was, too, but there were parishes excepted from the proclamation. They included New Orleans, so I figured these were the parishes that the Union Army, Mr. Colchester possibly among them, controlled. I didn't have a chance to consider this, because once the reverend finished reading the proclamation, the celebration began. I suppose it was something, despite the imperfections. And something was better than nothing. We needed to celebrate.

The day was clear and not cold, so everyone delighted in being outside in each other's company and enjoying the feast. Several hogs were roasted whole over large fires. Extra portions of coffee and bread went around. The soldiers who had recently returned from a march that had gone beyond the supply lines were especially eager for all the delicious food. They'd had nothing but water and hardtack for days. There was a lot of shouting and cheering. I don't know where it came from, but someone had a fiddle and played the most joyous, foot-stomping tunes. I'm not one for dancing, but I clapped my hands and enjoyed the bursts of singing that went on throughout the day. Emotional spirits ran high, and the liquid kind was plentiful too. Those who imbibed were warm and delighted with drink. But I admit a few soldiers did get ornery, as some drunks will do. Their army brothers, though, kept them from getting into too much trouble.

Sometimes I think about that barbecue and how it really was a perfect gift wrapped up and handed to us like a holiday bauble. It was like it was meant to settle us and give us a nice memory to look back on when the fighting continued. You could remember the day and think about the fellowship and the happiness and the gratitude and know it was all about what the fight was for. And I don't believe anyone that day was thinking about the fighting, even though it would have been easy to sit there and wonder who wouldn't be alive in six months. But you can't think that way and go on living. Wouldn't last a week with all that in your mind.

After that barbecue General Grant set his men to work cutting a canal around Vicksburg. He thought he could divert the river and use the canal to transport supplies, but again, I didn't see how that could work. For a different kind of river, maybe, like a smaller one. It seemed to me you'd have to dig deep and long to even make a dent in the Mississippi. And even then, with a river that big, you'd be more likely to cause a flood that might kill you. But they kept at it and, much to my disappointment, even got slaves from nearby plantations to help. While they were doing that, Mother B. and I were driven over to a hotel not too far away in a city that the Union soldiers controlled. We had to transform it into a hospital, where men would be taken once they had been stabilized at the field hospital. Mother B. had done this type of work before, and I followed her instructions. Being at the new hospital turned out to be a good place for us, because the rebels had turned the tables and taken to shelling the Union camps. At one point Colonel Eshton had all the nurses sent from the field hospital to the hotel hospital because the shelling was too close to their tents and he feared for their safety.

I saw fires burning in the distance and thought we were on the verge of battle. The whole valley by the river seemed to be in flames. There were clouds in the sky, and the fires were big enough to stain their bottoms with an orange coloring. It was an awful sight. I hurried to Reverend Grisholm, who was standing near his tent calmly smoking a pipe, to find out what was happening.

"No, Miss Bébinn, that's not a battle." He blew a stream of smoke into the evening air. "The rebels, God help them, are burning their cotton harvest."

"Burning it? Why? So our army won't have it?"

He nodded slowly. "Yes, so our army won't confiscate it."

I knew the will of the Confederacy was deep and stubborn, but to burn cotton? I realized then just how deep this fight was ingrained in them. I knew the blood and sweat of the thousands of slaves who had grown and picked such cotton. To burn it was another sad, senseless waste in the whole of the conflict.

Another fearsome sight: there were days when common people, white and colored, ran from the shelling and streamed past our tents. I'd been used to our regiments setting up operations in the woods. Now we were near a city, and I was stunned to see regular people who were not soldiers, people who lived right where the fighting was, fleeing for their lives. Some weren't even dressed and ran shirtless or in their night clothing. I saw one man who'd managed to escape with his unconscious wife in his arms. She must have fainted.

I thought of Poney and how he and I had stumbled into the middle of a battle. No one had shouted, *Stop! There are civilians on the battle-field! Cease fire!* It hadn't stopped after Poney had been shot or after the soldiers had seen me, a woman, driving through the artillery fire. They'd only told me which direction to go to get out of the way. The nature of the conflict, involving a question of how people, namely Southerners, lived their lives, could only mean, I supposed, that some of the fighting would take place in the fields and on the streets where people lived. And that meant ordinary people would be in the line of fire.

I didn't teach the groups of soldiers anymore. The fighting was different from before, so an orderly way of expectations, about when the soldiers would have time off or even when they would eat, was now impossible. The regiments were all over, on the water and the ground. Shelling and gunfire happened day and night. It was just one huge battle, day after day.

At the hospital we were fighting another vigorous enemy: illness. Yellow fever and typhus were regular occurrences in the South—I knew it all too well from Papa's illness and death. But with so many soldiers and all of us being so closely packed in at the camps, the contagion moved quickly through the troops. The yellow fever and typhus devastated us even more than a Confederate battalion. I felt sad that we couldn't do more for the sick. With a wounded man we could extract minié balls or perform amputations, which, though awful and unsightly, did save some of the men who were threatened by gangrene. But men lingering with typhus lay with fever and their skin sometimes covered in red lesions. Their stomachs would bloat from distemper. There was nothing we could give them. No medicine other than an opiate or whiskey if they were in pain. The only thing we could do was wait to see if they recovered or died. Both happened, but I think more died than got well.

I would inevitably see a familiar face in the hospital. Not from my previous life—no one from the Holloway Plantation or Catalpa Valley or even Fortitude. But even though I knew Mr. Colchester had gone to Louisiana, that didn't stop me from seeing him. I lost count of the times when I thought I had detected him reaching out for me from a stretcher. Or thought he was a body lying awkward and still after a shell blast. I craved the sight of him, and yet I didn't want to see him there, sick or wounded or both. I liked thinking about him being in Louisiana and wondered what the conditions were like for him there. In odd moments, like when I was waiting for the first wounded of the day to come in or doing an inventory of our supplies, I would see Mr. Colchester in my mind's eye strolling down a street in New Orleans or along the waters of the bayou. If I daydreamed long enough, I would be in the image, too, taking his hand and walking with him.

More often than not, though, the familiar faces that I encountered were from earlier battles and connections I'd made teaching the men. One of them was a Lieutenant Walter Stone. He had grown up in upstate New York, where his family owned an apple orchard. I guessed he was probably handsome when cleaned up, but like so many of the men, Walter had long gone unshaven, and his black hair had grown bushy and rough. One day he called to me from his bed and asked me to retrieve a book from the pocket of his uniform coat. It was *The Three Musketeers*. He had been an eager learner and an even more eager reader. When I first taught him, I remember thinking that, based on our conversations and his questions, he seemed like an intelligent man who probably would be in college if his family situation were different.

I pushed his hair back from his eyes, which were light blue. I smiled at the title. "Where did you get this?"

"I traded for it. Gave a man my ham sandwich." He laughed. "That sandwich is long gone, but I still got the musketeers!"

He asked me to read to him. I didn't know the book, but I could tell right away why it was a treasure to him. It was a story a boy would love, with sword fighting and brotherhood and intrigue and adventure.

> *"Four men traveling together would be suspected. D'Artagnan will give each of us his instructions. I will go by the way of Boulogne to clear the way; Athos will set out two hours after, by that of Amiens; Aramis will follow us by that of Noyon; as to D'Artagnan, he will go by what route he thinks is best, in Planchet's clothes, while Planchet will follow us like D'Artagnan, in the uniform of the Guards."*

> *"Gentlemen," said Athos, "my opinion is that it is not proper to allow lackeys to have anything to do in such an affair. A secret may, by chance, be betrayed by gentlemen; but it is almost always sold by lackeys."*

I smiled as I read. The part about the number of men traveling together looking suspicious reminded me of being with "Lynne" and "Jean" and the Dillinghams and how we'd known Silas couldn't go with us because too many men would be suspect. The musketeers were even staggering their departure times, as we had with Silas and Mr.

Dillingham. It was bittersweet, though, to think of Silas and how I had left him a second time. I tried not to dwell on it.

Walter had been shot through the shoulder and was still in a lot of pain. I noticed that as I read to him, his body relaxed, and his eyes half closed. He had gone into the story and was probably imagining himself as one of the characters. Learning to read must have given him a way to escape the nightmare of all the fighting as the war dragged on. It made me feel like I'd really done something. For all the men I couldn't help heal, I had taught some of them how to read. And now here was a kind of healing happening because of it. I decided to think of it as another one of those gifts that God surprises you with—another small bauble to help you feel good. It's like God just goes around and slips these gifts in your pocket. I'm grateful I notice them when they show up.

Come May, the generals decided that the fighting they were doing wasn't working. The canal turned out to be a failure, too, but not for the reason I had expected. The water level on the river that spring was so low that the canal's level never rose high enough to float anything.

The Union leaders had to attempt a new tactic on Vicksburg. Only it wasn't a new military tactic. It was an old one—the siege. I heard the generals even had to study historical sieges so they understood how one worked. When I thought about it, though, the strategy sounded simple, with just two pieces. The Union troops would surround the city and cut off supplies to the inhabitants, Confederate soldiers included. It would be like putting hands around a throat and choking the person to death. That is, if they didn't die from the second piece of the strategy: relentlessly bombarding the city with shells and artillery fire.

I must have slept during the siege, but it wasn't restful. No way it could be. Even behind the lines, we were subjected to the same noise—constant cannon fire and thunderous artillery. The Confederates returned the shelling, and many Union soldiers took shelter in caves they built into the hill below the white building called Shirley House that contained the regiment's headquarters. The citizens of Vicksburg had to do the same, and I was sad thinking of the women and children in those dark holes, hungry and frightened.

Late one afternoon the stretcher-bearers were bringing in another wave of wounded. I was directing them where to put the men. The ones who needed surgery went straight into the hospital building. The ones who could wait or, unfortunately, might not make it went to the cots under the pavilion. Sometimes I just didn't know and referred them to a doctor under the tent. I saw a young soldier who had taken a minié ball through the eye. I didn't know how such a wound could be tended, so I sent him to the doctor. Another man whose left leg was nothing but a mass of blood—he went to surgery. I moved as quickly as I could. I was able to be fast because such sights no longer horrified me. I'm sad to say it, but that's how it was. After a while it became a common thing to see a man's body mangled—limbs blown off, skulls shattered. But in a war, you don't look away. You can't look away. You have to look and look closely; put your hands on what's torn and broken and bloody and do your best to bind up what you can. Help lessen pain. Offer words of encouragement.

That day I happened to look at a stretcher-bearer and saw a familiar face. I directed him into the tent and followed him with my eyes. I couldn't remember his name. He had been a slave at Holloway's, a well-known fisherman who'd generously shared his catch beyond his family circle. He was also one of the faces that had stared silently and coldly at me when Fanny and I had walked to the big house each morning. His eyes were wide and dark, and he was short and squat in his build and walked slightly bowlegged. Fanny had said, "Don't mind Phocas. He don't mean nothing by it."

Phocas. It was him. He'd gained a few pounds, but his walk was the same. So were the eyes. When he went to leave again, I touched his arm. "Phocas. Do you remember me? From Holloway's?"

He frowned at me, and after a moment his expression cleared. "You that light girl. The one that didn't talk."

"Yes. Can you come back later? Tell me what happened?"

"You mean after you and Silas ran away?"

"Yes. I can make you a meal. Just come up to the hospital."

"All right."

My head buzzed with curiosity for the rest of the day. Really, I only cared to know about Aunt Nancy Lynne. Unless Phocas had run away, too, he had to know news about her. All the Holloway slaves knew Aunt Nancy Lynne. I made a simple supper of stew and bread in the hospital kitchen and waited at the window. It was possible Phocas wouldn't come. He might be sent on other duties. From Silas's work, I knew they often buried the dead at night. They dug huge holes and pushed the bodies into one massive grave. The men were dying by the thousands—there was no other way. But soon I saw Phocas down the road, making his way up the path to the hospital steps. I met him at the door and shook his hand.

"Thank you for coming, Phocas. My name, my real name, is Jeannette."

"So you can talk, huh?" He tilted his head like he would examine me.

"I wasn't supposed to. It was so no one would find out I had some education, that I could read. I didn't want to deceive you all."

He nodded.

I took him to the table and offered him a bowl of stew and bread. He started eating, and I sat across from him. I didn't want to interrupt his meal by making him talk right away. Instead of asking questions, I told him about me and Silas—how Aunt Nancy Lynne and I had spent months making clothes for us, how I had left the plantation dressed as a man and thought we'd be caught when I'd seen Boss Everett on the train.

"Sweet Jesus," he said when I finished my story. "That's why they didn't find y'all. They had those dogs out there for days, sniffing for miles around. Boss Everett 'bout pitched a fit when he came back from his trip and heard you was gone. But they couldn't find a trace of either of you. It was like you disappeared into the air."

I gripped my fingers under the table. "Aunt Nancy Lynne didn't get in any trouble, did she?"

"Oh no! She too smart for that. She went to Missus straightaway and said she upset and scared because one of her house girls was missing and that you might have run off with Silas."

"Yes, oh my goodness, of course." I should have known she would know what to do.

"She was just crying and crying, and there was Missus consoling her and telling her they'd find you and bring you back."

I couldn't help but laugh. Aunt Nancy Lynne was smart.

"And of course Massa was sad to lose his best man. I think that made them stuck on Aunt Nancy Lynne more than ever. Massa died in the summer of '60."

When I saw that he had finished his meal, I poured coffee for both of us. "How did you get here, Phocas? Did you run away?"

He shook his head. "Didn't run. But I came here because I knew there'd be food."

"There's no food at the Holloway Plantation?"

"There ain't no Holloway Plantation. Not anymore."

My hand went to my mouth. "What happened?"

"A few months ago Missus Holloway heard about the Yankees ransacking the big houses in the country. She had us go out into the backyard and bury the family silver. Then one day she and one of her younger boys—the other two are fighting with the rebels—went down the road to check on some neighbors she ain't heard from in a spell.

"She get there and didn't find nothing but ashes. House burned down. Clothes and furniture all over the place. Well, that done it. Just about lost her mind. She came back and called for me to bring her our big wagon. Made me dig up all that silver. While I was doing that, she had the rest of the family and Aunt Nancy Lynne loading up the cart with the silver, their clothes. They took the pictures off the walls. She even made them take down that damn chandelier and put it in the wagon! That big old thing from the front hall. Don't know why they'd want all that nonsense weighing them down."

"And Aunt Nancy Lynne! She's still all right?" It was so good to hear her name spoken.

Phocas chewed on a piece of bread. "Well, let me tell you. I get on a horse, and they all get in that wagon, Aunt Nancy Lynne with them. Missus said we were riding for the bayou. Wanted to get a skiff to take them west. Missus said if we could get west, we could catch a train."

"Did you find skiffs?"

"Yeah, they were down there. Missus takes her boy and her aunt and her daughter, and they go down to the skiffs to find one to take them. I went with them, and they left Aunt Nancy Lynne up on the road with the wagon. Took us a while. Had to walk a ways down the river. But they found a man who agreed to take them. We walked all the way back to the road. And you know what? Wagon was gone."

"Gone?"

"Yeah, gone. Aunt Nancy Lynne rode off with everything!"

I gasped. "You're sure? She could have been attacked by soldiers."

"Oh no. I know for certain! Missus was wild and screaming. She said, 'Go get her, Phocas! Go get her! She can't be far.' And I set my horse to running." Phocas laughed and slapped the table with his hand. "Yeah, I caught up with her. And we just kept going! What we gonna go back to them for? Aunt Nancy Lynne said, 'Ain't nobody gon' say we stealing because I'll tell 'em what's what: that I'm just collecting on an old debt.'"

"Oh my goodness!" I couldn't help but laugh. Of course she was. Oh, Aunt Nancy Lynne was so brilliant! "Where did you two go?"

"We got to a Union camp, and she turned the goods over to them and asked for help gettin' north. That's when I last saw her, with a regiment heading that way. She's probably nursing them just like you are. I stayed with the camp, though. Got a wife. Hoping to find her. Don't know if the slaves ran or what after Missus left."

"Do you think the Holloways went back to the house after Aunt Nancy Lynne left?"

"If Missus know what's good for her, they went back down to that skiff and kept going like they planned. Nothing for them left at that house. Who knows if it ain't burned by now?"

After Phocas left, I got ready for bed and thought about what I had learned. I thought about how I had felt about the Holloway Plantation after hearing about the Emancipation Proclamation and felt ashamed. Why wouldn't another slave feel the same way about Catalpa Valley— glorying in its destruction? I had been a child there, and my idealized memories didn't include the sound of lashings or the smell of burnt flesh from brandings. It must have happened there. Even if not during Papa's lifetime, I had no doubt Madame would have stirred up enough enmity after he'd died to make up for it. Dorinda had been whipped; she'd as much as told me that herself. And why wouldn't the Yankees consume Catalpa Valley like the plantations in Mississippi? I grew heartsick worrying about Calista and Dorinda.

The effects of the siege began to ripen in June. The people of Vicksburg were starving. It was not uncommon for a Confederate soldier, in a tattered and barely recognizable uniform, to sneak into one of the Union camps to beg for something to eat. Soldiers, on both sides, were dying so fast that the men doing the burying fell behind. Often they couldn't even retrieve the bodies because it wasn't safe—there was no cease-fire to allow for the collection of the dead. The ungodly stink of the corpses hung in the damp summer air.

It was so strange that with such hunger rampant up in Vicksburg, we at the hospital and in the camps wanted for nothing. Grant kept the Yankee camps well supplied. He was constantly sending the quartermasters out to forage for what was needed. They even jerry-built a rough road through the Louisiana swamps, a road reached by ferrying across from a plantation called Hard Times. The quartermasters traveled far and wide regularly and returned with bounty: barrels of bacon and cured pork, molasses, cornmeal, cheeses, salt, sugar, and whiskey and wines. One load included thousands of bars of much-needed soap, not just for our personal use. Mother B. insisted on keeping the hospital and the wounded as clean as possible. She would send notes to General Grant to complain whenever the stock of soap got too low. I happened to be walking down to the tents when Lieutenant Stone drove by on a supply wagon. He called out to me. "Miss Bébinn! Soap!"

He tossed a small burlap bag to me. I smiled. Small moments of grace and happiness comforted my heart, and I was glad of it. If such things no longer moved me, I would be in danger. This would be worse than losing my upset over the wounds I saw daily from the fields.

There were two bars in the bag. I pulled out a small fragrant brick and held it underneath my nose. On the surface of the bar I could see a shape carved or stamped onto it. I held it flat in my hand to study it. It was a flower of some sort, but then I saw that it wasn't just a flower; it was an insignia stamp. And I recognized it at once—a catalpa blossom. It was the insignia of Catalpa Valley.

I ran back to my room and shut the door so I could sit and study the soap again. I couldn't remember soap being made on Papa's plantation, but that didn't mean anything. This could be a new thing. Later Walter would tell me that they had brought 150,000 bars up the jerry-rigged road from Louisiana. That meant the soap had been made on a large scale; it wasn't just a hoarded supply stolen from a house. I saw the possibility, and it thrilled me: Catalpa Valley might be intact—intact and producing. But how? I felt hope, an energy that felt like life, which I hadn't experienced in a long time.

This moment of hope, though, was brief. When I woke the next day, my hands shook slightly and I was dizzy. I thought the dizziness was because I hadn't eaten, but I had no appetite. And I thought the shaking was nervous energy from having learned about Catalpa Valley. But my symptoms only worsened. I fainted in the hospital, and they took me up to my room. I didn't know if they didn't keep me in the infirmary because I was a woman or because they feared I might be contagious with a fever. I was too sick to understand much of anything. I slept— not a normal sleep. It seemed like I was tumbling into a dark hole. Waking up felt like trying to climb out of the hole. Only I couldn't do it. It was too hard—I couldn't reach the top of the abyss, and so I let go and tumbled back into darkness.

I sensed people around me. I was sure Mother B. was one of them. She consulted with a male voice—one of the doctors. They seemed to be concerned with time—how long I'd been sick, what would happen if I stayed this way too long.

One night I sensed a chill deep within me. The same chill moved about the room above my head. It swirled to the ceiling and seemed to come down to rest beside me. I was deeply afraid. But then the moment blossomed into a tiny flower of familiarity so palpable that my fingers moved to grasp it in my hand.

This is death, I thought.

I'd felt it before in Papa's room, and it had been over Fanny right before she'd died. It was like a thin veil that someone had tossed into the air, and now it was floating down to land over me. But it didn't fall entirely. It was suspended just above me, and a gentle hand held it aside, like holding a curtain open.

There was a question—I didn't hear words, but I felt a question. It was like a tingling from the top of my head to the tip of my toes. The question was suspended over me, just like the veil. I had to answer. A presence was insisting I answer.

"No," I whispered. "Not now."

I think I slept then. All that I had sensed before, the veil, the flower, was gone. I wasn't conscious again until I opened my eyes to see the pink stain of sunrise spreading through the sky outside my window. My forehead was damp with sweat, and I was thirsty.

"Oh, Jeannette!"

I heard Mother B. rush into the room. I realized then I must have been in some danger, because she had never called me anything but Miss Bébinn. I'd crossed a bridge.

"Water," I whispered.

She quickly poured a cup from the pitcher and helped me raise my head to drink.

"We were so worried, dear," she said. "Your fever's broken, thank God."

"How long have I been sick?"

"About a week, my dear. It's the end of June."

There was something different in the room that I couldn't place. The change confused me.

"Where am I?"

"In your room upstairs at the hospital." My room? Couldn't be.

"No," I said. "Something . . . missing. Gone."

"You're just weak. You've been sick a long time."

Her voice was so clear. Then it came to me. The strangeness was the quiet. There was no artillery thundering overhead. No shells exploding and tearing walls apart.

"Is the siege over?"

She nodded. "Yes, thank God. It ended sometime yesterday. General Grant is negotiating the terms of surrender."

By the end of the day I was able to take some soup. The following day I had a small meal and felt strong enough to get dressed and sit near a window, where I overheard details of the forthcoming surrender. From the raised voices I gathered it wasn't going well. General Grant wanted an unconditional surrender. The rebel commander, a man named Pemberton, seemed to think he could get better terms or go on fighting. He didn't care that it would mean more killing. He declared more Yankees would die before he would allow them to enter Vicksburg. He seemed to me like a bold fool. I knew how we were suffering on our side, and we were well supplied. From the rebel wounded brought to our hospital, it was easy to see it was the opposite with them. Their bodies were thin and racked with scurvy.

It took a few days, but the two sides finally came to an agreement that they signed on July 4. The soldiers were going into the city for it, and I was determined to go, too, against Mother B.'s wishes. I wanted to see for myself what forty-seven days of shelling and artillery fire had wrought. When I insisted, she agreed to accompany me. We rode in a cart driven by Union men.

The destruction broke my heart. I had expected to see a city. Instead I saw buildings torn apart; sidewalks crushed into pieces; houses whose fences and gardens had been trampled. Dogs and cats whined with hunger. The dogs ran to our wagon and leaped at the wheels. One of the soldiers aimed a rifle at them, but Mother B. stopped him from firing.

The rebel soldiers were to be paroled, and they walked into the city from their posts to get the papers saying they were free to go. Many of them had no shoes, and their uniforms were tattered with holes. Their arms and necks were spotted with red welts that I guessed were insect bites. As we rode on, I saw that the city's residents had built caves, like the shelters we had beneath Shirley House, to protect themselves from the shelling. Women and children, rail thin, with pale white faces and eerie hollow eyes, stared out at us as we passed.

"Who will feed them?" I asked Mother B.

"I'm sure the general will arrange it," she said.

One woman stepped forward from a cave and asked for food for her girl. The child's yellow curls beneath her small, dirty bonnet made her look so much like Calista I thought I would cry. I made the soldier driving the wagon stop, and I handed the woman some bread.

I decided, as the wagon moved on, that I wouldn't wait anymore. It was time to make my way home to Catalpa Valley.

That night I lay awake. The litany of Papa's land was on my mind and soon came to my lips.

Belle Neuve
Baton Bleu
Siana Grove
Chance Voir
Belle Verde
Mont Devreau
Petite Bébinn

I didn't know how I would make my way home, but the litany felt like a magnet drawing me on. If I just started walking, I figured, I would make my way there. I could take the jerry-rigged road the soldiers had built through Louisiana. By God's grace, I could make it. I got on my knees on the bed and prayed, but really it seemed all my thoughts, all my being, were already bent on this one prayer. I opened the drawer in my cupboard and took out my pistol. I cleaned it by candlelight and loaded it. I would have it with me from now on.

Chapter 19

In the early morning I awoke and wrote a letter to Mother B. I told her I was resigning my position so I could check on my family, if they were still alive. This was in Louisiana, I wrote, but I didn't tell her where. I didn't want her to have the burden of trying to conceal my location if she was questioned. I packed a bag and fashioned a sling for it from the cloth of my apron so I could wear it across my body. I put the pistol in my pocket and tied on my bonnet.

As I made my way down the road, I passed the porch of the house where some of the generals kept their headquarters. I caught the scent of a cigar and realized General Grant was sitting up there out of my line of sight. He'd never spoken to me before, so I thought I could walk on without his notice. But he called out to me in a calm, matter-of-fact way.

"Miss Bébinn."

"Yes, sir?"

"You appear to be on the verge of a journey."

"Yes, sir."

"May I ask where you're going?"

I looked up and could see him leaning on the front rail, his hat pushed back on his head.

"Sir, I grew up in Louisiana." I hesitated. I hadn't said these words complete, out loud, to anyone. "My papa owned a great plantation.

My half sister is still there, I think. I haven't been home since I was sold away a few years back. I want to find her." A sob rose in the back of my throat, but I stood firm. "I want to go home."

He knocked a bit of ash from his cigar onto the ground in front of the porch. "Is that wise? The surrender is still new. You may come upon rebels who don't know about it."

"I figured I'd take the road our men built out that way. I'm hoping our soldiers might be more plentiful in the area than rebels right now."

He nodded. "Come in, Miss Bébinn. I'd like to have a word with you."

"Yes, sir." I went up the steps, but I wasn't happy about it. It was clear he wasn't going to let me go. I had to figure out how to convince him or, failing that, devise a different plan for slipping away.

In his study, the general tapped cigar ash into a tin plate and sat himself on the edge of his desk. "You're right about that. There are probably more Louisiana men here and in Tennessee than there are in Louisiana right now. But that don't make it safe."

I shifted on my feet. "I still aim to go, sir."

He nodded and seemed to study me. "How long have you been nursing for the army, Miss Bébinn?"

"About two years."

"Have you received any pay?"

I shook my head. "No, sir. But I haven't wanted for anything. I was glad to have food, shelter. And I was grateful for the work."

"You've tended a lot of wounded, I'm sure."

"Yes, sir, but I can't count them all. So many."

"Do you know any of them in particular, I mean someone you're comfortable with?"

"I used to teach some of the men to read. Lieutenant Walter Stone was one of my students. He's a good man."

The general called out to one of his assistants, and a young man entered.

"Go find Lieutenant Stone and bring him here. Tell him to bring two good mounts."

The man left.

"Do you ride?"

After all I'd been through? Seemed I could handle a horse. "I can manage it," I said.

"I'm going to send you on your way, but I'm going to ask Lieutenant Stone to go with you. Consider the horse your pay."

"Oh my Lord," I gasped, stunned. "Thank you, General. Thank you so much."

When Walter arrived, the general explained his mission. Then he led us into another room and showed us a large map.

"These places"—he pointed to a series of red triangles—"are where you'll find Union camps. I suggest a stepping-stone approach. Make your way little by little, camp by camp, until you reach your destination." He and Walter mapped out the route, which would begin with us ferrying down the Mississippi.

"Godspeed," General Grant said when the horses were properly loaded with supplies and we were ready to go. "The United States Army thanks you for your service."

I shook his hand and smiled. Never before had I felt such gratitude. I was happy that Walter Stone would go with me, happy that I wouldn't have to navigate the journey alone. And Walter didn't question any of it, like crossing miles of strange territory with me was just an everyday matter. He even seemed eager for it.

"Come on, Miss Bébinn," he said, grinning. "We best get going."

Walter and I began making our way out of the camp, headed toward the river. We trotted the horses, so we were going neither fast nor slow. I noticed Walter kept his sidearm close. Every so often I placed a hand on my own pistol. I was determined to stay watchful for both of us.

We ferried south down the Mississippi for half a day before disembarking with our horses on the Louisiana side. I rode in wonder, thrilled to be on this land again. I felt hope for the first time in months as we arrived at a camp. More often I was whispering the litany to myself.

Belle Neuve
Baton Bleu
Siana Grove
Chance Voir
Belle Verde
Mont Devreau
Petite Bébinn

"What's that you keep saying?" Walter asked. "Is it a prayer?"

"Well, for me anyway, it's kind of a prayer. It's a list of names, the names of the parcels of land at Catalpa Valley." I told him about Papa's lessons and how he'd wanted me to know the land I would someday inherit. I'd had to recite the names to him more than once a day.

"He would make me study the maps and sometimes have me ride with him when he checked on the fields." I also told Walter how reciting the names had become a steadying prayer, something to hold on to—my hope that I would see those lands again.

"I know how you feel," he said. He told me about his family's land, how the orchards were a sea of pink and white blossoms every spring and heavy with red, pink, and green apples each autumn.

"It's the cycle of it all," he said. "Knowing that it's still going on, even though I'm not there. Some nights when I was in the hospital, my shoulder would hurt so badly, but then I would think about what month it was and what the apple trees were doing and what chores I'd be doing if I was at home. I'd be pruning trees or checking them for bugs eating at the bark."

"Yes, life going on. You're right. That's mighty comforting."

I wish the whole way had been as inspiring. But there was another day when Walter and I came upon the ruins of what must have been a great plantation. Shattered and blackened walls hinted at the original size of the great house. That and the tremendous chimneys that remained. The green lawns displayed the scarring from the hooves that had trampled it. The gardens were overgrown with weeds. Piles of rubbish stood where the perpetrators had burned whatever they couldn't take with them. At camp that evening, I tortured myself with wondering whether the soldiers hosting us had burned the plantation and whether they had done the same to Catalpa Valley.

About a week into our journey I saw a property marker with the image of the catalpa flower. I looked around and recognized the edge of the northernmost parcel of Papa's land.

"This is it, Walter," I told him. "This is where Catalpa Valley begins! Come on, we're not far now." I wanted to ride faster, but he made me slow down.

"Miss Bébinn, we don't know who's around, friend or foe," he said. "You don't want to startle anyone into taking a shot at you."

He was right. I reminded myself of my resolve to be more watchful, and I listened to him. I slowed, but my heart felt like it was already flying ahead of me. After many more miles I finally saw it in the distance and down the gravel drive: the great house, Papa's house, still standing. The oaks in front stood as they had before, but now they looked overgrown, with dried moss straggling down from their branches. Some soldiers guarded the drive. They took up their weapons, and one stood as we approached.

"State your business," he said.

Walter gave his name and regiment, and then he said, "My business is escorting Miss Bébinn here home."

"Miss Bébinn?" The soldier squinted at me. "You kin to our Miss Bébinn and Madame Bébinn?"

So Madame was still alive after all. I dismounted. "Yes. Is Miss Bébinn here? Is she all right?"

"Yeah." He motioned behind him. "She up at the house now, tending to her mama."

I ran. My feet flew. I found more Union soldiers sitting out on the gallery. One of them stood, but before he could say anything, the front door opened, and a tall woman with coppery-blonde hair and high cheekbones stepped out. Her dress fit oddly, and I could see why—it was roughly made with unfinished fabric. Her features had matured, but I knew my sister's face like I would know my own. She threw her arms open and ran down the steps, screaming wordless cries of joy. Finally my name spilled from her lips.

"Jeannette! Jeannette! Jeannette!" She grabbed me.

"I'm home! Calista, I'm home!"

I sobbed. I would have fallen to my knees, but she held me up, held me tight like she would break me with her love. Oh, how we cried! I hadn't known, not really, how much I had ached for this moment. Most likely I hadn't allowed myself to know it. How could I have borne this pain otherwise for twelve years without going crazy?

We must have been a sight. Calista spun me around like we were girls. For a while that was how it seemed—like it was just the two of us playing in the yard. No soldiers, no Madame. Calista held my forehead to hers. Here she was, my blood, my kin. How I had missed this. How I had missed her.

Finally, she wrapped an arm around my shoulders, and we moved as one toward the house. It felt like she would never let me out of her sight again. Her hold on me felt so strong and so good.

"Oh, Jeannette, how did you get here? Where did you come from?"

"Oh my goodness!" I'd forgotten about Walter. Where was he? I wiped my eyes with the back of my hand and turned to look for him. He was walking up the drive with our horses.

"Vicksburg," I said. I raised my chin in Walter's direction. "General Grant was kind enough to send this lieutenant with me."

The soldiers around us started to hear the name of the town.

"Vicksburg?" they asked. "Has it fallen?"

Calista and I looked at each other. I think she had forgotten the soldiers too. We recovered ourselves well enough to exercise our manners.

"Yes," I told them. "The Confederates surrendered. Lieutenant Stone here can tell you about it." I walked Calista over to him.

"Walter, this is my sister, Miss Calista Bébinn." I held her hand and said, "Calista, this is Lieutenant Walter Stone. He hails from upstate New York, and he's fought bravely this whole time."

His eyes widened, and he blushed and offered Calista his hand. She wasn't dressed well, and she didn't have her hair done fancy like I'd known it when we were younger, but she was a good-looking woman. I'm certain Walter noticed.

"How do you do, ma'am?" He stammered slightly.

Calista took his hand, but instead of bowing or curtsying, she embraced him. "Sir, you are welcome here. I will be forever grateful to you for bringing my beloved sister safely home. She's been gone for many years."

He was surprised by the attention, but he was smiling. "Miss Bébinn has been kind to me. I'm glad I could return the favor."

We walked up the steps to the gallery, and I turned to address the soldiers standing there. "Sirs, if you get Lieutenant Stone something to eat, he'd be glad to tell you about the siege. He was wounded in the action."

The men slapped him on the back and took him into their circle. Calista squeezed me to her again and led me into the house. In the foyer I removed my bonnet and took it all in. There was Papa's study on the left, where Madame had paid Amesbury to take me away. There was the parlor on the right, where Papa's body had lain in its casket. But there were now desks in both rooms, similar to the rooms General Grant had organized in Shirley House, and soldiers. But nothing seemed missing or out of sorts—nothing ripped from the walls. The tall ceramic vases still flanked the entrance to the parlor. The brass sconces were still in place.

"What's happened? Why didn't they destroy anything? How is it the house is still standing? I've seen nothing but rubble for miles." My legs suddenly felt weak, and I stumbled. "I'm sorry," I mumbled.

"Come sit." She led me to the dining room and called into the kitchen. "Annie! Please bring some coffee and bacon and bread."

A thin young woman with tawny skin and heavy-lidded eyes stuck her head out the door and said, "Yeah!"

I stared at Calista, and she took my hands. "Honey, Dorinda died last spring. The yellow jack came real bad and got a lot of our people."

Oh God. Not Dorinda.

I broke down then. It was all too much. Every ounce of tired I had ever felt collapsed in on me all at once. I dropped my head onto the table and sobbed. "Where is she?"

"I buried her in the family plot. Jeannette, are you all right? Oh, let me look at you!"

I lifted my head, but I didn't want to eat or drink. "I need to lay down," I said. "Please."

My feet seemed to have forgotten how to climb stairs. I leaned heavily on my sister as she helped me to a room. She unbuttoned my shoes and removed my stockings and dress. I fell back onto the bed, still in my petticoat, and fell fast asleep.

When I awoke, I couldn't tell whether it was dawn or dusk. The light outside was full of in-betweens—not dark or light, some pinks, some blues, air thick with water, but I couldn't tell if the dew belonged to the morning or the evening. Sitting up, I recognized the wardrobe at one end of the room and the purple brocade on the bed's canopy over my head. I was in Calista's room. My dress lay draped over the settee by the window.

I rose slowly and went to the window and opened it. The air that met me was warm—so it was evening, not morning. But was it the same day, or had I slept through to the next day? I didn't know. My hand touched the fabric of my dress, and I remembered Calista's words about Dorinda. I found the dress pocket that held the stone she had given me and pulled it out. I held it for a long time, turning it over and over in my hands.

Suddenly a spirit overtook me and I left the room, barefoot and wearing nothing but my petticoat. I ran down the back stairs, through the kitchen, and out into the gathering darkness. The family plot wasn't far, just down the drive and on the west side of the gates opening to our property. The grass felt warm and alive under my feet. It made me want to run faster, and by the time I reached the entrance to the cemetery, I was breathless. I stopped. A simple stone path split the two sides of the yard. I caught my breath while I searched for Dorinda's grave. Papa's grave was on the right side of the yard. I went to it and laid my hand on a wing of the small angel that sat atop his headstone. Its face, with the chin resting on its hand, looked thoughtful and quiet. I stood there and surveyed the area.

Her grave, the earth still rounded on top, was in the far corner of the plot. The stone, square and simple, bore only her name, **DORINDA,** and the years of her birth and death. I fell to my knees there and cried. I thought of her gentle care of me, of the moments we had laughed in the cart when I'd driven her away from Lower Knoll. She had been my mother. As best she could, that was exactly what she had been.

A light flashed behind me, and a shadow moved across the ground.

"Jeannette." Calista held a lantern, and she knelt beside me. I placed the rock in her hand.

"Dorinda gave it to me on the night Madame had me taken away. It's from her garden. She said it would help bring me back home someday." My tears flowed harder. "And she was right! There were times when I was so scared, and I would hold it and think about what she said. I wanted her to know it worked."

I wiped my eyes, and Calista caressed my face. "Dorinda and I were so happy when we found out you were alive and free. You should have seen her face. Nothing in heaven or hell was going to keep her from going to see you. She said you had to know that we hadn't forgotten about you."

"Yes," I said. "It was the best thing in the world, seeing her again."

My fingers dug into the earth, and as best as I could, I dug a small hole in front of the marker. I took the stone from Calista, dropped it into the dirt, and covered it over. I kissed the ground.

"Thank you, Dorinda," I whispered. "Thank you."

It turned out I had not slept through a night. It was the evening of the day I had returned. Calista had food brought to us in her room, and we sat in our nightgowns on the bed and ate and talked. She couldn't stop looking at me.

"Goodness, you were a girl, just a little girl when I saw you last," she said. "But I'd know this face anywhere."

"We were both girls." I bit into a buttered biscuit and drank wine from a cup.

"I'm sorry everything's not finer," said Calista. "We should be having a feast to celebrate. But everything has to be simpler now because of the fighting. I try to be careful so that everyone has enough to eat."

I crossed my legs underneath me on the bed. "That's wise. You don't know how many people I've seen starving. The people of Vicksburg, Confederate soldiers—so awful. I thank God for any food that's put in front of me."

Calista reached out and ran a finger along the scar on my arm. I could see the questions on her mind. I took hold of her fingers.

"Go ahead," I told her. "You can ask."

"Jeannette," she said slowly. "Where did you go when that man took you away? Can you talk about it?"

I sighed and looked out the window. The flames of our candles were reflected in the dark glass. I nodded. I sipped the wine again.

"Talk? That was the first thing. He hit me." I paused as the sting of that first blow came back to me. It was shocking how the pain could be so alive. I bowed my head. "He said I couldn't talk, could never talk where he was taking me. He was scared they wouldn't take a slave who sounded like she might be able to read. I had to pretend to be dumb. I couldn't do anything about it."

"Oh, Jeannette." Tears formed in Calista's eyes. I reached out and grasped her hand.

"He took me to Mississippi," I went on. "A plantation owned by a family called Holloway."

"I should have stopped Mama," Calista said.

"How? We were girls. What could you have done?"

She touched my arm again and ran her fingers along the long scar, still visible, from Missus Everett's whipping. "And this?"

I extended my arm on my lap so she could see it better.

"From a drunk woman," I said. "She was like Madame, angry that the girl I lived with was having her husband's baby. I was trying to get her out of the room, and she dragged me out into the yard and tried to whip me. But the worst of it was the girl, my friend, died." I began to weep again. "Her baby too. She was the only thing keeping me going every day. We were cold sometimes and hungry sometimes and tired all the time. But we were together. And she talked to me a lot about God." I stopped.

Calista crawled over and wrapped her arms around me. "Go on," she said. "I'm here."

I sighed and leaned against my sister. "When she died, all I wanted to do was run away. But an older woman helped me like Dorinda did. Made nice clothes for me because we figured if I could look right and get away and pretend to be white, no one would catch us."

"Us?"

"Yes, I left with another slave. I dressed as a white man, and he pretended to be my slave. We traveled all the way to Richmond. Abolitionists helped us after that. Sent me to a school in New York."

I looked around the room. I didn't want to think about Lower Knoll and Mr. Colchester yet. "I'll tell you the rest another time," I said. "It's just . . ."

"It's all right; you don't have to. I understand."

"Can I stay in here, with you?" I was afraid to wake up in the morning alone. Everything so far had felt too much like a dream. Would I be back in the field hospital when I awoke again? That thought seemed more real than Calista's arms around me.

She kissed me on my temple. "Of course. As long as you like."

Together we blew out the candles and settled under the covers. I fell asleep with my sister holding my hand.

Chapter 20

I spent the next day, at Calista's insistence, in bed. She worried I might get sick if I didn't rest fully after my long journey home. But I think she enjoyed looking after me, babying me. It was nice, though, to not have to get up for a day. I listened to the sounds of the house and tried to understand its rhythms, how it ran. The heavy shoes of the soldiers rapped on the floorboards downstairs as they came and went. But there was little upstairs activity—no one changing bedding or filling pitchers. I figured it was because there wasn't anyone but Calista and Madame in these rooms. The girl Annie brought me what I needed. I found myself, to my surprise, trying to hear Madame's voice. But I didn't ask about her. I wasn't ready to see her or even think about her properly just yet. Before I did, I needed to find that feeling I'd had back in Lower Knoll, of understanding her anger and despair. I would need that if I was going to approach Madame with my hands open, without a grudge.

On the third day of my being home, I was ready to get dressed and to move about the plantation. Calista and I walked down the drive after breakfast. She wanted to show me where the soap was being made, and as we walked, she told me more about the plantation. I still wondered about the condition of the place and how she had managed to preserve it.

"How long have the soldiers been here?" I asked.

"A little over a year. Oh, Jeannette, when I saw them coming, I thought we were done for. I knew New Orleans had been given up. And there was no one to protect us. All our soldiers got sent to Virginia and Tennessee and Mississippi, where they thought they could get the best of the Yankees. Mama was frantic. But when the Union soldiers got here"—she turned and pointed back to the house—"one of them, a captain, came up on the gallery and said the Union Army wanted to requisition Catalpa Valley and its functions for their use."

I shook my head. "It just seems like a miracle."

"I felt the same way. I didn't want to believe it. But it's been like the captain said. The cotton goes to mills in Massachusetts. The cane goes to New Orleans. We send food and supplies to the lines. 'Just keep doing what you're doing,' the captain said.

"A couple weeks after that he noticed Dorinda and some of the other women making soap. He said soap was needed and took most of them away from the housework and set to making it in larger quantities. We started selling that too."

We had reached the large yard near the slave quarters. Women were pouring the soap mixture into bar forms laid out across the grass.

"Yes!" I put a hand on her arm. "I got one in Vicksburg. When I saw it and the flowers stamped into it, I knew you might be all right, that Catalpa Valley was still here. But President Lincoln's proclamation didn't include all of Louisiana." I looked at the women. "Are they working of their own accord? At Vicksburg the soldiers made slaves help build the canals."

"No, they didn't do that here. The captain even said right away, 'There's just one caveat, Miss Bébinn. This place can't keep slaves.' I agreed, and I told him so. How someone dear had been taken from me and I hated slavery. I had never been in a position to do anything about it before because Mama ran everything."

"And she still did, right? What did she say to the captain?"

We turned and walked back toward the house. "Mama threw a fit," Calista said. "Was going on and on about how they had no right. I told her we had no choice. I guess you could say I overruled her. I asked the captain to help me organize our people. We drew up an agreement. I brought everyone here from the quarters, and we told them they were free, but if they agreed to stay, we would pay them. Not all of them stayed, but the ones that did work hard. We're doing okay. We manage to pay them regularly."

I looked at her with some doubt. "Madame allowed this?"

"She walked around here fretting for weeks. Then when Dorinda died . . ." Calista looked up toward the house. "Well, Mama had a stroke. Pretty bad. Been in bed ever since."

I took Calista's hands in mine. "You've had to take care of all this, and her, all on your own. How have you done it?"

"Well, I just do what I can. Look at this!" She twirled around in the rough-hewn dress she wore. "We haven't been able to get proper muslin or any other kind of fabric. The women and I took to weaving our own homespun! I sewed this myself." She laughed. "Not fashionable, I know, but I'm proud of it!"

We both laughed then. "Oh, Calista," I said. "I'm so proud of you. Papa would be proud of you."

Her eyes glowed. It felt so good to be with her again. I held her hand all the way back to the house.

When we got there, I paused and looked up at the windows.

"Where is Madame?" I asked. "In Papa's room?"

Calista shook her head. "She's in the red room. Hasn't stayed in Papa's room since he died and she had the nerve to sell you to that man."

"What has she said? About selling me?"

"She wouldn't allow anyone to speak your name. She wanted to act like it didn't happen. We often fought about this."

I sat on the steps and put my hands on my knees. I sighed.

"She had Dorinda whipped," I said.

Calista nodded and sat next to me. "Yes."

"And you refused to marry?"

"I couldn't, Jeannette. If I did, I'd have to leave here. I couldn't do it. There would have been no way to protect our people or to make her find you."

I bowed my head. "Calista, did Madame tell you anything about Papa's will?"

"No! Why?"

I stood, clasped my hands to my forehead. I walked a few steps away from Calista and back again. "She probably destroyed it," I said. "That's why she had to get rid of me, Calista. Papa left Catalpa Valley to us, just you and me."

"What?" She rushed over to me and took my hands. "You're sure about this?"

"She told me herself that night. She was angry. Said Papa had broken all his promises to her and that she would send me where I belonged."

"Oh my God." Calista looked like she was remembering something. "That's why she was so mad that I wouldn't marry."

"Yes. Having you gone, there'd be less of a chance of you finding out about the will. It would clear her way."

"What do we do?"

I shrugged. "I don't think we have to do anything. She's not in charge; we're both here. We just have to be who we are—Jean Bébinn's daughters."

She nodded. "Yes. Maybe we can pursue our legal rights after the war."

That made sense to me. But there was a thing I had to do, something to make sure I was all right within myself.

"I want to see her, Calista. Is that all right? It might bring on another stroke. Make her worse."

Calista laughed. "Or it could make her want to live just to spite you."

"Yes." I smiled. "That would be more like her."

"In which case you would be saving her life."

"I don't know which would be the greater burden."

She laughed and embraced me again. "I want her to know you're here. Don't pay no mind what it'll do to her. See her for your own peace of mind."

I nodded. "But not today. I'm not ready yet. All right? Maybe tomorrow."

"All right."

Walter joined us for dinner that evening. It wasn't fancy, just a roast chicken and potatoes. But Calista had Annie light all the candles so the dining room was bright and festive. I noticed Walter had combed his hair and trimmed his beard. When he wasn't laughing or telling a story, he sat with his left arm across his torso and held his right hand with the index finger and thumb touching and pressed to his lips. I'd seen him look this way in the classroom when he was studying or listening with care. Only now he seemed to be studying Calista.

After breakfast the next morning Calista and I went upstairs to the red room, which was in the same wing where Papa used to sleep and where he had died. I took Calista's hand, and we opened Madame's door. The room was heavy with deep August heat, but the bed was stacked with quilts. Madame, propped up by pillows, lay with the blankets pulled up to her chest.

"Mama," Calista whispered. She went to the left side of the bed and spoke closely into Madame's ear.

I was behind Calista, partly concealed by her taller figure. Madame's skin was as pale as cotton and seemed loose, like it was barely attached to her skull. The left side hung even more so, the eyelid bent downward and the corner of her mouth the same, as though those features were melting off her face. My nurse's heart responded, and I wanted to help her, but I didn't know anything about her affliction. There was nothing for me to bandage, no medicine I could give.

Her eyes fluttered open.

"Mama, Jeannette is here."

Madame's eyes moved around in their sockets like she was trying to focus. "Who?"

"Jeannette Bébinn. My half sister. Papa's daughter."

Madame twisted up the side of her mouth that could move. "No no no no," she moaned. "I don't know her."

"She's right here, Mama."

Calista stepped aside so I could be in Madame's sight line. Her eyes widened and took in my face and hair. She looked me up and down. For a moment, I thought she would have another stroke, just like I had said. Her body tensed up, and her paper-white cheeks briefly grew flushed with blood. I thought she was going to sit up and strike me, but then she had this calm come over her. She lay back and formed careful words.

"I don't know you," she said slowly.

I saw her retreating, and I knew well what an army did in this circumstance—pursue. I carefully grasped her wrist as gently as possible so I wouldn't scare her.

"It's all right, Madame," I said. "Because I know you." I paused. "And all that you've done to me. I don't hold you a grudge. I forgive you."

She didn't contradict me. Instead I detected a small wry grimace, almost a smile, set in the corner of her mouth.

"Nigger girl," she said.

I stood and stared at her. I thought of Fanny and focused on the memory of my friend's face and prayed to reach all my powers of compassion to help quell my anger. I took Calista's hand. I curtsied to Madame, and to my surprise, Calista did the same.

"I am the daughter of Jean Bébinn," I said quietly. "My sister and I give you leave to remain in our home. Rest assured, you may die here and do so comfortably. We shall see to it that you have all you need. Good day, Madame."

Calista and I left the room as we had entered it, hand in hand. Madame made a fuss, and it sounded like she was slapping the bedcovers. I think she was saying, "Give *me* leave? She gives *me* leave?" I didn't turn around. When we got downstairs, I embraced Calista.

"She's your mother. I honor her on that count, but I won't see her again."

Calista sighed. "It's all right. I understand." I saw the tears in her eyes. I put my hands on her face and kissed her cheek.

"Come," I said. "Let's sit in Papa's library. It'll help us feel better."

The room was vacant. Standing at the threshold of Papa's library, I put my hand to the locket at my throat. The room wasn't the same. Madame or the soldiers had moved things around. But I recognized Papa's books. And there were maps still laid out on the large table near the front window. I walked around and touched the spines of the books on the shelves and the surface of his desk. I sat at the table with the maps.

"I still don't understand how everything is here," I said.

Calista sat behind the desk, in Papa's chair. "It was all the captain's doing. He took me aside that first day and said he had a particular connection to the land; that he was bound and determined to see no harm came to it, and he made his soldiers swear likewise."

I frowned. "A connection? To our land? Who is this captain? Where is he?"

"He doesn't stay in the house. He built a small shack on one of the outer parcels, and he and some men guard that end of Catalpa Valley."

"Which parcel?" I stood and consulted the maps.

"Yours. The one Papa called Petite Bébinn. Here . . ." Calista came over, but I didn't need her to point out the area I knew so well. "I showed them the maps, and the captain noticed it like he knew it. He said that's where they would set up a guard point. I agreed because we needed it."

"Why? I thought he said the soldiers weren't going to destroy anything."

"No, but I'm sorry to say Southern men have tried."

I looked up from the map. "But the Confederate troops had all left Louisiana."

"They did. The men I'm talking about are deserters and ne'er-do-wells. Some of the damage you've seen in Louisiana was their doing, not the Yankees. It's how they sustain themselves."

"What?" It was too awful to consider. "There's no law and order?"

"In the more populated areas there is. But it's all they can do to keep things stable. And it's not like a sheriff or anyone else could get to a place in time once a gang got ahold of it."

I grasped Calista's shoulder. "Oh God. You've been at war too."

"Yes, but these Union soldiers take good care of us. They are a miracle, really."

We went out to the gallery. Walter was talking with the soldiers there. Annie was serving them biscuits and coffee.

"Good morning!" he greeted us cheerfully. I could feel the warmth of spirit around them. They were good men.

"Excuse me," I said. "Where is your captain? I'd like to thank him for bringing you all here."

One of the men stood and removed his cap. "Miss, Captain Colchester stays in the guard shack down at the southeast parcel. He's always there, so you'll find him right away."

My heart at once was a bird fluttering madly like it would escape from my chest. I thought I must have heard him wrong. "What did you say his name is?"

"Colchester, miss. He brought us this way from New Orleans right after we helped secure the port."

I looked at Calista, and I can only imagine what she saw in my face.

"Jeannette, what is it?"

Three days. He had been this close to me for three days. I couldn't wait another moment.

"Someone get me a horse! Now, please, get me a horse!"

Walter jumped up and ran down the gallery. I followed him down the steps and saw our horses tied to the post near the end of the drive. I outran him. He was yelling for me to wait, but I was on that horse and gone.

No one had to give me directions. I knew my papa's land. Had every road, every stream, and every field imprinted on my soul. And how could I not know the way to my own Petite Bébinn?

It was about ten miles away from the edge of the cotton fields. I could have ridden it blindfolded.

The shack looked to be about two or three times the size of a slave quarters. It was well made, though, like Silas's place. It had a small porch on the front, and two soldiers stood there with their muskets at the ready. When I saw them, I got off the horse and walked carefully the rest of the way. I didn't want to get shot. I must have looked wild, my hair windblown and my dress dusty.

One of them turned his head and seemed to say something. That was when I heard a voice come from inside. It called out loud.

"Who comes there?"

It was his voice! *His voice!* My heart thrummed. I responded.

"A friend without countersign!" I took a deep breath and added, "My countersign will have to be my face."

He appeared at the door in an instant. Within the next moment he jumped from the porch and ran to me. He was so fast and looked so healthy. It would have been enough to know he was all right, but to see him like this, to have him fold me in his arms again—I was overwhelmed with joy, consumed by gratitude.

He kept saying, "Ma chérie! Ma chérie! I knew you'd be here! Sometime, somehow, I knew you'd find your way home. Oh my God, Jeannette!"

For the longest time I didn't have words. I just wanted to take it all in: him, his hands in my hair and on my face, his lips on mine, his wild, beautiful eyes. Suddenly I was whole—whole like I hadn't been in years. It was a different kind of joy from what I'd felt coming home and seeing Calista. My sister and Catalpa Valley—these were restorations; elements that already belonged to me and where I belonged. But Mr. Colchester—Christian—was *part of me*, like my whole being—mine and not mine, only there by way of miracle. For him to be there did feel like a miracle, which is what he had always been. A gift that was there when I'd thought I had all that I could rightly ask for, like to come home again and to see my sister. I hadn't expected anything more. The voice came back to me, the one I'd heard so long ago:

Anything you want, ma chérie. Anything you want, Jeannette.

"Thank God, you're all right," I finally said. "I was so afraid! I saw Colonel Eshton at Shiloh, and I thought . . ."

"No, no, I'm fine. Shiloh? God, Jeannette!"

We heard a horse galloping, and the soldiers who had been watching us with some bemusement straightened at their posts.

"It's all right!" I told them. "It's all right. He's Union; he's with me." I wiped my eyes—I hadn't realized I had been weeping. When Walter approached, I was able to say, "This is Lieutenant Walter Stone. He escorted me here from Vicksburg. We arrived three days ago."

Christian held my hand and wouldn't let go of it as he moved toward Walter. He extended his other hand up to Walter, who was still mounted. "Captain Colchester at your service."

Walter shook his hand. "Lieutenant Stone, sir. General Grant said to extend his appreciation to whoever from this region has been sending us supplies. I understand now it's you and your men."

"Thank you, sir. But you are the one who has brought a treasure to me. I am in your debt."

Walter looked at me and Christian and tipped his hat. "I had no idea, sir. I was just bringing her home."

I laughed and burrowed my face into Christian's neck. He smelled the same—of warmth and musk and tobacco.

"You did, sir," he said to Walter. "You did."

Christian took hold of my horse and gave instructions to his men. We mounted the horse together and let it walk us back slow so we could talk. My hands were wet with sweat, so I was glad he held the reins. A late-summer haze draped the road in front of us, and the air was still.

I leaned against him. "I was going to start writing letters to find out what had become of you," I said. "I had to find out one way or another whether you were dead or injured. Maybe you'd even come through one of my field hospitals." I gripped his arm in front of me. "There were times when I thought you had."

"You've been a nurse, then?"

"Yes. Been at Vicksburg for nearly a year."

"A year! I've seen the reports. I hate thinking you've been through such hell."

My heart swelled as I saw the cane fields, the plants gold tipped and green, stretch out from both sides of the road. The last time I'd seen this parcel of Catalpa Valley, I'd been with Papa. The last time I'd felt this safe and loved had been at Fortitude.

"When did you leave Lower Knoll?" I asked.

"Only a day or two after you did. I was so afraid for you I didn't want to go. I even had Templeton do some riding around to see if anyone had seen you. Where did you go?"

"I left with Poney on the supply run and made him promise not to tell anyone."

"I couldn't wait—had to report to Colonel Eshton's regiment. I was gone from Lower Knoll before Poney returned."

"He got hurt, Christian. It probably took him a while to get back."

"Hurt?"

"Yes." I wondered if I should tell him how, but there was no reason to keep it from him. "We drove into the middle of a battle. He was shot. I managed to dress his wound and get us behind the lines to a field hospital. That's how I ended up becoming a nurse."

His arms tightened around me. "I'm sorry you have been in danger. If something had happened to you, I would have blamed myself. You left because of me."

"Please don't," I said. "I made the decision to go on my own."

"I wanted to look for you, but then I realized I didn't have to. I knew you would be here, at least in spirit until you came in person. I just had to find a way to get here."

"It was a risk," I said. "Coming south, this deep into the Confederacy."

I felt him kiss the back of my head. "Someone taught me that a person takes risks for what and whom one loves."

I smiled. "Yes."

Christian stopped the horse before we reached the house.

"Jeannette, please. I don't want to be in a room with other people just yet. Let me look at you and talk to you. All right? Only you."

I knew where to go. We tied up the horse at the post near the gallery, and I took Christian by the hand. We walked behind the house and down the lawn to Papa's gazebo, among the old trees where I'd sat with Calista. The small structure was in need of paint and care, but it was still there and sturdy. We sat, and Christian looked and looked at me like he couldn't get enough of the sight of me. He removed his cap. I wondered how it had ever fit, because his hair had grown long and bushy. His thick brown beard was also unkempt. If he hadn't been in uniform, I would have thought him as wild as his eyes. For some moments we said nothing. I reached out and touched his beard and stroked the side of his face. I didn't need for either of us to say anything. My mind was at peace and whole. I felt calm and clear. I was home. He was alive. It was enough for me to sit there acknowledging these gifts and to be content.

"You said you saw Colonel Eshton in Tennessee?"

"Yes. He said you had gone to New Orleans."

"I'd heard a group of infantry were headed there to attack the city. Eshton gave me a letter of recommendation, and I managed to find a troop that allowed me to travel south with them. Once down there we used shallow-draft transports to get us through the bayous. There was a fleet of ships ahead of us."

"How bad was the fight?"

"That's just it, Jeannette. There wasn't much of one."

"Why?"

"The force that was supposed to guard New Orleans got sent to Shiloh. The city was totally defenseless." Christian unbuttoned his uniform coat and removed it. The day was growing hotter, and he rolled up his shirtsleeves as he spoke.

"The people were dumping all the town's goods into the river. I couldn't believe it. They were burning the cotton, emptying the warehouses. They dumped molasses, sugar, even the wine and whiskey. Crowds got on top of the levees and were screaming at us, just howling with pure rage. You can imagine, Jeannette, how it felt to hear those screams. I kept thinking I should have been with them. Not as a rebel but as a citizen of New Orleans. I wasn't sure if I could fight them."

I did understand and took hold of his hands. "You must have been so torn," I said.

"Yes. I couldn't take part in destroying the city. I prayed constantly that I wouldn't have to. And then a man named Lovell—he was the Confederate commander—he knew he was badly outnumbered, and he withdrew his troops."

"Thank goodness."

"I was grateful, I'll tell you that. We established a headquarters. The commanding officers appreciated that I was from the area and knew the land and its resources. That's how I learned that the plantations were being raided—some of them even burned. There was a Major General Banks who knew about the raiding and the looting, and he was worried about the waste of cotton."

"Why would he care about that?"

"He was from Massachusetts. Had worked in a cotton mill when he was a young man. He said nearly two-thirds of the cotton mills in the North were closed because they couldn't get any cotton from the South."

"Calista said they've been making homespun here—the rudimentary fabric."

Christian nodded. "Yes, I told Banks about Catalpa Valley. I said if he could give me a regiment of men, we could ride west and secure it and its products for Union use. He liked the idea right away. And he approved of my plan to free the slaves because he thought it would be hypocritical if we didn't. We'd be no better than the rebels, he said. Within days I had my troops, and we made it to the property, found everything intact. We've been here since."

He pulled me closer to him. "Jeannette, there's something else I have to tell you."

"What, Christian?" I could see on his face that he was trying to work something out. "What is it?"

"My men know I'm not white. I don't hide it anymore."

I stood so I could hold his face in my hands and look at him. I wanted him to see my eyes, to know how proud I was. I kissed him on the forehead and held him to me. "How did you come to that?"

"There was a man named Pinchback among my troops. On one occasion at the campfire he shared his story with me. When his white father died, he left Pinchback's mother and the rest of his family penniless. He started working as a cabin boy and then a steward on the gambling boats on the Mississippi to help keep his family free.

"He reminded me of you, Jeannette. He refused to hide, was determined to honor both sides of his blood. In fact, he's not with us because he left to form a regiment of colored soldiers.

"Anyway, he and I talked a lot. I told him my story and about you. He's the only one who knew the real reason I wanted to come to Catalpa Valley."

"What did he say?"

"He said I was fortunate because I was in possession of my inheritance and that I should be confident about it. Once this war is over, he said, it will be important to hold on to what's intact. He told me not to be afraid. 'Don't make up fights that aren't there,' he said. 'Take care of what's in front of you, what you have now. Don't waste time being afraid.'

"He asked if I had planned to live in the North. I said I didn't know, and he said Louisiana is where I belong. That I should think about being here and being who I am."

"And have you?" I wasn't sure if I could bear to hear his answer. I already knew I wouldn't live anywhere that wasn't Catalpa Valley. I wanted this dirt always beneath my feet, the sounds of pelicans and bullfrogs in my ears. I craved the rhythm of the land's seasons, of planting and harvesting. If Christian didn't want to live here, I could not follow him.

He seemed to know what I was thinking and took my hands. "I have never felt more like myself than I do here," he said. "And I'm bound and determined to live as who I am. I will be here, and I will be who I am."

His eyes fixed on me with an earnest gaze.

"And if you'll have me, I'll marry you."

Already, I felt this was different from the last time he had asked me. There was no sense of bewilderment, nothing that made our love seem like a puff of a dream that might evaporate at any moment. I, too, felt like myself and more real and alive than ever.

I kissed him. I told him, "Yes."

How long we sat together like that in the gazebo, I hardly know. It had taken so much of me and Christian to get to that moment that now we were content to just stay there on and on until we grew old. But eventually I noticed the changing light and how the shadows of the trees were growing long upon the lawn. I took Christian's hand. "Let's go to the house," I said. "It's getting late, and Calista will be wondering what happened to us."

He gestured toward the house. "I'm sure Lieutenant Stone has told her you are with me."

"But I haven't told her about you. I wasn't ready. And I didn't know . . ."

"If I was still alive?"

I nodded and said nothing. We held hands and began walking up the lawn.

"When Colonel Eshton told me you had gone to New Orleans, I was so proud of you," I said. "I knew you were fighting for your home. I didn't think I'd ever get the chance to tell you that."

"Jeannette?"

"Yes?"

"This Lieutenant Stone. Have you known him long?"

"Since Shiloh. After the battle, Colonel Eshton asked me to teach the men who wanted to learn how to read. Lieutenant Stone was one of my students."

"And was he a good student?"

"Oh yes. He's very bright."

Christian looked down at me. "You like him?"

"He's a good man. I helped take care of him when he was wounded at Vicksburg."

"Then you've spent a good deal of time with him?"

"Quite a bit. And it was a lengthy journey here from Vicksburg. He looked after me the whole way. Still does. Today, when I rode off the minute I heard you were at Petite Bébinn? You saw how closely he followed."

"Yes," he said slowly. "I did notice." He paused. "Do you think him a handsome man?"

I smiled and suppressed a laugh. Christian was jealous. I would have immediately set him at ease, but then I remembered what he'd once said to me at Fortitude—how it was a luxury to behave as lovers do, to talk as lovers do. I took the opportunity, a delightful one, to tease him.

"You saw him for yourself," I said. "He is tall and striking. I'm sure once he's cleaned up and shaven that he is quite handsome."

Christian said words under his breath that I didn't catch. It sounded like "Damn him!"

But out loud, he only said, "You like him?"

I laughed then, unable to contain it. "You already asked me that! Oh, Christian." I kissed his hand. "Did you think I would have ridden out to you like a crazy woman if I weren't following my heart?"

"We've been parted a long time."

"And I've thought of you ever since."

"As I have you."

"Very well, then," I said. I kissed his hand again. "We belong to each other. It will always be so."

Chapter 21

We married.

    We married.

    We married.

    Christian and I didn't want to wait. We didn't see a reason for it. The end of the conflict was nowhere in sight—it was obvious hard times would continue. We wanted the comfort of each other to get through it. On the first day of autumn in 1863, Christian and I rode to the parish church and married there with Walter and Calista as our witnesses. That night, my secret fear that memories of Fanny would be a permanent barrier to my happiness melted away. I could truly be one with him, and in the consummation of our bond I felt my whole being magnified.

    Catalpa Valley endured multiple frightening assaults by Confederate deserters, assaults that finally lessened the following summer when Christian received reinforcements from Sherman's ranks after he defeated the Confederate general Forrest near Tupelo.

    Madame's doctor had once said that she probably wouldn't long survive the Confederacy. He had been right. She died in April of 1865, after General Lee's surrender at Appomattox but before poor President Lincoln was, to our horror, assassinated. Calista, I think, took Madame's death harder than she'd thought she would. Maybe she'd held out hope that the woman would repent for all that she had done to both of us. But Madame never would. Calista and I made inquiries at the parish courthouse and learned that Papa's will, unexecuted, remained in the records there. No one had ever pursued it because it was assumed Madame, as his wife, was Papa's heir. They didn't want to disturb a grieving widow.

However, the magistrates realized, if belatedly, that someone ought to have acted. Now, years later, it took some doing, but Calista and I ordered the resolution of Papa's will. The deed to Catalpa Valley was transferred fully and legally to Calista. This sparked another time of celebration, one that came amid much excitement and confusion. After the war, the Southern landscape was as wounded as its soldiers. There was so much to heal. Some areas were no different from before—lanes with quiet houses and small towns with banks, blacksmiths, and general stores. But in other places, the smell of the scorched land still stung the nose and the heart. The countryside was full of former slaves. Some headed north, some searched for family members who had been sold away, and some were simply looking for food and a way to make a living in the ruins of the Confederacy. Word had gotten out that Catalpa Valley was a safe place, and daily Calista and I received these arrivals, many barefoot and poorly clothed. We had to build more dwellings to house the newcomers. I turned some of the lower rooms of the big house into schoolrooms, one for children and one for adults, and invited all who wanted to learn. I did this until there were too many for me to instruct in addition to my duties of running Catalpa Valley. We hired two teachers, and they took over the classes.

Christian and I built a house on Petite Bébinn, a lovely structure with two floors and a wide porch from which, each evening, we could watch the setting sun. Though we visited Fortitude Mansion often, and the property remained in Christian's possession, Catalpa Valley was our home. Christian became a leader of LeBlanc, the parish he had protected so well. He eventually reconnected with the man who had been influential to him, P. B. S. Pinchback, and he encouraged Christian's participation in the revival of Louisiana during Reconstruction. Mr.

Pinchback would visit us, and he always listened carefully to my stories about teaching in Lower Knoll and for the Union soldiers. He visited the schoolrooms in the big house. Walter, who stayed on with us, told him how learning to read had changed his life. I like to think all this led Mr. Pinchback to supporting his first major cause: creating a state-supported public school system. He went on to become the governor of Louisiana, a tremendous achievement.

And yes, Walter stayed on. I'd suspected him to be in love with Calista from the moment they'd met. He probably saw in her the heroines in the books he read. They married and traveled to New York to meet his family. Fortunately he had a brother who'd also survived the war who could run the family apple orchard. They adored Calista, even more so when she was able to deliver the news of a grandchild forthcoming. I think she wanted very much to please them. It was the first time since Papa had died that she'd experienced loving parents. I am so happy for her. The Stones did indeed dote on their daughter-in-law, and they enjoyed coming to Catalpa Valley to visit.

This mention of parents, of course, leads me to think of Founder and of Missus Livingston. Christian and I wrote to each of them when we married. Missus Livingston had been happy to receive my letter from Vicksburg but hadn't known where to send a response. She was thrilled to hear I was alive and well and we were married. Founder asked some pointed questions in her response to Christian. I think once she realized I had properly inherited my share of Papa's estate and that Christian's inheritance wasn't at risk, she accepted our nuptials with a composure that satisfied Christian and me. Christian made it clear that Founder should have the run of Fortitude as its owner's mother. She accepted this but never changed rooms, preferring her third-floor apartment. I wasn't surprised. I knew how much she enjoyed the view from her balcony.

Lower Knoll, as Christian had hoped, thrived during and after the war. The villagers voted to officially incorporate the town in 1867.

Christian and I have visited many times since. Jelly, I'm proud to say, continued her education and earned a college degree from Oberlin. She became the superintendent of Lower Knoll School, which grew to have several teachers and, eventually, a large building with many rooms. I suspect the next time I hear from her, it will be to report she is marrying.

I never forgot Silas and thought often of what had happened to him. This mystery was solved when I received a letter that had taken such a circuitous route that it hadn't reached me for six months. The letter was from Carrie, my nurse mate. She had written to me through Mother B., but since Mother B. had long moved on from Mississippi, it took a while for the letter to find her in Indiana. Mother B. had to do her own research to discover where in Louisiana I could be. Once she found the location of Catalpa Valley, she forwarded the letter, which included a note of her own thanking me for my services and hoping I was well. I responded quickly. Mother B. would have been so worried after reading the letter I'd left the morning I'd departed Vicksburg.

Carrie's letter told me that she and Silas had reached Atlanta and they had married. She only succeeded partially in restoring his bright, brave way of seeing the world. They started a Baptist church, but Silas died of a heart attack not long after. She has dedicated herself to keeping it going. I've offered to assist her in any way I can.

Christian noticed the tears I shed as I read the letter. I told him all about Silas, how we'd escaped, how we'd separated, and how we'd found each other again during the war.

"Why didn't he ask to marry you?"

I put the letter down and leaned back in my chair. "He did, Christian. In fact, he was persistent about it. He wanted me to go to Atlanta with him."

"Why didn't you?"

I took his hand and kissed it. "I didn't love him," I said. "Nor did he love me. He saw me as a kind of partner, like I was always supposed to do this work with him." I looked at Christian. "And I loved you. I knew what it was to love. Even if I never found you, I wouldn't be with anyone else again unless I felt such love."

I kissed him.

We have now been married ten years. I live in the glow of our love and the love of our children, Jeremiah and Fanny. We are wonderfully close. Christian and I are as we have been, two parts of a whole. We talk constantly, even when he is away, because in my mind, always, I am thinking about what I will tell him when he returns, and I cannot wait to hear what has happened to him in my absence. All my trust is given to him; all his trust is devoted to me. He is my love as I am his.

I think about how this is and isn't the life Papa wanted for me. He wanted me to be protected, to have a home and not want for anything. That I am, and that I have. But I think he envisioned me as alone and obscure, a beloved china doll kept well and safe in a cabinet. Instead I am vibrantly full of family, life, and love. And I am myself, with nothing hidden or pretended. Christian and I don't fear what was, and we don't concern ourselves with a future that is impossible to see. We live, no matter what is happening, in a shining, perfect now. It is a gift handed to me divinely. I'm grateful to live it with the heart that Fanny showed me I have by nature—one bred of the love of my papa and tempered by trial and forgiveness.

Acknowledgments

I offer my heartfelt thanks to:

My friend Jane Wolfe for bringing me to New Orleans for the literacy program she created, Eat and Read at Melba's, and giving me the opportunity to continue exploring my fascination and love for Louisiana.

My friend and fellow Harvard graduate Peter Krause, who, because he loves his home so well, first piqued my interest in New Orleans.

My editor, Danielle Marshall, for caring deeply about Jeannette Bébinn's story.

The team at Lake Union Publishing, including Jen Bentham, Riam Griswold, Elyse Lyon, and Lesley Worrell, who worked hard and so well to produce a beautiful book.

My agent, Brettne Bloom, for believing in my writing.

Dawn Daniels, proprietor of Ballyhoo Books in Alma, Michigan, who read the novel's first draft.

My colleagues at the Alma College master of fine arts (MFA) in creative writing.

My family, Lynne Westfield, David Hicks, Jenny Lumet, Peter Wright, Robert Vivian, Mathieu Cailler, Donald Quist, Michelle Webster-Hein, Kali Van Baale White, Sarah Arthur, and Janet Simmonds, for their love and creative support and inspiration.

District New Haven, a beautiful shared work space that provided shelter and community when COVID made the university library where I once wrote unavailable to me. Most of this book was written and revised in an office there.

Bibliography

Brontë, Charlotte. *Jane Eyre*. New York: Modern Library, 2000.

Carnegie Center for Art and History. "Remembered: The Life of Lucy Higgs Nichols." Accessed September 6, 2021. https://www.carnegiecenter.org/exhibitions/remembered-life-lucy-higgs-nichols/.

Coddon, Karin S. *Runaway Slaves*. Farmington Hills, MI: Greenhaven Press, 2004.

Corbett, P. Scott, Volker Janssen, John M. Lund, Todd Pfannestiel, Paul Vickery, and Sylvie Waskiewicz. "US History I (OS Collection)." Lumen Learning. Accessed September 26, 2021. https://courses.lumenlearning.com/ushistory1os2xmaster/chapter/early-mobilization-and-war/.

Dumas, Alexandre. *The Three Musketeers*. Project Gutenberg, 1998. https://www.gutenberg.org/files/1257/1257-h/1257-h.htm.

Editors of *Encyclopaedia Britannica*. "Vicksburg Campaign." *Encyclopaedia Britannica*. Last modified June 27, 2020. https://www.britannica.com/event/Vicksburg-Campaign.

Fitzpatrick, Terry. "719 Words That Changed History: The Emancipation Proclamation." *Free the Slaves* (blog), December 28, 2012. https://www.freetheslaves.net/719-words-that-changed-history-the-emancipation-proclamation/.

Gardley, Marcus. *The House That Will Not Stand*. London: Bloomsbury Methuen Drama, 2014.

Gates, Henry Louis Jr. "The Black Governor Who Almost Was a Senator." Public Broadcasting Service. Accessed September 26, 2021. https://www.pbs.org/wnet/african-americans-many-rivers-to-cross/history/the-black-governor-who-was-almost-a-senator/.

Gore, Laura Locoul, Norman Marmillion, and Sand Marmillion. *Memories of the Old Plantation Home*. Vacherie, LA: Zoë, 2001.

Groom, Winston. *Vicksburg, 1863*. New York: Alfred A. Knopf, 2009.

Fine Print. "History of NYC—1850s." History 101 NYC. Accessed August 12, 2021. https://www.history101.nyc/history-of-new-york-city-1850s.

Hudziak, Mark. "The Shirley House Survived the Siege of Vicksburg despite Its Location on the Battlefield." *Iron Brigader*. August 21, 2018. https://ironbrigader.com/2015/07/28/location-battlefield-shirley-house-survived-siege-vicksburg/.

Jacobs, Harriet A. *Incidents in the Life of a Slave Girl: Written by Herself.* Edited by Nell Irvin Painter. Cambridge, MA: Harvard University Press, 1987.

Knowitall.org. "Conversations on the Civil War—1863: Vicksburg." Series | Conversations on the Civil War, 1863. Accessed September 26, 2021. https://www.knowitall.org/series/ conversations-civil-war-1863-vicksburg.

Lush, Kevin. "Duncarrick Mansion at Ray and Joan KROC Corps Community Center Dayton Ohio." Kevin Lush Photography. Accessed May 23, 2021. https://www.kevinlushphotography.com/ commercial-photographer-dayton-cincinnati-columbus/duncar-rick-mansion-at-ray-and-joan-kroc-corps-community-center.

National Park Service. "Civil War Timeline." Gettysburg National Military Park Pennsylvania. Updated March 5, 2021. https://www. nps.gov/gett/learn/historyculture/civil-war-timeline.htm.

Ohio History Connection. "Mary Ann Bickerdyke." Ohio History Central. Accessed September 8, 2021. https://ohiohistorycentral. org/w/Mary_Ann_Bickerdyke.

Ohio History Connection. "Siege of Vicksburg." Ohio History Central. Accessed September 26, 2021. https://ohiohistorycentral.org/w/ Siege_of_Vicksburg.

Taylor, Susie King. *Reminiscences of My Life in Camp: An African American Woman's Civil War Memoir*. N.p.: Big Byte Books, 2013.

About the Author

Photo © 2016 Rob Berkley

Sophfronia Scott is the award-winning author of multiple fiction and nonfiction books, including *The Seeker and the Monk*, *This Child of Faith*, and *Love's Long Line*. Her essays, short stories, and articles have appeared in various publications, including *Time*, the *New York Times*, *Yankee* magazine, and *O, the Oprah Magazine*. She holds a BA in English from Harvard University and an MFA in writing from Vermont College of Fine Arts, and she is the founding director of Alma College's MFA in creative writing. Find out more about Sophfronia and her books on her website, http://sophfronia.com.